Mr. Galaxy's
Unfinished Dream

R. GARCIA VAZQUEZ

Also by R. Garcia Vazquez

Beneath An Alien Sun
No Other Pearl - Stories

Mr. Galaxy's Unfinished Dream

R. Garcia Vazquez

SPINNING WORLD PRESS
TOMS RIVER – NEW JERSEY

FIRST SPINNING WORLD PRESS EDITION, DECEMBER 2017

Copyright © 2017 by R. Garcia Vazquez
rgarciavazquez.com

Published by Spinning World Press, Toms River, NJ.

This is a work of fiction. Names, characters, organizations, places, events, dialogues, and incidents are either products of the author's imagination or are used fictitiously. Any resemblance to actual persons, living or dead, or actual events is purely coincidental.

Mr. Galaxy's Unfinished Dream / R. Garcia Vazquez
Library of Congress Control Number: 2017910644
ISBN-10: 0-9991522-0-3
ISBN-13: 978-0-9991522-0-1

Printed in the United States of America.
10 9 8 7 6 5 4 3 2 1

For Ana

and

in memory of my parents

*Do you see over yonder, friend Sancho,
thirty or forty hulking giants? I intend
to do battle with them and slay them.
— Miguel de Cervantes*

*There is no easy way from the earth to
the stars. — Seneca*

Contents

Part One

Borders

Chapter 1

Something fell from the sky. Did anyone notice? Was it a bird, a plane?

Was it me?

In those days I was the last to arrive and the first to leave. I preferred the dim lights, the anonymity of the auditorium. I liked to sample the professor's spare words that echoed from afar. When Bruegel's *Landscape with the Fall of Icarus* was projected onto the large screen, I fixed on it and all else became a blur.

In my notebook I jotted down thoughts about the consciousness of falling birds, the ruminations of airplane crash survivors, the universal and pervading rule of indifference.

Outside, where it was bright and cold and windy, and Icarus was still gasping and flailing his arms, a muscular creature nicked my arm as it hurtled past knocking my books and papers in the air and hopscotching over ice patches.

Under different circumstances I might have cared enough to protest, but it was Friday and Jackie and Joanie were coming down from Montclair for the weekend.

Joanie Rand, my designated accomplice and partner in mutual exploitation, Joanie who came on to me within minutes of us meeting back in late September under Todd and Jackie's conspiratorial gaze, Joanie who never let me know where we were going or what we were or could be to one another, who didn't seem to give a hoot about that kind of thing (nor did I, I periodically told myself), who directed me to call her JR, who intimated, consciously or not, that our coolly efficient coupling was no more, no less, than a machine-like grinding away of life's perilous monotony.

At times Todd and Jackie would drive off to a secret place and me and JR would have the dorm room to ourselves. She talked more freely then and confided that she'd soured on Freud in favor of Masters and Johnson, who she said offered deeper insights into human nature. JR cited case studies in graphic detail as a kind of foreplay. Our first time I felt as if we were being observed through a one-way window by white-coated sexologists holding clipboards. The second time, and each time after, I found myself on both sides of the glass.

Despite the primacy of scientific inquiry in JR's world and her clinical approach to our relationship, there always came a tipping point—one I could discern in her drifting tortured features—when all observation and analysis became blurred by an aching hunger that flowed and rippled beyond the dictates of the flesh. At least that's how it was for me, and I think for Joanie too, though upon each return she was JR again, snatching whatever tenderness might have fluttered between us and sealing it in a jar for later analysis.

I don't know that I could have ever loved such a woman anyway, though in later times, during long boring drives across TriState, I sometimes—however rarely—conjured alternate plots that allowed me to contemplate the strangeness of someone like JR and someone like me together forever and the kind of world that would suggest.

Afterwards it was always a bit funereal and awkward between us. We shared no likes or dislikes, no passions or interests. I once asked her what she thought about love. Love? she said in disbelief and burst out laughing in an exaggerated ugly way. She had no time for fantasies, she said. And she never dreamed. I said that can't be and she said you're wrong, I choose not to dream, and when she saw that I was quietly scrutinizing what she'd said, she told me to go Freud myself.

I found it real hard to connect with JR, but it was nothing a good night's rest couldn't cure, and I always looked forward to those weekend blurs and hints of tenderness that in some alternate reality could be one and the same thing.

One evening I sensed her studying me while I wrote at my desk. She was lying naked on her side on my bed, her left knee drawn up, her hip smooth and round in the gray and silver light, her shoulder drawn in pressing one breast down against the other. Her relaxed flesh emitted a contemplative grace I had thought contrary to her.

My glance caught her off guard, and she immediately redirected my attention.

"That sock," she said pointing to the floor with an intense frown. "Isn't that yours?"

"No, that's Todd's."

"I thought so, I thought it might be Todd's."

I stared at Todd's sock awhile to assess the moment and to spare her, a twisted sweat sock grayed at the ball and heel, faintly scented of foot, JR's latest hiding place, I thought, and I wondered, should I draw her out?

"Joanie?"

She looked at me. *Don't*, she was saying without saying. *Please don't.*

"If I were a painter…" I said instead, and she got up and put her clothes back on.

One Friday morning in February 1977—crouching on a paved walk and flanked by glazed snow piles—I was clutching at errant pages and visualizing Joanie, her thoughts and flesh exposed too much, her index finger pointing at Todd's sock. When I looked up the man-beast was gone and the cold air was twisting up inside my thinning jeans and swirling over my calves, and suddenly the sun in my eyes was making me squint.

She came out of the bright light all bundled up measuring her steps like some benevolent alien from an old science fiction movie. She paused when she got to within a few feet of me, presumably so that I could stop what I was doing to look at her.

Close up I was able to observe the pricey fur-lined boots, the pale green flapping scarf and sleek hooded winter coat. The wind blew her hood back and her shiny chestnut hair flicked in the razor-sharp breeze. For a moment she seemed uncertain about covering her head again but decided against it. With a nervous casualness she asked me if I wouldn't mind sharing my notes. Then she smiled, nodding toward the ground where textbook pages were flapping and straining in the wind.

"If you don't mind," she said. "I missed the slide presentation."

I had first noticed her at the dining hall during work-study. The table with the laughing girls. At times she seemed to me separated by dream from the other three. In *Art Appreciation* she always sat in the third row, just to the right of center and next to one of her giddy dining partners, but not that Friday. I was surprised to see her under these circumstances and liked very much that she had approached me.

"I have no notes that would be of use to you," I said as if I were speaking to a tax auditor, but I quickly recovered and added, "because I have this severe tendency to daydream during class."

"I knew that," she replied without hesitation and laughed, and then I laughed, though neither of us was sure why the other was laughing. "Your papers are flying all over the place," she said and chased down and gathered up several loose sheets with difficulty because of her bulbous mitts.

"You write poetry?" she said.

I examined the sheet she handed me.

"That's not what I would call it."

"Would you mind if I read it, this one, whatever you call it?"

"*The Pigeon Lady.*"

"*The Pigeon Lady*, yes. If that's all right with you."

"You mean now?"

"No. Can't I take it with me back to the dorm?"

"Oh, sure."

"Don't worry, I'll give it back."

"I'm not worried."

"The next time I see you in the dining hall."

"The dining hall. Okay, good. We have a deal then."

She stuck out her mitt.

"My name is Callie."

"Really?"

"You find that amusing?"

"Callie, as in Calliope, right?"

"I prefer Callie."

"Lucas," I said and stuck out my cold bare hand and shook her puffy mitt. Something told me she already knew my name.

We walked down toward the girls' dorms without saying much more and then we said bye and I veered off toward Rickman Hall for *French Literature in Translation*. On my way there I pondered the nature of our encounter, which my gut was telling me had been inevitable. With a mindless euphoric finality I decided I must be with this Callie forever.

When later I told Joanie I could no longer see her she frowned and descended into thought, and with an almost reverential exactitude, began to remove her clothes.

She undid my belt and unzipped my pants and said, "I didn't come all the way down here for nothing. If this is about some other girl? You know what? I could care less."

"Joanie, stop," I said as I gently put my hands on hers.

"You're such a hypocrite."

She was right, but I still waited for that final nudge of permission. "Imagine I'm her if it helps," she said, "though you've never had any problem before, have you, Lucas?"

Later Joanie would gaze at me as if for the first time. Jackie drove her to the train station the next morning and I never saw or heard from her again.

"You looked so serious standing behind the counter in your white kitchen cap and apron. You put Salisbury steak, mashed potatoes, green beans and gravy on my plate."

"So that was our first ever encounter?"

"I said thank you and smiled, and you looked at me like I was a unicorn or something."

I laughed, held her face and kissed her pretty green eyes.

"You're my unicorn girl," I said, but she wasn't amused.

"At best you were in La-La Land, at worst you were just being rude."

"Could it be I was staggered by your loveliness?"

"I used to imagine what it might be like to approach you, and it made me nervous. Why doesn't this guy ever smile? I wondered, and I began to think something wasn't right and how unfair it was, whatever it was that stole away your smile, and then our first real day came and I made you laugh."

"You did, and you make me smile too, every day."

"Sometimes I'd start to tremble inside thinking about it, about being with you. I felt as if I were being whisked up the French Alps in a crammed cable car."

"Wait, are you saying you actually did that?"

"After Hadley's high school graduation. Mom and Dad, the four of us."

For long stretches I would trick myself into believing there was just Callie and me. There was no *Mom and Dad*, no *the four of us*.

"That morning I had it all planned out, but it was freezing and I lost my nerve before I even saw you, but then there you were on the ground in total disarray."

"Doing my Charlie Chaplin impersonation."

"I was a wreck. I took that first step and felt like someone had shoved me out of that cable car."

"I caught you, baby. You were light as a feather."

I thanked the god of man-beasts for the fallen books, which marked our first day. On our thirty-first day, in a moment of madness, I asked her to marry me, and when I heard her say yes, I touched her face to make sure she was really there.

Chapter 2

Like any urban sprawl Legacy City heats up like a frying pan from the center out. It lies within thirty miles of Copernicus University's main campus and less than a half-hour drive to the towering oaks of the old suburbs. Legacy feels like another country in the summer. Its brick concrete asphalt steel glass surface absorbs the sun until the bunched-up heat makes people forget how to walk and talk. Some say the summer heat in Legacy makes people love-drowsy, but it can just as easily make them want to kill someone.

It's a dicey proposition walking around parts of Legacy City in the summer. Back in the sixties it nearly all went up in flames. As a kid I could hear the shooting and the sirens day and night from my open bedroom window. There just wasn't enough love-drowsiness to go around. I watched Legacy limp into the seventies covered in ash and fatigued by dried up tears.

It came as no surprise to me that Callie wept the first time she drove from Colts Brook to my father's apartment to have dinner with us. She took a right off Lenape Highway, drove under the train trestle past a junkyard and spotted a man of indeterminate age picking his dinner out of a crumpled garbage can. That was something she wasn't expecting to see.

She told me about the incident months later. Farther up the street, she said forcing a smile, a woman walking on the sidewalk with a little girl in tow came to a complete stop. The woman stood holding the little girl's hand. The woman and the little girl watched her drive by at a snail's pace wiping tears from her face. What a sight she must have been, Callie said. How ridiculous she must have looked.

And then she laughed and shook her head. Whenever Callie wept or laughed over things like people picking dinner out of someone else's garbage or feeling that she'd made a fool of herself, her emotional response always left her feeling ambushed and it annoyed her to no end.

"I'm a sentimental ninny," she said.

I said, "There's a difference between emotion and sentimentality. Emotion is good. It's raw, it's honest. Sentimentality is, you know, kind of creepy and self-indulgent."

"But I *am* creepy and self-indulgent."

"Who isn't? It's all a matter of degree."

"A self-indulgent ninny."

"An emotional genius."

She smiled, already knowing the answer to the question she was about to ask. "When did I say that?"

"The first time we hung out at the pub together."

"At the pub, right?"

"After a couple of beers, you revealed your true identity to me."

I pictured it all very clearly, the woman, the little girl, Callie driving by in her sister's fancy car, that moment of strange mutual awareness bonding the two women and little girl forever. None of it surprised me. Moments like that are a dime a dozen for emotional geniuses.

CALLIE never did get to meet Marisol other than through photographs and stories José and I told her. And yet she was convinced everybody's life had been diminished by my mother's absence. I marveled at her ability to miss a woman she was only able to imagine.

But one evening after dinner and too much wine she went too far.

"So our kids are supposed to never know her?" she said like it was my fault. "Is that what you're saying?"

I wasn't saying anything, and what would she have me do anyway, resurrect my dead mother? I wanted to tell her that, and the words sort of loitered just behind my teeth waiting for me to give them the go-ahead signal, but I swallowed and walked away.

She followed me out of the room. It happened sometimes. Something would get in her head—a *spiritual prompting*, she called it—but this particular one had a practical component to it and I knew she was angling to make a life-altering point.

"Before the moon, the stars, before all flowers I have loved you," she said.

I took a deep cleansing breath. How long had she been planning this?

"Remember when you wrote those words? You said you wrote them for me. But that kind of love is so big, Lucas. I mean, bigger than me and us and bigger than death."

I turned around. I tried to be sensitive. You don't respond to an emotional genius by calling into question her vision of existence.

"Okay," I said.

"I feel her. Marisol isn't out there. She isn't not anywhere. She's right here."

"Okay, Callie."

She put her left hand over her heart and her right hand over my heart, and I was tempted to laugh it off, say something inappropriate, maybe ask her for a deck of cards so I could perform a trick.

Or I could have reminded her of how she had teased me when I first showed her those verses back at school. How she hadn't read any of this deeper stuff into them then.

Oh, you're such a romantic, she had said with enormous pleasure after setting aside the handwritten sheet and just before planting a quick kiss on my lips. A little like E.E. Cummings, are we? That was a pivotal moment because a minute later I asked her to marry me and she got swept up in the emotion and the madness and said yes maybe in part because I sounded a little like a dead poet.

Callie could at different times be crazy or spiritually prompted or a bit of a wine connoisseur, or she could be all those things at once and it wasn't always easy for me.

No matter how hard I tried to avoid it, her pretty words of resurrection and her love-inspired machinations only served to further harden my heart, and I decided it was best to keep my mouth shut.

I stood silently before her, and for the first time since we'd known each other she saw—really saw—the chasm that existed between us, and I caught a glimpse of fear in her eyes. It was just a glimpse, and I felt really bad about that, so I tried to smile but that probably only made it worse. She held me close and I let her hold me for as long as she needed me to, and we said nothing more about it.

AFTER WE returned from our honeymoon, José informed us his time in America had come to an end. His work here had been completed.

Juan was expanding his small carpentry business back in Spain and there was a job waiting for him. My uncle's shop was a twenty-minute walk to the cemetery where Marisol's remains had been laid to rest. Before Callie or I could open our mouths, José promised he would return to celebrate his grandchild's first birthday, whenever that might be.

For whatever reason—newlywed myopia, youthful insensitivity, raw egocentrism?—the possibility that José might one day go back to the old country had never occurred to us. And to do it so soon and without warning!

I glanced at Callie. It wasn't a conscious thing at all on her part, the wounded look on her face, I mean. It was just Callie's nature to want those she loved to be together always and forever. My father saw the wound but it was not going to change his mind for a second. In a mild defensive tone, he assured us that he loved us to the best of his ability. But all things considered, it would have served everyone best had he, not Marisol, been the one to perish. Nonetheless, he felt proud and privileged to be our father but again, to be clear, a father could never be a mother. Ah, classic José.

After a brief silence, and realizing that the poor man's circumstances presented no happy options, Callie and I tried to encourage him by spouting nonsense about the excitement of discovering new life and so on. I knew my father well enough to understand—even as he pretended to listen to us—that he was desperate for that day to come to an end.

At the airport, his face set like stone, my father stuffed several hundred-dollar bills in my shirt pocket before embracing me and disappearing.

Driving back alone to the apartment I clung to a singular childhood memory.

It is in the tomb-silent aftermath of one of their confounding quarrels. I watch him suddenly grab her from behind and begin to tickle her ribs. I can feel the table and chairs jump to attention when Marisol lets out a wild shriek. She twists and slaps at José's arms with shocking ferocity until she is able to squirm away. When she turns to face him, I seek and find the barely concealed smile. And then, at once, they both begin to laugh, and I am entranced.

Even now, when memory rages against time, I can see them facing off against each other like exultant warriors, tears in their eyes from laughing hard at themselves and at the wondrous insanity of being human.

Chapter 3

"I really don't think I should go," she said.

Ah, *think*.

A tricky word, at times an old friend that reminds you to slow down and take a breath. A word as full of possibility as infinity. An indispensable word that keeps savagery at bay but that can turn on you in an instant slithering over and under and all around your brain like a twisting vine, squeezing and squeezing.

"You don't *think* you should go?" I replied. "That's different from not wanting to go."

Callie looked at me and shook her head. "Why would I want to be away from you for two weeks?"

"It's just two weeks."

"You're being more silly than sarcastic. You do realize that."

She got up out of bed and marched to the kitchen. I got up and followed her.

"We've been married just over two months, and Grace decides it's the perfect time to whisk you and Hadley off to Paris."

Callie poured herself a glass of milk and started moving things around in one of the cabinets.

"You don't see anything unusual about that?" I said.

"Did you eat all the cookies? Oh wait, never mind."

"Why would Callie want to be with her husband in Legacy City to celebrate her first birthday as a married woman when she could be in Paris without him?"

"What can I tell you, Lucas? That's just Mom. She doesn't think the way we do."

"Oh, is that it? Okay, I feel better now."

"By the way," Callie said with a giggle, "you forgot to mention Dad. He's going too."

I had to laugh.

"Right, right, how could I forget Cam?"

It was the laugh more than what I said that gave her pause. The kind of laugh. She bit into a chocolate chip cookie that must have tasted like rubble to her. She put the cookie down on the counter. I could tell she was at a loss, weighing the pros and cons of pitched battle.

She took a deep breath and said, "This is all irrelevant. I'm not going. I don't care about Paris. Case closed."

Her green eyes bristled in defiance. I wanted to hold her face and kiss every bit of it, but something beyond my control rose between us like a glass wall.

"No, you're going," I said.

"No, I'm not."

"You said you didn't think you should go, not that you didn't want to go."

"My God, you are unbelievable. I just told you I don't want to go."

"*Now* you don't want to. That's not what you said before."

"I think you're dehydrated, sweetie. Here."

She offered me her glass of milk.

"Don't do that, I'm being serious."

Callie put the glass down, folded her arms and stared at me.

"Don't you get it?" I said. "Don't you see what this is all about?"

"Enlighten me, Lucas, why don't you."

"This trip, the timing, it doesn't strike you as underhanded?"

Callie covered her mouth to stifle a laugh. "Did you say *underhanded*? Sorry, it's just that—"

"You think Cam's going to Paris with you?"

"Everybody was yelling, 'Lauren, you're supposed to pitch it underhanded,' but she didn't see the point of that. Kept tossing it overhand. Never got the ball anywhere near the batter so we stuck her in right field. Best roommate ever and worst softball pitcher ever."

"You don't really think your dad's going to Paris, do you?"

"What are you talking about?"

"He's not going, Callie."

She hesitated. "Why would you say that?"

"Because I know he's not."

"Because he told you?"

Laughter was something I wanted to keep in check because of how ugly I knew it would sound at that stage of our discussion, but I laughed anyway. Couldn't control it. A bitterness reflex, I suppose, a condition I had developed over the last few months.

"Ha, you think Cameron Coldwell would talk to *me*?"

"Okay, I see. So that's what this is all about? You know my father's not the warmest person. I've told you. He's like that with everybody. It's not you. You just don't know him."

"Oh, but I do."

"Fine, you know him," she said and rolled her eyes.

"Don't do that."

"I'm not saying it didn't take my parents some time to adjust to you. I won't deny that. But they are over it for the most part."

"That makes me happy, for the most part."

"Telling them we had decided to get married after knowing each other for a month? Try to be objective for just a moment, can you? Think about it, their daughter, what she was entering into."

Callie's voice was starting to sound different to me. Analytical, unsympathetic, Coldwellian. My breath was starting to get away from me.

"What their daughter was getting herself into?" I said.

"I didn't say *getting* into. I said *entering* into."

"Oh, you didn't say getting into, but that's what you meant, right?"

"Stop twisting things, will you?"

I was sinking fast and needed to come up for air, even if it meant having to push her down to get up, push her down just long enough to catch my breath, long enough to save us both. All that time I had kept it to myself. I didn't want her to know. But I was drowning. I needed my wife to understand I wasn't a paranoid freak.

"They offered me five thousand dollars."

There, I said it. But it wasn't enough. It wasn't clear. She had no idea what I was talking about.

"A couple of days after you introduced me to them. They sent a man with an envelope. I'd never seen him before. He flipped the bills in my face, all hundreds. He said all I had to do was never go near you again. I told him to go to hell."

The way her mouth twitched I thought she was going to burst out laughing, that she was willing to play along, however ridiculous and distasteful the joke. But it all came together in her head soon enough. I watched her face change. I remember thinking she looked exactly how I must have looked to her, worn out, disgusted, wanting to be somewhere else alone and undisturbed.

"What do you want from me?" she said.

"You have to go to Paris."

She stared at me as if I had just slapped her face and locked herself in the bathroom.

An hour passed. I approached the bathroom door and listened, but I couldn't hear anything. I knocked. I said her name but there was no response. I knocked again, louder. "Callie, are you okay?"

For a terrifying instant I imagined she had slit her wrists. It was an outlandish thought, of course, but I lowered myself on all fours anyway and checked for blood under the bathroom door. I got up and knocked hard several times and raised my voice. "Callie! Would you please answer me?"

"Go away," she said. I went back to the bedroom and lay down.

A half hour later I returned and pressed my face into the corner of the door.

"You asked me what I want from you. I want all of you, heart, mind, soul and body, your voice, your smile, your thoughts, your breath, the way the world looks through your eyes, the way you hear the birds sing…"

I listened to her silence and wondered if she had already been taken from me.

"Something's wrong," I said in just above a whisper. "Something's wrong and I don't know how to fix it. Hell, I don't even know what it is. All I know is I hate myself for hurting you. I'm so sorry."

I was dozing off when she came back to bed. I felt her hand over my mouth, pressing down too gently to suggest she had decided to finish me off once and for all. When I opened my eyes, I saw that she was naked. She told me to be quiet and brushed my lips with hers.

COLDWELL backed out at the last minute and Grace got what she wanted. The night before the trip, Callie and I lay awake for hours. How many times throughout that interminable night did she say it's only two weeks?

I drove her to Colts Brook in the morning and walked her to the front door. She clung to me and I thought she was on the verge of backing out. I took her arms and gently pushed her away. Out of the corner of my eye I saw something move. Was that Grace behind the curtains?

"Go, I'll be fine," I said. "You're going to have a great time. It's better this way. It'll be good for both of us in the long run. And besides, it's only two weeks. Two weeks will come and go in the blink of an eye and we'll forget we were ever apart."

And so, she went.

Chapter 4

Like a lot of women her age, Marla managed to conceal her little pot belly with varying degrees of success. Overall, though, any objective person would tell you her extra weight was distributed nicely for a woman closer to fifty than forty. She dressed more stylishly than might be expected of a warehouse dispatcher and her presence among the techies lent an aura of tough elegance to our daily morning gatherings.

Through the big glass window of the Dispatch office Marla Tupo saw everything, and I had the impression no one knew more about *The Galaxy* than she did. The day after Callie left for Paris Marla came out of her office and walked up to me.

"Are you okay, buddy?" she asked me with a tilt of her head.

My response was out of character and an enduring source of embarrassment to me afterwards. I had just completed my first week as a field technician at Galaxy Alarms, Inc., and I found myself spilling my guts to this stranger as if I were a child abandoned on the street. I told her how much I missed my wife, how Callie and I had been married for only a few months, how this was the first time we had been separated since the wedding and so on.

Marla listened to my every word. Her determination to make me smile amazed me. Each morning she greeted me with an effervescent countdown to Callie's return.

Lucas, nine days left!

Eight days left!

Seven days, Lucas!

DESPITE Marla's efforts, that first Friday without Callie proved especially difficult for me. After work I squandered a couple of hours at the public library fidgeting over a paper I was writing on Eliot's *The Waste Land*. I stopped at a liquor store on my way back to the apartment and mixed myself a vodka and tonic to complement a late dinner of canned chicken soup and saltines.

The second time I poured less tonic and more vodka and found myself stirred by a restless melancholy. I walked over to the photograph of the Coldwell girls sitting on Callie's dresser. I kissed Callie's dime-sized face and watched with mixed feelings as the imprint of my lips lingered over Grace and Hadley's faces as well before evaporating.

Dazed and frustrated, I drifted away from the three sets of tiny eyes and sat on the edge of the bed. I was surprised at how easily Marla Tupo slipped into my thoughts. How nice it would be to talk with her again, tell her how much I missed my wife. How nice to revisit that sympathetic smile, hear those words of encouragement. If only I had her telephone number. But would I? Would I call her? It was a moot point. I didn't have her number, but in solitude I could ponder her thoughtful and optimistic nature at greater length, I could reflect on that oblique suggestion of passion I'd begun to glimpse in her now and again like the random gleam of a dewdrop…

I tried writing Callie a love poem but the words and sentiments were extravagantly unfocused. I revised and revised, reading the verses aloud again and again until I no longer knew what I was reading or why.

The ballgame held my attention for sporadic moments. Popups and strikeouts arrived and departed with agonizing regularity. Yankees and Indians plodded through grim blurry waves. I got up and down and up again to adjust the rabbit ears, coaxing the small black and white RCA television, pleading with it, cursing it.

Then the TV said to me, *But didn't you know chaotic reception is a spot-on representation of reality?*

AT WORK that morning Virgil Flynn and Barry Panko were singing the praises of a redhead who was the main Saturday night attraction at *The Milky Way.* Ginger Starlight, they called her. Virgil and Barry were making plans. Virgil said he got lucky. His wife and four kids were spending the weekend in upstate New York with her parents. He winked at me and reminded me I was free too and did I know how to get there?

I had that at least if I wanted, I reminded myself as Friday's darkness seeped in through the window blinds of the basement apartment. I was too emotionally charged to get into bed, so I stepped out the door and immediately was sucked into a warm, damp vacuum. There was no breeze, no sound, no scent, nothing to tell me I was there, somewhere, anywhere. I got in the hatchback and drove to nowhere in particular, like a camel-backed nomad churning through endless miles of sand, distancing myself from all human notice. Through a magic telescope I could see Callie strolling over freshly sprayed Parisian sidewalks deaf to my drunken moans.

The sky was being sealed shut by a thickening gloom of clouds. I couldn't ask for better conditions to wallow in self-pity. After years of mutual accommodation, why had loneliness turned so vicious?

But there! A woman strolling along Main Street in a red dress and high-heeled shoes! Marla, is that you?

I certainly had no intention to detain her. She was walking alone, absorbed in her thoughts, and I was coasting along in my car, one eye on the road, one eye on Marla.

Should I call out, "How many days left, Marla? How many days before I see my Callie again?"

Would the number be on the tip of her tongue? Or would she stop and stare, wondering who I was? And knowing, would she think me a fool?

Chapter 5

S aturday I got up late, went to the library just so I could get out of the apartment and spent a couple of joyless hours working on my Eliot paper, which was due Tuesday evening. I knew what I'd written was pure horseshit, and if I wanted I could leave it that way because Dr. Bloomberg was soft and always found some redeeming aspect or other in everything I wrote—maybe in deference to my ethnicity—when what I really wanted him to say was, "Mr. Amado, this is horseshit. You should expect more of yourself." Still and all, he was a decent man, and I wasn't going to hold his shortsighted, if well meaning, cultural bias against him.

The library closed early so I packed up and drove down to the park. I walked around awhile enjoying the pleasant breeze. As dusk began to settle the trees whispered go home, drink vodka, pay Ginger Starlight a visit, why don't you, and shoot the breeze awhile with Virgil, Galaxy's resident—if self-professed—spy thriller connoisseur. Virgil's preferred authors were John le Carré, Ian Fleming and Frederick Forsyth, and Amy agreed he could name their sons John, Ian, and Fred. It was the least she could do, he once told me half in jest, though he was clearly itching to say more but wouldn't or couldn't.

Virgil spotted me before I spotted him and waved me over. He talked the whole time but both his and Barry Panko's eyes were fixed on Ginger Starlight's hips. I understood maybe one of every five words Virgil said and quickly gathered I wasn't long for the place.

"Ginger Starlight, Ginger Starbright," Barry sang in a disturbing falsetto as he tore his gaze from the redhead for a moment to see if I was paying attention, "Ginger, I want you so bad tonight." I was paying attention, I guess, and yes Ginger was a light so bright so badly wanted, but within twenty minutes of seating myself and sampling one more drink, the ceiling started to dip and bob over my eyes and the floor began to float.

I felt my way to the Men's Room and, with the calm befitting a jeweler, knelt before what seemed to me an enormous toilet. I purged myself with unexpected violence and not a moment too soon. On the margin of my consciousness someone was gagging and I remember experiencing a modicum of regret and guilt.

I rinsed out my mouth and splashed water on my face and on my way out of *The Milky Way* patted Virgil on the shoulder.

"Darn, already? Hey, you going to be okay driving?"

I DROVE back to the apartment and parked around the corner on Herald Street. I stood for a while on the sidewalk imagining Callie in Paris with her mother and sister, the three Coldwell girls browsing shop windows, sitting at outdoor cafés, and enjoying the attention of admiring males.

The images were disheartening and I was glad for the distraction of a small white mark rippling and growing in the distance. I stared at it until my vision began to blur. I shook my head and looked again. It was still there, small and white, but not as small as it had been.

I rubbed my eyes and waited and the white mark continued to expand. I massaged my eyes and tried again to focus. The white mark was splitting, it had legs, and then it had arms. And then it sprouted a head. I watched a slight young man dressed in white moving toward me at a good pace down Herald Street. The man moved with purpose, apparently undeterred by my presence.

I held my ground. The man slowed his gait and then came to a stop some five or six yards from where I stood. He examined me head to foot, arm to arm. He was small and thin and wore a loose short-sleeved shirt, white work pants held up by a thin black belt, and black and white sneakers. He looked like someone who might work in a fast-food kitchen and looked to be about my age, early twenties. Suddenly he seemed at pains to understand why he was where he was.

I moved toward him guardedly. The man hesitated and then took a couple of tentative steps toward me.

"My name is Lucas," I said.

"My name is Angel."

"Angel?"

The man nodded and looked down at the floor, as if troubled by the sound of his name coming out of the mouth of a stranger.

I noticed numerous dark specks on Angel's white shirt. Splattered oil, maybe? I couldn't determine their color in the night.

"Are you lost, Angel?"

He appeared roused by my question and looked eagerly into my eyes. Did I have the power to resolve whatever had brought him out into the night?

"You have wife?" he said.

"I do."

"Then maybe you understand."

I now saw blood where before I had seen splattered oil.

"When he get lay off, her uncle come live with us. Six months! Orfeo a big man, he like to drink and he like to touch himself. He say bad thing in big voice like I no exist. He say he no can understand why Elisita marry a little *maricón* like me. He hold himself like this and say to Elisita, I know you want it, *amor.*"

Angel lowered his head.

"I sorry," he said.

"It's all right, Angel."

"I come home from work and Elisita on the floor screaming and Orfeo on top of her. I take knife from kitchen and stick it in his back. Orfeo a big man and he get up and look at me with crazy eyes but I stick knife right here in heart and he fall like a tree. Then I take his *pinga* and cut it off so he can no have it in hell."

Angel showed me his knife hand with great solemnity, displaying the fingernail gauges in his smooth young palm from squeezing hard enough to kill.

A sudden chill swept over Herald Street, or maybe just over me. I'd heard this kind of story before. It was the kind of story passed around like a bag of stolen candy by eighth grade boys hanging out on a street corner on a winter's night. A city boy story, hard and sour, enthralling in its brutality and assignment of power and self-determination and in its promise of street justice.

"Is your wife all right?" I said.

"Elisita say run Angel, you run *hijo*. She say she tell police Orfeo have money trouble. Bad men come for money but Orfeo drunk, he fight and they kill him."

"The police will ask questions. They'll know she lied."

"And what you know? Who you anyway? You say your name Lucas? You no Lucas, you like others, you no understand."

"I do understand."

He stared at me as if he'd never seen me before. In a flare of anguish, he turned and marched off, only to stop and begin to strike himself on the head with his fists. I ran to him.

"No, Angel!"

"*Ay Dios!*" he cried turning his tortured face toward me. "What I suppose to do?"

It took me a couple of minutes to calm him down. Then we walked back up Herald the way he'd come and stopped at the corner of Independence Street where the abandoned old church, Saint

Corbinian, stood with its grimy stained-glass windows that gazed across the street at Babylon Elementary.

He asked me how the fire alarm box on the wooden utility pole worked. I told him how and then he pulled down the handle that opened the box, and after a slight hesitation, depressed the small lever inside, transmitting a telegraph signal to the Legacy City Fire Department. Angel waved goodbye to me and lay down on the concrete sidewalk to wait for the fire trucks. He closed his eyes as if it were naptime.

On my way back to the apartment I heard the sirens. The fire trucks were coming for Angel. I stopped, overcome with remorse. How could I have left him lying there alone on the sidewalk?

I rushed back up Herald. Two trucks had sectioned off Independence Street, their red lights whirling. Firemen swarmed about the area. I couldn't see Angel anywhere.

One of the firemen saw me.

"Hey you, did you trip the alarm?"

"Me? No, I was just taking a walk, I heard the sirens."

"Sir, if you would, get the hell out of here."

I COULDN'T sleep. I turned on the bedside lamp and walked over to Callie's dresser and studied the photograph of Callie and Hadley standing like bookends on either side of their taller mother. In retrospect the thought of having kissed the photograph seemed almost comical. It was no more than an image, after all, flat, dry, and lifeless, stale paper suffocating behind glass, and yet somehow, against all logic, I knew someone was there behind the glass breathing and flipping invoices. She looked up suddenly and gazed at me through the glass in dutiful but playful compliance.

Four days left, Lucas!

Three days!

Just two more days.

Chapter 6

Callie made an effort to downplay the experience. The night she got home we had beautiful moments. The following evening I asked her—more out of a sense of spousal obligation than a genuine desire to know—to tell me about her two weeks in Paris. It was then that the full measure of her enjoyment became obvious to me. Oh, it wasn't that she had not thought of me, not missed me. It wasn't that at all.

I was the one who insisted she go, after all. I was the one who said it would be good for both of us in the long run, and for that one night it became easy to think nothing had changed and that we were destined to live happily ever after.

When Marla came over to introduce herself to Callie at the company picnic the following weekend, I found myself at a loss for words. Witnessing their easy banter and listening to their eager laughter I felt something like the prick of a needle just below my right eye. I didn't know what to make of the sensation and finally attributed it to the heat of the day and my dire need of a cold shower.

• • •

LIKE ANYONE else, Marla had her rough moments, but for the most part she was an engaging and accommodating woman. All the techies liked her. But you had to be careful in the way you engaged her because of Owen Borders, our misanthropic field chief. Marla and Borders were around the same age, so they had that in common, but publicly they didn't even seem to like each other all that much. Virgil said he stopped trying to figure out that relationship a long time ago. He said it was like trying to complete a puzzle with twenty percent of the pieces missing.

Virgil was the one who got me up to speed on Marla. Apparently, she had lost custody of her two sons and daughter though no one knew exactly why. When she first joined Galaxy there had been a great deal of speculation, most of it centering on the wealthy ex-husband, but no one thought much about it anymore.

Borders got in on the ground floor with her, so to speak, and the thinking around Galaxy was that there wasn't all that much interest anymore on her part, maybe just enough to keep the thing on life support until someone more suitable to her tastes materialized.

On one corner of her desk Marla kept a framed photograph of her kids getting ready for a day at the beach. The photo was taken a few years ago, probably by the father, and showed three attractive young teens leaning against a blue Ford Thunderbird, the girl in a pink bikini and matching flip-flops posing like a movie star between her older and younger brothers.

All three seemed carefree, and I thought looking at the photo that maybe Marla in some sad way was claiming at least partial responsibility for her kids' happiness, though I doubted she was playing much of a role in their lives at the time. A cynic might even suggest their mother's absence had no impact whatsoever on the kids' quality of life. I always resisted the urge to pick up the picture because then I'd have to say something about her children and I wasn't prepared to bear the awkwardness.

One morning an eight and a half by eleven wood-framed *Serenity Prayer* was displayed on the other corner of Marla's desk. It was a quaint thing with rustic letters etched over antique white inside a curvy pink border festooned with lavender, orange, yellow and white poppies. It was the kind of arts and crafts item you could buy at the mall and hang in a mudroom or on a bathroom wall.

> *God grant me the serenity to accept the things I cannot change; courage to change the things I can; and wisdom to know the difference.*

My first thought was Marla had gone out and got herself religion for under ten bucks. Or maybe she just liked pretty words surrounded by pretty flowers. Or maybe the framed prayer served as a counterbalance to what she had lost. But what did I know? I wasn't sure Marla even knew what she was thinking when she handed the cashier a ten.

Marla never talked about the prayer just as she never talked about her kids, but there they were on display for anyone to see. *Go ahead, ask what you have no business asking*, she seemed to say in those rare silent moments when she wasn't being her usual lively self, or wasn't being who I'd come to think she was.

Some guys liked that occasional flash of attitude, misread the nature of her defiance, thought it a kind of female gamesmanship. They talked about *The Marla Stare* and how they'd provoked and survived it as if it were a badge of honor. Marla was a warehouse goddess, but from the moment I saw that prayer displayed on her desk, I began to sense a deep vulnerability in her.

SHE PEERED over her reading glasses when she heard me come in through the back door but didn't smile. I wondered what was up. I plucked a box of fuses off a shelf as I walked to her office, a kind of ceremonial justification for my presence after normal office hours.

"How's Callie doing?" she said. "What is she now, seven months?"

"Just started her seventh. You know, good days and bad days."

"Oh, I know, believe me. I know bad days. Today, for example, is a very bad day. One of our customers called this morning to say they got broken into while on vacation. The wife had thousands of dollars' worth of jewelry stolen. The husband says our annual inspection is a rip-off, an exercise in fraud, so they're suing. I don't even know how to respond to people like that. And you know Ron Lester? He was the last guy there. He doesn't even work for us anymore."

Marla looked at me, waiting for me to chip in.

"How old's the system?" I said with just the right amount of tech expert empathy.

"Just over three years."

"I guess they never signed the maintenance extension?"

"Look, our salespeople talk it up all the time, we mail out reminders and sign-up forms. What else are we supposed to do?"

"A three-year old system, huh?"

"Right, it makes no sense. Maybe you get system failure once in a blue moon in some old rat-infested warehouse but not in places like Saddle Streams."

"Mr. Borders can't be happy."

"No, Owen is not having a good day. Roseboom called him into his office after lunch and read him the riot act."

I felt a little guilty about liking what I was hearing.

"But it's not his fault," I said.

"Oh, come on, it's *always* the field chief's fault."

She stared at me without blinking.

"I got a call from Owen's sponsor," she said. "He's been skipping his AA meetings."

I knew Borders liked his whiskey, but the AA part came as a bit of a surprise. Was she expecting me to be outraged, concerned, astonished?

Wait, was she glaring at me?

Marla straightened her back, crossed her legs and arms, and snapped, "I can't be talking to you about these things, *you* of all people."

Me of all people? I couldn't hold her stare, not that I wanted to. I wanted to leave, but I knew she'd be different tomorrow. She'd feel bad about snapping at me. Whatever this was would pass. Troubling, though, for sure. I picked up the artsy Serenity Prayer, pretended to read it, and put it back on her desk just the way she'd had it. I really did have to go, but...

"Marla, are you okay?"

She was staring at my right hand, had settled over it with her eyes that were like her hand over mine. She grew soft as I watched her dream about my hand or something remote and unrelated. It all happened so quickly, the harsh insinuation, the Serenity Prayer lifted, looked at, and put back on the corner of her desk, my right hand still held by her eyes...

"So how's Hester Prynne doing?" she said looking up suddenly.

I searched her face for traces of mockery. Instead, I got the understated smile of an Honor's student, the same one she always lavished on me when we talked about my graduate studies.

Hester Prynne and her struggle against the sinister power of those holier than thou morality peddlers helping transport Marla away from security system failures and missed AA meetings and bringing her back to me. And then in a flash Hester and her scarlet letter were gone and Marla was updating me on dates and locations of upcoming LSATs.

The more Marla talked about becoming a lawyer, the more I believed it was a ploy designed to show me she was more than your run of the mill dispatcher/divorced mom. I didn't mind it all that much. It was part of the game we played.

Sometimes as our words went back and forth, I'd glimpse a flicker of light in her brown eyes. I didn't know what that flicker meant. I wasn't convinced she would ever take the LSATs, or that she was even suited for a career in Law, or that she would ever summon the wherewithal to break away from Galaxy Alarms. I didn't know if it was that tease of a flicker, and her being stuck in a dead-end job that was making me angry, or if it was something else I hadn't yet figured out.

"Working in a place like this, Marla?" I blurted out, "sooner or later it'll make you want to kill yourself."

I immediately regretted saying it, but to my surprise Marla seemed to be pondering what I'd said.

"No, I get it," she said.

"My father worked in a factory," I tried to explain. "My mother was a cleaning lady."

"No, no, I understand what you're saying. There's no disrespect intended. My dad was a milkman. He drove a milk truck and left bottles on people's doorsteps. Daddy was really smart, you know, but he got frustrated with life sometimes. Once he told me he did what he had to do so me and my brother—God rest both their souls—could have opportunities he never had. Opportunities, my God. We shouldn't waste time, Lucas. We shouldn't waste time because life is too short."

It was one of the things I most liked about Marla, her working class directness, but the big things gone awry—such as the marriage and motherhood failures—and the weird mood swings and her incomprehensible relationship with Owen Borders… Well, these things were getting harder and harder for me to simply dismiss.

But in that moment—listening to her talk about her Dad—it was easy to overlook all the dysfunction. That moment was real nice, smooth and clean as a full milk bottle. I took and drank from it, and it was good going down. It got real quiet between us, and we became like two breeze-blown leaves dancing in a secret meadow. Maybe Marla was thinking along those lines when she flinched.

It was a nearly imperceptible movement of her head or shoulder, and maybe nobody would have noticed but me. She put her left index finger to her lips so that I wouldn't speak and picked up a pen with her right hand and began to write on a notepad as Borders stepped out of the hallway and into the Dispatch office.

As I saw it, whatever he might have heard or imagined hearing while standing in the hallway—who knows for how long—was less damning than the odor of intimacy that greeted him when he entered Marla's office.

Borders glared at me as he dropped a thick folder on Marla's desk with a loud thud. What a perfect time it would have been for the phone to start ringing.

But it didn't, and I didn't wait. I stepped past Borders and out the door without saying a word. All the way to the back door I felt his eyes through the big office window like two hook pins stuck in my head.

Chapter 7

J ohnny changed my perspective on life. I walked through the back door into Equipment and Dispatch feeling light-headed and exhausted. On that first Friday after Johnny was born the converted warehouse was transformed into something new. Not new as in a fresh coat of paint or reorganization of cabinets. No, we're talking newness of existential proportion, *The Galaxy* infused with brilliant light, flickers of hope like little banners flapping in the breeze of my imagination. That kind of newness, the kind that makes life strikingly beautiful even when it isn't supposed to be.

The techies were gathering in a circle around Borders as was the morning custom. The field chief was sorting the assignment and paycheck envelopes with his regular deliberation, though his expression was a tad more gloomy than usual for a Friday.

Marla had sent flowers and a quaint note to Callie on behalf of everyone at Galaxy Alarms, though I suspected she'd paid for the flowers herself without anyone else being involved. As thoughtful as Marla's gesture was, it fell short of formal company recognition, a detail that until recently had been of no relevance to me but that now emerged as a fundamental requirement.

Virgil said Mr. Roseboom made Borders do all the non-business announcements on paydays. When Ian was born, for example,

Borders read from a sheet, *Congratulations to the Flynn family extended on behalf of Mr. and Mrs. Roseboom and everyone at Galaxy Alarms, Inc.* Virgil said a small bonus had been included with that paycheck, which Borders made a point of mentioning to everyone in order to highlight Mr. Roseboom's generosity.

That was the norm, but Mr. Roseboom had a freak streak in him, as Virgil put it, and could change things up on a whim, so you could never know for sure how it might go.

Virgil said Mr. Roseboom was like one of those rarely glimpsed medieval lords who thought himself a father to his villagers. One of those soft-bellied hard-hearted horse-mounted delusional pricks who wouldn't think twice about selling your kid to a merchant in exchange for dragon teeth or doodling your wife just because he could. Mr. Roseboom wasn't anything like that, Virgil was quick to clarify, just the rarely glimpsed father figure type part.

I wasn't anticipating Mr. Roseboom would sell Johnny or doodle Callie, so when everybody was settled and Borders called out *Amado*—mine always being the first name called—I felt a tingle of pride in my belly like a lit fuse sparking all the way up into my chest and throat and filling my mouth with the sun as I walked to the center of the circle. My hands slid into my pants pockets before I could even feel them move and I couldn't help but break into a big smile. I was smiling in anticipation, not as a man smiles entirely for himself, but as he smiles when celebrating that which raises up with him all those present.

It was all Johnny's doing, of course, Johnny emerging from the cramped wet darkness of the womb into the spacious and noisy bright light, Johnny Amado who defied the void and all notions of emptiness, who gave flesh to the word *hope*, who was the son of Callie and Lucas Amado, who himself was the son of José Amado and Marisol Fernández and grandson to Rodrigo Amado and Isabel Rey and José Fernández and Teresa Neira, just for starters, and if we wanted we could go all the way back to forebears who rarely glimpsed their medieval lord, and farther back still to the farmers and fishermen and hunters and gatherers and loiterers who made us happen.

Were they all watching?

Maybe I was being too self-conscious, but I liked that I could see myself smiling that smile of communal regeneration. It was as though I had stepped away from the circle center to stand among my coworkers and from that vantage point been able to ascertain for myself the quality and legitimacy and purity of the smile on that young father's face. Such a smile could bring down walls, and that was all because of Johnny, and then I was right back in the center of the circle gazing at Borders with unanticipated tenderness.

Borders leaned in toward me and in a voice audible to only two or three others whispered, "That's *Ah-ma-dole* with an *A*, as in *Absolute Shit Hole*."

My smile bled away. I tried to work my way around the words, discover a lesser offense at play. The trailing stink of whiskey offered some mitigation, I told myself. And it would not have been the first time Borders had knocked one of his techies down a notch just for laughs, for the greater purpose of team building, as he liked to say. But this was different. It was personal. There was no immediate follow-up, no quick Band-Aid to soothe the humiliation, no attempt to let everybody know it was all done in good fun, an esprit de corps moment meant to set the tone for the day, meant to launch happy workers into the big open weekend.

I thought of Johnny opening his little pearl eyes and assessing the moving shadows of his big new world, and his first Friday had been forever sullied by a spiteful drunk.

My heart began to race, spurred on now by a sickening mix of disbelief, confusion and anger. I could hear voices all around me and sporadic chuckles of surprise as what Borders had said made its way around the circle.

I took a deep breath and stared into Borders's blue eyes, which receded into shadow. He looked away for several moments. Then, with a sigh of boredom he stretched out his hand and held out the envelope containing my paycheck and the day's assignments. I hesitated, then reached for the envelope. Borders jerked it back before I could grasp it. Someone laughed. Did I hear someone laugh? Was it Weller?

A phone up front began to ring. No one picked up. The beginnings of an inner trembling fury alarmed and dismayed me. The desire to hurt Borders badly, to make him cry out in pain simmered in my core, and my body tensed with barely restrained violence.

Slow. It. Down.

The phone kept ringing. "Jan doesn't get in till eight," I heard someone say in a half-whisper.

Borders grinned in dirty grays and yellows as he extended the envelope a second time, and in that moment my perception of what was happening changed. Power had somehow shifted from him to me, and the tension in my body dissolved away, and I saw the cloaked weakness and the conflicted pleading hidden behind the small eyes. His smile was a rotting mask that I peeled from his face for all to see.

Borders stood in the center of his circle staring at me like a lost wanderer paralyzed suddenly by overwhelming weariness. His grin wilted to a thin crumpled line. The envelope kept his arm suspended in the air stiff as the bloodless arm of a manikin.

I read his thoughts and for an instant was tempted by the grasping hope that at the last instant this would all go away, that I might find it within myself to play along and snatch the envelope from his hand finally and cry out "Gotcha, boss!" Then all the techies would let out a roar of relieved laughter, and all would be as it was before.

But how could it be? Amado was my father's name and his father's and it was my son's name, and what kind of son father man would I be if I let it all be as it was before?

I kept pity at arm's length and watched the fault lines of Borders's person deepen. I watched the man snap into fragments and drift apart. I took no pleasure in it, felt no satisfaction. I was glad my father was not there to see it, and that my son was too young to know about such things.

Borders drew his depleted gaze from me and exited the circle. He placed my envelope and all the other envelopes on a small table and walked back to his office.

Part 2

Marla

Chapter 8

The car doors thumped shut one after the other. From behind the steering wheel of the hatchback I watched Larry Griswold get swallowed up by the warehouse building followed by Louie Calabria, then Julian Mojica, Virgil Flynn, Barry Panko and other men, some young, some not so young. I watched them slow-walk in their navy blue work pants and sky blue shirts with golden arm badge patches depicting a tiny Saturn. They all got swallowed up one by one until there was none left but me.

The sign over the back door entrance read GALAXY ALARMS, INC. in washed out yellow letters suspended over a dirty black firmament. Saturn floated in the upper left corner of the sign dream-like creamy pink and gold and decked in gray rings and moons.

It was a joyless payday. The morning hung ashen warm and had a cloying feel to it, and the early discomfort promised a day of grievous toil and no doubt had something to do with the heavy-footedness of my coworkers.

Since the envelope incident two months ago I'd come to dread those Friday morning gatherings. We continued to assemble in a circle with Borders standing in the center doling out the paychecks and assignments. Each time he called out *Amado* we all observed a moment of silence, as if recollecting the ugly encounter, and I suspected I wasn't the only one wondering if today was the day he would even the score.

The prospect was always enough to make me stop halfway between the hatchback and the back door entrance. Would the earth stop rotating if I turned and drove away? Would the planets tumble out of the solar system?

I could go visit the Legacy City Public Library like I used to do when I was a boy. I could wander among the dense dusty deserted book stacks, and when I had drifted long enough among the thousands of stories and histories and recollections and ideas of men and women, I could sit at a big oak table beneath slow wobbly fans that hung from impractically high ceilings and write down my own stories and histories on a yellow pad.

I turned around and studied the small cramped automobile that doubled as family car and field technician vehicle, that spirited me thousands of miles east and west and north and south and all around TriState to the most extravagant and lowly dwellings and establishments, that fiendishly toyed with me, stalling for unknown reasons at the most inopportune times.

I looked for a sign, a headlight wink maybe? Something to let me know it was okay to drive away. It owed me one, didn't it? But there wasn't a wink to be had, nor the slightest nod of encouragement.

But even if there had been, how would I explain my truancy to Callie? Last night she asked me where I'd gone, and I felt as if she were testing me. Did she mean where did I go to instead of work, or where did my calls take me? Or did she mean it metaphorically, like where did I go while sitting at the kitchen table?

"Did you just ask me where I went?" I said, shoving away Borders's face.

She glanced at me with a look of abstraction.

I had an idea. I would tell her about Borders. About what he said and how badly I had wanted to hurt him. It would help clear the air. It would bring us closer together, the way we were before Paris... But how would I explain Borders without including Marla in the discussion?

"Oh, you know," I said, "here, there, and everywhere."

She was nursing Johnny when I said this, her attention already compromised. Had she heard what I'd said? Maybe she was just tired of my voice.

"There are these gaps in my head," I uttered with flagging energy, "like how the heck did we get from A to B."

I was staring at the center of the table when I said this, at nothing in particular, just the center, trying to fix the exact center point, maybe put my finger on it. How to get from A to B. It was a problem, a conundrum of sorts. How, Callie? How did we get *here*? She seemed always faintly annoyed with me now, and I seemed always faintly offended by something.

The baby had drifted off to sleep while I was talking. Callie frowned as if interested, as if pondering what I'd said. She shifted the baby, wiped his little mouth with a tiny cloth, kissed his soft little head and began to hum a lullaby.

She was sitting in the kitchen of our basement apartment humming a lullaby to our little boy. And then I was standing in Equipment and Dispatch wondering where Owen Borders was.

NO ONE knew where Borders was. Mr. Roseboom was nowhere to be seen. After Alfred the accountant handed out the envelopes, I walked over to the Dispatch office. Where was Marla?

Mrs. Grandie explained she was Miss Marla's new assistant and would be working part time helping out as needed and she didn't know where Miss Marla had gone but that no doubt she would be back soon. She didn't know anything about Mr. Borders either, as this was her first day on the job. She did say she saw Mr. Borders one time, two weeks ago, when she came to Galaxy Alarms to be interviewed by Mr. Roseboom and Miss Marla. She remembered Mr. Borders because he was wearing cowboy boots.

Marla walked into the office all agitated. Before I could open my mouth, she shook her head and raised a don't-even-think-about-it hand.

"I left two messages on his answering machine!"

She glanced wild-eyed at Mrs. Grandie and then settled on me in that unblinking way of hers. "He's been pissed at me. I overheard him tell Weller his pickup failed inspection, so maybe he's at the mechanic's, but he never put it on the calendar. He never said anything."

Under different circumstances I might have read her the Serenity Prayer, but Mrs. Grandie's presence introduced a measure of awkwardness I wanted no part of.

I had begun to worry about Marla and her morbid relationship with Borders. She had witnessed the envelope duel from her office and got Jay Weller to tell her what Borders had said to me. That morning she had waved me over as I was about to leave and apologized for Owen's behavior. I listened until she was finished, turned around and walked out of her office and left the building without saying a word to her.

Dissatisfied with how that had gone, Marla followed me out to the parking lot the following Monday morning and spent several minutes giving me a blow-by-blow account of her clash with Owen that Friday night and how she finally asked him to leave her apartment. She felt sick about the envelope incident and about the fight with Owen and had ended up contracting a feeling of intense dread the minute Owen stormed out of her apartment. She was just having the worst time shaking it. When she had no more to say I stared at her without blinking before asking her why she was telling me all this. All she could do was stare back at me with an expression of pitiful bewilderment.

So all that and Borders trembling on the edge of some emotional explosion was going through my head as I stood in the Dispatch office with Marla and Mrs. Grandie. And then it rushed upon me like a tidal wave of uncensored imagination, and in the very presence of the two women—flesh and bone witnesses—I watched Borders, his face contorted with rage, throw Marla to the floor, pin her down, and repeatedly call her a lowlife whore. I watched—rapt and helpless—as Marla thrashed while Borders tried to force his knee between her legs to pry her open. And when she continued to resist, he punched and bloodied her into submission.

The terrible vision blazed so fierce and real that I felt myself burn with shame from head to toe. I glanced covertly at Marla in search of cuts and bruises that weren't there, and then I peeked at her eyes and then at Mrs. Grandie's eyes, and I was relieved to find that neither woman had witnessed what I had.

"Of course," Virgil replied, as though he'd been asked if he paid his income taxes on time. "Are you kidding me? You think a wife and kids can spare you from loneliness?"

"No, of course, no one can," I said.

"Let me tell you something, rookie. Take my sweet red-blooded American wife. Amy's a great mom, the best, a hundred percent invested in the kids, which leaves, what? Zero percent for anyone else? The kids, man, their activities, functions, get-togethers, etcetera, etcetera... Hey, is this boring you?"

"Nah, man, I'm not bored, just pondering."

"Oh, yeah, how about pondering this? One day you're sitting at a big table with an aching scrotum and an overactive imagination. You're surrounded by people you don't know who are committed to boring one another to death, and your mind starts to wander and you start to wonder where the hell did Romeo and Juliet go. What happened to them, Lucas?"

He was staring at me and I couldn't tell if he was being rhetorical or expecting me to—

"'Grow up, Virgil!' I yell at myself sometimes, but it doesn't change anything, doesn't make me feel any better... I didn't know it would be like this, man. If I'd known, I mean, would I have run the other way if I'd known it was going to be like this?"

"I don't think so, Virgil, because you love her, right? You love Amy."

"Yeah, sure, of course, but the scary part is that one day—maybe after a few drinks—one day you start believing you no longer give a shit and all bets are off."

"But that's because of the bad voice talking in your ear," I said.

"But the other bad voice is shouting, 'No-no-no you can't do that shit!'"

"That's the good voice, Virgil."

"No, they're both bad. One says do something bad, the other says *don't* do something bad, but I've got to be able to breathe. Having no options is like having your head pushed down into a toilet."

"What?"

"It's like you're being drowned."

"Like drowning in loneliness, you mean?"

"But just when you're about to black out Lady Consolation grabs you by the hair and swings your head back up into the air, and water's flying all over the place and your eyes are burning and you do a double-take because that foxy chick sitting across the room next to the guy who won't shut up is flirting with you."

"With me?"

"My point, smart ass, is everybody needs consolation. But what works for one sorry soul may not work for another. Maybe you don't even need to respond in any way. Maybe it's enough to know that chick's looking at you the way you like being looked at, maybe it's enough for her to know you're looking back. "

"Maybe it's enough, but—"

"Yeah, I said *maybe*."

"It can get tricky, but I think you're on to something, Virgil."

"Shut up, Amado."

· · ·

WE GOT back to Legacy City from a grinding visit with Grace, made somewhat less onerous by Coldwell's absence. After Johnny stopped crying, after Callie fell asleep, after letting my mind float awhile—and inspired by Virgil's Lady Consolation—I sat down at the kitchen table and penned a brief rhyme.

Trees in a quiet forest we two seem
Together reaching, seeking newer light.
Gentle rotation of days as in dream
And restive earthworms mining day to night.

I slipped the sheet in my calendar book and kept it there until the morning. I sat in the hatchback in the back parking lot listening to the car doors thump shut and watching the men in blue disappear into the building and Saturn floating pretty with its rings and moons.

After they were all gone, I pulled the sheet out and read the rhyme aloud.

What in the world?

Disturbed by what I was hearing, I read the rhyme aloud a second time hoping to mitigate the damage but instead got the full picture in all its creepy gleaming plenitude.

There they were, Marla and Borders lying naked in bed together, breathless from laughing so hard, their pillow-propped flesh jiggling with merriment, golden lamplight glowing over Marla's opulent breasts and my wrinkled rhyme resting on Borders's crotch. Borders, grinning like a wolf, lifts the sheet yet again and reads the verses, channeling his inner Shakespeare in that phony drawl of his.

I tore the note into pieces and ate it, though I couldn't bring myself to swallow. I spit the wad into my hand and shaped it into a little ball that I rolled and rolled between my palms as I kept reciting to myself, "Nothing happened, nothing happened, nothing happened…"

Chapter 9

From up the road the flat-roofed ranch at 247 Hollow End Road looked like a matchbox. It sat by itself on a treeless, weed-strewn lot that had been baking in the sun all day. The ugly little house made my lips and tongue feel as hot and dry as that roof must have been, and I marveled that the house and my mouth hadn't yet burst into flames.

What kind of people were these Brinkleys? Would they offer me a tall cool drink?

The kindness of strangers, the good Samaritans, the givers of all stripes seemed to always be in short supply. I could get through one more customer, I knew, and barring a last-minute emergency call from Marla—something that wasn't likely—on my way home I would just hit the first 7-Eleven and grab an ice-cold Coke.

Marla had gone out of her way to try to make my life easier since the envelope incident. No more last second emergency calls. She was drawing guys from longer distances to do what I should have been doing. No one had complained, or noticed, that I knew of. Maybe I should have said something... I remembered the last time I got emergency call duty—if that was what they insisted on calling it—because it happened the day before Johnny was born and because of the bear.

I was in Staten Island saying goodbye to my last customer that day when Marla called the house and dispatched me to a two-story Dutch Colonial less than a mile away. The immense head of a bear hung on the wall over the fireplace in the living room. I think it was a grizzly. Whatever it was, it was unimaginably large, and it dominated the modest living room charging the atmosphere with a strange blend of menace and absurdity. It was so big it seemed fake.

"Oh, it's real," the husband had volunteered with a subtle brand of hostility, just in case I was harboring any doubts. He showed no interest in elaborating and appeared in a hurry for me to fix the broken magnetic contact on his mudroom window.

The Brinkley call was straightforward. Single level, two bedrooms, one bath, no basement. Fire system only. Check the control panel, replace the battery, test all the heat sensors, the smoke detector, the sounding device, and obtain the customer's signature. Piece of cake, thirty minutes tops.

The front door opened less than halfway and revealed the right half of a short, chunky woman split evenly down the middle. The musty air that was released by the breach buffeted my face, and the peculiar one eye, half nose, half-lipsticked smile distracted me from speaking.

"Mr. Galaxy, I presume?" the woman said.

"Uh, Mrs. Brinkley? Yes, I'm from Galaxy Alarms."

Mrs. Brinkley made no attempt to open the door any further. As I squeezed into the house sideways with my toolbox and testing equipment in tow I immediately understood why. I found myself at the threshold of a narrow trench whose walls reached nearly to the ceiling.

The weight-bearing portions of the trench walls were constructed mainly of furniture pieces, tables, shelves, a pool table, a ping-pong table, and a number of unused or unusable large appliances. Atop these were stacked drawers, cases and containers filled with dishes, cups, pots and pans, piles of books and string-bound stacks of newspapers and magazines. The uppermost layer was largely populated by carefully placed little statues of animals and lawn creatures and leprechauns and saints and figurines and long-limbed Barbie dolls and square-jawed GI Joe's complemented by vases and plaques and other assorted bric-a-brac, everything thoughtfully stabilized by a kind of fabric mortar mix of cushions, pillows and towels stuffed into any and all gaps and aesthetically unified, it seemed, by strategically positioned bunches of artificial flowers and ferns that lent to the little ranch a grotesque funeral home-like air.

I noticed that Mrs. Brinkley was staring at me, no doubt convinced that I had forgotten why I was there, what with all the wonders to behold...

But she was all business the next instant, pointing to a heat sensor dangling from the living room ceiling no more than a few inches from the head of a ceramic penguin.

"Are you going to fix that?" she said.

"Yes, absolutely."

"Are you going to fix everything, Mr. Galaxy?"

"Of course, Mrs. Brinkley."

"Everything?"

"I'm not sure I know what you mean, Mrs. Brinkley."

She burst into aborted laughter that sounded like a small muffled explosion but in an instant had regained her composure.

"Oh, don't mind me. I'm just having a little fun with you is all. I suspect you'll want to check the control panel first?"

Mrs. Brinkley led the way, flip-flops flapping rhythmically. Her ponytailed graying hair lay limp against her damp white back. She was dressed in an oversized turquoise tank top and billowing white shorts that highlighted the rhythmic roll of her big bottom.

I took note of a small gap in the trench wall to my left that revealed an air conditioner in what seemed the final throes of its existence. It was emitting a tepid moist breeze that was largely absorbed by the dense warm mass of pulp surrounding it.

In the dining room Mrs. Brinkley paused and directed my attention to a large framed print of a painting I'd seen before. I had always been seduced by its mysterious eroticism and felt heartened by its presence in the dreary little ranch. The painting showed two young naked huntresses moving through a forest, each accompanied by an eager, muscular white canine.

"*Nymphs Hunting,*" Mrs. Brinkley said, narrowing her gaze. "Grandpapa was a renowned painter, you know, an expat. He moved to Paris after Grandmamma died and after a time settled in Giverny where his remains are interred. Grandpapa never stepped foot in the United States again."

Did she expect me to believe her grandfather had painted this? "Your grandfather painted this?"

"Oh no, no, no, no!" she cried from a place of merriment.

But again, she was quick to compose herself. She cupped her right elbow with her left hand and held her right hand against her cheek as she studied my face for a few moments before speaking.

"Grandpapa and Julius were extremely close and great admirers of each other's work."

I wasn't sure where she was heading with that and found no good reason to probe and further delay my exit. I raised my eyebrows in a gesture of appreciation and smiled.

To my surprise—for other than our voices, Mrs. Brinkley's flip-flops, and the death drone of the air conditioner, I had detected no other sound—the first bedroom revealed a bony-shouldered teenaged boy hunched over a crowded desk.

"Julius, do come say hello to Mr. Galaxy," Mrs. Brinkley said. "Julius is named after Julius LeBlanc Stewart," she explained and tilted her head as she looked at me, "who painted *Nymphs Hunting,* of course?"

Julius got up from his desk, turned around, and smiled ingenuously. I was surprised at how tall and thin he was. He was wearing jeans and a camouflage t-shirt dominated by the head of a magnificent stag.

"My apologies, Mr. Galaxy! Hello!"

"Hello Julius!" I said trying to match the boy's enthusiasm, but my reply only seemed to distress him. Julius frowned and went back to whatever it was he had been interrupted from doing.

The control panel was located just outside the bathroom inside a towel closet. With some maneuvering and reorganizing of clutter, I was able to finally access and replace the battery and set the panel for testing, but already my goal of completing the call in thirty minutes was a pipe dream.

After fixing the dangling sensor and resolving a number of other random issues, I completed all the required checks and tests. I glanced at my watch: fifty minutes had elapsed. It could have been worse. I walked past Julius's bedroom and observed the boy hunched over his desk just as he had been when I first saw him. I thought it best to leave him undisturbed and went looking for Mrs. Brinkley, but with no success.

The day was catching up with me and I began to feel a bit woozy. I headed for the bathroom. Under the watch of the nymphs I set my toolbox and test equipment down on the floor and took a moment to admire once more the smooth white limbs.

I went into the bathroom and lifted the toilet seat with the toe of my shoe. As I relieved myself, I took in the enormous piles of smooth hardened soap scum laced with mildew and grime that coated the sink, the faucet, the faucet handles, and areas of the checkered black and white tiled floor. The opaque white, black and gray-streaked piles were like an architectural novelty, like miniature Gaudí structures.

Any thought of coaxing a handful of water from the repulsive sink vanished at the sight of the largest silverfish I had ever seen dropping from the ceiling into the basin where it squirmed and slid and struggled against the downward pull. My foot rose once more to depress the toilet handle, and I walked back out to the trenches listening to the tortured gurgles of bad plumbing.

When I got out into the hallway, Julius stood blocking my way. He was holding a smooth gleaming rifle. My pulse quickened.

Do not stare at the boy. Keep your eye on the gun.

Whatever my views on the commerce and purpose of guns, the boy's rifle was a thing of perilous beauty, like the nymphs in the forest. What perfection of irony it would be to travel this far in years and miles only to die at the hands of a troubled gun-toting teen on a street called Hollow End Road.

Where was the mother? I was poised to lunge and imagined young Julius and myself in a death struggle over the rifle, the two of us knocking about, our bodies bounding off the trench walls, ceramic penguins and stainless steel pots crashing to the floor.

Assuming I was successful in wresting the rifle from this pencil-thin boy, then what? Would Julius draw a bowie knife from the back of his belt? Would he bull rush me? Would I shoot him? Where? In the leg? What if I missed his leg? Would I shoot him in the chest and hope to miss his heart? Would I shoot at all?

To my great relief Julius grinned as artlessly as he had when he first greeted me. Even so, I wasn't ready to let my guard down.

"She's a Browning Safari, sir, right? You already knew that, right, Mr. Galaxy?"

Oh, how to answer that?

"I haven't spent all that much time with guns lately. But I'll tell you what, that rifle you have there in your hands is a thing of beauty. I don't believe I've ever seen such a beautiful rifle."

Julius pondered what I had said, his smile gone just like that. The rifle, which he'd held sideways to that point, was suddenly raised toward me.

"Would you like to hold her, sir?"

Other than a plastic Winchester rifle suitable for ages seven to eleven I had never before held a rifle, had never had the desire. Despite my aversion to guns, I received the rifle from Julius's hands with all due reverence. I couldn't deny that I experienced a strange pleasure as I felt the rifle's weight sink into my hands. It was heavy, slick and deadly, and I felt perfectly balanced holding it, confident and resolute. I could see how the rifle might impart a kind of moral authority to the bearer—however illusory—and how it might make a man feel twice the man he actually was.

"Browning Safari, Belgian made, .308 Norma Magnum caliber," Julius said.

I nodded, hoping to appear tuned in, but Julius seemed to expect more of me.

So I drew the rifle up with the utmost care and aimed it at the nearest heat sensor, rifle butt tucked against my shoulder. I simulated a couple of mild kickbacks. "Pow! Pow!" I said before handing the rifle back to Julius.

"No doubt about it, the perfect marriage of technology and art. I have to say, Julius, I can't imagine anyone doing a better job of maintaining this beauty."

"Ha! If only he were as keen about straightening up his room."

Mrs. Brinkley appeared behind me, round and bouncy and waxing ironic. I waited for her to break into manic laughter. I grinned anticipating her freewheeling disclaimer, which would go something like this: *Now really, Mr. Galaxy, how could you possibly think that I, ha-ha-ha, that I, oh my, just one look at this godforsaken place, ha-ha-ha. Really, Mr. Galaxy, where do you come from?*

But instead, with an edge to her voice, as though she'd grown weary of my presence, she demanded the invoice. She signed it with a flourish but then motioned to me with her hand in a come-hither fashion. I followed her into the kitchen.

To my astonishment she drew a pitcher of iced tea from the refrigerator and poured me a tall glass. The glass immediately began to sweat and the blurry smear of lipstick on the rim in no way deterred me. I turned my wrist just so to avoid Mrs. Brinkley's lip marks and down went the cold brown liquid in one long, noisy gulp. It was way too sweet, but it was cold and wet and refreshing and I was flushed with good will and gratitude.

We said our goodbyes and I walked out into the furnace of the dying day eager to get home to my wife and son. I was going to help her remember what we were like before—how we were the best of all dreamers and lovers and friends—and I wouldn't give up until we were all that again.

My mind was as clear as it had been all day, and I hadn't felt this flood of optimism in a long time. I started up the hatchback, rolled down the windows to relieve the compressed mass of heated air, and flicked on the air conditioner. I had just begun to pull away from the curb when I heard Julius cry out, "Mr. Galaxy, sir! Mr. Galaxy! Mr. Galaxy!"

The urgency in the boy's voice caused me to slam the brakes and the hatchback jolted to a hard stop and stalled.

The first thing I noticed about Julius was that he was unarmed as he bounded ostrich-like toward me. The second was Mrs. Brinkley standing at the front door entrance, her small white hand shielding her eyes from the sun. The third was long lanky Julius stumbling headlong and falling amid the dry weeds.

Chapter 10

"Owen is dead."

Wait, what did she say?

I waited to hear her say it again—just in case I'd misunderstood—but she didn't want to or couldn't, and her silence allowed what she'd said to knock around inside my brain in ghoulish echoes.

Owen dead? Owen is dead? Owen is dead as dead? Owen is dead as dead is dead?

Not a peep out of her. Why don't you say it again, Marla, let me hear that one more time just to make sure—but not a peep forthcoming—and in that stone silent lag I sampled muddled happiness that would have kept me contented if not for a sudden cold blast of guilt.

OWEN IS DEAD!

"Wait, what did you say?"

"Oh, Lucas."

"What happened?"

"You want me to repeat it?"

"What?"

"Never mind."

Even as Marla's voice faded away, I was retrieving Borders, visualizing the familiar distaste etched on his sullen, weathered face. I could almost hear the adopted drawl, the thin dry lips slogging through words of condemnation that landed on my head like methodical punches.

WHY – DIDN'T – YOU – JUST – PLAY – ALONG – AH – MA – DOLE?

Then Marla started to whimper in a fatigued manner, side-stepping the worst of it, I suspected, not allowing herself to be completely overwhelmed just yet by grief or rage or fear or whatever it was she was feeling, leaving herself room to breathe and sidle along on a less arduous path, keeping herself within reach, that's what it was.

She stopped weeping and I suspected she might be aware that I was working through a few things of my own, like images of Borders succumbing to a heart attack and wrapping his pickup around a utility pole or being beaten to death in a bar fight. Yes that, but also entertaining Virgil's conviction regarding the role of consolation in a person's day to day survival, and I thought right now—in the midst of this Borders shockwave—right now that's what I was for Marla, a consoling distraction, someone on the other end of the phone line being there to listen to her troubled silence just as she was listening to mine, the two of us making guesses at the other's interior turmoil.

"I hate to ask this of you, I do, and I wouldn't if I felt I had a choice. But Lucas, would you? Would you come by? Could you do that on your way home? Would you do that for me, stop at my apartment for a couple of minutes? Just to talk a little?"

Oh, such a dire request that shouldn't have been but was a jolt to my psyche, at some unexplored level more disturbing than hearing *Owen is dead*, though I should have seen it coming. How did I not see it coming? Because my head was filled with shifting panoramas of Borders's final moments? Because Callie and I were supposed to begin again? Because I had just downed a tall glass of iced tea with lipstick smudge on the rim and did Mrs. Brinkley put something in that tea?

"There's no one else I can talk to about these things," she said.

Oh Marla, Marla, in your world *these things* can mean anything. What things exactly? Borders things, Marla things, divorce and loss of custody things, you and me things, all of the above things?

"I hope you won't be angry with me," she said in a new steady voice.

"Angry? Why would I be angry?"

"I called Callie."

"Did you say—? Wait, why would you call—? You mean about Owen?"

"I lied to her, I had to."

"Slow down, Marla, please. What, what do you mean you lied to Callie? About what?"

Dead silence. Dead as dead is dead.

"I didn't tell her about Owen. I told her we got an emergency call, that you were the only one in the area. I told her the call wouldn't take long… I just couldn't stand the thought of her getting the wrong idea."

"The wrong idea? About what?"

"See, I knew it."

"The wrong idea about what, Marla?"

"I knew you were going to get angry."

"I'm not angry, I'm confused."

"I need someone to talk to, you know?" she said in an almost business-like tone, as though I owed her, and maybe I did.

"I'm not angry, Marla. I'm not."

"Someone who maybe might even give the slightest little shit and that I can look in the eye when I'm talking and know they're truly there for me. Look, I am sorry to ask this of you. This is so hard, Lucas, you have no idea. I am in such a bad place, and I just don't know how I'm going to—"

She began to weep softly.

"Listen to me, Marla. Everything's going to be all right. I'm coming over. Callie doesn't need to know, okay?"

"You are? Really? You've always been such a good friend, Lucas, I can't tell you. Do you know where Jackson Street is?"

"I do."

"I'm at 339, second floor."

"I'm heading right over. But tell me what happened to Owen."

"No, not now. I can't do this. We'll talk when you get here, okay?"

She hung up the phone before I could change my mind.

It was an easy number to remember, and I don't know why I wrote it down on my palm. I wasn't thinking about writing the number when I was writing it, and the *9* tail trickled off down toward my wrist like rainwater on a window pane. I only noticed it later, at home, when I was in the shower washing my face.

Chapter 11

Marla seemed surprised to see me when she opened the door. She had the absorbed look of someone suddenly pulled away from a compelling read.

"Lucas?"

Something was off. I gazed at her for a moment before doing a quick visual scan of the apartment. We had spoken less than an hour ago. Had I imagined our phone conversation? I distinctly remembered Mrs. Brinkley standing in front of 247 Hollow End Road and Julius tumbling in the weeds and a woman's voice on Mrs. Brinkley's phone saying *Owen is dead.*

"No one's here," she said with a curious smile. "Can I get you something to drink?"

I am in such a bad place, and I just don't know how I'm going to—

I stared at her, wanting her to cry.

"Something to drink, Lucas?"

"No, thanks."

"A beer?"

"No, nothing."

Then she smiled again—but now in a way I could understand—like I wasn't getting it, this whole thing, whatever it was. I glanced down the hall at her closed bedroom door.

"What's going on?" I said.

"There's no one here, only you and me."

"I'm here because you asked me to come, remember?"

She nodded. I glanced again at the closed bedroom door. I searched her face and she seemed puzzled by my scrutiny, but she wasn't puzzled at all, was she? I walked to the bedroom door and flung it open. An unmade bed, clothes on the floor, no sign of Borders. I went in and opened the closet door and looked for Borders's legs beneath the hanging garments and then got on all fours and looked under the bed.

I walked back to the living room. She was shaking her head, still smiling, but in a way I couldn't quite understand. "You know what? You need to take a shower because you stink."

Her face contorted and I felt a wave of nausea rush over me as I watched her shoulders begin to shake. I looked around. Did I miss something? Was he in the shower? She dropped down onto the couch as if the weight of hilarity were too great for her to bear standing. She covered her mouth with her hands and produced an awkward noise that could have been a guffaw or an aborted sneeze.

I dashed to the bathroom, my heart pounding, and swung open the shower curtain. What was happening to me?

I was at a loss as to what to think or do. For a moment all things seemed to have come to a stop. Even the hum of the refrigerator in the kitchen went silent. Nothing was ticking, buzzing, leaking, humming. All forms and colors seemed to quietly recede, deferring to some creeping madness or looming pronouncement.

Then from the deep belly of silence Marla let out a low grinding cry of rage and tottered into calamitous child-like wails. Her pain was sharp and vicious and of enormous comfort to me. I sat down next to her on the couch, incapable of anything but presence. Gradually she grew calm and her breathing became normal.

"How could you think such a thing?" she said looking at me askance.

"I'm sorry, it's just that what happened between me and Owen…"

"But how could you think that I would—?"

Do the unthinkable?

She turned and stared in disbelief at me a long time and shook her head in disgust and looked down at her hands and rubbed one over the top of the other so she wouldn't have to continue looking at me. I never felt so young and unsure of myself.

"The incident with the envelope," I said. "That time in your office when he walked in on us. I feel kind of, I don't know, like things needed to be resolved and they never were. I guess I'm having trouble accepting it, that he's gone like this, that we didn't have a chance to talk, reach some kind of understanding."

"You sure you don't want a drink?"

"I'm sure."

"Owen told me he found issue with you."

"Issue, huh? Okay. He never did like me, not from the first."

"No, he didn't."

"What did I ever do to him?"

"You missed your wife."

"I don't get it."

"If anyone's to blame it's me."

"What blame? This isn't about blame."

"I said things to him, okay?"

There was a tricky finality to the way she said that. It was like she was saying let's not talk about this anymore, unless you want to. But you did ask me what happened to Owen, didn't you? You wanted to know. But did I? I checked my watch. I could stay a few more minutes, give her some time to say whatever else she needed to say.

But she found a quiet place, and I started paying close attention to her breathing. Then, in a soft voice, she started talking about

Borders. She said nice things about him. Believe it or not Owen could be very sweet. Owen was actually pretty funny, you know. Owen used to collect rocks. When she drew close and lay her head on my chest, I told myself it was a sisterly gesture. Soon I could feel the pulsing of her blood getting mixed up with my own.

I hesitated before placing my hand on her shoulder. It seemed an okay thing to do. She sighed, not in response to my touch—I didn't think—but for the memory of Borders, whom she continued to eulogize as though nothing could be more important to her now than to vindicate the man.

"Owen was awarded a scholarship to Cornell. Did you know that?"

"I didn't. For engineering?"

"Electrical engineering, but he dropped out a week into his freshman year after his mother killed herself."

"Oh, geez, I had no idea."

Marla grew quiet again. I drew her close just for a moment in a gesture of support. She appeared not to notice. She smiled and started talking about Owen again and how he liked to tell stories about the kinds of people he would run into during his two years in Texarkana, Texas. He was living there with a disabled uncle—a World War II veteran—and his wife. His uncle got him an entry level job at the Red River Army Depot.

"There was a local pastor who visited Owen's uncle every Wednesday evening like clockwork, always with a bottle of whiskey and two shot glasses in his coat. They'd sit in the living room talking local politics and high school football. When they were finished the pastor would go in the kitchen to rinse out the glasses and dry them with his handkerchief and then put them back in his coat pockets."

"Did he ever offer Owen a drink?"

"You know, I never asked… Oh, and there was this old man who lived across the street who sat on his front porch all day complaining. 'Them three bitches turned my palace into a house of sin. Them whores just won't leave me be. Somebody better call the sheriff.'"

We both laughed and Marla shifted her body to get more comfortable.

"After his uncle died, Owen stayed with his aunt for a while. When the Korean War broke out, he signed up with the Air Force and when all that was over, he moved back east, brought that silly drawl and those cowboy boots with him."

She frowned after she said this and was quiet for a few moments.

"One day he blew my mind, Lucas. He told me he'd never loved anyone but me. I laughed in his face and said, 'Same here, champ,' but I was only kidding. I waited for him to say something funny, but he got real serious. He told me his head got damaged a long time ago. That's when he told me about his mother. He said that's why he could never marry me. He said he could never do that to me."

After a long pause, Marla looked up at me with tears in her eyes and said, "Can you believe that shit, Lucas? He could never do *that* to me?"

We sat in silence. I watched her wipe a cheek with the heel of her hand, the corner of an eye with a fingertip. Watched that same hand reach up where my hand rested on her shoulder and gently settle upon it, warm and moist and light. I kissed her hair.

A tingling warmth engulfed us. The world was quiet except for our breathing. Marla took a deep shuddering breath and began to unbutton her blouse. What she was doing seemed as beautifully ordinary to me as the pouring of water into a glass. I watched her nimble fingertips expose the curves and depths of her bosom like a fresh promise. She took my hand and guided it. My fingers slid under and cupped the generous flesh and felt pulsing within its warm damp weight dream and regret.

All that existed beyond that room seemed illusory. All people and things and past events seemed no more than shadows. Reality became concentrated in one small hidden place. Her breast in my hand was all that was real. When I squeezed her nipple, she flinched in pain.

"I'm sorry!"

"No, don't, it's nothing," she said trying to smile.

"What am I doing?" I said rising to my feet.

"Lucas, no—"

"I have to go."

But I didn't. I stood there watching her button her blouse. She smoothed over her skirt twice, three times. She wouldn't look up at me. She placed her left hand on her lap—so that it lay there like a sleeping kitten—and gently began to stroke it with her right hand.

I was sure I had noticed it before, but now her wedding band struck me as something oddly new and the cruelest of ironies, and I felt a kind of dispensation being bestowed on me. I knelt on the floor before her and she opened herself like a lily. She closed her eyes. Her mouth became bottomless and I couldn't stop falling.

Chapter 12

Virgil once told me one of the things he tried to remember every morning was to make other people feel important. Every person had a name and to hear someone say it in a friendly way was like putting a coin in that person's consolation meter. It might be just enough to help them get through another half-day. You could never tell and that's why it was always worth doing.

When Jan the receptionist was hired Virgil made it a point to take a minute to walk to the front desk that Monday morning and say, "Hi Jan, welcome to *The Galaxy*. I'm Virgil. Hey, do you sing? I'm just asking because…"

Jan was a thin, timid girl with a marvelous voice that was more suited to a recording studio than a receptionist's desk. Virgil's encounter with Jan was an example of building people equity, he had explained. And the equity ensured the occasional payout, like when Jan told Virgil she overheard Mr. Roseboom talking to Alfred the accountant.

Mr. Roseboom clearly wasn't being himself because he always closed his office door whenever he wanted to talk about important things, but this time he left it partly open, and Jan, whose desk was right outside Mr. Roseboom's office, heard every word exchanged between the two men as if she were sitting right across from Mr. Roseboom's desk.

Apparently, Mr. Roseboom had driven over to Borders's apartment building mid-morning that Friday and had asked the landlady to unlock Borders's door. Inside Mr. Roseboom took note of the unmade bed, the empty whiskey bottle on the floor and the closed bathroom door. Mr. Roseboom said the landlady knew about Owen's drinking problem and had a look of satisfaction on her face as she waited for Mr. Roseboom to go knock on that bathroom door and give Borders a piece of his mind. Instead, Mr. Roseboom walked over to the night table and picked up a blank Galaxy Alarms invoice with the words *Nobody's fault* written on the *Total Due* line. It was signed *Owen Borders – 20 July 1979.*

MOST OF the Galaxy folks showed up at the funeral home Tuesday evening to pay their respects to the family of the deceased. Mrs. Lefebvre, the widow of Borders's uncle with whom he had stayed after his mother killed herself, had come all the way from Texarkana, Texas. She stood to the left of the casket accepting condolences on behalf of any surviving family members, though whether such people existed any longer was a matter of pure speculation. I watched Mrs. Lefebvre talk to Alfred the accountant and his nosey wife and felt sad for all her troubles.

When Callie spotted Marla not far from Mrs. Lefebvre, she walked right over to her. I hesitated, then followed with reluctance, stationing myself in the general vicinity. I cringed as I watched Callie embrace Marla. I didn't know exactly how Marla would react, but given my own discomfort, I wasn't surprised to see her recoil when Callie rubbed her arm and began saying pretty words to her. Callie did her best to hide her surprise and seemed tongue tied for a moment. Before she could say anything more I went and got her and took her by the hand to Borders's casket.

We knelt on the red velvet kneeler and Callie prayed for Owen Borders's soul while I resumed the futile task of exterminating all traces of the man from my mind. At that point it didn't much matter whether it was an open or closed casket as Borders's probing gaze was like that of a hungry wolf monitoring my every breath and movement.

After Callie crossed herself, we extended our condolences to Mrs. Lefebvre and then I led Callie to the back of the room where I intended for us to put in a few more minutes of respectful observance before leaving.

"Shouldn't we be with Marla?"

When I didn't respond she explained, "She's hurting badly, Lucas. I never realized how close she and your supervisor were."

I wanted more than anything to disappear, but Callie wanted more from me, expected more, a word or two confirming what she had observed, an affirming nod, a movement of feet in the right direction. But I was giving her nothing. I didn't have it to give. Her concerned expression of inquiry quickly gave way to sharp-eyed impatience.

"Why didn't you say something to her?" she said.

"What should I have said that you didn't already say?"

She seemed to focus her eyes in order to see me more clearly.

"Why are you being so odd?" she said. "So cold, like you don't care or anything."

"What are you talking about? I do care."

"What's going on with you, Lucas?"

"Nothing's going on, I'm just being my regular cold and odd self, like you said. And in case it hasn't yet sunk in, that big shiny box? My boss's body is lying in that box. Guy killed himself. That's what's going on. Is that cold and odd enough for you?"

She stared at me like I was a crazy person. Then her expression turned analytical, as if she had gotten some kind of a foothold, and I started to feel invaded, like she was crawling up into my eyes, working her way around my eyeballs, getting behind them, owning them, and owning everything they had witnessed. I couldn't allow it. She had no right to be there. I opened my mouth to get her out.

"I hate to break this to you, but you know what the last thing Marla wants to hear is? That everything's going to be fine, that we're in God's hands and all that happy nonsense. Didn't you notice how she pulled away from you? Marla's always had it tough. Not everybody gets to fly off to Paris whenever they want. But that must come as a shock to a Coldwell, huh?"

I might just as well have struck her across the face. The weakening of her mouth made me want to drive a knife into my wicked nipple-pinching hand. She left me standing there and walked over to Marla and stood by her side without saying a word.

Borders had been right to detest me. The Coldwells had been right. They tried to warn their daughter. They even went the extra mile. I had to give them credit. I looked across the room at the two women, one a wounded angel, the other a prisoner of calamity.

I turned my attention to Mr. and Mrs. Roseboom, who were speaking with Mrs. Lefebvre. Not far from them was a small mahogany table displaying a handful of framed photographs. I made my way over there to look at the pictures. Owen pushing his uncle in a wheelchair. Owen with his uncle and Mrs. Lefebvre. Owen with a small group of young men in a bar, all wearing cowboy hats. And Owen by himself leaning against a pool table holding a pool cue upright between his legs and staring gloomily at the camera.

There were no pictures of Owen's mother. Had she burned them all? Had he? No sign of his father. Was his father even alive?

I should go ask Mrs. Lefebvre who looked dignified in mourning. She struck me as a woman accustomed to sacrifice, the kind of person who expects nothing in return. No doubt she had made sacrifices to come east knowing there was no other family to display those few pictures of Owen. Mrs. Lefebvre and Owen had shared no common blood, but for two years she kept dropping coins in his consolation meter.

I wanted to be closer to Mrs. Lefebvre, to whatever it was in her that hinted at holiness. I took a few steps in her direction but stopped.

"Owen was my supervisor," I whispered to myself. "He found issue with me. Tell me, Mrs. Lefebvre, did you ever see Owen smile a true and happy smile?"

That was how I might have begun talking to Mrs. Lefebvre. But why would I burden a good woman in that way? I went back to the rear of the viewing room to wait.

Chapter 13

Just before noon the following Saturday Mrs. Corrigan handed me her telephone receiver. It was Rolonda Belford, the weekend dispatcher. I couldn't keep up with all she was saying about Mrs. Bingham, my first customer that morning. I gathered there was some unresolved issue, possibly a question or questions concerning my interaction with the customer—a middle-aged widow—who may have been led to believe, or had possibly misunderstood, or who may have thought, or—

Just when I was about to insist Rolonda get to the point, her voice became rich and deep and her words processed out of her mouth with somber deliberation.

"Just so you know, Mr. Amado, I talked to Mrs. Bingham and I resolved your issue."

"My issue? Oh, that's good. Okay then. Thank you."

"Mr. Amado, I don't know you all that well, but what I do know is you a married man and a new daddy."

I waited for her to continue, but all I could hear was her labored breathing.

"That is correct, Mrs. Belford."

"Well, you have yourself a lovely weekend, Mr. Amado."

Rolonda's words stuck to me like warm tar. Just as I was preparing to leave, the phone began to ring again. Mrs. Corrigan picked up once more, exchanged a word with the caller, raised her eyebrows, and handed me the receiver.

"I've been trying to get through to you."

"Sorry, the phone was tied up."

"You did leave a message to call you."

"I did. I wasn't sure you would. Did Rolonda give you this number? I was just on the phone with her."

Marla waited several seconds before responding.

"I don't think we should meet," she said.

"I just thought we could—"

"You just thought?"

"I thought if we could just talk…"

The silence extended long enough that I was sure she had pulled the telephone plug from the wall.

"Marla?"

"I know where you are."

"Where I am? What do you mean?"

She clucked her tongue and sighed. "This is your last call today, isn't it? Okay, so meet me at two o'clock in River Park by the gazebo."

She hung up on me and the dial tone buzzed like the drone of swarming bees. Its unremitting hostility gave me pause. I set the receiver back in its cradle and waited a few seconds for alternate directions, maybe an *Oh, never mind* follow-up call that didn't come.

Since Borders's wake Callie and I had said little to each other. Talking with her about anything at all now seemed to me an exercise in self-incrimination. I avoided her. Our spat at the wake supplied the rationale for now, but the expiration date on that excuse was fast approaching.

Yesterday I told her I'd be working Saturdays, at least for the time being. I told her we needed the money. It was late notice, leaving no room for discussion. When I gave her the news she searched my eyes and finally just nodded her head and said okay. I knew she was annoyed with me, but I was feeling cornered and needed more time to figure things out. I had to talk to Marla, make sure we were on the same page regarding Callie.

But hell, who was I kidding? I woke up last night around three and turned on my side. I could see Callie's profile. She was staring at the ceiling. I pretended to be asleep. It was like she was staring at a maze, puzzling over how to get to me. But each trail led her to a dead-end wall that had the word BORDERS written on it in big bold block letters. Borders? she'd be wondering. I had never talked to her about Borders and yet there I was, rendered cold and odd by the man's death.

I watched her fall asleep knowing she would go to Marla. Who better to lead her through that maze? The inevitability of it made me sick to my stomach. My destruction seemed a foregone conclusion. Some vengeful god had already shot the arrow that would one day pierce my heart. One day I'd come home and find no trace of Callie or Johnny.

I got to the park around two. It was too hot to be outside. I tossed my work shirt in the back of the car and pulled a t-shirt over my head. The swampy scent of the Lenape River across the way hung in the oily humid air that softened the world's edges. Over a winding path a lonesome hunch-shouldered figure moved through patches of shade and sunlight like a ghost.

Meeting with Marla was a terrible idea, absolutely insane. I realized that now. What was I supposed to say to her? That Callie was our number one priority? That we had to protect Callie at all cost?

I made my way to the gazebo. Pigeons were ambling about pecking at crumbs on the concrete walk. I sat on a wooden bench and gazed at them. For a while I got lost in their world. I identified the most aggressive and aggrieved among them, named one Attila, the other Hester. An empty potato chip bag on the grass got me up on my feet. I shook out the last few crumbs—generating some excitement among the birds—and tossed the bag in a green waste-basket attached to a wooden post.

I sat back down and my watch showed 2:22. Marla wasn't coming. I felt relief and then I didn't. Where before I'd seen individual pigeons going about their business, I now saw a shifting iridescent mass. I couldn't find Attila, I couldn't find Hester. Did Marla's absence suggest there was nothing to discuss? That, in fact, nothing of consequence had happened between us? Or was she saying you're just going to have to deal with the consequences of your deplorable behavior, aren't you now?

A full-figured woman wearing a clingy pale yellow summer dress and white wedge pumps appeared from behind the gazebo. Her brown hair was tied back in a ponytail like a fifties' bopper. She wore big copper-colored sunglasses that concealed her eyes and large gold hoop earrings. Her skin gleamed in the humid river air like that of a young woman. She stopped and must have been staring at me though all I could see was some semblance of the world she was looking at reflected back at me in warped miniature.

Without uttering a word, she turned suddenly—her dress sweeping the air like a cape—and walked away. The ground shifted as I stood up. I planted my feet and called out her name and all the pigeons leapt into the air.

Part 3

Virgil

Chapter 14

Deep inside the gray matter I felt a pinprick. Up there something like a foil blade started to wag back and forth producing a stretchy rhythmic pain in my head. The blade snapped at the surface. I felt around but there was no nub to pinch and pull, no means to draw her out. Marla Tupo was infecting my brain.

"Hello there, anybody home?"

"Sorry, Virgil," I said scratching my head. "Run that by me again."

"You okay?"

"I'm okay. Go on, I'm all ears."

"There's something I haven't done yet, but maybe you have."

"What might that be?"

"I've never stepped in *bull* shit."

I wasn't in the mood for another of Virgil's linguistic escapades. But that morning in Equipment and Dispatch he had been more insistent than usual that I have a pint with him after work so I played along.

"Hmm, can't say that I have either."

"So why the obsession? Why not cut the *dog* shit? Why not don't be *cat* shitting me?"

"I would never *bird* shit you?"

"Dog, cat, bird, poop, plop, steam, stink, shoe, windshield, shoulder—and you tell me if I'm wrong—but unless you're hanging out at the ranch, you're not going to be stepping in *bull* shit, per se, am I right?"

"You're not wrong, Virgil."

That was as far as I was going with it and he knew it. I looked down to see how much beer was left in my mug.

"Doing anything this weekend?" he said.

"Maybe I'll take Callie and Johnny down to Point Pleasant for a couple of hours."

"I heard showers Saturday."

"Oh yeah?"

I stifled a yawn. I hadn't slept in days. I caught a glimpse of Virgil glimpsing my yawn and started to feel bad about him thinking my aura of discontent was his fault and with him working up to telling me something that might be important and all...

"Callie's mom planned a girls' night out for next weekend," I said. "Cousin's getting married next month. They're going to see a show on Broadway, *A Chorus Line*. Her mom even hired a professional babysitter."

Virgil grimaced but I couldn't tell if it was because of what I'd said or if he was as preoccupied and unhappy a man as I was.

"I get the feeling you've been wanting to tell me something," I said.

Virgil mulled it over.

"Speaking of Broadway," he said, "I once got my ass kicked because Amy couldn't keep her mouth shut."

"No kidding."

"Amy's cousin got her first bit part in some off-off-off-Broadway play. Me and Amy were walking in the city this one hot summer night on our way to see her and I catch sight of these tough guys lounging over a parked car like a brood of lizards. I thought about crossing to the other side but didn't want Amy thinking I was a pussy being that we'd only known each other for a week. So we're walking past and they're checking out Amy's ass, but I'm thinking, Virgil, it's a free country and as long as they don't say or do shit you're good. So I've got Amy by the hand and I'm pulling her along and just when I'm starting to breathe easy she stops, turns around with her eyes ablaze and says to the big guy who's got no shirt on, 'What's your problem, asshole?'"

"No way."

"I step between them and next thing you know I'm sitting in the Emergency Room with a broken nose and a concussion. And see this baby?"

He pointed to the crooked inch and a half long scar above his right eyebrow. "Landed my face on a piece of broken glass."

"I was wondering how you got that. Amy must have felt like hell, huh?"

"Uh, well, yes and no. After Freddy was born, she told me that when I was getting stitched-up it made her real horny. Said she wanted so bad to have my babies, knew I was the one. It took a week and me getting my ass kicked for her to draw that conclusion."

"Ah, she's something else this Amy of yours."

"Oh, she is that… But, you know, sometimes I wonder if love is enough…"

I could see him trying to slow things down, concentrating real hard. Then he looked at me with a smile of resignation and we clinked mugs. Virgil downed the rest of his drink and flagged a waitress.

"One more," he said staring at me like a gunfighter.

I hesitated, then nodded and finished off my drink.

"Sure, one more, but that's it."

"I do give a shit, you know. Most of the time."

"I never doubted it."

Virgil's eye twinkled for a moment and then he got all serious.

"I had this buddy named Leo Benavídez. Leo didn't look all that Puerto Rican but that's what his mom was. He also had an older half-brother and half-sister. When he turned seventeen his brother told him he, Leo, was the son of a rapist. Leo never did go to college. Right out of high school he started mowing lawns and shoveling driveways over at Leisure Village in South Apple. The old timers loved him because he treated them like gold.

"This one customer, a retired high school teacher, gave Leo a biography of Frederick Law Olmsted. The guy was like the patron saint of landscapers. So Leo got inspired reading the book and bought himself a small truck. He talked this eighty-year-old lady into putting a couple of beds in her front lawn with ornamental trees and shrubs and lots of nice dark mulch. Gave her a huge discount and a dozen red roses in a blue vase that she put in the middle of her dining room table."

Virgil smiled at the waitress as she set two fresh pints before us. He continued to watch her as she sashayed back to the bar before he resumed.

"The old lady's place got lots of attention and then everybody wanted Leo to do their front lawns because he was cheap and made their homes look real nice. Next thing you know adult children stopping by to check in on their folks started asking who's doing their lawns.

"One day back in '67 I ran into Leo at a 7-Eleven. He told me he got a call the night before from this bigshot who owned a financial services company up north. The guy and his wife had just installed a new pool in their Saddle Grove home and wanted to fix up the backyard for their daughter's wedding.

"It was a huge job and with short notice and all, but Leo wanted to take it on because his eye was set on bigger and better things down the road. He knew a couple of Mexicans who'd helped him out before and said he could use someone like me too. I was single at the time working odd jobs. I thought why the hell not? A little outdoor work wouldn't be the worst thing for my complexion and waistline, right? So we drove up to that beautiful horse country with the corrals and barns and met this Bradley Graddick and the Mrs.

and they seemed easy-going and friendly enough. They gave us an idea of what they were looking for. We got back to them with a good price and they said fine and put down twenty percent so we could start buying trees.

"We put in fourteen-hour days and finished the job one week before the wedding. When Leo asked Graddick when he thought we might be getting the rest of the money, the guy laughed and put his hand on Leo's shoulder. He looked him square in the eye like he was his son and told him to relax. He said he had to put in one last call to his broker and talk to his accountant. It was all standard procedure. He told Leo he'd be getting a check real soon.

"Leo's brother-in-law lent him money so he could pay the Mexicans. He'd already emptied his savings account to buy the Leyland Cypresses Mrs. Graddick was obsessed with, seventy-five five-footers that we planted in the northwest corner of the property.

"Leo was getting calls from Mrs. Graddick just about every night the week before the wedding. She turned out to be a royal pain in the ass, but we made all the changes she wanted and decided not to tempt fate by jacking up the original cost. We took care of the final details the evening before the wedding and left the place feeling like we'd recreated Shangri La, it looked so good.

"We figured we'd give them a week after the wedding to come back down to earth and if we didn't hear from Graddick by then we'd drive up on Saturday morning, knock on their big fancy doors, and show them a copy of the contract I drew up and that Graddick and Leo both agreed to and signed.

"Well, the days came and went and we told each other a week really wasn't that long considering such a big wedding and all, so let's give Graddick another week and if he doesn't get back to us by next Friday we'll definitely go up Saturday.

"The problem was Leo didn't have a confrontational bone in his body, and I wasn't much better. The thought of driving back to that place and getting in that guy's face was as appealing to me as a trip to the proctologist and having a stainless steel probe shoved up my ass. We waited for a call all week. I gotta be honest, it was humiliating as hell.

"We were eating cheeseburgers at McDonalds that Friday night and couldn't even look at each other. We needed to grow a pair in the worst way so I tried setting a fire under both our asses. I said, 'Fuck Graddick, Leo. We'll sue his sorry ass.'

"Leo looked at me like I'd just bit into a squirrel. He said, 'That's a great idea, Virgil, except for the fact Graddick's brother is the town police chief, and Graddick's other brother is an attorney, and Graddick's got more money than you and me and both our families put together are ever gonna have in our entire lifetimes.'

"That was the most words I'd ever heard Leo say in a row and he was right. Saturday was shaping up to be real ugly. All we could hope was Graddick had some trace of decency and would hand Leo a check when we got there.

"Amy called me when I got home. I told her I had a bad headache just so I wouldn't have to see her. She still wanted to know how things were going with the Graddicks, but I got really short with her and told her I'd talk to her tomorrow because I really had to take some aspirin and go to sleep since my head was killing me. If she knew how we were getting yanked around she would've dragged me and Leo by the ears up to Saddle Grove and banged on Graddick's door herself.

"It was still early after I hung up and I couldn't sleep, so I started reading *The Spy Who Came in from the Cold*. Then Leo called saying Graddick had called him and said to be in Saddle Grove at ten in the morning. I asked him how Graddick sounded and Leo said, 'Upbeat as usual.'

"So we got there and the double doors flew open before we had a chance to knock and three teenaged girls in bikinis dashed past us on their way to the pool. One of them shouted back all pissy and put out, 'Dad, the workers are here!'

"Graddick seemed pleased to see us. He motioned for us to walk with him and then had us stop to watch the girls take turns diving off the springboard. He was really into watching them splash and wrestle and scream in those wild, high-pitched voices. Those couple of minutes felt like a half-hour, but after all the hoopla died down Graddick turned to us and smiled. 'Good news, fellas. The money's been cleared. Just one last thing.'

"We followed him to the rear of the property. We were expecting another of Mrs. Graddick's bullshit requests to be the holdup. You know, like why don't we move that pear tree three feet to the right, but he led us to the cypress hedge instead. He pointed to the bottom branches of one of the trees, walked ahead and pointed to another, and so on until we'd walked the entire length and got a good look at all seventy-five of them. The six trees Graddick pointed out were browning just a bit in the lowest branches. 'They need to be replaced,' he said.

"Okay, so before buying the Leylands Leo had warned the Graddicks this might happen, but it just never seemed to register with them. Mrs. Graddick said the trees were elegant and perfect for the property, case closed. Leo tried to explain that yeah they were elegant and would be fine if maintained the right way. But Leylands weren't the sturdiest trees and you had to keep in mind they would occasionally need a little tender loving care, especially until they got established. But you got the feeling they weren't listening because they were important people with more important things on their minds.

"It wasn't that big a deal, nothing that couldn't be fixed with a little pruning and some fungicide spray. But knowing Leo the way I did, I knew he'd want to avoid complications. The guy was always bending over backwards to make customers happy and it pissed me off because I wanted him to show some backbone, but he just looked at me and I knew what he was thinking: let's just replace the trees, leave Graddick a gallon of fungicide concentrate, and write him down a few maintenance tips.

"The day was already shot to hell and I probably wouldn't be seeing Amy two days in a row now. I pictured Leo and me digging out the six trees and getting them back to the nursery before they shut down for the weekend. They were under thirty-day warranty so we'd do the swap, come back and plant the new ones, get paid and be done with it. If we busted our asses, we wouldn't have to come back Sunday. I wasn't happy about it, but we had a chunk of change coming our way and it would feel good to just get these people out of our hair.

"So Graddick says, 'When can you get it done?' and Leo tells him by the end of the day. Graddick looks all surprised and draws his head back to get a better look at us and says, 'All seventy-five?'

"That's when we knew he never had any intention of paying up. Leo got the original twenty per cent down payment—about $1600 out of a total cost to him of over $8000—which even today is still a lot of money. Hell, the Leylands alone cost him nearly half that. So I'm listening to Leo all soft-spoken trying to negotiate a compromise and Graddick's just standing there like a grim-faced statue. Man, I wanted so bad to crack his jaw. Leo never had a chance and it was pathetic the way he just went quiet at a certain point. I spit on the grass like that would unhinge the guy, but me and my spit were as irrelevant to him as one of those trees he wanted gone. Bottom line is we didn't replace the six trees—forget about the seventy-five—and we never saw another penny.

"Not long after that Leo moved down to Jacksonville, Florida. We haven't seen each other or spoken since."

"That sucks, man," I said.

"For a long time, I had these fantasies about what I was going to do to Graddick one day. It got so dark it started eating me up. I'd start yelling at Amy for no reason. She put up with it for a while because I'd finally gotten around to telling her, but one day she let me have it and I got a crystal clear picture of the asshole I'd become and told myself no more. You learn your lessons about your fellow man and you move on.

"Then in September of '74 I started working at Galaxy. I remember Marla Tupo coming up to me and introducing herself."

"Marla came up to you?"

The words slipped out of my mouth like a naked confession and with no way to cover them up or reel them back in. I tried my best to look casual, even borderline disinterested. Virgil, who'd been staring at my drink while he was talking, looked up at me when I said it as though he'd overheard somebody's deep dark secret, but he didn't miss a beat either.

"Yeah, good old Marla. That was a hell of a time. Laurie was born just before New Year's, which was a break because we got to add her as a dependent on our taxes, and Amy got laid off just before Thanksgiving, which sucked but actually kind of worked out."

Virgil closed his eyes and shook his head.

"But things haven't really worked out," he said with a mournful expression. "We got married too young, had kids too soon, four of them while we were still in our twenties. I should've done something, man, like taken night classes, not settled for an Associate's. I should've done more. I kept bouncing around from bad job to bad job making a pittance, and now I've been at Galaxy five years and my wife and kids are still living in a crummy apartment complex. Ah, man, it's been a huge disappointment. I don't mean the kids or Amy, I mean me. I just get tired sometimes, like I've got this tired heart and all I want to do is have a drink and watch pretty girls take off their clothes and dance around a pole. Does that make me a bad person?"

"No, no way. It makes you somebody with a tired heart, that's all. Virgil Flynn, man, you're one of the best on the planet."

"How many Virgil Flynns you know?"

"Don't get the wrong idea. I'm not saying you're perfect."

"I understand, but you want to know something funny? I'd forgotten all about Graddick until—"

"Don't tell me you ran into him."

"Not directly, but you know how you see or hear something and it takes you to a moment that happened a long time ago?"

"You mean like Proust?"

"Who?"

"*Remembrance of Things Past?*"

"Yeah, it's like you're right back there, like the time in between never happened. That's what happened to me."

"What do you mean?"

"Weller hands me my calls, right?"

"Okay."

"Guess where to?"

"Saddle Grove?"

"Last call of the day. Five years at Galaxy and I never once got sent there. Kind of weird, huh? You'd think in five years. It's like the gods were keeping me from self-obliterating, giving me time to mature in my way of coping with shit. Never, not once in all that time did I get sent to Saddle Grove. But still, even in the same town, what would be the odds of landing back in that house of horrors? I check the name. I check it twice, three times, four times just to make sure. It's not the cop, it's not the lawyer, it's, you know, Ass Face."

"And this happened yesterday?"

"Yeah, so I'm staring at the name and everything about that day in '67 is like suddenly all over me again swimming on my eyes, crawling in my ears, and I swear I could even smell the chlorine.

"Weller's doing the roll call but it's like he's invisible and all I see is Graddick standing there like a stone pharaoh and I hear the moment Leo's voice died and the excited jabbering of those three teenaged girls getting louder as they all drag themselves out of the pool at the exact same time dripping wet and squeezing water out of their long hair. Man, I'm just hating myself cause part of me wants to run away and hide but then there's this other me still aching to break Graddick's jaw.

"I didn't know what to do, Lucas. Tell Weller I couldn't do it? Tell him to send me anywhere else, Long Island, Cape May, Stamford, I don't care, anywhere, just not there?

"And then out of nowhere—I don't know if it was a demon or an angel that put the idea in my head—I started to see the thing in a whole different way."

Chapter 15

A commotion at the bar got our attention. A man in a jacket and tie was shouting obscenities at two women having drinks a few stools down.

The bartender with the huge hands warned the man, but the man saw no good reason to stop mouthing off so the bartender came around, grabbed him and tossed him out the door. The guy folded in on himself like a flimsy lawn chair as he was being dragged across the floor. He kept his mouth shut, but his feet were stamping in protest. Once he was out of sight the women began to laugh and joke.

It was nervous laughter, and I knew they'd be afraid going out into the parking lot later. Maybe we could get up to leave when they got up, but maybe that would spook them even more. I thought Virgil might say something about it, produce some pithy aphorism, but he got right back to business.

"When I got to the house this pasty-faced teenager with a serious mullet opened the door. He would have been about seven or eight back in '67 I guess. Kid showed no signs of remembering me. Turns out his parents were on a three-week tour of the Mediterranean celebrating their wedding anniversary.

"The kid was checking out my Galaxy arm badge with like this creepy reverence. He told me he was majoring in *Sociology* and minoring in *Poli Sci*—which his parents weren't crazy about—and wondered if maybe we could have a beer and talk a little after I was done. I said I didn't know, maybe. He shuffled off to his room looking dejected.

"The laundry room was the key to everything. It was on the ground floor, rear corner of the house, the perfect spot. I picked out the window nobody ever opens, did some quick rewiring to bypass the magnetic contacts and left the window latches in the open position. After verifying system integrity everywhere else I went upstairs. There's this open jewelry box sitting on the vanity in the master bedroom, pearl necklaces and gold chains spilling out, just begging to be swiped. It was like, come on, take me, there's more where this came from. I was tempted for sure, wouldn't need all that much to get back Leo's money, and with interest. It was right there, inches from my hands, but I left it alone because I had a plan.

"Then I went into Graddick's study and used a screwdriver to pull open the desk drawer and saw a gold money clip with a thick fold of hundred-dollar bills sitting there, three keys on a keychain, and a handgun. It was mindboggling, ridiculous, just too damn easy. I looked at the big armoire by the wall and had the feeling there was something real important to Graddick in there, and here were the keys, so go ahead, have a look, take what you want. I got it in my head that the only explanation was that the gods were testing me, like they had this wager going, and I didn't know which gods were for me and which ones wanted to see my ass dragged off to prison, so I played it cool.

"When I finished upstairs, I asked Jeremy if I could use the kitchen phone. He was wearing that needy look losers get. I could see he was the kind of kid that had trouble making friends. Other than his parents' money it didn't look like he had much going for him. Paunchy awkward kid, zero personality, bad skin, ludicrous mullet. You know, the whole package.

"After I hung up the phone, I told Jeremy I had no more calls that day and could have that beer with him after all. You should have seen how his face lit up.

"We sat in the kitchen and the kid started asking me questions about the working class like he was interviewing me for a school assignment. I tried to get him off the subject and to start talking about his family but he wouldn't bite. I checked my watch. The kid knew that mining me for school material wasn't going to cut it, so he tried to spice things up by telling me his roommate's girlfriend is the niece of an exiled poet from some Latin America country. He said he mentioned to Julio his roommate that he was going to have the big house to himself for three weeks in August if he wanted to stop by one day with his girlfriend, and maybe bring her cousin along, Rosalita, who he'd met back on campus.

"Turns out Julio called him last week and asked him about the availability of the house for August 18th. He said him and some friends were planning a party to commemorate the anniversary of some uprising and raise money for *La Causa*. Julio told Jeremy his Marxist buddies and the exiled poet and lady friends, including Rosalita, would be coming. Jeremy tried to sound cool as he told me all this, but I could see he was nervous and excited. He said I was invited too if I wanted to come.

"I said to him, 'Your parents okay with this?'

"His high-pitched laugh made my skin crawl but then he got serious and said, 'No way, but it doesn't matter because they won't know, and even if they found out, I doubt they would report me to the CIA.'"

"August 18th is next Saturday," I interjected.

"That's right," Virgil said.

"You going to that party?"

"The party fits the plan. The party is pure gift from the gods. I go the night before the party. Anything missing gets traced back to drunken Marxists and their hot ladies."

"So, you're really doing this?"

"Me and the kid, man, we're popping open our third beers and maybe my tongue got looser than it needed to be, but I was feeling free and easy and kind of in control because I could see how this was all gonna play out. I started talking Bay of Pigs and *La Revolución* and even toss the Founding Fathers into the mix along with the pursuit of happiness, and I say to the kid, 'So Jeremy, what do you think makes a man happy?'

"The kid hesitated, like wondering what the hell, and took a long swig.

"'I guess I'm being too general,' I said to him. 'What I mean is that probably what makes a rich man happy isn't the same as what makes a poor man happy, right?' and he says, 'Well, I suppose.'

"Beautiful setup, right? So I went right for the heart. I said to him, 'I don't know, like what makes someone like your dad happy?'

"'My dad?' The kid got this look on his face, like I was guiding a pair of pliers into his mouth to yank out a tooth. But here's where the full measure and worth of that third beer comes into play. After giving it some thought he says, 'My dad loves coins. He's been into them since he was a boy.'

"'Must have one heck of a collection.'

"'He sold a bunch of them at an auction a couple of years ago.'

"'So now he's collecting what, vintage comic books?'

"'Ha, I wish. Nah, he's just more particular. He only buys gold coins now. Some of them are pretty rare, worth tens of thousands of dollars, Liberty Head Double Eagles, St. Gaudens and such, upwards of forty and fifty thousand each.'

"He glanced up at me for an instant, trying to figure out what I might be thinking about all this.

"'You into coins too, Jeremy?' I said.

"'Not really, but I can see how some people might be. They're like miniature art pieces.'

"'Is that right? I don't believe I've ever held a gold coin in my hand,' I said. 'They must be pretty neat up close, huh?'

"He hesitated and then said, 'You want to see them?'

"'Ah no, thanks, buddy, that's okay.'

"'It's no big deal. My dad keeps them upstairs in his study. Sometimes I count them into one hand just to see how many I can hold before they start spilling, then I flip over my hand and watch them crash and splash like golden water. Yeah, I know, it's kind of weird… My dad for sure wouldn't approve of me doing that, but you could say it's his fault for not properly securing things. He's not really good at that. Neither is my mom. They're both kind of careless. I guess that's why they pay you guys.'

"'I guess.'

"'You've got to see these Double Eagles, Virgil.'

"'Ah, thanks, man, but I wouldn't feel right about it.'

"'Oh, yeah… I understand, no problem.'

"'It's been real good talking to you, Jeremy, and thanks for the beers.'

"I felt dirty walking out to my car. I heard him call my name. He was standing in front of the house holding a beer bottle in his left hand and his right fist raised in the air. 'Power to the people!' he shouted and then punched the sky with the bottle. Beer spurted out onto his face and spilled all over his hand and arm. The kid didn't know whether to be embarrassed or laugh, like he was waiting for me to decide for him.

"The whole time I was in that house I tried convincing myself Jeremy was going to be just like his dad one day just so my head wouldn't screw me over. And then there I was looking at the kid and trying to see Graddick instead of Jeremy, but it was like Ass Face kept flicking on and off but Jeremy was still there, like he wasn't going anywhere.

"I don't know, maybe Jeremy's going to turn into his dad one day, but he wasn't him yet. I laughed and it was like I was giving the kid permission to laugh and he did, and I didn't care that he had that high-pitched laugh that gives me the willies.

"Then I did it. I had to. I pumped my fist in the air. 'You got it, buddy,' I said. 'Power to the people!'"

Chapter 16

The whole time Virgil was telling me about Jeremy I started to feel I wanted in. "I'll be your second set of eyes," I heard myself say. Virgil raised his eyebrows like I was nuts and made a half-hearted attempt to talk me out of it, but I knew he was glad to have me and I just kept staring at him until he stopped talking.

With Callie away for the weekend the timing couldn't have been better. My reasons for wanting to do whatever it was Virgil was planning to do were probably all wrong and not all that clear to me, but I wanted in regardless, that much was clear.

I had nightmares all week long, but the days went by fast and before I knew it, I was pulling into Virgil's apartment complex. Thunderstorms and strong winds had moved through the region late in the day and left the sunbaked streets sizzling and steaming, and the drifts of fog in the night air made me see things that weren't there.

I got there early and parked across from Virgil's building, rolled down the car windows a few inches, tilted the driver's seat back and drifted off into light sleep. Mrs. Brinkley's son, Julius, who'd been a frequent visitor to my dreams all week long was leading me and Virgil to the rear of the Graddick property. Julius stopped and frowned as he pointed his rifle at the swimming pool. A kid roughly his age was floating face down in the water and appeared to be staring at something pinned to the floor of the pool.

Virgil made an obscure remark and I followed him to the edge where we were able to identify the lifeless form by the mullet floating in the water like a dozen tiny eels. From there we also had a good view of a pile of gold coins down at the bottom shining like a tiny chunk of the sun.

Julius then led us to the cypress hedge, which was brown and withered from top to bottom. Through the brittle branches we glimpsed a vast gray expanse. When a gunshot rang out in my right ear I jerked my head toward Julius and saw Virgil's face.

"Sorry," he said as he settled into the passenger seat.

"It's okay. What time is it?"

"One-forty. Amy kept me up telling me about these two moms who were secretly excluding Laurie from doing stuff with their kids. We're lying in bed, and Amy's correlating it with something that happened to her when she was a kid. I tell you, I was trying hard to be supportive, but I was dead tired and fell asleep while she was talking."

"Do we have enough time to do this?"

"We should be good. No traffic. Three hours total give or take. Hour to get there, hour to get back, hour to do what we need to do. We're back before five and Amy's still sleeping off the rage."

"You better hope."

"Assuming no one fiddled with the window or we run into a surprise."

We got on the interstate and headed north and west. When I began to lose sight of how fast we were going, Virgil suggested I drive no more than five miles over the speed limit. Last thing we needed was to get pulled over and have to explain the gear. Virgil smiled as he pulled latex gloves, pantyhose, and water guns out of a brown paper bag.

"On the off-chance," he said, jiggling the goods.

It was good to see Virgil in somewhat uplifted spirits but those were the last words we exchanged for a while. Images of flat-nosed, amorphous-faced burglars and chaotic encounters with sharply-dressed people occupied my mind as the dimly lit highway raced beneath us.

I tried shaking those images and thought of Callie. Despite the sleeplessness and the nightmares, we'd been doing better of late. She had kissed me on the cheek in the morning before leaving with Johnny for Colts Brook, nothing to get excited about, but a minor breakthrough nonetheless. Still, I was under no illusions.

Over the last few days, I'd been battling stomach cramps and migraines. I was desperate for boring days that yawned themselves to sleep. I wasn't stopping by after hours at Galaxy anymore, and Marla and I were avoiding eye contact. Our exchanges over the phone were brief and all business. If I could just hold out long enough for it all to go away, we might be able to begin again, Callie and me. But it wasn't easy. Maybe nothing would ever be easy again. Right now there was this, the dark road like a long, wicked tongue pulling us deeper into uncertainty.

Back in the old days sitting in the apartment in Legacy City having dinner with my parents—when life appeared to be more or less ordered—I would have regarded Virgil's scheme the product of a disturbed mind, and Virgil someone in need of aggressive medicating. And now? Now I wanted in. I wanted in real bad on some ineffable cosmic gut level.

In the morning I had collected my paycheck and assignments from Jay Weller and had touched base one last time with Virgil before heading out on my first call. Some interior nudge made me turn around as I was walking toward the back door. Marla was staring at me. Our eyes locked. It was a dare stare. We were like strangers in a bar staring at each other from opposite ends of the room thinking the same thing.

I felt a dark troubling thrill that needed correcting, so I took a few steps in her direction to dispel whatever was happening, to rectify or clarify—carefully, of course—without making matters worse. I was relieved when she began rifling through a folder as if I weren't there. I turned around and walked out to the parking lot.

"I don't know what to make of Marla," I said. The dark of night made it easier to talk about her.

"I was wondering when you'd get to that," Virgil said.

"Yeah, I know."

Virgil looked at me with anticipation and then prompted me, "She hasn't been herself since Borders died, that's for sure."

"I went to her apartment that night."

"To Marla's apartment?"

"The night Borders killed himself."

He was about to say something, but thought better of it and went back to staring at the road.

"Never mind," I said. "It's not important."

Virgil, who was quiet for about a minute, finally, in a voice flat and dark as the road said, "What did you do, Amado?"

I took a deep breath and exhaled.

"She called me at a customer's to tell me Borders was dead. She was really upset, obviously, like on the brink. She asked if I would stop at her apartment for a few minutes, just to talk. I was worried about what she might do. It was on my way home anyway, so I stopped at her place."

"And you talked."

"She talked mostly, and then I got up to leave. I was going to leave, I wanted to go, I did, but—"

"So you and Marla? Damn, I knew it."

"What do you mean you knew it? How did you know?"

"Wasn't that hard, the way the two of you hit it off from the start. Look, I'm not judging, and yeah, on a certain level… Hell, she must have been something back in the day. It's just that, you know, she's kind of like a big sister around Galaxy. And I'm thinking that for some of the younger techies like you, well, she's like a mother figure."

"What the hell is wrong with you, Virgil?"

"I'm just saying…"

"I don't know what to do."

I gazed at the white lane stripes as they whipped past the driver's side, each narrow flash of white like a consuming inevitability. Without taking his eyes off the road Virgil spoke in a soft but resolute voice.

"You can't dump this on your wife. You're going to have to live with it."

"But what about Marla?"

"You don't owe her anything."

"No, I mean, what if she tells Callie?"

"You think she'd do that?"

"I don't know. She's been acting real strange."

"Okay, say you tell Callie on the off-chance Marla's going to tell her, like a preemptive strike, right? You want her to hear your side of the story before anyone else gets to her. Okay, that's fine, but what if Marla was never going to say anything? What if Callie was never going to find out? Then you're screwed for no good reason."

"I'm screwed no matter what, Virgil."

"Listen, I don't know if this will make you feel any better. The misery loves company way of thinking doesn't work for me personally. Maybe it works for you. So I'm going to share something with you nobody else knows. I cheated on Amy four times, okay? Well, actually, more than four. I mean with four different women."

"So you never told her."

"Why the hell would I do that? To ease my conscience at her expense? After the first time I told myself I wouldn't do it again, but I did, and then I did it again, and again, and I had to take a good hard look at myself. I love Amy but sometimes I feel like I'm going freaking bonkers. So I made a decision that I would live with the guilt, okay? Not an easy decision, believe me, but the only one I can see myself living with right now. So far, I've been lucky none of those women know Amy or care enough about what we did to tell her. I still make her happy. I think I do, but if I didn't have the option of being a cheating asshole available to me, I don't know that I could."

I heard everything he was saying. I understood every word, but I was like two men, one listening to Virgil, the other trying to find secure footing for my wobbly soul.

"It's done," I said. "Never again. This thing's going to the grave with me."

Virgil stared at me.

"So, this is really why you came," he said.

I looked at him, trying to understand.

"This thing between you and Marla. I mean, you had to talk to somebody, I get that. I talk to you and you talk to me. That's how this works, right?"

"You're right, I had to tell somebody. It was eating me up. But this isn't just about that."

"You and me, Amado, we speak the truth to each other, right?"

"We do, but Virgil, you understand there's something just a bit off with us, right? Think about what we're doing, racing up to Saddle Grove in the middle of the night to break into some big shot's house to make him pay for something that happened a dozen years ago when you were single and with no wife and kids and I was in the seventh grade."

"You getting cold feet? Maybe we should just turn around and head back home."

"That's not going to happen. Look, what I'm saying is this is really lost in space crazy. This thing you want to do—whatever it is—I want to do it too because my brain keeps feeding me this crazy logic that says this is as necessary to you and me as it is ridiculous. It's like a tailor-made quest for disturbed young men of humble origin."

"How lyrical is that? Tell me what you've been drinking, Amado, and did you bring enough for me?"

"I've been drinking dreams, Virgil, strange dreams. I don't know what any of this means, but I'm feeling it's no longer about the money."

Virgil got real quiet and small. I remembered the day Borders got reamed out by Mr. Roseboom because of the lady who got her jewelry snatched. I never looked into it, never wanted to bring it up with Virgil. I glanced at his profile and slowed the car down. I pulled onto the shoulder and put the car in Park. Virgil didn't say a word. I wanted him to say something. I waited.

"It's not about the money," he murmured. "Happy?"

"Right, because it can't be."

"Why can't it be?"

"Because you and me? We're not like Ass Face."

Virgil exhaled like he wanted no part of anything that was inside him, like he wanted to expel himself from himself so he could start all over.

"Shit! Shit! Shit!" he yelled. He looked more miserable than I'd ever seen him.

"You having a nervous breakdown, Virgil?"

"Ha, you're funny."

"You see, undertaking a quest can be unsettling for even the best of men."

"Nah, man, I'm good. I was just thinking how grand you'd look riding a donkey."

"I would need to put on a few pounds."

"Yep, you fat and happy on a donkey and me on a horse."

"An old beaten down arthritic horse."

"Whatever, man, but you on a donkey and me on a horse."

Chapter 17

"There it is," Virgil said. "Slow down. That clearing over there? Pull in there."

I looked back after we had walked out of the grove. There was no sign of the hatchback.

"No stars tonight," I said. "Hard to see."

"That's a good thing. Hey, you okay?"

"I'm just following your lead, man."

"Here, stick these in your pockets."

Virgil gave me a pair of latex gloves, a nylon stocking, and a black plastic German Luger water gun.

"When we get there we'll put the gloves on. We're taking no chances."

"No chances, huh?"

"You know what I mean. You hear anything out of the ordinary you pull the nylon down over your face. Scares the shit out of people, induces paralysis."

"We'll be like thugs in a Batman comic."

"Yeah, the guys he beats the shit out of in alleyways."

"Too bad we're not Batman," I said.

"No, not tonight. Tonight, we're thugs."

"There's this lady down the Pine Barrens who kept calling me Mr. Galaxy."

"Ha, no kidding."

"Yeah. 'Mr. Galaxy, I presume?' That's how she greeted me. She asked me if I was there to fix everything. The way she said it, like with a kind of expectation, but in a faint mocking way, not malicious at all, but like, hey, can you fix this mess, can you, will you? You should have seen the place. A national disaster area. Piles of crap stacked up all along the walls. Real unhealthy environment. The place should be condemned. She was just kidding around, she said, but on a certain level—"

"On a certain level she was saying, 'Mr. Galaxy, forget about this mess, I want you to fix me. Me, me, me. Fix me the way you know how, big boy.' Man, you *are* young, aren't you?"

"I'm not *that* young. Okay, so maybe she was flirting a little, but boy, she was one rare bird. No trace of a husband anywhere. A weird teenaged son, real tall and skinny kid. I'd ask her a question and she'd start laughing hysterically like I was the looney."

"I was thinking of Jeremy and he reminded me of Julius, her son. Different kinds of kids but about the same age. Julius had this rifle. While I was waiting for you I dozed off and dreamed about that rifle and a dead boy floating face down in a swimming pool. I knew it was Jeremy because of the mullet. I saw the cypress hedge you told me about, all brown and eaten away. I could see through it out onto this big gray desert."

Virgil stopped and looked at me.

"Go back to the car. You don't have to do this. No big deal. Drive by the house like in a half hour or so until you see me."

"Forget it, I told you I'm all in. I think all I'm saying is just that we really need to be careful."

"Mr. Galaxy, I'm so scared. Oh, Mr. Galaxy, please fix me."

"I'm not kidding, Virgil. You're no Batman and neither am I."

"Gotcha. Come on, man, lighten up. It's going to be okay."

The big properties with their corrals and flood-lighted barns were staggered across Saddle Grove and separated by thickets and knolls and hedges and post and rail fencing, all of which we easily negotiated. The houses were set back from the road a couple of hundred feet and had long lit driveways. After walking a while in a contemplative haze, we stopped to listen to a low rumble. The road behind us tilted forward under the weight of light. We ran onto a lawn and stood motionless by a tree. The car roared past and faded into the night.

Virgil was right. I did need to lighten up for both our sakes. I hadn't seen Virgil this alive in a long while and I didn't want to bring him down. I said to him, "There's this guy named Lucius who does magic, right? He's bored to tears with himself so he decides he wants to be a bird. He snaps his fingers, but something goes wrong, shockingly wrong. Not only did he fail to become a bird, he was no longer even a man. He was an ass instead, you know, the four-footed kind."

"Yeah, four-footed, I figured as much."

"The distinction's important because the ass has all these misadventures."

"Got it. So the ass is trotting around town, and—?"

"My point, Virgil, is that we are who we are. Magic can't change that. An ass is an ass is an ass."

"Yeah, but..."

"But what?"

"Of course we are who we are and magic can't change that."

"That's what I'm saying."

"No, you're saying an ass can't be a bird."

"What?"

"What *I'm* saying is *you* can be a bird."

"So you're saying I'm an ass?"

"What I mean is *you* can be a bird because the bird's inside you, like you made room for it to be there so it's there, but someone like Graddick? I don't know. Maybe he can only be an ass because at some point in his life he decided being an ass suited him just fine, and that decision left him no room to ever be anything else."

"Interesting. By the way, Virgil, I see the bird in you too."

"Let me ask you something. If you could wave a magic wand, who would you want to be?"

"I don't know, a better me?"

One time Callie was talking about *metanoia*, and at first I thought she meant some type of insanity, which it may be to some people, but it's really about fundamental transformation of mind, heart and so on. So, what if I could be a bird for Callie? What if I could leap into the air and fly, free myself of all the stultifying stagnating stuff that keeps me stuck to my conflicted old self?

I didn't want my heart to get tired. I wanted wings. I needed wings in the worst way.

"I want to fly," I said and Virgil just looked at me kind of funny.

We then started to walk in earnest, like marching soldiers, left, left, left-right-left, but marching toward what and why? What the hell were we doing? I should have stayed home in bed. I could be dreaming of Callie in my arms. I should have talked myself out of doing this.

A dull thumping sound got our attention. A Yorkshire terrier was rebounding like a basketball off the glass of a big bay window to our right. Within moments housedogs everywhere were bounding and baying with such exaggerated rage and despair you'd think an asteroid was speeding toward Saddle Grove.

"I'm sure people here are used to this kind of racket," Virgil said looking a little worried. "All the damn fox, deer, and raccoon roaming around serving no purpose other than to piss off the dogs."

We picked up the pace. When we saw the Graddick property all lit up inside and out, we paused to evaluate the situation. A copper-colored Pontiac Firebird sat in the driveway, Jeremy's car. We heard no sound, detected no movement. All those lit indoor lights at that hour suggested the presence of a mindless slumbering teen with a huge house all to himself. We slipped on the latex gloves and adjusted the nylons on our heads like berets.

The overgrown rhododendrons that covered the rear of the house where the laundry room was situated served as a natural cover. Virgil briefly struggled with the window but got it open. He stuck his head into the dimly lit room and began to hand me several hand-painted pots that had been placed on the worktable that stood right beneath the window.

"These weren't here before," he said. "Just lay them on the ground. We'll put them back on our way out."

We drew ourselves through the open window onto the top of the table and carefully lowered ourselves to the tiled floor, the idea of quest suddenly overshadowed by the reality of breaking and entering. The light coming through the partly opened door from the kitchen seemed a portent of ruin.

Virgil pulled the stocking down over his face and nodded to me to do the same. We beheld each other with a kind of awe, each presenting to the other a monstrous countenance. We drew our plastic Lugers and approached the door. I followed Virgil, mimicking his every move. The kitchen was clear but for a fly strolling along the rim of an open peanut butter jar sitting on the countertop.

Virgil opened the pantry closet door and stuck his head inside.

"The kid never turned the system on," he said. "Wait here. I'm going to rewire those window contacts back into the circuit."

I was impressed by Virgil's attention to detail, no doubt nurtured by all those spy thrillers. There was to be no evidence of tampering, no way of tracing anything that was going to happen tonight back to his original service call. Virgil was being diligent, and I was glad to see it.

It took him a couple of minutes and then we were back on track gliding through the dining room. I thought I smelled pot as we stopped for a moment at the threshold of a large recreation room that looked out on the swimming pool some forty yards away. The pool was illumined by sprays of gold-colored light emitting from wrought iron post lanterns set along an extended perimeter of the pool.

Behind the pool and all around across the darkness lay acres of quiet mystery. I wondered how different life might look to someone when viewed daily from such a room. I imagined what the pool would look like tomorrow night with swarthy radicals standing around drinking beers and talking revolution and naked Latin girls diving off the springboard into cool glittering water.

"The stairs creak," Virgil whispered. "Walk on the ends where the treads are tighter."

We slipped the Lugers inside our belts and began our climb along the right end of the stair treads clutching the handrail for balance. With each step the odor of pot intensified.

The study was to our left, adjacent to the master bedroom at the end of the hallway. Three more bedrooms lay to our right. We advanced to the right quiet as monks through the brightly lit hall-way. We moved as if through chest-high water, pushing against a pressure that threatened to lock up our muscles and brains.

I kept glancing back as though expecting to be ambushed from behind. Were there others in the house? Early bird guests? We peered into the first bedroom, saw no one, and slid past an empty common bathroom. Then the second bedroom neared, like a land-mine. We pushed open the door. No one, nothing. Before reaching the third bedroom we stopped and gazed at each other like Russian roulette contestants anticipating a head explosion.

The door of the third bedroom hung partly open. The room, shrouded like an abandoned cave, seemed quite large. When our eyes adjusted to the half-light of the desk lamp we observed—like a large lump of pale twisted wax—a naked half-man, half-child lying sideways on the bed. He was staring at us. In a grotesque semblance of courtesy, we waited for him to make the first move. We waited for him to draw a gun from under his pillow and shoot Virgil and me in the face.

But Jeremy's eyes were shut, a condition that at first seemed favorable to us but that rapidly became worrisome in itself. He wasn't breathing, we realized, and a raw terror seized us. We entered the room crouching like dubious shamans begging the boy back to life.

He surprised us with a sigh and shifted his top arm and leg, and seeing that he was asleep we started backing away with small sound-less steps.

Everything came increasingly into focus as we retreated. Beer bottles and ashtrays littered the desk and night table. Copies of *Hustler* and *Penthouse* were strewn about, the centerfolds yanked out of the magazines and arrayed on the carpeted floor beside the bed.

Once out of Jeremy's room we made our way to Graddick's study. Virgil went directly to the desk. He checked all the drawers but came up empty. His gloved hands moved quickly over the bookshelves and the books and in the gaps between the books.

"Everything okay?" I whispered after peeling the stocking from my face.

"I can't find the keys, and the money and the handgun are gone."

I tried not to think about the gun.

"Are you sure it's locked?" I said.

Virgil walked over to the armoire and opened the doors. Inside, the keys lay before a leather-bound metal case that looked like a miniature armoire, almost an exact replica of the furniture piece. He drew the case out and placed it on the desk. He unlocked the gilded case doors and pulled out the first of a dozen trays.

Beneath the concentrated white light of the desk lamp the first set of coins leaped up at us from their dark blue felt holders like gorgeous obscenities. We stared in silence for a good while at the half dozen identical profiles of the grave gold-bearded man. A half dozen more South African Krugerrands were embedded so as to display the obverse side of the coins, one springbok more radiant than the next.

Virgil slid each tray back into its slot and drew out the next one with the utmost care, as though he were handling delicate embryos. Each new group of coins demanded our complete attention. The hard shiny pieces were instigators and survivors of empires and revolutions and industrialization and the senseless rupture of *The Great War*.

We identified Prussian Marks and Austrian Coronas, French, Belgian and Swiss Francs, Russian Rubles and British Sovereigns— their golden auras as enticing as the darkest secrets of colossal wealth.

The lower trays displayed United States gold coins. Virgil used the smallest of the three keys to open the last tray, which contained the Double Eagles Jeremy had mentioned—Liberty Heads and St. Gaudens—all ten of them in near mint condition.

I got inside Virgil's head for a moment. Leave eight, take two, it said, one for Leo, one for Amy, that being *twenty percent*, which represented the hard beauty of poetic justice. So easy now, and despite what we'd earlier professed...

Virgil picked up one of the Liberty Heads and frowned as he drew it close to his face. He studied the coin with the intimate air of a lover. The attraction was formidable, I could see, and though I'd hoped things would go a different way, I understood, knew time and circumstance had a way of changing perspective, and I fully expected Virgil to slip the Liberty Head in his pocket, and there was nothing I was going to say about it. He might have briefly entertained the thought, but to my surprise he put it back in the tray. Then he performed the exact same ritual with the St. Gaudens.

After we memorized all the coins in all the trays, Virgil returned to the bearded man and the springbok for a little while longer before sliding the tray forward and closing the case.

"Put it back," he said.

I hesitated a moment and then carried the coin case to the armoire, placed the keys on the case and shut the doors. I went back and stood beside Virgil. He was sitting in Graddick's chair printing camouflaged words on a pad with the concentrated care and primitive dexterity of a five-year old.

> WE KNOW
> YOU'RE NOT A MAN

The faint, indistinct noises had been coming from somewhere far away. They were part of a wilderness chorus that barely registered with us even as I read aloud in a minstrel's whisper what Virgil had written.

We know you're not a man.

And then the noises converged into one plaintive sound, like the *bah-ing* of a lost sheep nearby.

"Bah! Baaah!"

Where was that sheep? Louder and louder the cries grew. We glanced at each other in confusion and pulled the nylons down over our faces. We'd come so close to finishing, but we'd gotten careless.

"Mah! Maaah!" Jeremy cried and crumbled into hiccup-like weeping.

We waited. After a couple of minutes we heard Jeremy sigh and all became quiet again. Virgil finished writing his note.

> WE KNOW
> YOU'RE NOT A MAN
> BUT AN ASS
> WITH A HOLE
> ERGO
> BRADLEY ASSHOLE
> IS WHO YOU ARE

"Where are you going to leave it?" I said.

"Where Jeremy isn't likely to look. Get a book, will you?"

I went to the bookshelves and started to do a quick scan of the titles.

"How's this?" I said.

Eye of the Needle. Virgil nodded, inserted the note in the middle of the book, and slid the book to the back of the top center drawer of Graddick's desk.

"No!" Jeremy groaned.

They sounded like elephant feet pounding the hallway. For a moment we thought he was coming at us, handgun waving in the air. But he stopped and the double bang of a rebounding toilet seat marked for us a change of fortune.

In the midst of groans and heaves and splashing sounds Virgil motioned to me with his head to follow him. We hurried through the hallway and down the stairs, the rapid patter of our steps covered by Jeremy's violent purging.

As we reached the main floor, and as I glanced one last time at the pool, it struck me that there was to be no party in Saddle Grove, no congregating of radicals and lovely Latin girls, and no Rosalita.

We jogged past the recreation room and through the dining room and kitchen, and in moments were climbing out the laundry room window. I handed Virgil all the hand-painted pots and he put them back on the worktable before lowering the window.

Like beleaguered spirits we glided over the wide dimly lit lawns back to the hidden hatchback. All the long way back we were pursued by grave bearded men and springboks and lost lonely boys.

Part 4

Bear

Chapter 18

She was standing in her office with Mrs. Grandie during what appeared to be a teaching moment, Mrs. Grandie nodding and asking follow-up questions. The next time I looked Marla was on the phone wearing that little smile she occasionally got when dispatching became flirty and effortless. She never did look for me through the glass, not that I could tell. It was like watching her from afar through binoculars. In Marla's world I no longer seemed to matter or even exist, and just maybe—if that were the case—then neither did Callie and what happened never happened and how fortunate that would be for everybody.

That was Thursday morning and the scenario I had envisioned with such high hopes was shot to hell by the time I got home Thursday evening. Callie wouldn't look at me either, wouldn't talk to me. I felt invisible and after a few hapless words I just stopped trying, and maybe my silence was an admission of guilt.

When I got home the next day after work my dinner was on the kitchen table, just like yesterday. The plate was hot, just like yesterday. It was courtesy of the most devastating kind. I would rather she had scratched out my eyes, wept and moaned, anything but this. And now Friday night was becoming Thursday night all over again, long and miserable, poked awake now and then by Johnny's half-hearted whimpers.

I knocked and opened the bedroom door. She was feeding him. She didn't look up. She didn't say hello, hi darling, how was your day, sorry about yesterday. I was afraid beyond all reason to say *I love you* for the more wrenching silence it might unleash.

I stayed up until they were both asleep and then I crawled into bed leaving plenty of space between us. She had made the idea of distance very clear without having to say a word. I watched the ceiling until I drifted off into new arenas of nightmare.

The morning heat and a distant voice woke me. Johnny was issuing cautionary complaints. Callie rolled away in a gesture of relegation. I got up out of bed.

"What gives, little man?"

His pretty mouth was partly opened, his eyes not quite shut, one hand suspended near an ear, tiny curved fingers with tiniest fingernails touching the wing of a butterfly.

Four months ago, I was watching him through the hospital glass, his little body—as frail and beautiful as the first flower—lying in a bassinet. The small sign at the foot of the bassinet identified him as *Amado* and that pulsating vision anointed in pastel blue made me feel a little disembodied.

I remember pressing my forehead to the glass. Even now my taste buds tickle at the memory of tears rolling down to my lips. How incapable I'd been of understanding his long-anticipated appearance. There I'd stood, stilled by wonder and battered by collisions of joy and sorrow, euphoria and dread.

"You're going too fast," she warned. Those were Callie's first words to me since Thursday morning.

The speedometer read 81 miles per hour.

Yes, I was going too fast, but if only she could see what was closing in on me. I depressed the accelerator, pushing the hatchback up to a rattling 87 miles per hour.

Fly, fly, fly. Oh, if only we could fly away, my love, my baby and me.

"You're scaring us!" she screamed and okay, maybe I was, but it was her shout that made Johnny cry.

I slowed the car down and drifted into the right lane. Callie turned around to reassure Johnny, then sat back in the passenger seat and stared at the road. She didn't look like Callie anymore. I had changed her.

In northeastern Pennsylvania—not more than a dozen miles from our destination—the hatchback died on a country road for no apparent rhyme or reason while sailing along at a forty-five mile per hour clip.

The Budapest twins who serviced the car had always gone out of their way to let me know they believed what I was saying, like I was some crazy man in need of reassuring. The issue was they had no way of determining cause of failure. The car drove flawlessly every time for them. *A nigma*, one of the twins would say as he shrugged his shoulders and wiped grease from his hands with a blackened rag. *A crazy poozle*, the other would agree with a look of pained cheerfulness.

I directed the car's momentum toward an old white oak, got out, popped the hood, removed the air filter, lodged a screwdriver under the choke flap, got back in the car, turned the ignition key and pressed the gas pedal just so. The car grumbled and wheezed and with a lurch went silent.

We were in for a bit of a delay. I had a blanket I kept in the back of the car for moments such as this and laid it under the oak tree for Callie and Johnny to sit on and went back to my familiar routine. After each failure to start up I took a deep breath and waited another fifteen minutes before trying again.

An hour passed in the midday heat before the engine spurted back to life. We'd given ourselves extra time to get to the church, but we had lost our entire margin for error, which guaranteed we'd miss the beginning of the marriage ceremony. I can't say I was too upset about that.

"It's off this road, right?" I said several miles later.

Callie ignored me. It didn't help matters that the air conditioner had been reduced to emitting only a memory of cool air. The directions card was balancing itself on my thigh, and I remember glancing at it with scorn, its mute speckled guidance more irritating than useful on a day that reeked of random antagonisms.

Tell me what YOU think is wrong.

Oh, sure, I could begin like that and just wait for her to stare at the side of my face and say nothing, and the thought of her silence and her wounded gaze penetrating to the depths of my filthy soul filled me with grief as vast and dark as outer space itself.

Callie, talk to me. You have to tell me where our love went. Did tears wash it away? Was it carried in the belly of a river, lost in the ocean blue?

I was already in some kind of altered state, and the sun and heat made the asphalt and my mind undulate all the more. A stretch of illusory road puddles vanished and appeared again up ahead. I became lost in the desert, and in a kind of wishful delirium I thought I heard Callie speak.

There, she might have said, might have pointed.

And though I couldn't see any church or road sign—did I miss the sign?—Callie's single word, or what might have been a word, or her thought of maybe speaking a word—regardless of a possible last second retraction—was like a sip of cool water.

I spotted a white sign with big red letters and an arrow pointing to our gathering place: *Fellowship of the First Rapturous Church.*

We took the right on Crawford Farm Lane and within moments were turning into the parking lot. The hatchback rolled over the crackling gravel surrounded by luxury cars and stopped with a doubtful air, as if evaluating its wretched options.

I stared at the only place left to park, a fringe, sun-battered area. I drove toward a towering pine. It was midday and what little shade the pine produced eluded all human endeavor. No one—not even Johnny—spoke a word as I parked the ugly little car.

It seemed to me an unlikely place for moneyed folks to have a wedding ceremony, but the modest setting offered me no happy assurances. I was trying hard but all self-correcting failed to spare me from the dread of faces I would see, the gazes I would endure, the conversations and silences I would hear. I could be the most irrational of men at times, I knew, but rationality had nothing to offer me just then.

It was a long shot but I tried. I took my right hand off the steering wheel and placed it on my thigh and waited for Callie's hand to respond—as it always had before—in a silent gesture suffused with the power to override all chaos and hurt. I waited, reconstructing the sensation from memory, imagining in her touch my wife's tender longing and forgiveness.

But she was far away, I could see, hands occupied with the minutiae of being a mother and a Coldwell late to her cousin's wedding ceremony.

I took a deep grating breath to keep from saying something inappropriate. And then I felt it, not the gentle soothing hand I wanted, but a damp and desperate hand like my own, and in its subtle turbulence and hints of ruinous loss I again entered into reluctant communion with Marla Tupo.

The high noon sunrays drilled my back as I wrestled with the car seat straps and buckles as though they were living squirming things and my hands a pair of paws. A bead of sweat raced down from my forehead and dripped off the tip of my nose onto Johnny's eye. The boy, who had until that moment observed our family silence, began to whine and wave his tiny fists and feet. As my own misery increased, Johnny's sorrows intensified.

Callie murmured something and the wailing escalated with surprising speed to desperate, breathtaking howls. It was as though an invisible imp had jammed a needle in our little boy's bottom. I watched in dismay as Johnny snapped his head side to side and kicked his rigid little legs out with a violence disproportionate to his size. After each lingering howl he paused to catch his breath, his eyes enlarged and fixed upon some tormentor only he could see. With each breathless interval it seemed his little heart would burst.

Callie reached for him across the back seat from the other side of the car, issuing desperate entreaties, but Johnny was having no part of it and resisted all attempts at consolation.

What was happening in seconds seemed to me to extend over long exhausting minutes. I dabbed Johnny's eye with my handkerchief, but he raged against me. I drew my head out from the car to collect myself, took a deep breath and squinted up at the boiling sun. Callie came around intending to complete what I had been unable to, but I lifted my hand in the air to let her know my job wasn't finished.

At that very moment a sparkling white Jaguar pulled up and parked about a dozen feet from us. A large, burly man with small concentrated facial features stepped out from the driver side, followed by a tall, abstracted woman wearing a short clingy silver dress and ankle-strapped stiletto sandals. Her cropped platinum hair, ivory complexion and lofty indifference gave her a strikingly cosmic, almost alien, look. Neither of them was in any hurry to get to the church. The man lit up a cigarette. They leaned side by side against the Jaguar and observed our little drama.

I wiped the sweat from my brow and ducked my head back into the small furnace of the car. My fingers moved nimbly now and within moments I was holding in my arms my drained and whimpering baby son.

Johnny's appearance into the searing light of day seemed to animate the woman. She walked over and with unsmiling, almost scientific, interest said, "What a pretty little man. Come look, Bear."

She ignored Callie and me as if we were just happening by with no relation to the child.

"Come on, Artemis," Bear commanded, and took her by the arm and led her off, her heels stabbing at the gravel more forcefully than necessary.

Then the man the woman called Bear said just loud enough for me to hear, "Nice car."

Chapter 19

G race Coldwell stood well over six feet in regular high heels and might still have been described as regal by the occasional observer of a bygone era. She was quite a bit taller than both her daughters but lacked their feminine grace and allure. Grace was possessed of a humorless self-awareness bordering on arrogance. Her features overall were harsh when compared to those of her girls, her mouth less shapely, her jaw more rigid, but both Callie and Hadley had inherited their mother's most striking feature, her exquisite green eyes.

Grace stared at me with those marvelous eyes, bewildered by my comment about September weather, my forced and ill-fated attempt at small talk. She glanced away in a gesture of barely controlled contempt.

"Danielle and Chad are a stunning couple," she said finally, but the observation served more as a recrimination than as an attempt at small talk.

"Beyond words," I replied.

She tilted her head as she took a closer look at me. Had she detected a touch of sarcasm?

"For the life of me," she said, having decided she could now dispense with chitchat. "I find it inconceivable that Callie would not be on time to see Danielle's entry."

"It was unfortunate, but it couldn't be helped."

Grace studied me with distaste for a moment more before glancing at her husband.

Cameron Coldwell appeared behind me like a sudden flare. He was about an inch taller than Grace in her high heels, and his face was smooth pink from the golf course. Curly waves of dyed yellow hair crowned a high disapproving forehead. Small gray eyes bore into me.

"Didn't you have directions?" he said.

The question took me by surprise. I found myself scrambling to reconstruct the interior of the hatchback, my thigh, and the location of the directions card.

"We did," I said, recovering just enough to be vague. "It wasn't a matter of getting lost."

Coldwell turned to his wife as though seeking a cogent explanation which I, evidently, was incapable of providing.

"They were delayed, Cameron," she said. "Apparently, it could not be helped."

Coldwell shot a glance at his wife indicating too much effort had already been expended on the topic. "I'll pull up the car," he said.

Standing there with Grace, waiting for things to happen—for Callie and Johnny to return from the Ladies Room, for Coldwell to pull up his car—did nothing to brighten my outlook on the day. I was stuck. I knew Grace had noted her daughter's unhappy state the moment she saw her despite Callie's best efforts to conceal her misery, so I braced myself.

I sensed a hesitation on her part. I would have liked to think her conscience was tempering her message, but I knew better.

"Callie is an exceptional young woman," she said drawing close, her expression emotionless and practical, as if she were responding to my earlier comment about the weather. "You should know this is very difficult for her. Difficult for all of us, for the entire family. Oh, you cannot begin to imagine. No, how could you?"

It took me a moment to realize Grace was not referring to my infidelity—which she would have no knowledge of—nor to my failure to get Callie to her cousin's wedding on time. No, in its unsettling intimacy this was something new, a fifteen-second confession of loathing doubling as a lament for my calamitous intrusion upon the Coldwell universe.

I wasn't immune to the sting, though the sentiments came as no surprise. But why unload on such a special day as today, a day when we should all be lifting a glass to the stunning newlyweds, Danielle and Chad?

A refreshed Johnny announced his presence and Grace instantly became someone else. She turned around with an open-mouthed smile and took my son from Callie and held him awkwardly for a few moments as if she were holding a soiled puppy. She bobbed him up and down singing, "Oh my, look at you, oh my," and Johnny, to his credit, tolerated the encounter with diplomatic flair.

I noticed a slight tremor in Grace's right hand after she handed Johnny back to Callie. It was something I had observed before, but nothing anyone appeared to regard as noteworthy, or at least nothing anyone ever spoke about in my presence.

As Coldwell's brand new Continental pulled up, Grace clasped her hands and said, "I have an idea. Let's all go together in the new Lincoln."

"Mom," Callie said.

"So we can catch up," Grace said. "You know how it is now at these wedding receptions with these new bands. You can't hear yourself talk."

"Mom."

"Oh, why not?" Grace said.

"The reception hall is almost an hour away," Callie said.

"Is it?" Grace said and dipped her head toward the passenger side window. But Coldwell showed no interest in the exchange and sat in the driver's seat staring straight ahead.

"I'll go get the car seat," I said to Callie, who refused to look at me. "You and Johnny go with your parents. I'll follow along."

"Oh, dear," Grace said, swatting the air with her hand. "Of course, what was I thinking?"

She put on her sunglasses and gazed across the parking lot in search of the hatchback.

"Mom, we'll follow you and Dad. We can talk later."

"No," I said. "It's fine. You and Johnny go. I'll be right behind."

"Oh good," Grace said with a smile. "See, it's all settled."

I didn't have to see his face to know that Coldwell's level of irritation was beginning to peak. After I strapped the car seat in the rear of the Lincoln and everyone got in, Coldwell drove to the edge of the parking lot exit and waited there.

I hastened back to my car but slowed my step when I noticed unnatural movement inside the Jaguar. I opened the hatchback passenger side door and pretended to look for something in the glove compartment. I sat down and left the door wide open to secure an unobstructed view. I watched Bear's back shift from side to side. He reminded me of a large animal mauling its prey.

Suddenly Bear flopped back against his seat, raised his elbows in the air and dropped his hands with a violent thump on the steering wheel. His cheeks filled and emptied with a forceful rush as he blasted air out of his mouth.

In the shadowed recess of the Jaguar's interior, I made out Artemis. She was leaning in my direction. She seemed almost inanimate, like a blanched nautical figurehead on a ship's prow. As I began to see her more clearly, I realized with a start that she was staring directly at me. Was she speaking to me or Bear? As I puzzled over her strangeness the Jaguar's driver side window rolled down and Bear's knowing gaze became fully trained on me.

"You want to stick her, don't you?"

What did he say? My right hand touched my right ear, as if to verify I possessed such a thing, or to correct a malfunction that had caused some sound distortion.

At a loss for words, I groped toward civility behind the faint grin of a fool. A remote suspicion that Bear was one of those edgy fun guys who liked to shock people failed to get traction. Maybe what he had said, or the way he'd said it, had been just beyond my grasp of appreciation. Maybe it was a matter of mishearing—did I want a sticker?—or a misconstrued inflection. Maybe a smile somewhere in those tiny eyes of his had escaped my notice.

"Oh, uh, I didn't mean to," I stammered, "I was just concerned something might be wrong."

"Wrong?"

"Sorry about that, it was a misunderstanding, I mean on my part."

"What could be wrong?"

Bear frowned and wagged a thick finger at me. He was shaking his head. "There's no misunderstanding. She told me everything. She saw it all in your eyes, man."

He studied me awhile and then broke into a big wide grin, his little eyes sparkling. I exhaled, but before I could begin to relax, his car door swung open halfway and his left foot crunched the gravel. The foot shifted slightly, then settled and locked. My throat thickened and my heart began to race. I stared at the foot, which remained bolted in place like some weird museum artifact. I looked up and saw that Bear's head was turned back toward Artemis. They were talking.

I felt trapped inside the hatchback. I needed space. Just as I moved to get out of the car the bulging black wingtip disappeared back into the Jaguar, and the door slammed shut and the window rolled up sealing me out of their world.

The Jaguar screeched and spit gravel as it backed out of its space and appeared to leap as it exited the parking lot. I leaned back in the passenger seat to take a deep breath and for an instant forgot what day it was. Then I remembered.

The Lincoln!

I jumped out of the car, scanned the empty parking lot, scrambled into the driver's side, took a quick right out onto Crawford Farm Lane, and in moments found myself racing to keep up with Bear and Artemis.

Chapter 20

I followed at a discreet distance. We were going west and north, racing past farmhouses, silos, and fieldstone walls that seemed to have been duplicated and pasted at random across the country-side. We rolled through once-quaint colonial type villages with their skimpy antique shops in need of paint jobs and cramped two-story homes with rotting front porches.

Mile after mile I saw no living thing and gave myself over to pondering uncertainties. Did Callie protest when Coldwell decided to drive away? Did Johnny cry? Who invited Bear and Artemis? Did Marla call Callie?

I followed the white mark, teasing it into brief disappearance with the vague satisfaction reserved for some absorbing irrelevance, like that of watching a sailboat vanish on the horizon. When the white was gone too long, I shook my head to rouse myself and depressed the accelerator pedal and pushed the hatchback until it rattled like an old shopping cart.

There it was again, but just as it began to enlarge it descended below my line of sight on a road decline and was gone. In seconds I was cresting the slope, and I could see the road dip and then rise ahead for a good distance. They were gone. Bear had either turned at a crossroad or pulled into the woods. I passed a narrow clearing to my right, drove on ahead a short distance to rule out nearby crossings and doubled back.

I drove to the opening and saw tire tracks in the dirt trailing into the woods. I parked a short distance away, tight against the woods, and walked back to the clearing. It didn't take me long to spot the Jaguar angled forward like a beast sniffing at some slumbering prey. I crept toward it, impelled by a sense of moral duty compromised by perverse compulsion. At about twenty feet I hesitated. The glare on the rear window was obscuring my view. Were they inside the car, the mauling beast and its prey?

A rocking scream and a blast of wings seemed to erupt from a common well of terror. My eyes followed the flash of black bird springing from a low bough. Was it the bird wailing? "Oh God! Oh God! Oh God!"

I whirled in confusion.

"Don't! Don't! Don't!" The cries landed as fast and hard as a plunging knife and I couldn't move.

A fluttering sensation in my upper chest triggered a coughing fit. I peeled my feet from the soft ground and slogged toward the Jaguar. The car was empty, the keys were in the ignition. I cringed at the screams that assaulted me from all angles.

"Oh no! No! No! Please, no!"

I doubled over clutching my belly and felt a surge of loathing for the coward in me. "Damn you, get up!" I cried. I scrambled about, my eyes scouring the ground, my hands sifting through rotted leaves and dirt and pieces of decaying trees in search of a rusted tailpipe, a fist-sized rock.

What sounded like a final desperate plea quickened my hands. I clasped a broken branch and ran through the trees toward the cry of death, leaves and dirt flicking off the crooked limb.

At the sight of her I staggered to a stop. The woods behind her were thickening like a gathering mob. She was bound upright against an oak tree, her arms pulled back, her stretched bare breasts peering at me like large dull eyes. The sick bastard had stripped her naked but for her fine jewels and stiletto sandals.

In too casual a voice she said, "What are you going to do with that branch?"

Did she speak to me? Was that mouth real? Did it move and utter words? I touched my own mouth. All I needed to do was open it to remind myself to wake up, and I would.

Wake up, Lucas!

"Are you the forest ranger?" she said.

She tilted her head, frowning.

"What is this?" I said in a loud voice intended to make her vanish.

"Oh look, Yogi Bear is here," she replied. "He wants to talk to you about the importance of safety."

The cocking of a rifle bolt seemed to quiet nature, seemed to make the trees shimmer.

"What the hell did you do to her?" Bear said.

Artemis sighed and gazed up at the oak boughs.

"I'm talking to you!"

I turned with my hands raised. The rifle was aimed at the middle of my chest.

"What the hell do you think you're doing, Ricardo?" he said. "What are you trying to accomplish?"

Ricardo?

"Sorry," I said. "I didn't mean to barge in on, on whatever this is. A game?"

"A game? Does this look like a toy to you?"

"No, it certainly doesn't. Wow, what you must be thinking, I mean, I was supposed to follow my in-laws and wife to the reception hall. I had the directions card and then, and then I didn't."

"Bullshit."

"No, I'm telling you the truth."

"Ah, Ricardo, she told me the truth."

"I think you're confusing me for someone else. I'm not Ricardo, and please could you stop pointing that gun at me?"

He frowned in surprise, and then smiled in disgust as he shook his head.

"What is it with you people? Second Amendment ring a bell? How in hell am I supposed to blow a hole in your chest if I don't point this gun at you?"

I searched his small eyes for signs of levity, but it was like being swept into a rip tide.

"I got distracted. We were the last ones in the parking lot, remember? So I had to follow you because I lost the directions card."

Bear drew close and began to sniff me.

"You have to give us something," he said.

"What do you mean, *give you something?*"

Bear raised his eyebrows, looked at me, glanced at Artemis, looked back at me.

"I'm giving you a way out, moron," he said.

"I don't understand."

Bear waved the rifle in Artemis's direction and turned me around with a firm shove.

"She told me all about you, Ricardo."

Artemis pretended to be asleep and began to snore.

"I don't know what you mean. Do you mean because I was glancing over at your car? Okay, I could see how you might get the wrong impression, but—"

"*Wrong* is not a word, don't you understand?"

"No, I don't, that's the point. This is all a misunderstanding. I misunderstood what was happening back at the church parking lot, but now you're misunderstanding me."

Bear appeared to mull over what I said.

"I appreciate a good lie as much as the next guy," he said, "but sometimes lying is just a piss poor idea. Now, for example. What does trying to convince me you're a choir boy get you? Belly laughs for everyone and three bullets in your chest? You can't lie about what's inside you any more than you can lie about the color of your skin. It's always there, it's always the same. Once you understand *that*, Ricardo, everything else falls into place."

"I'm not Ricardo."

Bear gazed at me in disbelief and then shoved me with such force that I stumbled several steps back toward Artemis.

"I pull all this shit together to bring you up to speed and what do I get for busting my ass on your behalf? A lack of gratitude. You make me sick, man. You're a disgrace, Ricardo, a disappointment of epic proportion."

"I'm not *Ricardo!*" I yelled as I turned to face him.

Bear's mouth shaped itself into an oval of astonishment. I thought he was going to knock me to the ground, but he pressed his lips together and studied me with the relaxed intensity of a portraitist.

"*You* need to know something," I said, urged on now by his sudden passivity, and eager to recover a measure of personal dignity. "I am as American as you are, *Ricardo* or not, and with all the rights bestowed on me by the United States Constitution. And right now you are infringing on my rights as a citizen and you are breaking the law of the land."

Bear stared at me with a mix of amazement and revulsion, as if he'd just come upon some bizarre sea creature rolled up on the beach. The absurdity of what I'd said didn't hit me until Bear started to roar with laughter. But his mirth quickly evaporated and he turned serious again.

"It's no secret, Ricardo. We all know how much you want it. She didn't have to tell me, but she did anyway. She doesn't understand, you see, that some things are best left unsaid."

I snuck a glance at Artemis, who closed her eyes, licked her lips and started writhing like a tree snake.

"Come on, let's go," Bear said. "Get over there and drop your pants."

His gaze seemed to travel over every part of my face, as if gathering data, taking snapshots of my thoughts and emotions.

"You can't be serious?" I said.

He shoved me again with greater force this time and, after a second or two delay, jabbed me in the back with the butt of his rifle, knocking me down on all fours and igniting a deep fire between my shoulder blades.

"Give her what she wants, asshole!" he growled.

"Bear," Artemis cautioned.

I rose to my knees. The hard tip of Bear's rifle pushed deep into the hot spreading pain.

"Bear, stop it!"

Before I could imagine my chest exploding, I watched Artemis release herself from the tree. She took off her sandals and marched barefoot through the rotting leaves back to the Jaguar. When the rifle tip was extracted from my back I cringed and covered my head in anticipation of a parting blow.

Then I heard the violent rustle of dead leaves and it was a most lovely sound. I stood up and watched Bear shuffling away like some claw-footed beast that haunts the lonely imagination.

Just when I thought I had escaped lasting damage, Bear stopped and turned around. His nostrils flared as he took aim at my chest.

"Pow!" he spit out as he mimicked the rifle's kickback. And then he disappeared.

Chapter 21

I pretended to scan the reception hall. Would she come to me? She was holding Johnny when she glanced up and saw me— though she assumed me unaware—and I knew that for just an instant she thought it was me, the other Lucas, her Lucas, the one she thought she was getting when she signed up for *till death do us part.*

The music stopped and more lights were turned on. In the stark and bustling reception hall Callie handed Johnny over to cousin Lilly and made her way toward me in a blur of wounded movement. But her steps failed to shorten the distance between us. She might just as well have been walking in Paris or on the Moon. She stopped and stood beyond my reach like a gloomy stranger. I tried to smile but couldn't as I saw that all trace of recognition had vacated her person.

"How's Johnny doing?" I said for no other reason than to hear her speak.

She stared at me in disbelief. Implying what? That I had relinquished the right to ask about my son? That I wasn't fit to be a father?

"How is he?" I insisted, and the edge in my voice took her by surprise. It surprised me too, pained me like an accidental wound, like a nail running through the bottom of my foot. She whispered something I couldn't hear and turned to look back at the table she probably wished she'd never left.

Johnny was sitting on Lilly's lap, facing the girl, his arms clasped by her hands. She was dipping him back and pulling him up, back and up, over and over. The boy was all giggles and frowns, perfectly adjusted to a world that was unraveling.

At the table Grace turned and said something to Coldwell. Whatever she said made him get up. Without a word he walked away and faded into the crowd.

"Please talk to me," I said.

It didn't matter now, I realized—what I said, what she said, what they said. What more did I have to lose that I wasn't already losing? Callie turned around and crossed her arms, her gaze fixed on my crooked tie.

"I don't know what you heard, but we need to talk," I said.

She looked up and stared into my eyes for several moments. I waited for a word, any word, but all she had to give was cold grieving silence. She turned and walked back to the table, and I hesitated before following her.

I nodded to Callie's unsmiling sister, Hadley, and her indifferent husband, Brock Penny, said hello to Lilly's parents—Audrey, who was Grace's younger sister, and her husband, Ed Rollo—and to Grace's cousin, Adeline, and maybe the only other person in the place as ill-fitted to the occasion as myself, Adeline's husband, Stan Yoblonski.

I took Johnny from Lilly, excused myself, and headed for the bar. Grace's voice was like a scraper file grinding against the back of my neck as I walked away. "I don't know how much longer we could have waited," I heard her say.

I ordered a vodka tonic and took note of my son's intense scrutiny, which seemed to pose inexorable questions: Who are you?

Who am I? What are we doing here? I drew back my head a few inches to get a better view of him, to frame and record and store the image of his indisputable dignity. I could see Callie's mouth and Marisol's brow etched on his little face. I needed to hold on to that. I kissed his cheek and felt his soft wispy hair against my temple.

That was when I noticed Coldwell a short distance away talking to an attractive woman who appeared to be in her mid-thirties. The woman laughed in response to something Coldwell had said. She touched his arm and her hand slid all the way down and over the top of his hand in a fading phantom-like caress. Coldwell paused for a moment, surprised, and flashed the rarest of smiles before resuming his discourse. The woman clasped her hands and her laugh trailed off as she looked up at Coldwell from a secret place.

It came as no surprise to me. I'd always had my doubts about the Coldwells. I downed the rest of my drink in one long swallow and watched Johnny's lips move in a simulation of sucking. I ordered another drink and took it with me and Johnny back to Table 5 and wondered where Callie had disappeared to.

Adeline got up and took my son so that I could eat. My mouth was watering before the first sliver of prime rib had touched my tongue. I was shocked at how hungry I'd become.

"God works in mysterious ways," Adeline said as she bounced Johnny on her knee. "I often marvel at it all, don't you, Ed? Don't you marvel at it all?"

"I know a ghost writer you should talk to."

"I bet you do," Adeline said glancing at me and smiling, and then reiterating for my benefit. "Young man escapes Nazi-occupied Poland, works on a Norwegian trawler headed for Newfoundland and ends up in Toronto. He learns English, becomes a Canadian citizen and manages two businesses. Then of all things, he falls in love with a New York gal, and here we are all these years later."

"Compelling," Ed said, nodding, "especially the scene with the heart to heart between the young fella and the old dying queer. I have to confess, that got me right here in the heart, and in a big way."

"Ed, really," Adeline said.

"I'm only going by what you told me."

"If I thought you were being malicious, I'd get up and punch you in the nose right now. Peter was a lovely man."

Ed winked at Stan.

"Oh, but Ed is always thinking in marketing terms," Stan said. "It's why he has so much money."

"Well, *so much* is a relevant term, isn't it?" Ed said.

"Agreed, but back to your marketing strategy, Ed: tortured homosexual widower grooms young protégé. Am I on the right track, Ed?"

Ed laughed. "Yes, yes, exactly. Grooms. I like that, Stan. Yes, grooms."

"Stan, please don't encourage him," Adeline said.

"In all seriousness," Stan said, wiping wine from his lips with a napkin, "Peter was a kind and generous man and very much a second father to me."

Stan and I exchanged a brief glance. He smiled at me with such dedicated gentleness that I felt my face grow warm. I looked down at my plate and cut another piece of meat.

A silky wounded voice that reminded me a little of Billie Holiday was easing into *Blue Moon*. At the microphone a delicate woman-child wrapped in gold foil from neck to ankles like a piece of coffee-colored candy was swaying to the lazy rhythm. Seduced by the little moon goddess, couples migrated to the dance floor, quickly filling it and spilling out from the hardwood onto the carpeting.

"Where has Callie disappeared to?" Grace said sounding cheerfully irritated.

As if on cue, Hadley and Brock got up from the table and headed for the dance floor. I scanned the hall in search of Callie certain it was Coldwell's absence, not Callie's, that was irking Grace.

Despite Grace's intrusion, an impromptu feeling of optimism had sprung in my mouth and begun to ripple out and down to my fingertips and toes. My body began to tingle, and I thought how good life was going to be when Callie returned to me. How good it would be, I thought, as I scanned and chewed, revitalizing blood juice slithering over my tongue and teeth and sliding down to my core. I took another sip of vodka. If only we could talk in a quiet place, Callie and me. If we could just talk it would all be okay.

I looked all around for her from behind my plate of meat and potatoes and then focused my attention on the drama of the moon dance, the bodies revolving and rotating like crowded planets, the floating faces that spoke of escape, desire and dream, the multitude of secret anticipations streaking like comets across the little galaxy of the reception hall. I saw Artemis emerge from the shifting mass, her arm pulled free of Bear's grasp, and then, after the moon goddess stopped singing, I watched Callie and tuxedoed Steve walking through the crowded dance floor back to Table 5.

"Everybody having a good time?" Steven Vandeway said.

"Why, hello there!" Grace cried out with almost desperate delight. "Where have you two been all this while?"

"We were just catching up," Callie said.

"My goodness," Grace said. "Just looking at the two of you, I can't help but imagine…"

I was the least surprised or embarrassed, I think. The least inclined to imagine what Grace wanted us all to imagine. The resulting silence, as oppressive and awkward as it was for the others, had no immediate impact on me that I could tell.

"Refresh my memory," Grace continued. "When did you two stop being an item?"

Steven seemed willing to say something innocuous but couldn't quite come up with any words.

"Mom," Callie warned, and I wondered why she bothered.

"Oh, you know what I mean," Grace said lifting a glass of red as if ready to propose a toast.

"Actually, it will be three years in December that Callie and I went our separate ways," Steven said. He tossed a quick glance my way, but I was paying more attention to the tremor in Grace's right hand, a tremor that now, I realized, had found its way inside me.

"Then *this* guy swooped in before I could get her to change her mind. Hello there, Lucas."

I got up, nodded, and shook his hand. "Hello, Steven," I said.

I took a quick glance at Callie, who had turned her head and was watching the band milling about. I wondered how much she had told him.

"I'm so glad you're all here," Steven said. "I know Chad appreciates it so much. The fellas devised a tongue-in-cheek fertility ritual for the newlyweds. Something tribal, I've been told. Mad as hatters the bunch of them. Hey, I should get back. I need to stay in the loop so I don't stick out like a sore thumb when the curtain goes up. Should be lots of fun. Hope you all enjoy it!"

Steven Vandeway flashed a big white smile and headed off to be briefed by the mad-hatters.

I sat back down in what had become a parallel universe. I could hear distant muffled voices. Grace talking to Audrey. Adeline trying to hoist Lilly out of her descent into hopeless boredom. And Hadley minus Brock saying something to Callie about a dress.

Stan and Ed got up and went for a walk. I stayed behind and cut green beans in half and pushed them across my plate like chess pieces.

The moon goddess faded into the background, and the amped-up band leader now took command and revved up the crowd with a couple of crude wedding night jokes before launching the band into a preposterous rendition of *Whole Lotta Love*. A circle comprised of thick-necked men in their late twenties and early thirties formed in the middle of the dance floor with the groom pinned at the circle's center. I noted Bear's integration into the elite circle with special interest and recalled something Callie had once told me about the groom.

A few years back Chad Vandeway, starting quarterback at Wall University, had been accused of participating in the gang rape of a local high school girl during a campus frat party. Not surprisingly, the case was settled out of court. When Danielle started seeing Chad, Callie grew concerned and took the initiative to meet with her. Since that encounter Danielle barely acknowledged Callie's existence.

Most guests had probably heard the story, but there was no indication that what happened in the past was in any way tempering their celebratory enthusiasm, and maybe the mystique of a rapist groom added a little zip to the festivities.

Chad Vandeway danced like a man without a care in the world. His buddies crouched and swayed from side to side lavishing him with lewd encouragements and allusions that elicited laughs from several of the guests.

The groom tossed his limbs about with such abandon that at one point he lost his balance and stumbled. A burst of appreciative laughter and applause went up as his former teammates shoved him back to the center of the circle where he stood sweating like Elvis, one raised arm pointing at the ceiling, the other dangling between his spread legs.

"Danielle!" went up the shout like a clarion call. In moments the crowd had taken up the chant. "Danielle! Danielle! Danielle!"

One of the groomsmen peeled away from the circle and danced his way to the bride and groom's table. He led the bride back by the hand, and guests applauded warmly as the newlyweds were reunited. A loud, nostalgic *Hut! Hut! Hut!* chant ensued and spread across the reception hall. From what must have seemed to him the center of the universe, Chad initiated a series of odd maneuvers meant to coax his bride into a pantomime of copulation, but she pulled away with a nervous laugh when she realized what he was trying to do. A few chuckles among the guests were followed by uncertain clapping.

"What I'd give to be that age again," I heard one man say.

The Zeppelin tune continued like a broken record for what seemed eternity until the groomsmen tired of it and the circle broke apart. The music petered out and everyone caught his breath. The bandleader, running his hand through his sweaty locks, exhorted the guests to applaud the newlyweds one more time for knowing how to put on a show and for being such good sports.

Grinning faces wafted by as guests returned to their tables. I said her name loud enough, but she pretended to not hear me. I gazed on the face I loved most as I felt myself release her. The moment's festal din and banter, its social dictates, its sweat and heat all rendered the delicate complexities of love untenable. The simplicities of lust and vanity that were barely concealed beneath the extravagant gowns and expensive suits won the day and simmered in anticipation of impending rewards.

My newfound optimism now seemed a childish exercise in wishful thinking. All sense of purpose fled from me. I got up and walked away from the table. Did Callie turn her head? Was she thinking how she'd gotten it all wrong with me?

Loss of purpose could feel a lot like freedom when it didn't feel like death, and it became easy for me to slip into another frame of mind and linger over things that might otherwise have seemed ill-advised, like the prospect of plucking forbidden fruit from an oak tree.

I collided with a man I at first mistook for Coldwell returning from his tryst, and I bowed in extravagant apology. As I walked toward the bar I chuckled at the absurdity of my predicament and ordered another drink.

From there I was able to locate her seated at a nearly empty table. She had her back to me and was talking to a sour-faced woman whose glum countenance reminded me of Borders. I emptied my glass in one swallow and walked toward them. I stopped at a short distance to better view the smooth curve of her left cheek, the flutter of fake eyelashes, the pronounced bulge of her left breast.

Was there a human heart in there somewhere? I wondered as I settled in the seat behind her. Her distracted listener glanced at me with a blank expression and redirected her attention back to the speaker.

"It's enough to make me want to kill him," Artemis was saying in a loose alcohol-tinged voice. "It frustrates me like you would not believe. 'Art, shut up,' he says, 'you don't know shit about art. If I hadn't taught you what makes art, art, you'd still be auditioning at Syphilis Studios.' He thinks he's so clever saying things like that. Well, I don't do porn, Jeanine, not anymore. I take my art seriously and I will not be talked down to like that. One night, while he's asleep, I'm going to take that gun of his and shove it up his ass."

Jeanine motioned with her head toward me.

Artemis turned around. "Oh!" she squeaked.

It took her a moment, but then she seemed pleased to see me.

"You know him?" she said to Jeanine.

"I don't," Jeanine said.

"Tell me the truth, good sir, are you a PI?"

"Am I a pie?" I replied.

She burst out laughing and with her hand over her heart said to Jeanine. "God, he's funny. A pie! Don't you think he's funny, Jeanine?"

Her laughter was encouraging and made me feel better about myself in some illicit way. The smell of vodka coming from her breath was familiar and of comfort to me and suggested new possibilities.

"Tell him I went to the Ladies Room, if he asks," she instructed Jeanine as she rose from her seat. Her fingers felt light as a breeze as they swept over the top of my hand.

"Come on you," she whispered in my ear.

As I walked with her out of the reception hall, I heard a voice like that of a museum curator explaining an exhibit to a patron. It sounded like Ed, but I didn't look.

If it was Ed, Stan would be there too, part of him listening to Ed and part of him watching me walk by with a pale, long-legged creature from outer space.

Chapter 22

The wall rolled up and down my spine, tailbone to cranium, cranium to tailbone. But for all of the wall's movement I remained stuck, my gaze fixed on the Ladies Room door, my mind a quagmire of inchoate thoughts and jumbled emotions.

Coldwell's girlfriend appeared in the parlor and disappeared behind the door in an instant. I imagined a large mirror teeming with decorated hands and touched-up hair and makeup and lipstick and glittering jewels and fine purses and adjusted bras and girdles and garter belts. Reconstituted perfumed ladies emerged from that magic place like clockwork, forming and disbanding transitory pockets of discussion, the occasional male attaching, detaching and drifting away without fanfare.

Then I saw Lilly—but it wasn't Lilly—speed-walking with a blood-stained napkin pressed to her nose and mouth. She picked me out and looked at me with big round eyes before slipping behind the door. A woman—her mother?—burst out of the reception hall in silent pursuit.

How did this happen? Did a man beast's wayward elbow strike her face? Beneath the bloody napkin I imagined tender lips cut raw and swollen lumpy-blue, teeth outlined in thin lines of bright blood, and blood smeared like cherry jam over her lips, nose and chin. How helpless I felt, how incapable of doing whatever it was I needed to do to change everything, to heal the anguish of Callie's mouth that was a deep widening gash in my heart.

How I missed her mouth, her words and kisses. If life were solely a matter of words and kisses... If life were solely a matter of words and kisses and believing that a woman's mouth is a sanctuary that offers life to the fullest, then all the bleeding would matter little.

I walked over to the glass walls and gazed beyond the terrace out onto the course. And beyond the course, on the horizon, a descending arc of the sun was saturated with the orange velvet hue of a dying ember, and the muted green topography crept toward the darkening woods.

Behind me I heard Artemis. I turned and saw her standing with a woman who walked away after nodding in agreement with whatever Artemis had said.

"You can't be doing this," she said as she walked toward me.

"But didn't you say, 'Come on you'?"

She took a quick glance all around and said, "Let's go outside."

My yen for forbidden fruit had waned, but for lack of a plan I followed her out onto the terrace to the marble railing. Beneath the terrace and the grass and the soil the world was boiling.

I placed my palms on the rounded top of the railing and the world's heat rose up through the marble and into my hands and up through my wrists and arms and shoulders and settled in my head in a slow simmer that warmed my ears as I stared at the horizon.

"I didn't want to do that scene," she said looking at the dying sun.

"The scene in the woods you mean."

"I knew it would get complicated."

"But it was just a game."

"No, not *just*."

"It was a *complicated* game."

"When he saw you following us in the rear view, he said the movie gods had dropped you in his lap."

"I'm going to be in a movie?"

"He wanted to see it up close and personal for the sake of art. That's what he said, anyway. Like the female lead not being told she's going to be raped in the next take, only this time keep the man in the dark. Bear said he wanted unrehearsed shock, fear, confusion, humiliation, blind lust, and so on. He said he wanted to see what a man's face looks like when he's trashing his own so-called human dignity, or having it trashed by someone else."

"I'm reminded of the girl, the actress in *Last Tango in Paris*. She was nineteen years old. They didn't tell her a thing."

"I have to pick my battles. I really wasn't in the mood, but in truth I was a little curious to see what you would do, how far you would go. You failed to comply and it made him kind of irritable. He wanted more from you, he was itching for more."

"How much more?"

Artemis laughed.

"It gets complicated with Bear," she said. "He gets to play whenever and however he wants because of his daddy. His daddy owns this place, for example. His daddy owns so many places, people and things it would make your head spin."

"So does this mean I *am* going to be in a movie?"

"You need to be careful. Like coming to our table before? That was insane."

She placed her hand over mine and smiled.

"Not that I don't find the willingness to die for a cause sexy in a man," she said.

"*Viva La Causa!*" I said.

"The only cause Bear supports is Bear… Look, don't tell him I said this, but Bear no longer has a pair, if you know what I mean."

She batted her eyelashes at me. I drew my hand away but she wasn't finished. She ran her hand down my arm to my wrist and kept it there. I had the feeling Bear was watching, taking notes.

"If he sees us like this, he *will* hurt you," she said.

She stared at me with an expression of grave concern, and then suddenly began to giggle. "You do understand he will hurt *you*, not me, right? Bear wouldn't hurt me, but he might kill you. He might. He could. He wouldn't get into any trouble, you know. Don't tell anyone I said this because I will deny it, but Bear has descended into madness."

She smiled like a radiant cheerleader as she squeezed my wrist. Her cool blue eyes sparkled with pleasure. I looked at her hand, white as milk against my skin. I wondered if evil was the color of milk.

"He's watching, isn't he?" I said, pulling my arm away.

"What kind of woman do you take me for?"

I scanned the terrace and the glass walls. Bodies were milling about, but no Bear in sight. I scanned nearby shrubs and trees. No Bear sightings anywhere.

"You don't know what it's like to be with him. He makes me read everything he writes and expects me to ooh and ah and when I don't, he tells me I have no concept of what makes art, art. You can see for yourself how hard it is for him to process reality."

I stared into her inscrutable eyes.

"What do you want from me?" I said.

"What does anybody want from anyone?" she said but gave me no time to respond. "I don't know if you were there when I lied to Jeanine, but the truth is Bear never hit me."

"Good to know."

"You don't believe me, do you?"

She stepped away from the marble railing and stood facing me, her back to the building. She exposed her neck and stretched her arms and flicked her wrists and said, "Not a mark, see." When she lifted the hem of her dress above her waist it took me a moment to realize she was wearing nothing beneath the silver fabric.

"No marks anywhere," she said showing her big white teeth. "I'm clean as milk."

I shot a glance at the building as she dropped her hem and wiggled her body. "So where is he?" I said.

"You wouldn't be referring to my husband, would you?"

I pondered that bit of information.

"You should go, unless you want to get me killed," I said.

Artemis chuckled and came to my side. The two of us stood leaning against the railing like a couple of coworkers on lunch break. "Oh, don't worry, he's off somewhere with his boyfriends doing blow."

She turned and pointed to a grove on the course a couple of hundred yards away. "How about you and I meet in those trees in a half hour?"

"To do what?"

"That's a secret I will reveal to you and you alone. Not even Bear will know."

I gazed at the trees.

"To be honest, I did lie before," she said. "I really was telling Jeannine the truth when I said Bear hit me. He punched me right in the face. And you know why? Because I embarrassed him in front of his boyfriends. I don't even remember what I said. He broke my nose and two front teeth. I was out cold for ninety seconds."

"You should be the one writing the scripts."

"It happened three years ago, Smarty Pants. I needed plastic surgery, okay? That was no walk in the park, believe me."

"I don't. I don't believe anything you say. Artemis and Bear. What are you, cartoon characters?"

"You can be so rude and obnoxious, did you know? For your information, my daddy gave me that name for whatever reason. You would have to ask him. I never did, but he's dead anyway. Believe what you want, I don't care. I can't make you. Now it's your turn, Ricardo. I want to know what your real name is."

"I'm Mr. Galaxy."

"Oh, wow, I love it! I bet your pretty little wife calls you Mr. Galaxy every time you do it."

"You're a piece of work, aren't you? It's obvious you don't know the first thing about love."

"Oh, did I touch a raw nerve? Love? How romantic, how sweet and all. But I have to tell you in all sincerity—and you'll have to pardon my French—love is a crock of shit, a fallacy perpetrated by whomever for whatever reason, greeting card companies and such and so forth, and as a service to mankind the word should immediately be removed from the lexicon.

"I've got something better for you anyway. Unlike Bear, who only thinks of himself, I'm going to give you an out of this world one of a kind present, but before I do, I'm going to let you look forward to it for a tiny while so as to build up your excitement. It's the least I can do after that awful time he put you through."

"Go away."

"Oh? Okay, I'll go, just make sure you meet me in the trees at sunset for your exciting present."

She winked and started walking back to the clubhouse.

"Why would you marry a bear without a pair?" I called out.

She turned around and placed her hands on her hips in mock bewilderment.

"Oh, Mr. Galaxy, you are simply a hoot, aren't you?"

She disappeared into the building. I was glad to be free of her. With any luck I'd be free of Bear too.

I walked back into the cool indoors and settled at the entrance of the reception hall to take a look. Adeline was holding Johnny, tapping him gently on the back while talking to Audrey. Lilly was there too, her head resting on the table over her crossed arms. There was no one else at Table 5. The little moon goddess was swaying again. Her voice made it okay to not think too much.

When the band transitioned from *Natural Woman* to a disco medley, I turned my attention to the crowd of dancers. From the shuttling mass of couples emerged Callie and Steven Vandeway. The tuxedoed gentleman escorted my wife back to Table 5.

. . .

NO ONE saw me. I retreated to the terrace. A thin hazy sliver of sun clung to the horizon as dusk began to settle. Off to the side one of the groomsmen had a bridesmaid pinned against the marble railing. They were devouring one another like starving animals. I strode past them onto the course and headed for Artemis's grove. I walked close to the tree line to my right, like a vessel navigating along an unmapped coastline.

In the deepening gray, snickering spectral forms appeared and disappeared behind the trees.

"You sons of bitches!" I cried out. "Go back to hell! I'm not afraid of you!"

I shambled deeper into the woods and found a dead spot where I stopped and stood among silent gloomy giants. There was no country club, no celebration, no electric lights, nothing to remind me I belonged to a civilized world. I had no sense of north nor south nor east nor west, nor of time.

I thought of Callie and Johnny and it made me sad that I might already be dead and that I'd left them in such a lurch. But as I listened for whispers of life I detected a faint rhythm within me, and I touched my chest and found that my hearts still beat.

My hearts? One within, another without, its sound and rhythm like that of plodding footsteps. I turned and saw a large shadowy figure bearing down on me. My leg muscles twitched but I remained stuck in place. Everyone knows you can't outrun a bear anyway. You have to face the bear and make yourself big. I waved my arms and shouted, but the bear kept coming. I jumped up and down cursing in a newly invented tongue, and finally the bear stopped in its tracks.

It bore a rifle, and after pausing as if to reconsider, continued coming, walking now in an almost conciliatory fashion, the rifle carried sideways across its broad waist. It stopped within an arm's length of me, so close I could smell its sour breath.

"You are one crazy ass son of a bitch," the bear said with a hint of admiration.

"You may be right, but you are one lousy ass writer. Which is worse, man? You tell me."

The rifle butt swung like an axe in a compact arc, striking me above the left ear, hurling me into dark breathless space.

Part 5

Nigma

Chapter 23

Heavy-headed heavy-handed situation down here where the gray muck folds and rolls and the words hide inside, so me scratch and claw and wipe and stir up filth clouds that tease the words nearly free but not quite, not quite. Filth is stubborn as all hell by nature and likes to float back down and settle, so me scratch and claw and wipe and stir up clouds for the rightness of words, but filth is stubborn as all hell by nature and...

So long so deep in chlorinated waters me arms swell up like saturated loaves, me head's a *nigma poozle* conundrum heavy like a hammered anvil and up above so high me got puppet feet float-dangling.

But then *swoosh!* just like that my head's shooting up into the water's face like a bound log cut loose, then *whoop!* down and up I go, then *whoop!* down and up and I'm gasping, coughing, apprehending Mrs. Brinkley's flip-flops flip-flapping. She's running strong and steady by my side, right hand on the stretcher cart, barking white dog at her heel. Stan is trying to keep up singing songs of exile in a pitiful fade.

Who are these people, these faceless people shaped and colored all different ways tugging, stretching, mauling me?

Marisol is upstairs singing songs of old. In Madrid the flower girls sing and the birds are chirping, chirping.

In the hallway downstairs I hear the crackle of pork chops frying in a pan. The kitchen windows are wide open, and I know so well the summer breeze and the scent of meat cooking in olive oil drifting down the apartment stairwell.

I met a girl, Mamá. Her name is Callie.

In Madrid the flower girls sing and the birds are chirping, chirping…

Marisol covers her mouth with her hands. A woman in blue puts her arm over her shoulder and they walk away together.

Where are you going, Mamá?

Men with hollow eye sockets dance in ragged circles while the techies watch in blue. The groom tosses cowboy boots back over his shoulder into a crowd of blind scuffling men. And there's poor Adeline holding her hollow belly with one hand, her chin with the other.

Gravity makes the brain swell downward against the brain stem, says who, and I sink into a crawl. Through a thicket toward the light I crawl, flopping hand dispersing clouds of gnats and fog. A lamp post rises, its bulb like an enormous shiny beetle stuck in a pod. I check my watch, it says zero, colon, zero, zero. The road stretches both ways in a hazy blur.

"Boy stupid as stupid can be."

"*Chica*, what you mean he run into a tree?"

I didn't run into a tree.

"Ah, *sí, hija*, the police say he run into a tree."

"But, *chica*, his head cracked this side here, so how that can be?"

"Maybe he run sideway like this, you tell me."

I didn't run into a tree!

"*Ay, pobre!*"

"Run sideway like a drunk goat."

"I think boy drink to forget."

"Forget what, *hija?*"

"What he don't want to remember."

"And she sit there looking at that poor cracked head with tears all dried up."

Why didn't you wake me?

"She love her goat boy but she tired, you can tell."

"Use up all them tears then what you got?"

"Then you no cry no more—"

"—no more, no more, no more, no more."

"And boy, don't you come back *no más*."

"Ha, *chica*, is not even funny."

Off the midline, on the outer limit of flickering light in the thinning fog, some small low thing is saluting me. A car races past, illuminating and displaying and my throat shrinks dry. I lick my cracked lips and listen to barking dogs.

"I understand this may not be the best time nor place, but I think we're beyond such considerations at this point. I am just having such difficulty processing all of this. We need to talk about your future and Johnny's. Clearly—"

"Oh, Grace."

No, Adeline, let her talk.

"Mom, please stop."

Callie, we need to talk, just you and me.

"I understand, darling, I really do. This is so difficult for you. Of course, it is. Don't you think this is difficult for me too?"

Here I am, Callie. Not that dead thing! I'm right here, Callie!

I stumble back onto the grass. A car sways at the last instant evading the creature. Its small pointy face turns idly after the headlights and I feel a sudden hideous burden.

"Your friend is in a medically induced coma. The high pressure caused by swelling to the brain depletes the oxygen, causing some areas of the brain to starve. We have addressed that. The induced coma allows the brain to rest and the swelling to subside, which in turn reduces pressure. Gradually, normal oxygen flow returns to the brain. We can't rule out the possibility of brain damage, but we remain cautiously optimistic."

"Can he hear us?"

Of course I can hear you, Virgil. I'm standing right here.

"Each patient is different. We don't know how much Lucas can hear, or how much of what he hears, if anything, he comprehends. Some induced coma patients report having had vivid dreams and visions. Some have been able to recall conversations in great detail. Others may even see themselves standing in the room conversing with their visitors."

"So he could be standing right here next to us, listening? Talking to us?"

What did I just tell you, Virgil?

"Yes, in his mind it is possible, though highly unlikely."

Would you please turn your head and look at me?

"What happened to you, Lucas?"

I was at the bottom of Graddick's pool clawing and scratching to get at the words, but the filth kept swirling and I couldn't see them.

"Who did this to you?"

They're saying I ran into a tree, but I knew you wouldn't buy that.

"Who did this to you?"

I don't know, somebody.

"Who did this to you, Lucas?"

You want me to say me? You want me to say I did it?

Waving away the fog to assess the tiny black eyes that look but don't see and the bright agitated splats of blood and pulp simmering on the asphalt.

Do it. You have to, it's not even a choice.

K-I-L-L spells KILL.

Primordial word, old as life, bold and neat as an axe.

KILL!

Act of mercy, Amado, feel it tighten round your throat like a big dry hand.

I go in search of a killing stone and settle for a broken branch the size of my arm. I snap off the dry shoots, linger and speculate. That car speeding by, the people inside were invisible as ghosts. Where were they going so fast and what were they saying? Who said you had to go fast anyway? I take my time to breathe, speculate and string together conjectures, assumptions and theories. I give nature time to slow-cook all that's extraneous to me, and if I play my hand just right, I won't have to kill. I'll let nature run its course. I'll bide my time speculating and theorizing.

But the thing won't die. All the speculating and theorizing and the thing still won't die. Nature turns its heat on me like I was any other forest creature. I check my watch, it says zero colon zero zero.

I loom over her like a doubtful Goliath holding my kill club like a gentle wand meant to nudge awake sleepers. Her blood is fresh and nervous bright, cooking on the hot pavement, makes me think how moments ago she was heading back to her young after her nightly foray, her movements guided by scent, her world immediate, gloriously odorous and tactile, and then…

It gives one pause. I bend toward the creature, angered suddenly by its mute serenity.

KILL the damn thing! I hear them shouting inside the speeding car that's miles away.

I lift high the club and the head swells in collaboration. You can't miss the head now it's so big and death is sure to be quick. So why are you waiting? Flex that shoulder, lift it high, high, high and put your back into it, and now swing, boy, swing like your life depends on it!

I can't and the roar and flash of steel hurls me onto my back flat and from low down on the damp ground I register the piteous squish-splat.

"Johnny and I have been staying with my parents."

Oh, Callie.

"They're going to bring you out of the coma tomorrow. They'll keep you under observation for a period of time…"

I'm not that, I don't need to be observed, I don't want to be observed.

"I don't know if you can hear me, Lucas, or understand what I'm saying."

I'm not that thing. Look at me, I'm not that thing.

"I fell in love with you. I put you on a pedestal. Maybe having expectations of anyone is unfair. I thought our differences would help make us better persons. But I was kidding myself, I can see that now. We don't think the same way, we never did. We just don't believe the same things. That's why I can't be with you. How can we raise children together when we can't even agree on what's right and what's wrong?"

I'm not that thing, I'm not, and anyway, don't you believe in forgiveness?

"I don't know…"

"Oh, don't go! Please, Callie! I'm not that thing, I'm not…

The stars are dead and it's so damn cold.

From my low vantage point it could be a discarded hand puppet, a kid's tattered toy tossed out the window of a speeding car. I need to verify. I need to get closer. The head's intact, all right, and normal sized. What are the odds of that? And what am I supposed to take from that howling black oval with sharp little teeth?

My insides lurch, so I dash into the woods. I bend over, purge, shake it off, spit, wipe, straighten up and walk then run because my head is going to burst—oh, I just know it—it's going to burst like a small mammal under the wheel of a two-ton car.

I dash through the trees holding my sloshing head that feels like an overripe watermelon. Across a clearing and toward a ragged brown hedge I run, my hands and arms aching from holding up too much.

Someone is whispering in my ear, *Break through to the other side! Break through to the other side! Break through to the other side!*

Brambles tear and claw at me, and I'm snagged like a wild, thrashing animal.

Chapter 24

She walked into my room with a nurse early afternoon. I'd spent a good chunk of the morning piecing together who I was and what had happened to me and finally getting around to thinking about her and Johnny. But the first thing that popped into my head when I saw her was that she'd just come from discussing whatever she'd decided with Steven Vandeway.

She looked at me but didn't smile. Her lack of joy at seeing me didn't bother me as much as her look of worry, which reminded me of a mother fretting over a sickly kid. We said very little and then she left.

I began a period of physical therapy and a series of sessions with a counselor, a dual effort directed at easing me back into the world, though it was a much different world now. One morning Callie came back to the hospital to pick me up and drove me to our basement apartment in Legacy City.

We sat across from each other at the kitchen table. She had insisted on this. It was important that she see my eyes when she spoke to me, she said, that she be convinced I understood what she was saying. And it was important that I not touch her. She was trying to be tough but she was coming across jittery. The encounter was costing her in a big way, but I couldn't pinpoint why. Regret, sorrow, fear?

The words had already done their job the first time she said them while I was comatose. They'd left a wound in me deep and wide as life itself, though there was no way for her to know this, of course.

"I can't be with you, Lucas."

No surprise there. I handled it better than I thought I might. Maybe the weakness in her voice, like a lack of conviction, also had something to do with it. I was already numbed and tired anyway. If I'd had the energy, I would have asked her how she found out about Marla, just for the sake of curiosity, though it didn't matter now. No excuses, no mitigating circumstances. She'd made her decision, right or wrong. Gotten advice from an old friend, right? To hell with forgiveness. So that was that. What else was I supposed to think?

"Lucas, do you understand what I'm saying?"

"My family didn't find out, did they?"

"About us?"

"About me being in the hospital."

"No, I'm sorry... I just couldn't bring myself to..."

I took a long look at her, trying to understand.

"It's fine," I said. "It's better this way."

"I don't know what happened to me. I was terrified of talking to your father. I prayed every night that you would be healed and that you'd wake, but—"

"It's okay."

"No, it's not. Five weeks, Lucas. I should have called him... I was afraid of what I would say, how I would—"

"Forget it. It doesn't matter. I want to see Johnny."

"Of course, Lucas, but do you understand what I mean when I say I can't be with you?"

"Yes."

"I need to say something more... This is so hard."

Divorce? Lawyers? Custody? Really? My first day home from the hospital?

I'd had enough for one day. I got up from the table and walked to the street side of the apartment. I stood for a while in front of the bedroom window. My line of sight was at foot level. It was noon and the sidewalk was a busy place. I watched different legs and feet go by, bare legs, covered legs, trousers and skirts, sandals and shoes and sneakers, left to right and right to left, some fast, some slow, some purposeful, some aimless.

Callie got up from the kitchen table and stopped so near I could feel her warmth behind me. I thought I sensed in her remorse or a kind of guarded respect. Was it possible that in these last couple of minutes she had reconsidered? I didn't want to be stupid about it but I kept thinking that maybe, just maybe, she had glimpsed in me a trace of stoic nobility, some link back to what she once imagined me to be. I pressed my hand against the window and watched the legs pass over my fingers, left to right and right to left, legs and feet of all shapes and colors and inclinations.

Callie caught her breath and began to cry. I turned around and saw my life suddenly restored in her tears. The moment of reconciliation had arrived at last, and in the most unexpected way. I opened my arms and stepped toward her, but she raised a hand in alarm and stepped back away from me.

"I'm so sorry, Lucas."

"It's all right, darling."

"No, please don't."

"What is it?"

She started taking quick breaths and seemed on the verge of hyperventilating. She held up her hand again to stop me from touching her.

"Your father is dying."

Then she broke with a deep groan. The words she spoke were so alien to me that an image of Bear and Artemis flashed before me, and I thought how all the world seemed permeated with bad theatrics. Hadn't death already—much too soon—visited us?

My legs began to weaken and I dropped to the floor.

"I'm so sorry," she said wiping tears from her face. "I am so sorry, Lucas."

She sat down on the floor next to me. I could feel her hesitate and then place her hand over mine. But I felt nothing. She drew her hand away as if she'd touched fire.

"Who told you?" I said.

"Tío Juan left a message a couple of days ago. I only saw it yesterday when I came by the apartment."

She paused and breathed and tried to steady her voice.

"I called him and we talked a little and I explained that Johnny and I were staying a few days at my parents' house while you were away on business, and then he said José has colon cancer... It's in his lymph nodes, and lungs and liver and oh, Lucas, it's everywhere."

"Why didn't anyone tell me?"

"But I—"

"Hell, Callie, why didn't anyone tell me?"

"But Lucas, how could I?"

"Ah, shit..."

"Juan said your father didn't want us to know he was sick."

I smiled and shook my head. "How much time does he have left?"

"Days."

"I have to go to him."

"I'll drive you to the airport."

"No, I'll take a taxi."

"But I can—"

"I'm taking a taxi."

"Please tell your father I love him," she said and her mouth tightened with grief. "Will you?"

I took my bag out of the bedroom closet and began to fill it with little thought as to what should go in it.

"Tell him," she said.

I stopped what I was doing and stared at the articles of clothing in the bag for a few seconds before gazing at her.

"I'll tell him, Callie. I'll tell him that you love him. But now go, okay? Please, I need to be alone. Just take care of Johnny."

I walked to the bathroom to gather toiletries for the trip. I could hear her footsteps behind me, firm and angry now.

"Why, Lucas?" she screamed. "Why?"

I stopped what I was doing and turned to face her. Her eyes were wild and desperate. She looked more beautiful than she'd ever been. But she was separated from me by a glass wall, and she became less real with each passing second, like an impression on a window that fades away.

"I don't know why," I said.

She was shaking her head in bewildered rage. I put my hand up, as though to touch what remained of her vanishing image, and then she was gone.

Part 6

José

Chapter 25

The small quiet man carried my bag to the front of Tío Juan's house, accepted the tip I gave him and shook my hand. He shrugged his shoulders in sympathy and slipped back into his taxi. I stood in a drizzle watching the black Seat until it disappeared around the corner.

Before opening the door, I paused to listen to the muffled, animated voices of men inside the house. I felt as if I was about to walk into a Spanish bar back in Legacy City where even the most mundane conversations tend toward ferocity.

It just seemed too normal and I began to wonder if Callie had misunderstood Juan's creative mix of Spanish and English and had gotten this dying thing all wrong.

I opened the door and there was Adriana in the hallway frozen like a statue. Then some button in her must have been pushed because she rushed me with open arms, and I felt her belly before anything else.

"You look so old," she said taking two steps back to get a better look.

"And you look so… pregnant."

She smiled with her sad, dark eyes and stroked her belly. "Seven months last Monday."

"Andresito."

"Yes, Andresito, your nephew," she said, her voice a little unsteady.

"And Enrique?" I said, but I was thinking of my dying father.

"Enrique couldn't stay any longer. He went back to Zurich yesterday. He said goodbye to Papá."

She shook her head and did her best to compose herself. "I'm really just the most pathetic sister a guy could have."

"I'm sorry I missed Enrique. I wish I could have been here sooner."

"Some things can't be helped. How are Callie and Johnny?"

"Fine, fine."

"Lucas is here."

It was the voice of a young girl. She stood a few feet away, studying me with a shy but earnest expression.

My sister waved her over and put her arm around her waist. "This is Penelope, Elena's eldest. Isn't she a beauty? She just turned thirteen. Last Saturday, no?"

Penelope nodded.

When Adriana saw the look of confusion on my face she said, "Elena, Lucas. Our cousin, Elena, Tía Pilar's middle daughter."

Before I could recall what Elena looked like—and as I was exchanging kisses on both cheeks with Penelope—a number of women and children appeared in the hallway.

"There he is, *el Americano*," Tía Pilar said with a smile so bright it bordered on inappropriate. "Inés, your brother's here!" she called out in a loud voice.

Inés was coming down the stairs, and for a moment I mistook her for Marisol. She made her way toward me then stopped and searched my eyes.

"Papá didn't want any of us to be here, you know," she said and embraced me gently, thoughtfully.

"Inés?"

"What is it?"

"For just a moment, I thought—"

"You thought I was Mamá? You're not the first to say it... And Callie? Johnny? And you?"

"They're fine, I'm fine. We're all fine. How are Grant and the kids?"

"Back in Seattle like ducks in a pond, as Grant likes to say. Rain, rain, rain, like here, though I've been told the bad weather has arrived here earlier than usual this year."

My uncles grew silent as I approached them. In the hallway outside the living room that counted my father's final days Juan, Eliseo, Rogelio, and Paco regarded me with somber affection.

"Julián, *el doctor*, was here earlier today," Juan said as he embraced me. "He'll be back tomorrow."

"Nephew, be prepared," Eliseo said. "Your father is much diminished. You won't recognize him."

Paco put a big hand on my shoulder as my uncles walked away. Rogelio glanced back to speak a word but only nodded, as if indicating agreement with what his brothers had said.

I crossed the threshold into the dying room alone. What kind of world had I entered? Who was this prone withered figure being devoured from within? I stared long and hard trying to reconcile this poor soul with the image I'd always had of my temperamental hard-working father. His eyes were shut and I accepted his uneasy slumber as a small mercy, and for a moment—because he seemed to have stopped breathing—I imagined him dead and felt relief before I felt regret.

But José wouldn't want to die like that. There were things, lists to review, loose ends to tie up, last words, a final check of the lights and the doors and the stove and the leaking toilet in need of a handle jiggle.

I stared at his partly opened mouth and his breathing returned. I began to piece him back together. Among the sharpened bones of his face I glimpsed the once handsome husband and father. I counted his breaths and the seconds between his breaths.

On the wall above him hung a wooden cross with a bronze corpus, on the night table a pitcher of water and a tray with folded white towels. I wet one of the towels and dabbed my father's dry lips. José took a deep rasping breath and sighed and began to stir as though having been set upon by a predator. He opened his eyes and blinked in confusion. He frowned and leaned and twisted his torso trying to lift himself.

A gold scapular medal and crucifix on a chain swung loose from inside his pajama shirt. He grimaced as though the chain were slicing into his neck. His hand clutched at the air trying to get a hold of it. After a couple of failed attempts, he pointed to his chest and said without looking at me, "Take it off."

I did as instructed and placed the chain on the night table.

"Your mother," he said, and shook his head in resignation.

José groaned suddenly as he pitched sideways and projected a brownish stream onto the parquet floor. The loud splash was like the hard bang of a cymbal and it made me jump from my seat. Distraught, he gestured with his hand that I should leave the room and struggled to draw his reed-thin legs over the side of the bed, groping at the air that now stank of death as though to remove the foul slop by force of will.

I gathered him up like a child and put him back into bed and covered him.

"It's okay, Papá, it's okay."

"My poor one," cousin Pepita said as she strode into the room with a bucket and mop. "Your father, even now. Such modesty! Such courage!"

Pepita wiped José's mouth with a clean wet towel. When he had closed his eyes and returned to his waiting place, she leaned over and kissed his forehead.

Tía Pilar and Inés came into the room to help with the clean-up. When Adriana returned from her errand Tía Pilar and Pepita left us to be alone with our father. After a while Adriana attempted to lighten the mood by relating a Swiss alpine joke Enrique had heard at work, but she began to stammer with emotion and had to stop.

After a late dinner, Inés took me upstairs to one of the bedrooms.

"Try to sleep a little," she said.

"I have to be there when he…"

"Of course. The three of us. We'll come to wake you. What is it?"

"He thought I was going to be an architect. I told him once, I don't know why I did, maybe because that's what he wanted to hear? He couldn't look at me when I went to him, couldn't even bring himself to say my name. I've been a disappointment to him, and now it's too late."

For a moment I thought my sister was going to slap me across the face.

"What did you expect from a man dying of cancer, Lucas? Tell me, what did you expect? That he would jump out of bed and run to you with open arms? Too late you say? Is it too late for you to understand such things?"

I looked down at the floor and shook my head.

"It was a stupid thing to say."

"My God, you have no idea."

"I'm sorry."

"When you came into the world Papá cried, did you know?"

"Yes, I knew, I did, but Mamá confessed that he had cried out of frustration, that he was devastated by the development."

"You're such a liar," Inés said with a half-laugh. "She confessed no such thing. Papá was ecstatic. He finally had a son."

"Sure, sure, but didn't he also cry when you and Adriana were born?"

"So we were told, but it was just a little white lie, actually, Mamá hedging her bets, making sure we wouldn't be jealous of the baby."

"But it didn't work."

"Maybe we were a little jealous in the beginning, but then we fell in love with you. It didn't take that long."

Inés smiled, handed me a pair of Juan's pajamas that looked far too big for me and kissed me on the cheek. She turned around before closing the door and said, "Yesterday Papá started asking everyone, 'Where is Lucas? Where is my son?'"

Chapter 26

The lumpy mattress felt cold and damp, and I woke up thinking I'd wet myself. I got up and turned on the overhead light. The mattress and my pajama pants were spotless as could be, and I didn't see any stains or cracks or leaks on the ceiling.

On the Galician coast of Spain, the rainy season seeps up through the old foundations like some clammy ocean spirit and penetrates wood floors and tiles and permeates the plaster walls. It settles deep within mattresses and pillows and blankets and sofas and towels and everything you touch and even what you don't, like your bones and brain.

I remember my father saying the electric heating system in the old house had been installed above the ceiling as an afterthought and was good for warming the top of your head down to the ears, depending on how tall you were, of course, but not much more. And Adriana, who should have been a meteorologist, said that on dry winter days in Santa Rosalía you were always better off on the street than indoors because—as she was happy to explain—the Gulf Stream current that swept across the Atlantic from the Eastern Caribbean brought with it mild air to dry your bones.

But dry winter days were as rare as springboks in these parts, and though officially winter was still a few weeks away, I knew my bones weren't going to dry any time soon. I got back into bed and assumed the fetal position to hoard heat to the best of my ability and dozed off for maybe another hour before waking with a start. Disoriented, I scanned the dark shadows in the room until I was able to reconstruct where I was and why, and the unhappy knowledge got me back up on my feet.

For a few hazy seconds the world seemed a place of quiet mystery, and I took my time walking down the stairs, my head floating one or two steps behind my feet. But the sudden explosive *Ra-Ta-Ta-Ta-Ta!* belching of a motorcycle racing past the front of the house jarred me into a state of bitter wakefulness. What kind of miserable jackass, at this hour? I stood barefoot on the cold tile floor of the center hallway taking deep breaths. When I felt half normal again, I went to check on my father. A thirty-something woman was keeping watch.

I cleared my throat. She turned around, her lips moving in uninterrupted prayer. It was my cousin, Julia, plying rosary beads. She looked into my eyes with a perfunctory expression, as though to communicate she had registered my presence, and then turned around to continue her whispered offerings.

I walked around to the other side of the bed and stared at José's poor face. I studied his labored breathing. I sat down on a chair and took the measure of his shrunken body, his bony hands, his distressed brow.

But there's still a lifetime of why's to investigate, José, a long list of why's. Your daughter-in-law asked me why and I didn't know why. Maybe you know why…

"Callie loves you," I whispered. "She wanted you to know she loves you."

Julia snuck a quick glance at me and then looked at my father's face as she made the sign of the cross. I wondered what she was thinking as she stared at that pinched sallow face.

I'd never had a conversation with her that I could remember. *Hola*, how are you, so good to see you, and so on, but nothing of substance. She'd always seemed to me a bit of a sourpuss. She had once been engaged to be married. Years ago her fiancé went to Germany in search of work. In Berlin he got a job and met a German woman and they married and started a family there. I had never paid all that much attention to Julia, so I didn't remember what she was like before her heart got broken.

She stayed with me, without uttering a word, until Tío Paco appeared. We left my father's dying room together. In the hallway she handed me my father's chain with the scapular medal and crucifix and told me to get some sleep. Apparently, me sleeping was a family priority.

"Julia," I said as she walked away.

She stopped, hesitated, and then turned to face me. A slight frown creased her forehead. She stared at me, at pains to understand what I intended to do or say.

I walked up to her and hugged her. "*Gracias*," I said.

When I released her, she managed a smile, and I knew sorrow could taste sweet sometimes, and maybe even be a form of happiness.

"*No hay de que*," she said, not at all.

A faint sigh escaped her as she touched my cheek. She stopped by the front door to take her umbrella from the large ceramic vase and then walked out of the old house into the cool drizzly night.

Chapter 27

Tío Juan's wife, Vicenta, prepared me a breakfast of milk and coffee, eggs with a light sauce of chopped tomatoes and onions, and thick toast with butter and peach marmalade. I had just finished eating and had stepped into the center hallway on my way back to my father's bedside when the front door flew open and in stepped Don Martín Ravelo. Martín looked like he had been plucked out of the stormy high seas by Poseidon and plopped inside my uncle's house.

At first glance he could have been another grim, wild-haired uncle. He wore the dark gray trousers of the middle-aged men of the region and a charcoal gray knit sweater and carried a brown bag in one hand and an umbrella in the other. He closed the umbrella and shoved it into the vase by the front door.

Upon seeing me he paused for a moment, as though to formulate a proper greeting. Without saying a word, he walked up to me, squeezed my arm, and stuck his head in the kitchen.

"Vicenta, take this, fresh from the bakery," he said in Galician and handed her the bag.

"Martín, Martín, what am I going to do with you?"

"You're going to do nothing with me, Vicenta, because you're a married woman."

Don Martín went inside my father's room and addressed Juan. "When is Julián coming by?"

"In the afternoon, around seven or so."

"Very well, then. And did you talk to Esteban?"

"Mother of God, Martín, how could I not have talked to Esteban?"

"Yes, yes, of course, Juan. Of course you did. Good, good. Well then."

After checking on my father and exchanging a few more words with my uncles he came back out into the hallway, took my arm and led me to the empty dining room.

"Sit with me," he said switching to Castilian. "You remember me? Ah, how could you? You were a child when I left for Africa."

"I do remember."

"Ah, good, very good. I have been back from Ceuta for two years now. You were playing marbles there on the floor with Jorge Villar's boy when I last saw you."

"Yes, I remember playing there with Javier."

I noticed the small white rectangle of Don Martín's Roman collar peeking up from behind his gray sweater and black shirt and I realized, against all logic, that its appearance made me feel somewhat constrained.

"Javier has a good job in Bilbao," he said, "civil engineering, and a wife and son, like you."

"We haven't seen each other in a few years, but we've kept somewhat in touch."

"One week a year I would return to visit my family. Javier and I coincided a couple of times. He always asked me questions about theology and philosophy. For a time, I thought he was going to be a priest, but look how things change."

"We thought my sister Adriana would become a meteorologist and she became an accountant."

"A meteorologist? Is that so? You see what a mystery life is… Did you know that your father and I went to school together?"

"Of course, Don Martín."

"We are good friends."

"I know you are. He often spoke of you."

"Yes, yes, very good, of course, of course… So tell me, how are things in America? How are your wife and baby son?"

I hesitated. Don Martín smiled and nodded in a manner of encouragement.

"Separation," he said. "Very difficult to negotiate. But it is important to cultivate positive thoughts."

I may have nodded, I don't remember. Surely, he meant separation in the broader sense, didn't he?

He stared at me, as if trying to divine my thoughts.

"Difficult, very difficult, to be separated from those we love," he continued, "and yet inevitable, and so we must make our peace."

My eyes were drawn again for an instant to the Roman collar. A faint expression of forbearance appeared and vanished like a passing shadow over Don Martín's face.

"Last week your father and I were reminiscing about the old days," he said, "before the Civil War. How good it was to be young, to play *fútbol*, swim in the bay, flirt with the girls during Sunday *paseo*. He remembered a good deal, your father. He was quite lucid. I took the opportunity to ask him if he would be making a confession. He said nothing and I did not press him. We spoke of others things. But later he returned to it. He said to me, 'I want to confess my sins, Martín.' It was a good thing for him, a relief, an opportunity to unburden himself."

Don Martín waited for me to say something.

"Does it surprise you?" he said.

I'm not going to confess my sins to you, Don Martín.

"No," I said with a smile, "Mamá told him he wasn't to die until he had spoken to a priest."

Not that I was being flippant, but shouldn't my lighthearted tone have suggested to the priest we move on to another topic? His focused gaze told me no, that it would not be enough, that he expected more of me. It felt a little dangerous to say more, but to my surprise I found, in fact, that I did want and need to say more.

"One day my parents were having a heated discussion," I said. "I was in another room watching television. I walked into the kitchen and said something silly to make them laugh, but they ignored me. They were so consumed by what they were debating that I don't think they were even aware of my presence. My mother was insisting that my father promise her that after she died, he dare not leave this world without confessing his sins to a priest. After she said that she realized I was standing just a few feet away. She covered her mouth with her hands, as if she had blasphemed. She tried to smile and Papá tried to make a joke, but it was too late. But all that is irrelevant now. No, Don Martín, it doesn't surprise me that my father would make a confession. Who would deny Marisol her final wish, after all? And you being his friend…"

"Your mother was such a bright light," Don Martín said with a sad smile. "So many boys had a crush on her, but she chose José. Yes, your father confessed his sins to me, though I served only as a facilitator. God is the one true confessor."

Martín's attire, his directness of speech and coarse benevolence spoke of blood that was dear to me and so, out of respect, I tried to remain ideologically detached.

"I mention this not to console you in some artificial way," Don Martín said, "nor to minimize your loss. But I believe it is important that you be aware of your father's most recent state of mind."

"His recent state of mind? Given the circumstances, it seems to me that my father reached a point of *resignación*, as Tía Pilar might say."

Don Martín gave what I said some thought before responding. "It is a word too often tossed about, too often misunderstood. True resignation does not bow down to death. It embraces trust unreservedly."

Why couldn't he have just slapped me on the back, blessed me, and been on his way?

"Trust, you say? Trust in what, Don Martín?"

He seemed taken aback by my uncharitable tone for an instant, and despite my dim, guarded state I felt a twisted sense of triumph.

"Trust in love, of course," the priest replied in a soft voice.

Ah, the pretty words again, come to brighten our day. I should put them on a sign and hang them on my neck for the benefit of humanity. *Trust in love, you all.* I shook my head and suppressed a grin. I noted the concern in Don Martín's eyes, and I looked away in search of an excuse to leave the room.

Don Martín scratched his jaw and began to speak in a pragmatic tone.

"A teacher of mine, Don Sergio Márquez—prompted by a question from one of his students—confessed to a classroom filled with thirteen-year-old boys that he did not know if the God of the cross existed. But he had met people who were capable of making extraordinary sacrifices for others. How is sacrifice possible without love? he wondered aloud. And where does love come from? Is it a trick of the brain? An accident of nature? Can what is best and most noble in a person be dissected like a frog and analyzed?"

I've heard it all before, Don Martín. Just tell me how in hell you reconcile this loving God with humanity's daily portion of horror?

I didn't have to say it for Don Martín to hear it. He looked so tired suddenly that I began to sense the enormity of his chosen path, and in that moment, I wasn't all that certain that he did believe. To my surprise, his burden pressed down on me and unsettled me. He stared at me, ensnared by my uneasy silence. Then he glanced at his watch.

"I have to go to Fontevila to see a mother of four who is dying of cancer. Your uncles and aunts know the Rodríguez family. I will say my goodbyes to your father and go, but first I must leave you with this, *amigo* Lucas. Long ago I wrote down something Don Sergio said, not because of the words themselves so much—at the time I did not fully understand what he meant—but because of how he said them, with his eyes closed, as if he were communicating to us a special message from a faraway place. He said, 'I regret to tell you, my friends, there are no happy endings in this world. But there will always be new beginnings. Think of how the flowers return each spring after the cold and dark of winter. Dear boys, you are the flowers of our land.'

"In July 1936, after the Fascists took control of Santa Rosalía, Don Sergio was seen leaving a barbershop. Three men shoved him into a car. The next day a laborer found his body in a field an hour's drive from town. We knew the murderers, but no one could say a word against them. They were Francoists and regular communicants at Sunday Mass. Word spread that Don Sergio had been a purveyor of atheistic Marxism and a contaminator of young minds, and that he had been possessed of an unhealthy fondness for boys. Lies, all lies. You see how corrupt men can become when driven by ideas rather than love.

"I stayed awake imagining how I would kill those three men, one at a time. Don Sergio would not have approved of such thinking. In time my hatred and rage passed. I refused to become like those men. My teacher would have been surprised to find that I became a priest because of things he said and that his death contained for me the seeds of new life."

Don Martín smiled and squeezed my shoulder as he stood up. I followed him into the dying room. Everyone grew silent as he held José's hand and bent forward to speak to him. I could not make out what he was saying. He turned his head to better hear whatever my father was murmuring, made the sign of the cross over him, and kissed his forehead.

Then he walked out of the room looking straight ahead, his lips pressed together. He walked like a man determined to see all things through no matter how fierce and deadly the tempest.

Chapter 28

A devotional air permeated Tío Juan's home in the wake of Don Martín's departure. I thought I smelled incense, though I may have imagined it. All sound and movement in the house now seemed vested with a liturgical spirit.

The hours passed. We waited for *el doctor*. My cousin Elena got up from her chair and with a glance indicated I should take her place. She touched my arm and whispered in my ear what sounded like, "Your father has left you something. He has entrusted Penelope to give it to you when the time comes. She is a little afraid, but she said she must be the one to give it to you."

Then I felt a man's hand on my shoulder. It was Tío Arturo, my mother's surviving brother. He had driven down from Ferrol in the far north Galician coast. I rose from my chair to embrace him. Arturo tried to smile but his mouth twisted in a familiar kind of agony. We held each other and then Arturo kissed my cheek and released me. He placed his hand over my father's chest and said something to him and nodded, though it was not clear to me that my father had recognized him or was able to respond in any way to what Arturo had said. I saw Marisol in Tío Arturo's remote gaze as he walked out of the dying room.

Finally, Doctor Julián Ventoso arrived. He acknowledged me with a stern nod when he came in. He checked in on José, and gathered my uncles about him in one end of the hallway. I drew near to listen.

"Your brother is half in this world, half in the next, as if wondering whether to stay or go," Doctor Ventoso said.

"It is time, Julián," Tío Eliseo said.

"Yes, there is no remedy," Doctor Ventoso said with a trace of bitterness.

Shortly after *el doctor* left, José's breathing slowed, and the strain that had carved gashes across his forehead and between his eyebrows softened. His body's thin, ashen skin seemed to settle upon him like a delicate membrane. I wanted to believe impossible things. If I could just peel that membrane, beneath would be revealed a new and healthy José Amado eager to begin again, eager to feel the sun on his face and to gaze upon a full moon.

One by one they said their goodbyes to José and left the room, uncles, aunts, cousins, and friends. Juan was the last to leave, but it was José I saw walk out of the dying room, the final exertions of my father's struggle hacked onto his older brother's face.

Then we were alone with him, my sisters and me. I counted his breaths and the seconds between his breaths. We didn't speak. Each of us, I imagined, was thinking back to moments and particularities that were unique to our relationship with José.

In the presence of his dying, it was as though the dying itself were the means by which what was best in him became permanently sealed in my mind.

Oh, my father was no more a saint than I was. The drama of dying didn't erase his past sins—nor whatever harm he'd done to each of us by misbegotten word or act or omission—though all of that had long ago been forgiven if it needed to be forgiven. But now the dying—the unique and fundamental event of dying—was like a purifying fire, and all but the inextinguishable breath of love was being burned away.

It wouldn't end too quickly. The final hours passed among memories and prayers and shadows. When he called to us, we all thought we were dreaming. It wasn't a word we could understand, if it was a word at all. It was more a gesture, a faint entreaty, a request issued from a dream. He barely moved, if he moved at all. He barely spoke, if he spoke at all, and yet the three of us rose to our feet in response to something we may have collectively imagined.

The second time we knew it was a word.

"What did he say?" Adriana asked, looking first at Inés and then at me.

José strained to raise both his hands from the bed in an attempt to explain but could only lift his fingers scant millimeters.

"*Fuérteme*," he groaned.

"He created a new word," I said with hope, as if that word held some healing power. "*Strongme*, like be strong for me, or give me your strength."

"Yes, that's it, he wants us to hold him," Inés said.

Adriana was the first to get on the bed, then Inés, then me. We put our arms around our father's sharp ribs and caressed the bones of his face.

José was greatly relieved. He closed his eyes, and as he sank into a cloud of dream he sighed and said his last word, "*Así!*"

There!

The shadow of a smile on his lips became our sole focus. Nothing moved, but he lingered still, no doubt sorting through nebulous fragments of reminders and precautions that yet needed to be issued but could not be.

"Papá," Inés said finally, "it's okay to go now. Mamá is waiting for you."

He must have heard her—Inés or Mamá—from very far away, from a distant shore, from across a great ocean.

I counted each rare fading breath to the last, and then the seconds flew one after the other into infinity, and I saw with my own eyes that José Amado Torres was no longer a prisoner of the dying room.

Chapter 29

The time of death was 1:03 AM Sunday morning. Esteban the undertaker and Kiko, his assistant, appeared soon after to clean and prepare the body. The casket was delivered to the living room where my father's body would be kept until the funeral Mass and burial on Monday.

José's death seemed to make the rain come down harder and it rained all of Sunday. The people with their umbrellas came in great numbers after the morning Masses. In the slippery tile-floored living room the women sat in chairs or stood against the walls around the closed casket in focused silence or prayer. The men mingled in the center hallway or in side rooms speaking in reserved tones.

Javier appeared suddenly before me. After a moment of awkward silence, we embraced and all the years apart were like a single day, and despite so much loss, a bit of me was recovered.

Don Martín arrived after the noon Mass. He was pleased to see Javier and the two of us together like in the days before Africa but was soon all business moving from person to person asking questions and confirming details.

When one of the women alerted him to the continued downpour expected Monday during the burial, he dismissed the thought with a wave of his hand, "And why do you think they invented umbrellas, Gabriela?" he said in Galician. "For sunny days?"

After he had completed various appointments to his satisfaction, he entered the living room and led the women in a rather animated rosary of *The Glorious Mysteries*.

On his way out, he pulled me aside and said, "Would you like to say something at the funeral Mass?" He took a quick glance at Javier and noting my hesitation added, "Ah, no, no, it is not obligatory. Some families prefer that the priest say a few words."

The eulogy hadn't even crossed my mind. Public speaking wasn't my thing and my Spanish was a bit rusty, and anyway, I was the baby of the family, wasn't I? I thought of Inés and Adriana. Had he asked them?

As though he had read my mind, Don Martín said, "I spoke to your sisters before you arrived. Understand, I have no issue with women speaking from the pulpit, none whatsoever, but I thought about José, about the kind of man he was, and all the years I'd known him, the conversations we'd had... Call it an intuition. Your sisters agreed I should approach you, but if you feel that you would rather not do it, understand there is no obligation, and no one will think twice about it."

"I should do it."

"Ah, you *should*?"

"Yes, I should, but I also want to."

"Well then, very good. It is very simple. After the Gospel reading, I will say a few words and then I will nod to you. You will go up to the lectern where the readings were proclaimed and speak into the microphone. When you finish, go back to the pew and we will continue with the Liturgy. Would you like to ask me anything?"

"No, Don Martín."

Javier and I watched the black explosion of the priest's umbrella as he exited the house.

"He remembers how we used to play marbles in the corner of the dining room," I said.

"Martín has a prodigious memory."

"Maybe so, but he didn't remember how you swindled me of my shiny glass marbles."

"Oh, don't you believe it, he remembers all right. Everybody remembers thanks to Adriana. He teased me about it last summer when Amelia and I were here. He scolded me in front of my wife for taking advantage of *el Americano*."

"He didn't mention that to me."

"Of course not. Why do you think? To uphold your honor. Who wants to be reminded of having been duped?"

"Yes, Javier, who?"

"*Hola*, Penelope," Javier said as my cousin's daughter approached. "You've grown four centimeters at least since I last saw you. You'll be taller than Amelia soon."

Penelope shook her head in mild disagreement but said nothing and stood there staring at the floor with her hands behind her back. I knew she was shy, but this was excessive, and I thought something might be wrong with her, some psychological condition no one had alerted me to.

She stretched out her right hand, avoiding my gaze, and stared at the object she was holding. It was small, flat and rectangular and wrapped in a white envelope. "Tío José told me to give this to you."

Elena had alerted me, and yet I found myself unable to move or say a word. Penelope looked up at me with a worried expression. Had she done something wrong? I smiled and took the item from her.

"Is it a cassette?" I said.

She nodded.

"A cassette, like for recording music?"

She hesitated before nodding again.

I remembered my father's modest LP record collection back in Legacy City, his favorite pieces playing on the bulky wooden console, Spanish *coplas* sung by Imperio Argentina and Sarita Montiel, *zarzuelas* and arias sung by Alfredo Kraus, Puccini's *La Bohème* and *Madama Butterfly*, Falla, Albéniz, Granados…

I noted the clean schoolgirl script, *Para Lucas*. I took my time peeling the scotch tape from the envelope, preserving the girl's careful workmanship.

"Did Tío José tell you anything about this cassette, about what is on it?"

"I know what is on it," she said in a barely audible voice.

I glanced at Javier who seemed as puzzled as I was.

"You were with him when he recorded this?" I said.

"Yes, but..."

"Do you like Tío's music?"

"Very much, but there is no music on this cassette."

"Oh?"

"Only Tío's voice, and mine too, but mine only a little."

I felt something rush through me, like the wind, or fear, or hope. Can gratitude be a response to terror? Mary and Martha, what did they feel as they watched their brother walk out of the tomb wrapped in burial cloths?

That is, if we were to believe such things.

Oh, I never saw this coming, but there it was, José like Lazarus rising from the dead before we could even get around to burying him. José coming back because of unfinished business.

All I could think to do was hug the young girl. I kissed her and thanked her. As I separated from her, she threw her arms around me and clung to me with fierce desperation, her head pressed hard against my chest.

I gave her a few moments and then stepped back and held her hands. I soon found myself indulging the clever tricks of grief, the altering of attitude and perspective and language.

"Penelope," I said, "Tío José suffered a great deal. God rescued him and reunited him with Tía Marisol. Imagine how happy they must be! And how happy we are for them. One day, though I think not for a very long time, we'll all be together again in Heaven. That's what we have to look forward to. It hurts so much now, I know, but all will be well in the end, Penelope, I promise you."

I caressed her cheek and let her go. I think my words soothed her, though she may have been pretending for my sake. She was a special girl, a smart and sensitive girl. When she was gone, I realized Javier was staring at me in an odd way.

"What?" I said.

"She'll sleep better tonight."

"I hope so. I wanted to lift her spirits, say something useful to her."

"Useful is an interesting word."

"Shouldn't we be useful, Javier?"

"Of course we should."

"How strange this journey. One day I'm on the floor playing marbles with you, the next I'm playing messenger of God."

"Lucas Amado, hometown prophet."

"More like hometown fool. I know pain when I see it, but I don't know a damn thing about anything else."

Javier embraced me and patted me hard on the back, more like a fisherman than a civil engineer.

"Go find a cassette player," he said. "I'll see you tomorrow."

Chapter 30

B efore I was born Tío Juan put up two walls in a corner of the attic to enclose a small office where he kept his papers and documents, listened to news from Europe, and carved dolphins from pine wood remnants that he'd hand out to family and friends. Against one of the walls stood the same Formica kitchen table and vinyl and metal chair that I remembered from my expeditions there when I was a small child. On the table sat the Philips Jupiter 543 tube radio made in West Germany the year I was born.

Juan assigned—or so it seemed to me for a number of years—an epic importance to the coincidence that saw the Philips Jupiter delivered to his home the exact same day Marisol was giving birth to me back in the States.

"This radio is named Philips," he said while teaching me how to tune in to a station in Vigo. "He came from Jupiter, like you, Lucasito, and both of you have been given special powers to communicate secrets from other worlds."

I was a recent graduate of kindergarten at the time and found the remark unsettling and the cause of several nightmares. As it turned out Juan hadn't been serious at all about what he'd said, but that would only occur to me a few years later after I'd acquired a better understanding of adults and, in particular, of my uncle's peculiar sense of humor.

I gazed at the Philips Jupiter for a long time. The silence of the attic room grew deeper and more distressing by the moment. I was tempted to fill the emptiness by unleashing the stored metallic chatter and static, and my fingers circled the radio's power knob as if it were the means to alter reality. But did I really want to summon the loud eager voices of Paris, Madrid, and London to a house of mourning?

I sat down on the old chair and loaded the cassette player. My index finger hovered over the *Play* button even as my attention veered off to the two piles of world almanacs pushed up against the wall. A Spanish-English dictionary and a small New Testament lay nearby. I grabbed the 1978 almanac from the top of one pile and set it before me on the table like a dinner plate.

When I was a boy, my father would give me a five-dollar bill to run to the corner candy store to buy the latest edition of *The World Almanac and Book of Facts*. Once a year I would bring it home and present it to José who would let me keep the change. After flipping through the almanac for a couple of weeks, he would then ship it to his brother. Juan never debated demographics or river lengths or international merchant navy capacities with his buddies without first consulting the latest edition of the almanac.

I got up and carried the '78 edition with me to the window that overlooked a small concrete patio and a rectangle of black and green earth where Tía Vicenta picked lemons from the lemon tree in the summertime.

I gazed at the old well jutting up from the left border of the yard. When as a child I first saw it, stony gray and patient as a kidnapper, it had demanded my respect and fear. How many times had I imagined myself falling down inside its dark wet throat? Then I learned to draw water from it, and it was no longer threatening, and with time the well became quaint and familiar, like an old relative who prefers silence to conversation. The well was always silent now. I would have liked to draw from it, but there was no longer a bucket. Where did the rope and bucket go? I wondered.

It struck me that my father would no longer see Tía Vicenta cut lemon wedges in the patio and squeeze the wedges to sprinkle the juice over the *merluza a la gallega*, and though I myself had never been a big fan of fish dishes, Tía Vicenta's hake with potatoes and *chorizo* had no peer on the Iberian peninsula, or so José—who to my amazement had always preferred fish to meat—once assured me.

But José also loved to spar with his sister-in-law. "What is the point of having a clothes drier, Vicenta, if you never use it?" he once chided her as he winked at me.

"*Hombre*," she replied without missing a beat, "you've been in America too long to understand such things. Clothes are like people. They want room to flap their arms and legs. And if they had gums they would enjoy flapping those too, like you."

Was this the last almanac my father had held? The last he'd sent my uncle? I flipped through the pages looking for signs, something written in a margin, a bookmark with a scribbled note, a folded corner of a page. But there was nothing. I placed the almanac back on the table and pressed the *Play* button.

The steady sustained hum of the recording strip as it unwound began to make me feel ill. I grew so perturbed by the sickening sound that I became convinced that somehow Penelope had failed to press the *Record* button at the same time as the *Play* button, effectively producing a blank strip.

I closed my eyes and pressed the heels of my hands hard against my temples. I walked back to the window squeezing my head, and as I stood looking at the old lemon tree down below, I heard a loud grinding noise followed by what sounded like the thumping of half-filled boxes being hurled against walls. Then all the noise died and I heard a man speak in Castilian, "Ready now? We can begin?"

It was my father's voice, distinct enough, yet different. This was a thinner voice, sapped of its virility by the cancer and yet freer somehow.

"Yes, Tío. You can begin."

"Very good. Thank you, precious."

José coughed and paused before speaking.

"Don't be troubled by what you've seen or heard, Lucas. It's nothing. This is nature taking its course, nothing more. But I do regret not organizing my thoughts sooner, when my mind was clearer. Maybe I would have written a book, eh? Ah, well, the book-writing I leave to you and your sisters, so nothing is lost.

"The machine is recording, yes, dear?"

"Yes, Tío, it is recording."

"Good, good... Let me see, what can I say to you, son, that you don't already know? That ego is a burden? How long did it take me to learn that when I am wrong, I am wrong? Why waste time denying the truth? In fact, we should thank those who show us our errors. We should buy them a drink and toast them for doing us the favor of fixing our bad thinking."

José stopped to take a couple of breaths.

"Remember how I always complained about your long hair? Your mother always sided with you. 'José, this is a new generation,' she would say. 'They have their own ideas, let your son be.' So I left your hair alone, but the radio? Ah, that was another matter. One Saturday I came home from having the car serviced. You were eating a sandwich in the kitchen. You expected that I would turn the radio off, for I could not abide such sounds, but this one time I let it go. I went down to the basement to do some work. You were in shock, I think.

"Interesting, no? The things one remembers. The small radio sitting on top of the refrigerator and those words all these years later. When I met your mother, I knew them to be true. When your sisters and then you were born, I knew them to be true. When I die, I will know better than I do now that they are true."

José paused to breathe and began to cough, and it seemed the coughing would not end, but it did.

"All you need is love, how true, how true...

"One summer in Legacy City you were reading a book of poems by Antonio Machado. You were just a boy, eleven or twelve, and the poems were in Spanish. It must have been difficult for you. I felt so proud, though I may not have said so. Do you remember? You asked me what the poet meant. *Caminante, no hay camino, se hace camino al andar*. Traveler, there is no path, the path is made by walking.

"I told you that each person chooses who he is to be. He makes his own path, he becomes who he is step by step, decision by decision. And now I tell you that the measure of each step and the motive of each decision has to be love. It must always be love if we are to be *human* in an inhumane world.

"Since Mamá died, I have tried to pray in my own clumsy way, but how difficult it has been for me. As you know, your mother never forced me to go to Mass with her. She understood she could not turn me into a believer any more than she could turn a chicken into a rooster. Yet, despite our disagreements, I came to respect her steadfast faith."

José cleared his throat and mumbled something to himself. The words came with greater difficulty now. I turned the radio volume up.

"I could not console her in the end. I had no strength for it. In her final moments she tried to console me... It's been a long six years, son. When I came back to Santa Rosalía I brought with me all your mother's religious books and items. I have prayed on my knees with her rosary beads before a crucifix and felt only emptiness..."

For what seemed too long, all I could hear was the faint hum of the recorder. What was happening to my father?

"Oh Penelope, how sweet you are. Your cousin has put her head on my chest to console me. But I am fine, precious. The problem is I've been spoiled by too much love. How much is left on the cassette, dear one? Ah, good. Enough for one more chapter then."

I pressed the *Stop* button and got up and went back to the window. Somebody was standing down below in the patio beneath an umbrella smoking. I walked out of my uncle's office and went to the stairwell. I sat on the top step and listened to the subdued voices of family and friends two stories below. I wanted to run down those stairs. I wanted someone to show me where I could find the clay marbles.

After a while I got up and walked back to Juan's office. I sat down and pressed the *Play* button once more.

"Yesterday Vicenta forced me back into bed. I had been doing well. She was right to do it, though. Sometimes I get delusional and think I am Superman. The good woman propped me up on pillows and handed me your grandfather's copy of *Don Quijote*, which I'd begun to read in spurts when I arrived from America. But I could barely lift the page and told her to take the book from me.

"I fell asleep and woke up in Legacy City. The old apartment was empty. I looked everywhere for your mother. I began to claw at the walls and only stopped when I remembered she was gone. I went to the window and saw people coming out of all the buildings. Thousands were walking out onto a wide avenue, everyone moving silently in one direction, and I found myself among them.

"We walked for many days and nights and gradually lost sight of each other. All the cities and towns and roads were gone and all that remained was an area as vast and dry as a Moroccan desert. I became diminished with each step, smaller and smaller, vanishing a little more with each breath until I became as insignificant as an ant.

"Then I stopped to listen to the thunder. Far away I saw thick black storm clouds and bolts of lightning. I continued walking for what seemed many days before I came upon another city. But it was not a city. As I approached, I came upon a group of weary men holding swords that were dripping blood. They were all staring at me, but without malice. Behind them, all was covered in smoke. The wind came and blew away the smoke and I saw piles of broken bodies stretching to the horizon.

"Then I saw the King standing among his battered angels. He had five wounds red like roses. I lowered my head and fell to my knees and said to him, 'I know this terrible battle was fought for me, but why? I am a man of no importance.' I was afraid, but the King said my name and I looked up. He was gazing at me with such tender love that I could not help but fall to weeping."

For a few moments I listened to the hum of the recorder. Then I heard Penelope say from faraway, "There is very little space left on the cassette, Tío."

"Ah, then…"

I listened closely, anticipating a final word, but my father said no more.

A few seconds later the recording strip reached its end and the *Play* button popped up with a loud clunk. I took a pad and pen from the shelf above my uncle's table and began to write my father's eulogy.

Chapter 31

The tall front entry doors of the church were left wide open. I could hear the rain from inside. Don Martín nodded in my direction from the presider's chair in the sanctuary. I rose from the pew and stepped into the center aisle, pausing to touch the top of my father's casket.

The women of the family were all seated in the pews opposite us across the center aisle. They were all watching me. I glanced to the rear. Men and women in grays and black and white stood crowded in the narthex behind the pews. They extended back to the rear walls and flowed out onto the plaza where cobbled black umbrellas covered the people who couldn't fit inside the modest nineteenth century church.

What was *el Americano* going to say?

I was composed and focused as I positioned myself behind the lectern. I drew the folded sheets from the inside pocket of my jacket, looked out at all the faces, and felt like I could see each one. I had the sense—however unrealistic—that I could linger over each facial line or sag or gleam of a cheek for as long as I wanted. No nervous blur, no racing of time threatened me. Before me flowed blood histories that intersected with my own and familiar faces framed in anticipation of the words I was about to deliver.

"You don't know what tomorrow will bring. What is your life? You are a mist that appears for a little while and then vanishes."

My Castilian was sound and my voice clear and imbued with a measured authority I had not anticipated.

"So wrote the Apostle James. My friends, there are no guarantees. Wealth, power, fame, youth? None of these offer guarantees. Like the mist we are here and then we are gone. People are dying even as I speak, being taken suddenly and unexpectedly from their loved ones. This very moment entire families are being thrown into disarray, their lives turned upside down by shock and grief. Everything can change in an instant, and so we must consider carefully how we are to be."

I was stunned when something like an iron finger poked me in the back. I knew it was nothing I could see or touch or feel other than in my mind, but that made no difference. It took me by surprise and the moment started getting away from me.

The Apostle James? Are you shitting me, Ricardo?

I resisted the urge to swing around. I looked up from my notes but saw no familiar faces now, detected no blood histories. The church began to fill with fog, like poison gas being piped in from a dozen inlets. I looked to my right toward the women and could see only my sister, Inés, but it wasn't Inés.

Mamá, is it you?

Oh, how concerned she looked.

I glanced at my notes but the words had begun to leak and deform and my eyes pulled away. My father's chain felt like a blade of ice against the back of my neck, and the crucifix and scapular medal hung like cold lead on my chest. I saw myself keeling, stirring up clouds of concern and confusion in the house of worship, and it drove me to the edge of panic. I snatched at a remembered line the way a falling man throws his hand out at a ledge.

"Father, why have you abandoned me?"

My voice trailed off with a faint tremor.

You and I, Ricardo, we need to sit down and have a talk.

I stared at my wriggling notes. I frowned and shook my head in anger, and I must have looked deranged for a moment, but the letters began to reclaim their identities and the words, like soldiers, began to fall back into formation. I looked up and the fog was dissipating, and my gaze drifted past the congregants out to the black umbrellas and the rain. I breathed in the cool damp air and felt myself suddenly removed. The words came now from somewhere else, and it was as if I were back in the pew seated with my uncles and cousins listening to a young man I barely recognized.

"'Father, why have you abandoned me?' Jesus asked. Death does not discriminate. In his awful loneliness, even Jesus questioned his father.

"All separation is a form of death, and all the separated die a little. I remember when my mother, Marisol, died, how we all suffered, how we all, in some way, died with her, but no one more than my father. José suffered the most, died the most."

And then to my surprise I said, "He grew so distant that I wondered, is there no love left in you for us, Papá?"

On an impulse, perhaps initially to distract, I reached inside my shirt and drew forth the crucifix and medal and displayed them to the people. My notes, which had seemed a lifeline just moments ago, had become superfluous.

"This crucifix, this medal. José wore these on his deathbed. Marisol gave them to him to wear, and so he wore them. I wear them now because my father entrusted them to me. But neither José nor I have been the most ardent believers, if we have been believers at all…"

I glanced to my right. There were Inés and Adriana, and all the women of the family, and there before me, my uncles and male cousins, and beyond them all the faces and blood histories, the living, the breathing, all waiting for my next word.

"And yet death changes everything. Death draws people closer to God or pushes them farther away from him…"

I hesitated, felt myself again on the edge of a precipice. I expected, or maybe hoped, that someone would come to lead me away to a safe and quiet room.

"I feel God's presence in this place."

The words took me by surprise.

I feel, I feel, in this place, in this place.

What? What did I feel?

I felt probing eyes and leaning bodies and lips parting as if to formulate words that would be spoken later in other places.

Or was it my imagination, my own conspiracy to create and elaborate a custom consolation, an antidote to my grief and greatest fears?

I glanced again at my notes.

"Death makes you think of things you may not normally think of. What person, for example, thinks often of his father or mother while he is busy navigating his own hurried life? The years pass quickly and this day comes, and you find that you must think in a new way.

"I have thought much these last hours about José and what he has left behind. I have tried to understand him better. He left me this crucifix and medal, but these are only signs of what I've come to learn from him, of what I consider my true inheritance to be.

"José was a temperamental and exacting man. He could drive one mad with too much orderliness, but my father has left me a portrait of self-sacrifice, loyalty, and respect for others. He has left me a way forward, a way to be.

"He has also left me a dream that I want to share with you. I think he would want me to because you are his friends. In the dream José was walking across a great wasteland, and after many days came upon a band of bloodied warriors. Behind them he could see dead bodies piled high one upon another all the way to the horizon. Something happened to José, like a light flashing in his mind, and he saw the King standing suddenly in the midst of his battered angels. My father fell to his knees and said to the King, 'I know this terrible battle was fought for me. Why? I am a man of no importance.' He heard the King call him by name, and when José looked up, the King was gazing at him with such tender love that all my father could do was weep.

"As we lie dying, what will be our response upon seeing the face of God? Will we weep, like José, overwhelmed by his love?

"Then we won't care about money, nor power, nor things, nor think about worldly consolations and achievements. In the end one thing alone will matter. Love is all we get to keep, my friends, it's all we ever needed. It's what the dying know better than those left behind."

I slipped my father's crucifix and medal back inside my shirt, stepped away from the pulpit and walked off the altar.

Chapter 32

I heard my footsteps and the patter of rain against the umbrellas. There were no other sounds. I saw and smelled the lilies, carnations, and roses surrounding my father's casket. Had angels arranged the flowers while I stood at the pulpit? The weight of death seemed to have been lifted as by some heavenly host. For a few tantalizing moments I moved like a pious monk embracing and believing all I had said.

The rain had turned to mist by the time we carried the casket out to the church plaza. We small-stepped our way toward the old hearse. One by one the umbrellas shut themselves with a *whoosh*, and the hearse began its unhurried two-kilometer climb to the town cemetery.

We passed by the town hall plaza, its privet hedges framing five palm trees shipped to Santa Rosalía from the Canary Islands right around the time William Randolph Hearst decided blaming a declining Spain for the explosion of the USS Maine was a splendid little way to sell newspapers.

Don Martín was wearing his priestly vestments—a white alb, purple chasuble and stole—and walking several feet behind the vehicle with a breviary in his hands. About two-hundred people processed behind the priest with my family in the vanguard.

"I love the Lord, who listened to my voice in supplication, who turned an ear to me on the day I called," Don Martín read in a loud defiant voice from his breviary, seemingly immune to the diesel exhaust and its nauseating odor. "I was caught by the cords of death; the snares of Sheol had seized me; I felt agony and dread. Then I called on the name of the Lord, 'O Lord, save my life!'"

Up the hill we climbed, the hearse slow as yoked oxen. Along the way people paused in doorways and on sidewalks to watch.

"The Lord answered me when I called in my distress."

I should have eaten breakfast—Tía Vicenta had warned me—but the looming task of delivering my father's eulogy had taken away my appetite. I was paying for my lack of foresight now. An irrational terror seized me as I imagined breaking ranks and dashing to the side of the road to vomit. I kept turning my head from the exhaust fumes seeking relief. I covered my mouth and breathed in my cupped hands to buy time.

"What is the matter, nephew?" Tío Paco said.

Up the hill, where the houses were spaced farther apart, a strong wind had begun to flow through the open spaces. It arrived just in time, blowing the exhaust fumes sideways and away from the processors. I looked up at the fast-clearing sky. Cumulus clouds floated across the expanding blue like heavenly balloons.

"Nothing, Tío, I'm fine."

The cemetery was surrounded by a thick fieldstone wall dappled with yellow and green lichens and moss. The hearse stopped outside before the open cast iron gates. We assumed our positions and carried the casket into the cemetery to its niche location. Tall cedars, firs, and pine were sprinkled among the tombs. The treetops swayed in the wind like restless souls. Most of the gravestones and niche edifices were scrubbed clean. A young woman with a little girl stood praying before a gravestone covered in white carnations. A diminutive widow dressed in black placed fresh flowers in a blue and white vase. The undertakers helped us guide José's casket headfirst into the open niche.

Oblong picture holders the size of my hand were secured to most of the gravestones and niche plaques. The majority of the photos portrayed men and women during their more sanguine middle years, regardless of age at time of death. A smaller number showed the faces of the very old and of children and babies.

The picture of Marisol—the one my father had chosen for all to remember her by—once again surprised me with the memory of her last birthday party. The three of us were in my parents' apartment back in Legacy City. Marisol had just blown out the candles and made her wish. I had snapped the picture with the Canon camera my parents had given me as a high school graduation present.

A week later the freshly developed photo showed Marisol at her most wistful. Already she seemed separated from us. Did she know what was to come? And what had been her wish? I left for Copernicus University to begin my freshman year soon after and never saw her again.

I stared at her picture and considered the irony of a birthday image displayed on a tomb. I looked at her name, and for a moment it seemed someone had made a mistake. If there was one mistake, who was to say there weren't more? Who was to say with any certainty that my mother's remains lay in that niche? Who was to say she was dead? Who was to say anything at all was as we assumed it to be?

Marisol Fernández Pérez, 20 Aug 1927 – 3 Sep 1973.

Who was this Marisol Fernández Pérez?

There I was again, indulging the tricks of grief. Of course it was her, her name, Marisol Fernández Pérez, just as my father's name was José Amado Torres, and my name was Lucas Amado Fernández. How sad the tricks of grief.

I looked at my father's open niche and stared at the foot of his casket. What shoes was he wearing behind the gleaming wood? Which suit? How was his hair combed? Were his hands folded? Had Julia threaded rosary beads between his fingers? Why couldn't I remember?

I heard Don Martín issue the concluding benediction. We all made the sign of the cross. We all said *Amén*.

The mason began to spread mortar and lay bricks over the opening of my father's niche as we watched. The trowel seemed a magical instrument, plopping and spreading and scraping and grooving the mortar, row of brick quickly set upon row of brick. With growing discomfort, I imagined my father crying out from his tomb, "For the love of God, Lucas!" But my father was dead, wasn't he? I was there. I heard his last spoken word, saw him die with my own eyes, felt with my own hands the life leave his body.

In a few days a plaque would be sealed over the brick, just as had been done for Marisol. My sisters and I would find a suitable photograph of José, an image to stand the test of time.

My uncles led us back out through the gates of the cemetery. The people were waiting there. The men of the family stood to the left of the entrance, the women to the right. We formed a line beginning with Tío Juan to my left, and to my right Eliseo, Rogelio, Paco, and Tío Arturo, my mother's brother. One by one the men grasped our hands and without the slightest variation repeated the same words, *Te acompaño en el sentimiento.*

I am with you in your sorrow, I am with you in your sorrow, I am with you in your sorrow...

The ritual was strangely consoling. All hands became one hand, all voices one voice, all the living were as one mourning all the dead who were as one, the living and the dead joined one to one in improbable communion.

Afterwards several of the women came up to me. They kissed me on the cheek. Some touched my arm or hand. Some looked a bit undecided, incapable of articulating what they were feeling. Others said I had spoken from the heart, and oh, how such words had needed to be spoken and heard in this age of despair and cynicism, in these times of darkness.

A few of the men also commented on what I'd said. Tío Rogelio, a man of few words, confided that he'd been given a new perspective to ponder. He asked if I could make him a copy of the eulogy so that he could discuss it with his friends. When I told him that much of what I'd said was different from what I'd written, he seemed amazed. He nodded gravely, patted me on the arm and continued to stand before me until I said yes, that I would make him a copy.

What did Don Martín think? I wondered. He didn't really say anything to me. A brief glance of acknowledgement, that was all. He walked the two kilometers back to town with my family. He had removed his vestments and carried them and his breviary in his left arm. I noticed that he was wearing the same trousers and sweater that he had worn when I first arrived. They were speaking in Galician, Don Martín and my uncles. It was all business, confirming all the remaining details about the niche and the plaque and anything else he could think of. The tireless overseeing and attention to detail reminded me of my father. They would have made great battlefield commanders, I remember thinking.

Javier walked alongside me. We said little to each other. When we reached the town hall plaza, Tío Juan reminded Don Martín that he was invited to eat with us. Juan had reserved the lower level of *Maria's* restaurant for the occasion. Don Martín said he had a few matters to attend to first, but that he hoped to be able to make an appearance. When the priest left, Tío Juan approached us. "Javier, you will join us, yes?" he said, and patted him on the shoulder.

At the house, Adriana gave me another massive hug. "That was amazing," she said. "I had no idea you were such a gifted speaker."

Inés followed with a more sedate embrace. "You are a surprising young man," she said as she studied my face.

"Actually, I surprised myself. I guess being married to someone like Callie, I mean, sometimes we'll be talking and she'll bring up some Scripture or other to make a point. She's got like five different Bibles lying around the apartment. I found a pocket-sized New Testament in Spanish up in the attic. That's where I got the St. James quote."

"Interesting," Adriana said. "And Papá's dream? I never heard it before. When did he tell you that dream?"

"Yesterday. I mean, I heard it yesterday on the cassette."

"The cassette?" Adriana said.

"Yes, the one Papá left with Penelope."

"Did you know about a cassette, Inés?"

Inés tried to appear unsurprised. "No, I wasn't aware."

"After Papá died she gave it to me."

My sisters stared at me waiting for me to say more.

"She sat with him one day. There were things he wanted to pass on to us."

Javier coughed into his hand, a reflex reflecting my own discomfort. I looked into my sisters' eyes but detected only surprise and curiosity.

"It's upstairs," I said. "I'll rewind it so you can listen to it."

My sisters glanced at one another for a moment.

"Papá always had a reason for every decision he made," Inés said.

"Yes, and Don Martín told us he thought of you for the eulogy," Adriana said. "I'm sure he and Papá discussed it."

"It was helpful, right?" Inés said. "The cassette was a help to you, all the things Papá said that Penelope helped him record."

"It was helpful. I did get diverted a bit when I was up at the podium, but yes, it was a big help to me in writing the eulogy. I'll make copies of the cassette for each of you, okay?"

"Oh wonderful, I'd like that," Inés said.

"Absolutely, make us copies," Adriana said, "but remember to be at *Maria's* no later than two-thirty, and you too, Javier."

Chapter 33

The long, jagged pier extended out into the bay like an arm gathering water. Beneath the flashing head light, the curved top of the stone wall was damp, cold and bumpy against my palms. A trawler powered up the coast from the southwest opening of the *Ría de Arousa*, the largest of the Galician estuaries. A flock of squawking seagulls hovered over the boat like a tethered cloud.

"Hake," Javier said, pointing, "and lots of sardine for the grill."

I kept my eyes fixed on the gulls.

"I said too much in church."

"Too much? What do you mean too much? Too many words?"

"No, you know what I mean."

"So you made people think a little. You gave a little hope."

Javier turned away from me and I gathered he wasn't up to talking about things like the various shades of hope or the nuances of hypocrisy. I turned around so that we were both leaning with our backs against the pier wall, the two of us staring at the drowsy harbor with its docks and moored boats and lazy dark glowing waters, and everything looked magical and lovely along the promenade with its softly lit street lamps and muted facades.

We all came from here, all our families, the people at church, the people watching us from their doorways as we climbed to the cemetery. We went back generations, back so far we probably started out as the same one family—all of us covered in dried mud and filth and lice—lugging carcasses into caves before we figured out how to harvest mussels and clams or stay afloat long enough to catch hake and sardines. Santa Rosalía was a modern port city now, and the day we buried my father was coming to an end.

"I wasn't pretending to be someone I'm not."

Javier stared at me. "And you think I was thinking that?"

"I listened to my father's recording. When I was at the pulpit time seemed to stop. There were moments when I wasn't even sure it was me up there. It was like the words had their own life and wanted to be released, so I let them go. I don't know what happened to me up there, but I wasn't pretending anything."

Javier seemed to ponder what I had said and then smiled.

"Your father always got here a few weeks later, after you had turned brown and wiry from being outside all the time. You with your mother and your two pretty sisters would always appear in late June, just before the *Fiesta de San Juan*. Do you remember the first time I took you to the bonfires in the *Campo de la Feria*? You watched us leap over the flames without saying a word, and then you jumped. When I saw you do it I knew you were one of us despite being so quiet and shy."

"And gullible?"

"Ah, there you go again. The enduring saga of the clay marbles. I'll have to live with it for the rest of my life, I suppose."

"I wasn't that shy."

"No, you're right. The girls were very curious about *el Americano*, and you seemed to find your voice with them. It was uncanny, actually."

"You were convinced—still are apparently—that you had pulled a fast one on me."

"Ninety shiny glass marbles for fifteen ugly clay ones? Like you Americans say, nothing personal, just business."

"Your selling point was that yours were handmade. But you didn't have to convince me. I liked the inconsistent sizes, the shades of tan, gray and brown, the dents and gashes. When you said, 'You want to trade?' I couldn't believe my luck. I tried not to smile as I handed them over to you."

"You smiled like a little dimwit, and I felt sorry for you and I almost gave them back to you."

"But you remembered it wasn't personal, it was just business."

"Yes, exactly, I remembered…"

Javier seemed to become lost in wistful recollection. I wondered what he was thinking. I would have liked to know, would have liked to have the time and leisure to pursue random trains of thought and unconventional subjects with my friend. He caught me staring at him and I must have had the same wistful look on my face that he had on his, and it was kind of like looking into a mirror and it made us chuckle like tired old men.

"We're allowed to laugh?" I said.

"Laughter's always permitted and highly recommended. But when was the last time you laughed so hard you fell on your ass? What happened to that kind of openness to joy?"

Along the promenade two boys were kicking a soccer ball back and forth to each other as they made their way. A man on a bicycle threaded between them, waving an arm in the air and barking out some warning. One of the boys raised his arms to the sky as if he'd just scored a goal.

"I don't know if I ever told you, Javier. My wife Callie had a boyfriend for three years before she met me. They were going to get married after she graduated from college, but one day she realized she wasn't in love with him, never had been, so she broke off the engagement. That got her a lot of grief from her family because in their eyes the guy was perfect, like one of your glass marbles. And then later, of course, they got me instead, a clay marble, so you can imagine the turmoil and consternation that caused.

"Callie and I don't always see things the same way. One day she told me our meeting wasn't a coincidence but what she calls a God-incidence, an act of divine providence. She said it like a joke, laughing, but only because of who I am, not because she didn't believe it."

"So, what's the problem? Let her believe it."

"Of course, for her own sake, but now I've made everything too difficult for her."

"Bah, all marriages have issues. I could spend forty hours straight telling you about my own squabbles with Amelia."

"Squabbles are one thing, betraying her with another woman is something completely different. In her eyes I committed an unforgiveable act."

Javier looked confused for a moment, as if I'd spoken in Arabic.

"Unforgiveable?" was all he could think to say.

He frowned and seemed on the verge of saying more but said nothing. Instead he turned back toward the ever-darkening bay.

"She took Johnny and went to live in her mother's house," I said. "I've done some real damage, Javier, maybe the kind neither of us will ever recover from."

His face was in shadow. He mulled over my words for a few moments and said, "No, no, I do understand what you're saying, but *hombre*, love doesn't flee at the first sign of trouble."

I knew he was trying to be helpful, but there was an unintended dismissiveness to his response, some reflexive Iberian bravado, some let's-not-drown-ourselves-in-a-glass-of-water posture that might smack of insensitivity in some other culture. I understood it, I took it all into account, but it still irked the hell out of me. I made a poor effort to modulate my voice and to choose my words with care.

"I can't tell you how tired I am of hearing bullshit clichés," I said.

He glanced at me with a look of concern but said nothing.

"Callie doesn't trust me anymore, don't you see? I'm no longer the man she fell in love with."

From the time he was a boy, Javier had always had a way of diffusing and neutralizing other people's bad energy and of dismissing their insults and recriminations as if he were waving off a disoriented fly. He pulled my arm to make me face him.

"One more cliché for good measure, then," he said. "Good things can come of bad things."

I sighed congenially, "You sound like Don Martín."

"He told you the story of his murdered teacher, Don Sergio?"

"He did, and I remember my father mentioning something about that long ago."

"It can happen, you know, cliché or not. Sometimes good things do come out of bad things. It has everything to do with one's disposition."

"My disposition needs fixing," I said.

"And mine."

"Look, it's okay, I'm fine. We don't have to get into this."

"Not so fast, not so fast. You're not off the hook yet, *amigo*. I need information. Tell me, how often did you go to the well?"

"One time," I said.

"Only once? With one woman?"

"Yes, but a friend."

"What kind of friend?"

"Maybe not so much a friend as a friendly acquaintance, a coworker, someone Callie liked a great deal."

"And you say you're no longer the man Callie fell in love with?" he said.

"How can I be?"

"I agree, you cannot be. That poor devil's gone forever, vanished the instant he dropped his pants. Listen to me carefully. If you want your Callie back, you must reinvent yourself, there is no other way through this."

I was trying to understand exactly what that meant when he glanced over my shoulder and added, "How is it you Americans put it? To *think outside the box*, yes?"

I turned around and gazed down the length of the pier. An old man wearing a black beret was strolling back to town.

"You mean like that old man?" I said.

"No, I don't think so," Javier said. "Maybe, it's possible. What I mean is you must be like the carpenter's son."

"Wait, what?"

Tío Juan's son, Seve, who was a notary, immediately came to mind, but obviously Javier was not referring to my rather boring cousin.

"Now believe me when I tell you that I say this with all due respect, but the truth of the matter is that your innate charms have proved insufficient for the hard work of love. Henceforth you must appeal to Callie's higher appetites."

I fought the impulse to smile.

"So to be clear, you're suggesting that if I pretend to be like the carpenter's son, I'll win back my wife."

"No, not quite. What makes this such a challenging proposition is that pretending doesn't work."

"Ah, I see. Tell me, then, must I master the art of walking on water?"

"Lucas, *hombre*, let's not be ridiculous."

Out in the bay the lighthouse was blinking in a mockery of time. I gazed down at the breakwaters and for several moments stared at the relentless little waves lapping the big rocks.

"Hmm, the carpenter's son," I said.

"You mustn't overthink it," Javier warned.

I imagined Callie levitating above the bay and staring at me with the kind of modest interest reserved for observing a circus dog or dancing elephant.

"Live like you believe and end up a believer," Javier then said with an ambiguous grin.

"Pascal's Wager?"

"I myself reject the wager. Maybe not reject out of hand. Postpone, delay? For now, I'm content to stand on the shore watching the tides come in and go out."

"You're afraid to go in the water, aren't you?"

"The waters in these parts are cold as hell, you know that."

Clouds began to creep over the region. Heading back to town I felt suddenly exhausted. The gloom of separation was once again descending upon me. Life in all its pieces seemed to be chipping off and drifting away from me in all directions. I recalled a homeless man in a supermarket parking lot in Legacy City back in the sixties during my early teens, before the riots. The man was snatching at the air like a child trying to catch soap bubbles. I thought it comical at the time, but how different it all seemed to me that evening on the pier.

Where the pier broadened into town, we passed the old man with the black beret. He had stopped before a large docked trawler and was staring at the name painted in dark blue on the bow of the boat, *Angustia*. Would that be me in fifty years? Would I be standing alone reading the story of my life in the hand-painted name of a boat?

Our last few minutes together Javier and I said nothing. We embraced and went our separate ways. After a dozen steps or so we turned to wave to each other as had been our custom from the first of our many farewells.

That night I lay awake in bed in my uncle's house thinking of Callie and Johnny and wondering if Johnny would remember me, and if Callie still loved me. I thought about the things that could go right and the things that could go wrong.

I had to stay a few more days in Santa Rosalía. There was the tiny flat José had been renting and where my sisters were staying and my father's few possessions and all the paperwork that had to be completed and signed, and plenty of other loose ends that needed tying up.

Part 7

Cosmo

Chapter 34

The Iberia 747 jumbo jet hovered like a reluctant beast over the cosmic spill that was coastal New England, tilting south and west on its Legacy City Airport trajectory one thinning cloud after another.

No one said anything. Were we all speculating, theorizing, taking inventory of our countless miscalculations? Did we fear ourselves stuck in the sky and that the sun would melt our wings? The overhead vents hissed and the engines grumbled, but not an organic word, not a chuckle, not even a sigh. We were falling in stale air with minds thin as clouds. Had we all stopped breathing?

The door to the basement apartment opened wide like an aggravated wound. Someone might once have written that there are as many shades of loneliness as there are shades of blue—maybe it was me—and upon seeing it I thought how dark the mottled blue of the old carpet was. I dropped my bag and tossed the mail onto the kitchen table.

An envelope from Galaxy Alarms called out to me. I left it on the table unopened along with all the other mail. There were no messages on the Phone-Mate answering machine Grace had bought Callie.

I couldn't stay inside, it was too blue. As I drove to Colts Brook, I prepared myself for failure.

There was a bite in the air. Thanksgiving wasn't far off. I rang the doorbell a second time and waited and rang once more and then knocked until my knuckles throbbed. I rubbed them and walked up and down the front of the house and around the back peering through curtain gaps but saw no sign of life. It was just as well because I was hardly at my best just then and it was dark and getting colder by the minute.

I got back to the apartment in under an hour and sat down at the kitchen table and went through the mail. The Galaxy envelope contained a sympathy card showing a brook surrounded by wildflowers winding its way into dark woods.

Our Deepest Sympathies was embossed in shiny gold calligraphy in the upper left corner over a patch of pastel blue sky. I opened the card and recognized Marla's handwriting.

Dear Lucas, the Galaxy Alarms, Inc. family extend our most sincere condolences to you and your family for your grievous loss. Please let us know if there is anything we can do for you. Your friends at Galaxy Alarms.

I could see her peeking at me from the dark woods that bordered the winding stream, Marla, whose name I'd called as I stood amid the leaping pigeons.

I unpacked, heated up a can of soup and wrote notes to my two professors. By the time I finished it was after 3:00 AM Spanish time and I fell into a fitful sleep.

JAN THE RECEPTIONIST always clocked in at 8:00 AM. I waited until then before calling the office. She seemed surprised to hear my voice because I'd never called her before. I suspected she'd heard a thing or two about me. Maybe I was being paranoid.

In any case, I called her, not wanting to talk to Marla, at least not yet. I told Jan I'd be back at work Monday morning and to please pass on the information to Jay Weller, the new field chief.

Within five minutes of ending my conversation with Jan the phone rang. I didn't want to pick up but I did.

"Back to work Monday, huh? Thing is, Panko and Garvey called in sick this morning, the typical Friday bullshit I have to deal with. I need you to pick up some of the slack."

"I just got back from burying my dad, Jay."

"How about this afternoon? Two Baytown calls, a twenty-minute drive. Customers took time off from work, expect us to be there, we can't afford any more bad press."

"I've got some stuff I have to take care of this morning," I said. "I'll do the Baytown calls, just the two, no more."

"Got what you need?"

"Think so, yeah, I should be good."

"Okay, grab a pen and write this down."

Chapter 35

Every time he swept the barber's cloth under my chin and settled it over my chest, with the flair of a matador, *Senhor* Cardosa uttered the same five words, "How is our champion today?" It didn't matter whether I was four or twenty-four.

Those five words, perfectly autonomous and detached from all context, had been addressed to me over the course of twenty years and delivered in the same unrelenting Portuguese accent. I knew they weren't the only English words Cardosa knew, but for some reason they were the only ones he felt comfortable saying to me. Over time the question had attained a morbidly playful permanence in my mind, like a riddle engraved on a tombstone.

Some places are carved out of the everyday landscape to serve as escape hatches from time and circumstance. *Cardosa Barbershop* was that kind of place with its big street windows and unflinching observance of the changing seasons, with its ageless mirrors and chairs, its outmoded head sketches tacked to the wall depicting haircut styles of a bygone era, with the same *Benfica FC* pennant hanging just beneath an autographed photograph of the legendary Eusebio scoring his second goal against Pelé's Brazil in the 1966 FIFA World Cup.

But my favorite thing on the wall was a cutout from a magazine showing Mickey Mantle and Roger Maris during a skit on the Perry Como show in October 1961.

When I asked about it my dad—who was there when it happened—told me one of Cardosa's customers had glassed and framed the page and given it to Cardosa to hang on the wall. The customer suggested it was good for business to have first generation kids associate him and his barbershop with Mickey Mantle and Roger Maris so they wouldn't think he was just some guy off the boat who didn't know squat about America or the New York Yankees.

Cardosa was nothing if not consistent and so when he saw me enter the barbershop he nodded, smiled and kept clipping away without interruption. Later, after I'd settled into the barber's chair, he said, "How is our champion today?"

For the first time in twenty years I really wanted to answer that question, I mean in a raw unadulterated way. Should I tell him about José? About Callie? I'd always suspected there was a kind of father figure and friend to be had buried somewhere inside the man, someone who might listen and offer the occasional word of insight and encouragement.

And maybe there was, but not on that day. I replied in my best Portuguese—the way José had taught me from the very first haircut—"*Bom, e você?*"

I pointed to the picture of the M & M boys and Cardosa's eyes grew large for a moment and then he nodded and began to cut my hair very short. Wavy locks rolled down the white cloth over my chest and tumbled to the linoleum floor, revealing hints of fresh scarring above my left ear that Cardosa seemed to abide like any other cosmetic imperfection. In the big wall mirror I could see the veteran barber smile and frown as he clipped away, his hands, scissors and comb hungry little machines.

• • •

AFTER having a cup of coffee across the street at the *Habana Café*, I drove to the Legacy branch of Copernicus University and walked to the English Department. It was Friday and the place was quiet as a library. I slipped the notes I'd written under my professors' closed office doors. I heard movement inside Dr. Greene's office but I didn't press the issue. The best I could hope for at this point was a phone call or a letter, some kind of arrangement to make up the lost time, though I wasn't optimistic. Most likely the semester was lost and I'd have to repeat the courses, meaning those six credits were going to cost me double. But that was the least of my concerns, and I was somewhat relieved that I wouldn't have to face Dr. Greene nor Dr. Bloomberg that Friday morning.

"Mr. Amado?"

I turned around and there was Dr. Greene standing in the hallway holding my note like a limp napkin.

"Dr. Greene, I didn't mean to interrupt you."

He seemed to be fanning a flame as he motioned for me to approach him.

"Come inside," he said. "Please sit."

Except for the diffused light of an elongated bronze desk lamp, the surrounding space of the windowless office gave the impression of being suspended in a dim vapor. An open book of verse lay where the light was brightest, and a telephone waited to the side half in shadow.

The old Medievalist looked the part with his thin-rimmed glasses, red bowtie, white shirt and plaid suspenders that held up his bulky gray wool trousers. After closing the door, he took his time walking around his desk back to his seat, affording me ample opportunity to check out his scuffed white sneakers. What little hair he had left was wispy white and neatly parted from the side, left to right.

One day two of my classmates were on line in the cafeteria discussing Dr. Greene. They were joking about him being a pretend Oxford don and such, an old fool, in other words. Dr. Greene could be a little quirky but pretend wasn't part of his makeup, which I pointed out to them. Did they know the old man had served with distinction in *The Great War*? That he'd been awarded a Rhodes scholarship and had spent two years at Merton College, Oxford working on his doctorate? That he was one of J.R.R. Tolkien's first students when the legendary author began his teaching career at Oxford?

No? Oh, I see.

They didn't ask me how I came to know all this and I didn't tell them. In fact, they didn't say another word while I hovered near. I walked out of the cafeteria thinking that what my classmates had learned about Dr. Greene that evening had suddenly made their own lives just a tad more interesting.

"You wish to know what, if anything, can be done to salvage the semester," Dr. Greene said, his right hand tapping the top of his desk.

"I was wondering, sir... Maybe I could do some independent study while resuming my regular course work?"

"Yes, of course. I would be happy to arrange something with you."

"I can't tell you how much I would appreciate that, sir. These last two months I've—"

"No need to explain, Mr. Amado," Dr. Greene said, raising his hand. "Your wife contacted me several weeks ago. She said you would have to suspend your studies for an indeterminate period pending family matters. She did not elaborate."

"I've been away and returned just yesterday."

"I trust things are progressing?"

"More slowly than I'd like, sir."

"Let's not further complicate your life then. You may find writing a paper discussing the influence of Boccaccio on Chaucer worthwhile. Say five-thousand words, due in two weeks or thereabouts. Limit yourself to no more than three examples each from *Decameron* and *The Canterbury Tales* to develop your thesis. We can discuss what you have in mind and any other details before next Thursday's class."

"Thank you, sir, that's more than reasonable."

Dr. Greene peered at me over his glasses with benign interest.

"Now that that's settled, Mr. Amado, allow me to ask you, what is your opinion of Pope?"

"The poet?"

"Yes, Alexander Pope."

"I haven't yet read him, I'm embarrassed to say."

"To err is human; to forgive, divine."

Dr. Greene's face suddenly contorted and he began to laugh like a lunatic. The laughter trailed off into a series of diminishing snorts.

"Oh my, forgive me, Mr. Amado, I do beg your indulgence. What you must be thinking. But oh, Mr. Amado, your expression was absolutely priceless. I don't mean to suggest you are erring for not having read Pope—no, no, no—nor that I am forgiving your imaginary transgression, heavens no."

"Are you sure about that, sir?"

Dr. Greene chuckled. "Ah, Mr. Amado, you have found me out!"

"I do remember hearing a few things about Pope. He was quite a mess, actually—if I might use that word, sir?"

"Oh yes, mess, very much so. A mess of lifelong fevers, headaches, respiratory and abdominal difficulties, inflamed eyes, which for a writer, well, you can imagine. A four-and-a-half-foot tall hunchback Roman Catholic mess living in Catholic-hating Protestant England. The beleaguered man wasn't the most agreeable fellow to begin with, being possessed, as he was, of a superior aristocratic disposition. Add to that a tendency to lash out with unmitigated cruelty at his critics, his verse regarding the divine nature of forgiveness notwithstanding. But for all that his enemies could not deny his genius."

"I'm sorry to have interrupted your reading."

"Nonsense, not at all. I woke up this morning wondering why Pope was on my mind. I must have dreamed of him. When I got to the office, I picked this volume off the shelf. I was re-reading *An Essay on Man* when I saw your note sliding under my door. If I may, Mr. Amado…"

Dr. Greene picked up the book, cradled it like a baby, and began to read.

> *He hangs between; in doubt to act or rest;*
> *In doubt to deem himself a god, or beast;*
> *In doubt his mind or body to prefer;*
> *But born to die, and reasoning but to err;*

He carefully placed the volume back down on the desk and smiled.

"A race of grotesques, each and every one of us conflicted and deformed in one way or another, to greater or lesser degree, even the most brilliant and beautiful among us. We are in constant struggle with ourselves, with others, with the gods—or with God, if you prefer. And wouldn't you know, Mr. Amado, it is our conflicts and deformities that make us infinitely more interesting than the angels. We make for wonderful subjects, wouldn't you agree?"

"I do, and I look forward to reading Pope."

"Yes, of course, and remember, Mr. Amado, you and I are capable of extraordinary things—good and evil of the highest order and magnitude."

Chapter 36

On my way home from Baytown I stopped at the market for bread and cold cuts and picked up a bottle of wine at the liquor store. I washed down a ham and cheese sandwich with three glasses of cheap Chablis and stared at the kitchen sink until I thought I would begin to scream if I stayed one more minute in that blue apartment.

Outside it was cold but less oppressive and I could breathe a whole lot better. I was leaning against the brick stoop column of the apartment house remembering the day Callie tried to teach me *The Jesus Prayer*. "Breathe in *Jesus*," she said, "and breathe out *Mercy*."

I had played along just to please her, and she knew I wasn't really getting it the way she wanted me to, but it made her smile anyway because she saw that her smile was what I was after all along.

I tried the breathing and the words again but saw no payoff so I began to walk.

The sidewalks were empty but for the occasional longshoreman or construction worker dragging himself home. The street lamps cast a spectral light that gave the neighborhood a sinister air after sunset, especially as the days shortened and winter drew near.

A long time ago someone planted trees thirty feet apart on both sides of Sycamore Street. Someone else lay concrete sidewalks and curbs and left small squares of dirt around the trees so they could breathe and drink. When Tío Arturo arrived from lush mystical Galicia to work on a construction crew he stayed in a room down the street for three years. To my surprise he suggested the sycamores lent a kind of rustic elegance to the cramped and homely working class neighborhood I grew up in.

By then I'd already begun to look at the trees in a different way, imagining them as sentient creatures straining against the hard surfaces. Over the years I watched the dappled branches stretch and reach across the street toward one another, their restless roots lifting and cracking the concrete slabs though never enough to break free.

I remembered Angel who had torn himself from bondage only to destroy himself. I walked down to the corner and turned left on Herald Street and continued to where I'd first seen him months ago, but there was no one there.

I walked to Independence Street and stopped at the corner in front of Saint Corbinian's. I stared across the street at Babylon Elementary, the place where I'd had an ill-fated crush on Miss Bellucci, my kindergarten teacher, and where three years later they informed us our young and handsome president had been shot in the head and we had to go home.

The firemen had reset the alarm box and no one was lying on the sidewalk awaiting the fire trucks. I never did figure out where Angel went that day. I placed my hand over the alarm box and studied the little pane of glass on the white handle plate. My view was obscured by a layer of dirt and grime. I worked the tiny window with my fingertips, rubbing away at the filth.

The loud stuttering *whoop-whoop* of a police car siren froze me. High beams flicked on and the night danced in pretty red and blue whirling lights. My hand, the alarm box, the wooden utility pole, and everything around me became illuminated as if for the holiday season. I shielded my eyes from the bright glare and noted the Legacy City Police Department patrol car idling at a short distance. A cop stepped out of the passenger side and stood with his right hand on his hip observing me. I could hear the staccato voice of a Police Headquarters dispatcher.

"Sir, put your hands straight up over your head… I said straight up!"

I knew not to haggle. I'd heard too many stories growing up in Legacy City. There was a history. Guilt, innocence? That wasn't always relevant. Things could escalate from the trivial to the deadly with the slightest ordinary word or gesture. Street wisdom dictated you keep your mouth shut and you speak only when spoken to.

When the driver emerged from the patrol car, the first cop started walking toward me, to my left, his right hand still on his hip, gunfighter-like. When the other followed, approaching on my right, I felt pinned and helpless.

"Keep your hands straight up over your head, sir. Slowly walk to the wall to your left and place your hands up against it. Hands up higher, sir!"

The other cop checked me up and down, asked me for identification, and walked back to the patrol car. I could hear him talking to the dispatcher. After a couple of minutes, he came back.

"Mr. Amado, you can lower your hands and turn around. Here's your driver's license."

"Thank you, officer."

"Mr. Amado, what were you doing with this fire alarm box?"

What was I doing?

"I went to school here, officer. In eighth grade firemen came to talk to us about fire safety—"

"Sir, what were you doing with this fire alarm box?"

"Oh, I was on my way to the pharmacy to buy aspirin. The little window on the panel was dirty. I stopped to wipe it, that's all. I know it's a strange thing to do."

The two cops stared at me.

"Mr. Amado, are you aware there have been several instances of fire alarms being recklessly activated throughout this ward over the past few months?"

"No officer, I was not aware."

"Did you know a homicide was recently committed a couple of blocks from here?"

"I think I heard something about that."

"Where were you today, Mr. Amado?"

"I got a haircut. I ran some errands. In the afternoon I went to work."

"In the afternoon? Where do you work, sir?"

"I work at Galaxy Alarms."

"You install fire and security alarm systems?"

"Yes, sir, some installation work, but mostly maintenance and repair service."

"But you didn't go to work today?"

"I did, officer, but only in the afternoon, as I stated. You see, I just got back from Spain yesterday. My father died. We buried him this past Monday."

The two police officers continued to stare at me for some moments before glancing at one another. The driver went back to the patrol car.

"Our condolences, Mr. Amado," the other cop said as he turned to leave. He stopped and looked back. "A word of advice. As a general rule, when the sun goes down, you should either be in motion or indoors. It's never a good idea to be standing outside alone in the dark, especially not in this town."

The patrol car followed me until I entered the pharmacy and then sped away. I bought a small bottle of aspirin just so I could say I did what I said I was going to do. There was no point in taking any chances.

Chapter 37

Before dawn Saturday morning I pulled into the Coldwells' empty driveway, leaned back my seat, closed my eyes, inadvertently dozed off and woke up to the drone of the garage door going up. The sun was somewhere behind me. I checked my watch. I'd been asleep for a couple of hours. Coldwell walked into the garage from inside the house carrying an overnight bag. He looked intense and focused, itching to undertake some momentous task.

My presence took him by surprise but I could see he was making an effort to appear unperturbed, to act as though I wasn't there, or if I was, that I was there only in some ineffectual, insubstantial way, and it was just a matter of seconds before I would go *poof* and disappear.

He tossed his bag in the trunk of his car and stood with his back to me. I got out of the hatchback and slammed the car door shut for effect. Coldwell turned around and we stared at each other for several seconds without saying anything.

"You need to move your car," he said.

"I want to talk to Callie."

"There's no one here. You need to move your car."

I felt a tightening in my chest and throat that would be of no use to me. I had to relax. I took a deep breath.

"Where's Callie?" I said.

"I told you no one's here. Move the damn car."

"Where you going, Cam?"

"Excuse me? Are you out of your mind?"

"I'm not moving the car until you tell me where Callie is."

"I don't know where she is."

"Where's Grace?"

"Oh, for the love of..."

Coldwell shook his head and checked his watch. He took a couple of threatening steps back toward the house—to do what, call the police?—but then stopped and looked at me as if he didn't know what to do next.

"Where's Grace?" I repeated.

"I don't know."

"How can you not know where your wife is?"

We glimpsed the irony in each other's eyes, and I thought there was a smile somewhere on his person, not a friendly smile, though not a totally unfriendly one either. Coldwell looked away and then gazed at me again, this time with something like melancholy, as though he were observing from a distance an old acquaintance that reminded him of a less complicated past. Then his shoulders seemed to sag a little and his features seemed to grow heavy.

"Lucas, please move your car," he said in a strange almost tender voice.

It was a voice I'd never heard, a word I'd never heard come out of his mouth, *Lucas*. It was a vulnerable voice—one that nearly touched me—but ultimately, I knew it was a self-serving voice, its attempt to reach that place of sympathy in me more a sign of congenital indifference than trusting intimacy, and maybe that was a reason to mourn too, a reason to return to the quiet hilltop, where by now a plaque would have been installed over the brick covering of the burial niche, and where an oval photograph the size of my hand would have been fastened to the plaque. No longer his eyes or mouth to see but in frozen images and dreams.

My father, Cam, his name was José. Did you know of him?

I knew that whatever power I thought I had in that moment was no power at all. I got in the hatchback and backed out of the driveway and watched Coldwell drive off in his Lincoln. I listened to the hum of the garage door as it went down and then drove the five miles into town to empty my bladder and eat a cheeseburger. I bought a pad of paper and a pen and drove back to the Coldwells' and parked in their driveway.

At the top of the pad I wrote, *There are no happy endings, but always new beginnings*, and I began to sketch out the story of Don Sergio Márquez as well as I could remember from what Don Martín had told me.

When I had tired of writing I got out to ring the doorbell three more times. I knew no one was home, but I rang the doorbell and knocked on the door. I knocked until my big knuckle split open and started to bleed.

Chapter 38

Borders set up camp in my head the moment Marla informed me of his demise. At random times the old field chief would walk out of the tent he'd erected in my brain so he could stare at me. Sometimes he gritted his teeth and clenched his fists, muttering words that were barely audible and which I couldn't understand.

For the most part he just glared at me until his eyes got tired. His slicked back gray hair, the deep facial folds that ended at the corners of his mouth, the overall lupine effect of his countenance and bearing were brazenly clear. Sometimes his image was so real I had to touch the air where I thought his face was so I could convince myself I was only imagining him.

He did pack up and go away for a time. During my coma I felt suggestions of his presence in my dreams and visions, like a wraith wandering through night woods. In Spain he disappeared altogether without a trace. But he was back now, though at least for the time being in a less oppressive capacity.

I was sitting in the hatchback listening to the car doors thump and watching the techies getting swallowed up by the Galaxy building. I was thinking of the day Borders killed himself and how before Marla broke the news to me Mrs. Brinkley had anointed me

Mr. Galaxy, and Julius had showed me his Belgian made Browning Safari, which was beautiful and deadly.

It should have been funny how young Julius had stumbled and fallen among the weeds kicking up a cloud of dirt. If only I'd moved faster, pulled away from the curb before I could hear or see the boy, or at least far enough to believably pretend to have not noticed him. If I'd been able to pull that off Marla wouldn't have been able to reach me and I would have gone straight home and Callie would still love me.

Virgil spotted me as soon as I walked in. He came over and gave me a hug.

"Hey, man, so sorry to hear about your dad."

"Yeah, thanks, Virgil."

"Losing a parent really sucks."

I nodded in agreement and snuck a glance at the Dispatch office window. Marla was talking on the phone.

"Hey, so how you doing?" Virgil said. "Last time I saw you, you were in a freaking coma. You feeling okay? And what's with the hair?"

"Yeah, oh yeah, I'm fine, the hair's fine. The occasional headache is all. Nothing out of the ordinary. Getting my bearings back, dealing with stuff."

"Hey, how's Callie doing? Ah, never mind. We can talk later. We do need to talk, you and me."

"So this here Mr. Galaxy?"

I looked at Virgil.

"Uh, yeah," Virgil said. "Lucas, meet Cosmo Etienne, one of our new techies. Cosmo, Lucas Amado. I'm Cosmo's mentor for a couple of weeks."

Cosmo extended his hand. His grip was firm and eager.

"Virgil been showing me round the Galaxy."

"I've been taking Cosmo with me on calls. I was telling him what oddballs some customers can be, like that one lady calling you Mr. Galaxy."

"Sound to me like the lady craving your sexual consideration and affiliation," Cosmo said with a wide grin.

I was too distracted by Marla to fully appreciate Cosmo's engaging manner. I chanced another glance and caught her studying me. To my surprise she smiled and waved.

"Yoh, Lucas," Cosmo said. "Virgil give me the news about your old man. My deepest sympathies, yeah."

"Thanks, Cosmo."

"Just got to keep putting one foot before the other, right brother?"

"Yep, that's right… Excuse me, I just need to touch base with someone real quick."

I walked away to collect myself and lingered in the Men's Room for a good couple of minutes just wanting the day to die. I was surprised when I heard a flush and watched Jay Weller walk out of one of the stalls. We washed our hands on opposite ends of the vanity without saying a word to each other, and a few seconds later I followed him out and joined the techies who were forming yet another Borders circle.

After all the calls were distributed, I walked over to Dispatch. The office door was open but I held back. Despite Marla's apparently friendly demeanor, I took a couple of deep breaths before issuing a courtesy knock.

"Can I come in?"

"Hey, hi you! Of course, you can come in. Wow, you cut your hair really, really short."

"Too short?"

"No, it looks good, gives you that bright-eyed schoolboy look."

"I'm not sure how to take that. I was aiming more for the no-nonsense major league look."

"Oh, I'm just teasing you… Lucas, I am so sorry about your dad."

"Thank you."

"You've been through the mill, buddy. I was so worried about you. Head injuries can be real tricky."

"I guess I was lucky."

"You have a very strange notion of lucky. You didn't look so lucky when I went to see you in the hospital."

"You saw me?"

"Not a pretty sight, I must say."

I felt a little embarrassed but liked her like this, bold and cheerful and direct. It was like having the old Marla back. I regarded her with cautious affection. Was this the voice that had ripped apart Callie's heart? No, I wasn't buying it. There had to be something else going on, someone else.

"So where's Mrs. Grandie?" I said.

"Lois? Oh, she and her husband moved down to Florida."

"Oh, they did."

"Yep, nice lady, though less helpful than you might think."

I nodded in empathy and wondered about Mrs. Grandie, and how she remembered Borders because of the cowboy boots, and all those hours and conversations she and Marla must have had. I stuck my head out into the hallway for a moment to make sure nobody was within hearing distance and closed the door.

"Marla, I really screwed up big time."

She frowned as she weighed my words. Was really screwed up big time adequate phrasing?

"You don't have to say anything," she said, but I detected the faintest trace of dissatisfaction in her voice.

"I just feel like... Ah, hell, I should get going. Oh, by the way, thank you for the sympathy card."

"You mean the Galaxy Alarms sympathy card?"

"Yeah, that one. I'll be talking to you, okay?"

"You be careful out there, buddy."

She was right about being careful, right to remind me—however ironic the advice—because talking with Marla Tupo could sometimes be a little like walking across a minefield covered in wildflowers.

Chapter 39

Jay Weller was as unlikable as ever and nearly as unapproachable as his more colorful predecessor. Weller didn't care about colorful. I don't know if Weller cared about anything. He could have been a closet neo-Nazi for all I knew. But Weller never gave anyone any reason to think that, and that's what made him so hard to figure out.

The guy had been Borders's right-hand man, and who knew what kinds of things Borders had told him about me, things that might or might not be true. There was no evidence Weller harbored any affection for Borders. His loyalty was entirely self-serving, or at least that's the way it looked to me.

It was a stretch to think Weller had been so torn up by Borders's suicide that he'd want to make me pay somehow. It made no sense because Weller was indifference personified.

After the day's calls were handed out I made another visit to the Dispatch office. Marla was standing at an open file cabinet flipping folders. She was wearing a snug lavender sweater over a white collared blouse, a modest gray skirt and low-cut black suede boots. She smiled when she saw me. She had a contented innocent schoolgirl quality about her that day, despite her forty-seven years, and her hair appeared to be just a tad darker than it was yesterday.

A minute ago, it had seemed easy enough to walk over and suggest to her that we needed to talk, maybe meet at a diner or a coffee shop after work.

"Hi," I said.

"Hi to you too, mister. North by northwest today, huh? The thought of it makes me shiver."

"Sussex County always does seem to be at least twenty degrees colder."

"Oh, it doesn't *seem*, it is," she said and looked at me with a frowning smile. "Was there something you wanted to ask me, Lucas?"

It was the perfect opportunity, and before I even said another word, I was already regretting not having taken it.

"Actually, I just wanted to wish you a stress-free Tuesday and, uh, maybe you can see your way to not assigning me any emergency calls today?"

"Well, mister, I may be able to arrange that, but only if you behave yourself."

The words clutched at me like a pair of claws. Was I misreading that smile? She took note of my discomfort—maybe because she was anticipating it?—and smoothly shifted to her pragmatic dispatcher tone.

"You've got a long day ahead of you, buddy," she said. "You better get going. It's going to be cold out there."

I felt mildly violated as I walked out to the parking lot, but it wasn't a totally unwelcomed sensation. I was feeling confused, torn, unmoored, and strangely excited.

"Virgil!" I called out.

He said something to Cosmo and came walking toward me.

"You all right?" he said.

"Yeah, like I told you yesterday, just working out a few details. Weller's got me going up to Sussex."

"It was eighteen degrees up there when I got up this morning. That's not right, man. We just got started with November."

"On my way back I'm stopping at my in-laws' place, which is just off 206."

"So Callie and the kid moved out, huh? Have you heard from her?"

"How did you—? Never mind, no, I haven't. I saw her dad Saturday. He says he doesn't know where she is."

"What about her mom?"

"She wasn't there. He said he didn't know where she was either. I think I believe him."

"What the hell's going on?"

"He was tossing an overnight bag into the trunk of his car on his way to somewhere. He was all tensed up, unsure of himself. That never happens with this guy. It was like things had gotten out of his control. I saw him talking to this younger woman at the wedding a couple of months back."

"You mean the day of your accident?"

"Yeah, the day of my *accident*. She slid her hand down his arm while he was talking, you know, like all sultry and suggestive. They exchanged these secret smiles. I'm thinking Callie and her mom took off somewhere. He wouldn't say where. I don't think he knew. The guy looked discombobulated."

"Wow, discombobulated. Maybe they went back to the house now he's gone?"

"That's what I'm thinking."

"Okay, wait, go back just a bit. You saying you didn't have an accident? I mean the way you said *accident*."

"It's a long story, Virgil. I don't want to get into it right now."

"I've got to get going anyway. Cosmo's waiting. Guy is one serious techie. Says he's shooting for Weller's job. Wouldn't put it past him. Lot more ambitious than I've ever been, tell you that much. Hey, don't forget, we need to talk. Call me, or I'll give you a call."

"Sure, okay."

"Stay warm, pal."

• • •

IT WAS COLD enough to get my attention but not as cold as I'd expected for most of the day because there was barely a breeze blowing and the sun was shining bright as could be. But as daylight waned the temperature again began to plummet.

On my last call of the day, I couldn't convince the old guy to swap out the obsolete outdoor alarm for a new one and found myself spending way too much time standing on a rickety old ladder as the sun was setting scraping out generations of wasp nests and readjusting and rewiring the big old relic. By the time I finished my fingers were curled and red from the cold and my nose felt sharp as a razor.

I was glad to be back on the road heading south in a car that still remembered how to warm me. But I could feel in my gut that something pivotal was going to happen soon. One moment I was seeing Callie open the door of her parents' home and throwing herself into my arms, but the next she was standing beneath the driveway lights telling me it was over.

Because I no longer love you, Lucas…

The hatchback must have been as sick of me as I was of it because it decided to go dead right then. I forced the steering wheel to the right and redirected the grinding heap of junk off the road. I was nowhere, and nowhere was icy dark. A road lamp in the distance was winking at me. I closed my eyes.

I didn't want to get out and feel my blood thicken and stall on its way to my extremities, nose and eyes, didn't want to shiver all over again repeating the same life-sucking steps required to resuscitate the vampire machine, didn't want to hang around like an indentured servant waiting to hear okay, now you can go, and wondering where the hell my wife and son were. The whole scenario made ice churn in my entrails and frayed my nerves. I banged the steering wheel with my fists, whipped my head side to side, cursed and howled like a tortured dog.

I paused to take a breath.

That wasn't how my parents raised me, but in that cruel moment my excesses seemed as natural and necessary as any other corporal function, eruptions so perfectly raw and dense with anguish and self-pity that I would have no need of others for a long while. Whatever comfort they provided me—the easing of pressure inside my skull, for example—was paid for with a torn throat.

I pressed my hand, like a compress, against the pain and made an effort to steady my breathing, but by then nothing but further self-inflicted pain seemed warranted.

I lowered my head to the steering wheel and began to tap it with my forehead, at first in an exploratory, centering way, and then a little harder, a little bit harder, harder still, and the next thing I knew I was in a kind of self-flagellating rhythm, and I don't know if I would have kept going until I slipped into another coma but for the clinking sound of metal against the hard unforgiving steering wheel. The clinking sound made me stop. I gathered the medal, crucifix and chain and dropped them back inside my shirt.

My head felt on the verge of splitting right down to the bridge of my nose. I opened the glove compartment and took out the bottle of aspirin I'd bought a couple of days ago when the cops were questioning me about the fire alarm box. I swallowed four pills and sat in the car waiting for a wave of nausea to pass before getting the flashlight and a screwdriver out of my tool case. The stars seemed all over the place and I started to shiver as soon as I popped open the hood. I lodged the screwdriver beneath the choke flap and tried to start the car but nothing happened.

A lot of effort went into managing my head and throat pain but I was still conscious of cars whipping past. It was too dark and too cold to stop for a stranger, I understood, though wasn't that when a Good Samaritan was most useful? But who was I to judge? I understood the reluctance, the fear... I waited fifteen minutes more and tried again. The engine roared to life like a happy beast. The sound surprised me and I teased the accelerator pedal, feeding the steel animal and securing my gain.

A rush of euphoria, like good wine, coursed through my body, warming me and making my head feel just a little better. The stars began to realign and I found that I no longer felt anxious about what I might encounter when I got to Colts Brook.

Even so my newfound serenity failed to soften the shock of a realtor's *For Sale* sign on the front lawn.

The exterior lights and a single living room lamp were lit. I rang the doorbell and knocked, and when there was no answer I peered inside through the cracks between the curtains, but it was evident the house was empty. I got in the car and drove to the nearest neighbor's house a football field and a half away. A well-groomed, middle-aged man opened the door just wide enough to eye my golden arm badge patch surrounded by azure blue.

"Your neighbors, the Coldwells?" I said.

"Don't know them."

"Did you happen to notice a young woman with a baby?"

"Don't know anything about that."

"So you did see them?"

The man closed the door without saying another word. He wasn't rude about it, or anything like that. It was a routine and necessary act, like closing a refrigerator door.

What would be the point of knocking again? I had no desire to see another patrol car emerge out of the dark, its high beams flashing, so I headed back to Legacy City.

Chapter 40

On my way to Callie and Johnny I got lost and the hatchback died for good.

Worst way to wake up, but a shower, a cup of coffee and a fistful of cheerios made me feel better. I went outside in my work blues and stood on the sidewalk and stared at the scruffy little car, which if I were still dreaming would be me staring at me, according to any number of dream experts.

I got inside the hatchback—inside myself?—and said relax, breathe, tease the life force pedal, keep the gas-blood circulating, and put one foot before the other like Cosmo said.

Last night I looked everywhere for Callie's address book. Buried at the bottom of her night table drawer I found an old one from college. I dialed Hadley's number. A recording told me the number I was calling had been disconnected. I tried again with the same result before remembering that Hadley and Brock had moved to Connecticut.

Not sure why I bothered dialing Ed Rollo's residence but I did, three times. Each time as I listened to Ed's peppy recorded greeting, I imagined him staring at the phone with his jaw set and Audrey gazing out a window having already been warned not to pick up.

This had nothing to do with some hypothetical Coldwell mandate. It was much more basic than that. You just couldn't count on Ed. His Lenape Hills mansion was pretty much off limits and I suspected Grace had learned that well before I did. Strangest thing too. You would think that with Ed being a backslapping encourager of souls, good-natured kidder and so on…

But no, so Grace and Callie and Johnny wouldn't be staying at Ed and Audrey's any more than they'd be staying on Pluto, but I left Ed three messages anyway.

I WAVED HELLO to Marla but she either didn't see me or decided to ignore me, so I kept my distance wondering what happened since the last time we talked.

Virgil was waiting for me in the back parking lot. Cosmo was leaning against Virgil's car staring at the Galaxy Alarms sign. His African profile was accented by frosty puffs of breath that projected a kind of cinematic heroism.

"Not so good last night?" Virgil said.

"Does it show?"

"You're not your usual perky self."

"I think they went up to Connecticut, to Hadley's new house. It shouldn't be this hard to find my wife and kid, you know."

"You'll find them, just take it one step at a time, okay? Who's Hadley?"

"Callie's sister. They moved a few months ago. I can't get a hold of anyone."

"Changed their number?"

"Changed and unlisted."

"Reeks of conspiracy, if you ask me."

"That did cross my mind."

"I was just kidding, man."

"Her husband's a bank president. He got offered a job up there. I think the bank's in Greenwich. I remember Greenwich being mentioned. I'm heading over to the library later. There's got to be a Connecticut phone book there, I would think."

"Marla's got all the phone books in her office."

"Yeah, I know."

"But the library should have what you need too."

"I'm going up to Connecticut Friday. I'm going to lay it all out to them. I'm not going anywhere until they tell me where my wife and kid are. I'll sleep on their front doorstep like a dog if it comes to that."

"Hey, easy, it won't come to that. Not to change the subject but, see Cosmo over there?"

"Yeah?"

"Go talk to him."

"About?"

"You know."

"What are you talking about?"

"The guy knows."

"Knows what?"

"About Callie finding out about you and Marla."

"What? How would Cosmo know anything about that, Virgil?"

"Talk to him. He said he'd be happy to talk to you."

"Happy? He used the word happy?"

"No, I used it."

"Wait a second, so you told this virtual stranger about Marla and me?"

"No, of course not. What the hell is wrong with you? We're talking about two different things here."

"What the hell is wrong with *you*, Virgil?"

"Maybe three things, like how he found out about you and Marla, and also how he found out how Callie found out, and also how he found out about other stuff too."

"Are you playing word games with me, Virgil? Are you playing freaking word games with me?"

I heard Virgil say something as I turned away, but I wasn't paying attention. I marched over to Cosmo. I could feel Virgil behind rushing to keep pace.

"So what's this all about?" I said.

Cosmo straightened up and with a dignified air said, "It sure ain't about me."

"You know who talked to my wife?"

"Yes, sir."

"Was it Marla?"

"No, sir. Well, not directly."

"What do you mean not directly?"

"It's complicated."

"Is that right? Well, maybe you could un-complicate it for me?"

My tone was all wrong. Cosmo shook his head and looked away. I thought he was going to tell me to go to hell and slip inside Virgil's car. But he didn't move and I had the impression he was going to milk the moment, wax poetic, teach me a life lesson. He was about Virgil's age, mentor, sponsor, big brother age. I needed to relax.

"Sorry, man," I said. "No offense intended, I'm just trying to understand."

Cosmo looked everywhere but at me, nodding his head as if he were listening to recommendations from a cloud of invisible witnesses. Then he began to speak to different parts of my face.

"In fifth grade I saw the future, man, and it was ugly. I promised Cosmo I'd lead him out of the shithole life he was born unto, wrote it all down in a notebook for future publication."

I wasn't seeing the point and he must have deduced as much because he added, "No need for you to know the precise details of Cosmo's emancipation proclamation, only that you talking to a serious man."

I nodded.

"I understand, and I appreciate your willingness to help me sort things out."

"Because I'm driven to make Cosmo Etienne beholden to no one, I make it my business to learn all I can about people and institutions so as to put myself in a most advantageous position."

Cosmo paused when he heard the back door open. He waited for the techies to pass and then drew closer.

"So when I hear about folks working weekends I begin making targeted visits to further educate myself. That's how I come to meet Mrs. Rolonda Belford."

"Are you suggesting Rolonda talked to Callie?"

Cosmo raised his hand as though he were about to take an oath.

"Mrs. Belford not the easiest woman to talk to, but she appreciative of my rectitude and respectful nature. The second Saturday I come by I get her to open up to me. But hard as I try guiding her to the matter of Chief Weller she rather talk about Chief Borders and his terrible fate. All knowledge is good but then she stop talking altogether, and I know she wrestling with a demon because of her Christian conscience. So I put the burden on me. I say to her, 'What, Miss Rolonda, what you keeping to yourself that rightly should be brought into the light?' She hesitate, but then she so glad to relieve her soul of that heavy weight that she tell me everything."

"What do you mean *everything*?"

"Everything pertinent to your involvement with Miss Tupo."

"Am I wrong to think Rolonda takes pleasure in prying into other people's affairs?"

"Oh, you right about that but don't make it any less true what she know and say."

"So, she talked to Callie, huh?"

"Yes sir, that be a fact, like you and me talking right now, but there more about Miss Tupo you ought to know."

"According to Rolonda."

"Like why she lose custody of her children."

"Sounds to me like Rolonda is something of an oracle. Is that why you believe her? Because she's an oracle?"

Cosmo shook his head and crunched his features. "Come on, man," he said in a mournful voice, as if he were embarrassed for my sake.

"I'm being serious, I'm curious to know. Why do you believe her?"

"I don't know what you implying, Lucas, but I got no bias against no one regardless of race or creed. Her skin color don't mean shit to me other than I could use it to find out information for my own personal benefit and by happenstance yours too."

"But you still have not answered my question, Cosmo."

"Why do I believe her? Maybe cause her Christian soul answerable to God Almighty."

"Oh, I see, her Christian soul…"

"Whatever you want to believe, brother, is your business. Now I'm going to lay on you what Miss Rolonda say to me that is directly related to you. She say Miss Tupo leading you down the road to perdition. She say she know you know she know what been going on between you and that Marla woman because she talk to you on the phone following the tragedy befallen Chief Borders, but that knowledge evidently proved insufficient to make you pay attention because she know what you did with that woman and how you still associate with her. Miss Rolonda so troubled by all she discover and the potential further calamity lying in wait that she take it upon herself to call your wife in the hope your woman smack some sense into your dumbass head to keep you from further disgracing yourself and ruining your marriage for all eternity. Miss Rolonda say it cause her great distress because your wife a lovely young lady and not deserving of such piss poor treatment."

"Rolonda's a crazy woman. She doesn't know anything. It was just Marla and me in her apartment, nobody else. Nobody saw us, nobody knew. So explain to me how Rolonda Belford managed to get the inside scoop."

Cosmo chuckled in a benign way, as if he'd just won a friendly bet.

"Oh, that part easy, Lucas. Miss Tupo tell her."

The words had a strange locomotive effect on me—*Tupoteller, Tupoteller, Tupoteller*—like an unstoppable engine chugging along inside my head on its way to the edge of a bridgeless cliff. Just then the back door swung open and out came Jay Weller and Walter Dunst.

"Much appreciated, Lucas," Cosmo said. "That is a piece of good information for me to know and apply."

Cosmo snapped off a military salute and slipped into Virgil's car.

Weller and Dunst tossed sour glances our way as they walked past. We waited for them to be out of earshot before saying another word. Virgil beat me to it.

"There's one more thing you need to know. Marla used to teach high school up in Buffalo. She was involved in a scandal back in 1967. Sex with one of her students, a sixteen-year-old boy. The parents found out. She got off with a fine but lost her job. That's why her husband filed for divorce and why he got custody of the kids."

"Hold on, sex with a sixteen-year-old? Marla?"

"I know, but listen, Rolonda did some snooping around. Marla's resume does show she taught high school math up in Buffalo from 1958-1967. I didn't know she was a teacher, did you? Someone here—probably Roseboom—drew a circle around *1967* on her resume and put a question mark next to it. Kind of weird Marla never mentioned to anyone she was a teacher, don't you think?"

"That doesn't prove anything."

"Wait, there's more. Rolonda had her son drive her up to Buffalo. Walked into the main library and pulled up microfiche from a couple of local newspapers dating back to the Spring of '67. And there it was, sure enough, right in the news."

"What was?"

"The scandal, Lucas. Marla and the kid."

"So, Rolonda's got proof of this so-called scandal?"

"Oh, yeah. Unfortunately, she wasn't able to make copies."

"What a surprise."

"It's microfiche, man. She couldn't print the stuff so she wrote it down."

"She wrote it down? Virgil, come on, you buying this? Look, I understand Marla's got her issues, but there's something seriously wrong with this Rolonda woman. I mean, driving up to Buffalo to check up on a coworker? You kidding me? And I'm not saying she didn't do it, she probably did, but what does that say about her? And we're expected to believe some crazy stuff she wrote up?"

"You need to read what she wrote, Lucas."

"The bottom line is she hates Marla. The guys love Marla because she's personable and attractive, everything Rolonda's not. I bet she thinks she deserves Marla's job too. It must be really hard for her, I mean, being Galaxy's morality watchdog and all..."

Virgil stared at me in silence a few seconds before pulling several folded sheets out of his back pocket.

"Here's what Rolonda gave Cosmo to give to me to give to you. She wanted you to have it so you could verify for yourself that it's all real."

I flipped through the pages. It was all one big annoying blur. To make matters worse, I couldn't shake Cosmo's words, *Oh, that part easy, Lucas. Miss Tupo tell her, Tupoteller, Tupoteller, Tupoteller...*

"Why would Marla tell that woman anything?" I said. "Why would she give Rolonda more ammunition? It makes no sense."

"The whole thing sounds crazy, I know. Who knows what happened between those two? Hey, I have to get going, pal. Read the sheets, man, you owe it to yourself. Read the sheets. We'll talk some more later, okay?"

Virgil jogged off and I watched him and Cosmo drive out of the parking lot.

Read the sheets...

At the top of each sheet were notes identifying the newspaper item, including date and page number, followed by the full title and neatly scripted blocks of tiny words.

I read the first sheet.

ERIE COUNTY TEACHER CHARGED WITH ENGAGING IN SEX ACTS WITH UNDERAGE STUDENT

> An Erie County High School teacher was arrested in Lackawanna last week and charged with engaging in multiple sex acts with an underage male student. West Shore High School teacher Marla Humphrey, 35, of Buffalo, was arrested Thursday. Mrs. Humphrey is slated to appear in Buffalo Superior Court Wednesday to answer four counts of sexual intercourse with a minor, two counts of oral copulation with a minor and one count of distributing matter deleterious to a minor with the intent to seduce. The Math teacher was placed on administrative leave by district administrators.

On the bottom right of each sheet, inside a circle she had drawn, Rolonda had added, *This is Marla Tupo, which is her maiden name. It's definitely the Marla Tupo in question who works at Galaxy Alarms, Inc. because I saw her picture in the newspaper.*

Marla Humphrey was released on bail the day of her arrest, spent no further time in jail, was fined $500 and then fired from her teaching job. I sat in the hatchback and read from beginning to end until the words began to dance, and I didn't know who to pity more, Marla or Rolonda.

I wished Dr. Greene were sitting next to me in the passenger seat to shed some light on the matter, help me put things in perspective.

If I may, Mr. Amado… Consider, if you will, the loneliness of souls swelling before us like a sea of mirrors. See how such a sea reflects and prompts the me to ask, is what I see at sea my face, multiplied over time and space?

Greeny laughs and taps the hatchback console three times, then slaps his thighs in rhythm and fast time.

Is it Marla I see, Dr. Greene? Is it me? Is it you, he, she, we?

Oh yes, yes, yes, yes, yes, and yes, Mr. Amado, it most surely be.

Part 8

Water

Chapter 41

The sun felt good on my eyelids and nose and cheeks and warmed my forlorn lips. The way the sun felt on my face made me think back to Johnny's first Fourth of July and me pushing the stroller on the boardwalk on a hot sunny day, and Callie walking by my side with her hand over mine, and the rhythmic rumbling tide receding and leaving all that fine Jersey sand pressed smooth moist-white like vanilla ice cream, and red white and blue pennants flapping in the warm breeze all along the boardwalk, and the two of us sparring over the merits of chocolate chip mint versus peanut butter chocolate swirl even as that wonderful hour was steeping in our ignorance of Borders putting an end to himself two weeks into the future and me ruining everything.

The muted roll of a fine car pulling into the parking lot brought me back to Greenwich Connecticut and Brock Penny's bank. The BMW was suffused with a brilliant aura during the seconds it took for my eyes to adjust from the blaze that had flared behind my eyelids. I watched the car cool to cobalt blue and come to rest near the bank's front entrance. And then a good-looking woman with chestnut hair like Callie's emerged into the sunlight, and it took me a moment to realize it was Hadley.

I slid back into the rental and watched my sister-in-law sashay into the bank and was heartened by the knowledge I'd be able to eliminate Penny from the equation and just follow Hadley back to the house.

It didn't take her long to come back out, and she was looking real sharp and purposeful and well acclimated to her new surroundings. She drove the BMW out of the parking lot and I followed in the Dodge Colt. It wasn't that they looked all that much alike, but there was enough of Callie in her big sister to make my heart race and ache just a little more than usual.

A couple of blocks down the street she lurched to a stop and angled the car in reverse and did the back and forth dance of parallel parking with the tedious precision of a space-docking maneuver. When I got the chance, I slid the Colt past her and came to a stop several car lengths away and watched her emerge with a burst from the BMW and disappear into a building a few doors away.

The five minutes I was anticipating turned into a half hour so I left the rental and walked down to see what the delay was all about. I stopped outside *Cleo's Beauty Salon*. Through the shop window I could see two rows of women facing each other with their heads trapped inside immense hair driers and Hadley sitting unattended, her head uncovered, an open magazine up against her face.

I was hungry and thirsty. I walked a bit farther up the street and found what looked like a luncheonette. They didn't have cheeseburgers or sodas, though, so I ordered a ham and Swiss bagel sandwich with spicy hot mustard and a tall iced tea to go. I headed to the Men's room while my lunch was being prepared and felt that life had become a tad more manageable by the time I walked back to the counter.

The lady at the counter was busy with another customer, so I took the opportunity to stick my head out the door and was stunned to see the BMW nudging itself back and forth.

"Sir? Sir?" the lady at the counter called out, but I was already shooting through the doorway and sprinting down the street.

"Sir, you left your food and change!"

The BMW pulled free and slowly started to distance itself. I stopped with a stutter step and was bemoaning my lost opportunity when the car came to another abrupt stop.

Hadley got out, removed her sunglasses and leaned her head forward a bit to get a better look at me. Then she either cursed or said my name or both because I could see her mouth move though I couldn't hear what she'd said.

She started walking toward me but stopped and went back to close her car door. She spun around and shot a glance at her fingernails as she took several steps in my direction before setting her feet and fixing her full attention on me. I began a slow cautious jog worried that at any moment she was going to change her mind and get back in her car and drive off. When I got to what I felt was a close enough non-threatening distance I stopped and lifted my hand a few inches in an aborted wave.

"Lucas," she said with disgust.

"Hello Hadley."

"She's not here. You should have called."

"Your number's unlisted."

I searched her unsympathetic face and glanced down at her sandaled feet and cherry-red toenails, and I noticed her toes were wiggling around the tiny foam wedges that were squeezed between them.

"You don't have to believe me," she said, "but it doesn't change the fact she's not here."

Despite her hostile demeanor I had to smile. "How is she? How's Johnny?"

"I told you, they're not here."

"All right, Hadley, suppose for a moment that's true. They're not here. Just don't tell me you don't know where they are."

"You should have called. It would have saved you the trip."

"Couldn't, didn't have the number."

"Oh, well."

She turned and started marching back to her car but with a few quick strides I was right behind her. Before she could open her car door I said, "You leave and I'm walking into your husband's bank and raising hell, I'm making a big ugly scene, I'm yelling, 'Brock Penny's a pedophile!'"

Hadley studied me with renewed interest.

"Brock's not in there," she said.

"We'll see about that."

"He's not. He got home yesterday from gall bladder surgery."

She gazed at me for a few seconds more. "I need to move the car off the street. I'm serious, I'm not going to drive away."

With the same agonizing patience she exhibited earlier, she worked the interstellar apparatus back and forth until she got it aligned to her satisfaction.

"Are you hungry?" I said.

"No, but I suppose I could have a drink."

She wasn't smiling when she said this, but I could have kissed her.

We sat at a small table near the back, too close to the rest rooms but suitable for my purposes. A teenaged boy brought over my lunch and an iced tea for Hadley. He must have been around the same age as Marla's schoolboy. I wondered why he wasn't in school.

"Gall bladder's gone, huh?" I said.

"Uh-huh… So I heard about your dad."

"Oh, yeah…"

"My condolences."

"Thank you… Hey, you know, you can live a normal life without a gall bladder."

"Ha, we'll see. Normal is different for everybody. Brock's not used to this kind of normal."

We stared at each other.

"You and Callie have very similar eyes," I said.

"Hmm."

"So, Grace is doing well?"

Hadley sighed.

"I went to your parents' house. I saw your dad. He said they weren't there. I drove by the house a couple of days later and saw the *For Sale* sign on the front lawn."

Hadley shook her head and jabbed her finger in the air at me.

"You!"

"Me?"

"She gave everything up for you. The way she talked about you, like you were something special. It was sickening, actually. We thought she was out of her mind, and then she springs this marriage nonsense on us. Of course we tried to talk her out of it."

"Yeah, of course."

"We went through that whole Catholic thing with her, which was interesting in and of itself, but this? This was worse. It had disaster written all over it. She was so out of touch with reality. You know what she said to me?"

"Tell me."

"Oh, nothing special, only that she was worried about me. *She* was worried about *me*, got that?"

Hadley tried to smile as she looked down at her fingernails, all shiny and red. She spread her fingers wide apart and turned her hands for my benefit.

"Know how much I paid to have these done?"

"I couldn't even venture a guess."

"More than makes sense, even for a rich girl."

She sighed and shook her head.

"I was there for the big fight, okay?" she said as if conceding some crucial point.

She looked at me expecting some acknowledgment, I suppose, but Callie never told me anything about a big fight. I was in the dark and Hadley must have picked up on that because she seemed uncertain suddenly, as if debating with herself on whether to cross some forbidden line.

"It doesn't matter now anyhow," she said, "who cares?"

I knew immediately what was coming wasn't going to be for my benefit. Hadley was going to satisfy a need in much the same way Grace had in front of the church the day of Danielle's wedding. Who cares? I didn't care. I welcomed Hadley's sudden, if hazardous, openness. I wanted to hear what she had to say maybe as much as she wanted to say it.

"Daddy got in from work and stepped right into the fray. Callie and Mom were arguing and he told them to be quiet and said he didn't want to hear any more talk about this marriage nonsense. There wasn't a sound to be heard after that, and we thought case closed but then suddenly Callie goes nuts."

Someone behind us knocked over a drink and let out a high-pitched yelp. Hadley didn't turn her head but I did and one of the two lustrous ladies sitting there was dabbing at the spill with her napkin and sighing as if to indicate the rebellious beverage was to blame.

"She started to cry she was so angry and saying crazy things, like that we couldn't possibly understand what she was feeling. *Couldn't possibly understand.* It didn't register at first, what she meant by that, but then I realized she was saying we didn't know what it was like to be in love, not Daddy, not Mom, not me…"

Hadley's voice trailed off. She let the thought wither away and then she spread her hands before her on the table and looked at them with affection. She began to speak in a subdued tone to each of her fingernails.

"Daddy poured himself a drink and locked himself in his study. Callie started banging on his door until Daddy threw it open and then he just stood there staring at her, and I knew he was wondering how this girl could be his daughter. She told him he had no right— I still cannot believe she said that—that he had no right and that she was getting married with or without his blessing. And you know, that's when all this started, and Mom and Daddy haven't been the same since that fight."

"Don't put that on Callie."

"Oh, I'm not. I'm putting it on you."

Hadley pressed her lips over the top of the straw and took a slow sip of her iced tea while keeping her eyes fixed on me. Was I that much of a threat to the Coldwell universe? I didn't know whether to laugh or beg forgiveness.

"So what happened?" she said.

"Didn't you and Callie talk?"

"I want to hear your version."

"I don't have a *version.*"

"Come on, tell me."

"It was a woman at work."

Hadley's entire person seemed to rise to an almost voyeuristic level of attention.

"You cheated on her, of course you did. Is she prettier than Callie?"

All I could do was shake my head.

"I'm not surprised. What happened, did you get bored?"

"Stop it, will you? She's an older woman, a divorced woman. Boredom had nothing to do with anything."

"Oh, that's interesting."

"Her lover committed suicide."

Hadley started laughing. "You are such a bullshit artist, I had no idea."

"They found him dead in his apartment. He left a note."

"Now that is sad. But tell me something, what did he say in the note? Did he say he killed himself because she wanted you more than him?"

What did I ever do to her or her family other than fall in love with her kid sister?

"She called me on the phone. She sounded terrible. I thought she might do something crazy. I was really worried, so I went to her place thinking I might be able to help her get through a bad moment."

"How dashing of you. You're a regular knight in shining armor, aren't you, riding your stallion across town to rescue that poor woman from doing the unthinkable. Oh, I bet you got her through that terrible moment, and in spectacular fashion. Well, kudos to you, Lucas Amado!"

She was looking deep into me, and for the briefest moment I saw Bear grinning behind those green eyes.

"I screwed up. It was a one-time screw-up. It's never going to happen again."

"Never? Hmm. This guy I know told me he couldn't stop cheating on his wife. He said it was like eating ice cream. He just couldn't put his spoon down."

She had the strangest smile on her face when she said that, and I thought how different she and Callie were.

"You don't want to go around saying stuff like that, Hadley. People might get the wrong idea."

She laughed off my remark. "Of all people, you giving me advice, how comical."

Then she grew silent. I thought she was going to get up and leave but instead she said, "So then you went and unburdened yourself on Callie?"

"She really didn't tell you anything?"

"My sister's so misguided, the way she's always protected you… But, you know, actually, I don't think it's that so much anymore. I think she's finally beginning to realize we were right about you all along, and she's having so much trouble coming to terms with that. You can imagine, can't you? It's as if her whole life turned out to be a lie."

I felt like I had slipped and fallen into a slimy river, and Hadley was all alligator, slippery, strong and hard-toothed, impossible to handle. She was thrashing up my old doubts, tearing open my old wounds. Was she privy to her sister's secret thoughts?

At a glance I could see that she understood full well the damage she was inflicting, that possibly she had gone a bit too far, and it seemed to me some nudge of conscience, some subtle sense of shame kept her from raising her eyes to look at me. She stared down at her drink as she sipped through the straw.

"No, I never told Callie," I said.

Finally, Hadley looked up. "So, who told her, the grieving old whore?"

"Look, I need to talk to Callie."

"I told you, and I'll say it again, she's not here. They were with us for a couple of days, that's it. She and Johnny and Mom. But they aren't here anymore."

"You have to tell me where they are."

"I don't have to tell you anything, and besides, she does not want to see you. Do you understand what I'm saying? Callie does not want to see you."

"Where are they, Hadley?"

"I have to get home. Brock's wondering why I'm taking so long."

I slapped a five on the table to cover Hadley's drink and the tip, got up and ran out to the street. By the time Hadley got to her car I'd already blocked the BMW's exit with the rental.

Hadley stormed up to my driver side window.

"I'm counting to ten," she said. "If you don't move your stupid car I'm walking into that pharmacy and telling the attendant I'm being harassed by a man with New Jersey plates and would he please call the police."

She began counting in a loud voice but by the time she reached *seven* she stopped with an angry groan. I got out of the rental and faced her.

"You are a pain in my ass!" she cried.

She drew a pen and small notepad out of her purse and scribbled off a few lines. She tore the sheet and thrust it at me.

"Whose address?" I said.

"Oh my God! Adeline's, who else's would it be?"

"Up in Canada?"

"Spare me the melodrama. It's Niagara Falls, not Saskatch-ewan."

I stepped toward her to kiss her cheek but she recoiled. I backed off feeling like a fool. She stared at me for a few seconds and seemed on the verge of saying something, but then she got in her car.

Before driving off I glanced over at her. She was sitting in the driver's seat with her sunglasses on, hands on the steering wheel and staring straight ahead, and for a moment she looked just like Callie.

Chapter 42

The telephone rang while I was in the bedroom checking the expiration date of my passport. I ran into the living room.

"Hello?"

I grimaced at the sound of my desperate voice and pressed my ear against the ocean-like drone. She was there somewhere in the middle of that vast and distant place. I could sense her hesitating.

Don't hang up, darling.

"Callie?"

Callie, please.

"Callie?"

An indistinct movement and then—

"Remember when you said we needed to talk?"

"Talk?"

"You don't remember?"

"Marla?"

Her voice was suddenly so clear it almost had fingers and breasts and I could have sworn she was in the apartment standing to my left. I whirled and saw my passport flipped over on the floor in the bedroom.

"It doesn't matter," she said, "just meet me at River Park tomorrow at 2:00, okay? You know where."

But I don't want to see you.

"Okay?" she said. "Did you hear me?"

"No, wait…"

Someone told her I knew everything, and now she was going to tell me her side of the story. But I didn't care about any of it, not Rolonda nor the boy, nor what she did all those years ago. I had to go find my wife and baby son. I didn't need or want any explanations.

"What's the matter?" she said.

I don't care, don't you understand? Just let me be.

"Lucas, are you there?"

No, I'm not here. Please go away!

The phone grew heavy like steel in my hand as I imagined her ample figure spread over that couch in dreamy repose, her chiseled nostrils breathing me in, the fingers of her free hand curling a strand of long brown hair round and round and round—and the phone grown cold and heavy like a knife in my hand—and those nimble cherry-tipped fingertips releasing one slow button at a time, her eyes like turbulent waves pulling me down.

I shook the phone and the image vanished and my teeth stopped grinding.

"Lucas, what is it? Please don't be angry with me. I won't be bad, I promise you."

"For God's sake, stop talking like that. I'll be there, okay? But you have to stop talking like that."

After a few moments of silence, she hung up the phone.

AT FIRST glance she was a young dreamer sitting at the same park bench where I had waited for Marla back in the summer just days after Borders's funeral. She wasn't completely alone. Pigeons were strutting about in front of her on the concrete walk, their polished little heads bobbing. She had brought with her a bag of bread-crumbs for the pigeons.

Her right leg hung over her left, the tip of her low-cut black suede boot curled up just a tad baiting the cloudless sky. She wore a denim skirt and light gray down jacket with a fur-trimmed hood thrown back, and her dark brown hair looked soft and full, probably from having been washed and dried earlier that day. Her head was turned away from me.

It was a lovely and disturbing image. I suspected she had arranged this view of herself, pigeons and all. She'd customized it for me the way a skilled photographer might arrange his subject for optimal visual impact. She must have seen me coming from a distance before I even knew she was there.

What kind of person orchestrates such scenarios? A dreamer? A faker? A fantasy maker? She was trying to shape reality to her preferred form and texture. And by being there, wasn't I helping her perpetuate her fallacy?

I slowed my pace. Maybe I was reading too much into all of this, maybe I was the dreamer faker fantasy maker conjuring up my own preferred forms and textures, my own special little world in which to crawl and hide from time and circumstance.

She uncrossed her legs and stretched them out in the air before her, toes curled up toward the sky. I stopped to watch. She drew her hands from her coat pockets and rubbed them together and then brushed them over her thighs several times from waist to knees before her heels touched ground again.

Without intending to—maybe without wanting to—I felt again inside me the warm, pulsing silence of that convoluted evening and found myself revisiting that place of doom.

I closed my eyes and begged for cold blood to displace the heat coursing through my body. It should have been Callie on the phone, not Marla with her sordid secrets and family ruins and Serenity Prayer encircled by cheap little flowers.

She say Miss Tupo leading you down the road to perdition.

"Hey, Mister!"

She was walking toward me, hands in her coat pockets, smiling as if our phone conversation had never happened.

"Hi, your hair, it looks nice," I said.

"Thanks, I've been trying this new peppermint conditioner."

"Oh, yeah, peppermint."

"I wanted to change things up a little... So what were you thinking?"

"Excuse me?"

"Oh, I mean now. You were standing there with your eyes closed. I was watching you. You didn't even know I was here. What were you thinking about?"

"You know, just stuff."

Marla turned serious.

"I heard about Callie moving out. How is she?"

"I haven't really had a chance to talk to her much since I got home from the hospital."

"Right, right, I understand. Hey, do you mind if we walk a bit? I was just starting to feel cold."

"Oh, I'm sorry, I thought you said two o'clock."

"I did say two. I got here early. I wanted to think over what I was going to say to you, like when people practice where they're going to give a speech before they give it."

"So you've prepared a speech for me?"

"You're funny. No, not a speech, just a couple of things I wanted to tell you."

I looked into her eyes in as kindly a manner as I could manage, despite my growing discomfort, and we walked in silence.

"People say all kinds of things," she said a short while later after coming to a sudden stop, her tone hinting at indignation.

I slowed my pace but kept walking a couple of steps ahead thinking she would follow, but she was waiting for me to turn around.

"Please don't do that," she said. "Please don't act like you're totally in the dark."

I walked back and stood in front of her feeling a little confused and a little exposed.

"I saw you talking with Virgil and Cosmo."

I stared at her, trying to buy a few seconds.

"Yeah, that Cosmo is quite a character," I said.

Marla sighed and brushed back a strand of hair.

"I don't know what you've heard about me, but I can tell you I am so finished with putting my trust in people."

She stared at me. I think she was just waiting for me to respond, but I had already decided it was in my best interests to keep my mouth shut, at least until I knew exactly what she was talking about. I nodded my head in vague affirmation and she continued.

"The week before you ended up in the hospital? That Saturday morning, I went to the office really early to get my journal. With everything that was going on I forgot to bring it home and I couldn't remember if I'd locked it in my desk drawer. Stupid, right, like why is she telling me this."

"No, not at all, go ahead, I'm listening."

"I'm telling you this because of Rolonda Belford."

"Right, right, Rolonda the weekend dispatcher."

Marla looked at me with mild suspicion before resuming.

"She doesn't have her own desk. She uses mine. And, by the way, did you know her husband's a dentist?"

"No kidding."

"So what's she doing at Galaxy anyway?"

"What do you mean?"

"She doesn't need the money. Plenty of other people could use that money. Why is she at Galaxy? I don't understand it. And besides, I'm the kind of person who gets along with everybody, but not her. It's like she was put there to punish me. I get there first thing to avoid running into her, right? But guess who shows up early, like she was planning for me to be there? She doesn't say a word, just stares at my journal like it's a bag of stolen money. I'm thinking to hell with this and walk right past her without saying a word. But this woman just cannot help herself. She shakes her head like this and says, 'Uh-uh-uh.'"

"That's all she said?"

"Oh, she's a regular wordsmith that one, does it all the time to me."

"Did you ask her to stop doing that?"

Marla sighed and shook her head.

"I was so tired of her trying to make me feel like I'm this evil woman that I absolutely knew I was either going to zip her mouth shut right then and there or stab her in the face with a pen."

"Whoa, easy there, Marla. So I'm assuming you zipped her mouth shut, right?"

"I did, Lucas."

"How did you manage it?"

"I confessed."

"You confessed? What did you…? I mean, you don't have to tell me."

"You have to understand, Lucas, she had pushed me to the limit."

"I do understand, and if you think it would help you to tell me what you said to her…"

"It would help me a great deal, actually."

"So…"

"I've been wanting to tell you, but…"

"It's okay, tell me."

"I told her, I told Rolonda."

"Right, you did. You told her?"

"About us."

"Okay, you mean about—"

"Yes, that."

"Right, I understand, but how did you tell her? I mean, how did you put it?"

"How did I put it, Lucas?"

"I'd like to know what you said to her."

"Exactly what I said to her?"

"Yes."

"I said exactly this. 'Rolonda, because you love sticking your nose where it doesn't belong, you'll be happy to know Lucas Amado and I fucked each other's brains out on my living room couch.'"

I don't remember my mouth opening at the sound of those words until the cool autumn air nipping at my teeth and gums brought it to my attention.

"So maybe it was selfish of me to put it like that," Marla said with an edge to her voice. "Maybe I could have said it in a nicer way. I'm sorry that you think I went too far, but you don't know what it's like. I couldn't bear it any longer, so I did what I had to do to make her stop. You should have seen the look on her face."

I licked my lips. I'd known it was coming, and yet...

"I'm sorry, okay?" She shook her head and stared at me. "I guess I'm an evil woman like Rolonda said. I guess I must be a witch. I should be tied to a post and set on fire."

I had nothing of value to say to her. I spoke out of sheer inertia.

"It's done, we did what we did. Nothing we can do about it now."

She looked confused, thrown for a loop.

"Is that all you have to say?"

"I don't know, maybe going forward, maybe we can control things better going forward."

"But there are things I have no control over, Lucas."

She looked away and shook her head. Then came the smile, bitter as a lime. She was laying the groundwork, prepping me, gearing herself up to tell me the rest of the story.

"There's something else I need to confess," she said.

"You really want to do this?"

"Yes, I want to and have to."

"Are you sure, Marla?"

"You've seen for yourself, Lucas, how selfish I am."

"We're all selfish to some extent."

"But what I did to you, and to Callie, it's unforgiveable."

"Stop it, don't say that. I'm the one that screwed up. I told you already, didn't I?"

My words smoothed away the edge in her. She gazed at me with almost childlike expectation, the way Angel had, I realized.

Can you fix my life?

Seduced by her need, and by the erroneously conceived idea of life-altering power residing within me, I said, "Despite all that's happened, Marla, I believe there's a more beautiful you waiting to emerge." The words slipped out of my mouth with all the forethought of a groan.

"Oh, wow, you *are* the sweetest one, Lucas, did you know that? And your hair, I wonder why you cut it so short. I've been thinking about it, you know, how it makes you look like a boy. Do you mind if I touch it? I'd like to touch it so very much. Are you sure? I don't know that I've ever met a boy as sweet as you."

She touched my hair where Bear's rifle butt had struck me. I felt her fingers briefly explore the fresh scarring. I wanted to say stop, please, but I couldn't or wouldn't.

When she drew her hand away, she smiled like Mona Lisa.

"I thought I was doing the right thing," she said, her features darkening suddenly.

I gazed at her with growing anxiety.

"I thought I could make it better, but I've come to realize there are so many things I just don't understand, so much of life and living I just don't get."

"We're all trying to figure it out," I said.

"That woman of God who goes to church every Sunday and sings in the choir. She's got it all figured out."

"Are you talking about Rolonda?"

"Who else have we been talking about, Lucas? Didn't Virgil tell you?"

"He told me that Rolonda called Callie after you told Rolonda about us."

"And?"

"And what?"

"They didn't tell you what happened afterwards?"

"I'm not sure I know what you mean. Cosmo told me that Rolonda called Callie after talking to you, but apparently that didn't happen until the following Thursday, like she couldn't decide whether she should or not. That's when Callie stopped talking to me."

"Well, just so you know, she called me after talking to Callie, okay?" Marla said.

"I don't get it. Why would she do that?"

"To tell me."

"That she called Callie?"

"Yes, and to light a fire of lies."

"What do you mean a fire of lies? What lies?"

"A fire of lies to consume me."

"What are you talking about, Marla? What lies? Maybe she just told Callie the truth."

"She called to tell me she told Callie everything, and she said I was going to burn in hell."

"What do you mean she told Callie *everything*?"

"She said I was going to burn in hell, Lucas."

"Marla, that's ridiculous, and what do you mean she told Callie everything?"

"Everything could be anything, don't you see, like you and me being lovers from the beginning, from that first weekend when Callie decided to leave you to go to Paris."

"Callie didn't decide anything, I made her go. She didn't want to go. But that aside, you didn't tell Rolonda that, did you?"

"Oh, my God!"

"No, of course not, of course you didn't."

"I wasn't about to take any chances, Lucas. That's why I called her. Believe me, it was one of the hardest things I've ever had to do."

The left side of my head—where Bear had struck me, where *Senhor* Cardosa had paused briefly, where Marla had touched me—immediately began to throb. I located the center of pain with my fingers and pressed down and worked the pain.

"You called Callie?"

"I'm sorry, but I felt I had no choice. I was so concerned. What if Callie believed all those made-up things?"

"Made up things? So you called Callie?"

"I had no choice."

"What did you say to her, Marla?"

She shook her head, as if too much was being expected of her.

"What did Callie say?" I said raising my voice.

"I tried, I really did. I tried to explain everything, but she didn't say a word to me. I could hear the baby fussing in the background, but Callie didn't move. She didn't hang up on me. It would have been better if she had just slammed the phone down, but she kept listening to me talk and never said a word. It was awful. I finally gave up and said good-bye Callie, I'm so sorry. What else was I supposed to do?"

I started walking away from her and she hurried to catch up.

"Please don't be angry with me," she said touching my arm.

I stopped and glanced at her strange excited face. I don't know what she saw in mine. Hatred, pity, sorrow? All of the above? I resumed my disembodied stroll beset by numerous doubts.

There was no way of knowing what Marla had said to Callie, or what Rolonda had said to her. I suspected Rolonda might have embellished a bit, but I didn't think she'd blatantly lie. Of course, Marla's colorful confession didn't help matters in that regard. There were too many variables. Rolonda's story and Marla's story and Callie's interpretation of each of those stories, and how each of those stories impacted one another inside Callie's head, and there was my own story and all the questions and speculations and fears and weariness that come from walking in a world littered with ruined lives and cheap clichés.

It's never too late it's never too late it's never too late...

How tiresome it all was. She was tired, I was tired, we were all so damn tired of trying to be better or saying to hell with it or being stuck somewhere in between, in a kind of conscious coma, all of us dragging heavy legs across the dry and empty expanse of the seventies, all the weary conflicted and deformed destined to toil amid the drought of imagination and compassion that had calcified what was most human in us.

Wish I had a pen, wish I had a pad and pen to jot down my foolosophical meanderings. *Hey Marla, got a pen, got a pad and pen?* I started laughing at myself and at Marla and at the theater of thinning rust-colored boughs floating above and all around us.

"What the hell is going on?" I shouted out to the sun that was peeking at us through the thin colored patches of dying leaves. I laughed even harder hearing my own peculiar-sounding voice cracking through the silence, shaking awake the sleepy grass and giving squirrels a moment to pause and reflect.

Marla turned to me with a hopeful and perplexed expression. She saw that I was smiling and shaking my head like someone who'd just heard the best joke, and she was encouraged and delighted by the development. She slapped my forearm and cried out, "First one to the tennis court wins!"

Before I could caution her Marla ran off in her low-cut black suede boots. She was the kind of woman that never, ever, looked quite right running, and probably never did even in her youth. The boot heels proved averse to such shenanigans and served only to compound the awkwardness of her strides. Before long her right side collapsed and she tumbled to the concrete walk. I ran to her side. She was crunched in pain, her hand groping at her ankle. I resisted the urge to say are you okay?

"Come on, Marla, let me help you get to that bench over there."

She wouldn't move. She wouldn't speak. She lay in a twisted heap, her freshly washed hair obscuring her features. Her right hand hovered over the bad ankle and her rigid left arm kept her from tilting over.

"Marla, let's try to get you up, okay?"

I took her hand and arm but she wouldn't budge. Her hair hung like a dark veil over her face. I knelt in front of her and parted her hair. She lifted her head just enough for me to get a close look at her swollen, tear-streaked face. As I watched, the youthful-looking hair seemed to change before my eyes, grow lusterless and limp, and her features seemed to grow heavy with age.

"Come on, buddy, try to get up," I said.

She got up and I helped her over to the nearest bench. Two ten-year olds raced past on stingray bikes crying out "Ha-ha! Ha-ha!" in a vile imitation of honking ducks.

"Can I take a look?"

I took her unresponsiveness for a yes and carefully removed her boot.

"It's beginning to swell up. I'm taking you to the Emergency Room."

She shook her head. "No, it's nothing, it's not that bad."

"Are you in a lot of pain?"

She took a deep breath but said nothing.

"Okay, look, I'll take you to your apartment. We need to put some ice on that ankle and keep it raised."

"I can drive. I can get myself home."

I helped her get up and she tried to walk without my assistance but collapsed with a sharp cry.

"That's it, I'm driving," I said. "We'll go in your car. We'll see how you do at home. I'll hang out a while until I know you can stand up on your own. But if it gets worse, I'm taking you to the hospital."

She felt heavier now as I put my arm around her waist and helped her up again. She hung her arm over my shoulder and we made our way to her car.

"God hates me," she said in a whisper. There was no terror in what she said or how she said it, no self-pity, no obvious marks of devastation. It was a dark statement of fact issued with resignation, the way one might feel when recognizing the opportunity of a lifetime squandered. Hell awaited her, like Rolonda suggested, or maybe hell was here and now.

I could pretend I hadn't heard what she said. Or I could assure her, No, Marla, God doesn't hate you. He can't because he's not paying attention. Would that release her? Would it release me? Would it set us both free?

You will know the truth, and the truth will set you free.

Ah, the truth...

A couple of times she came to a stop and I thought she was going to say something or begin to sob or just give up and drop to the ground. I thought I was going to have to carry her to her car and then up the stairs to her apartment, and I wondered if I was physically up to the task, and if not, what would we do? But each time when it seemed her misery had peaked, she bit her lower lip and soldiered on, and each new crisis was followed by a trembling breath.

"You're wrong about God," I said.

She stopped, we stopped. She wanted to know, she had to know.

"Don't you know how much he loves you?"

She didn't respond in any way. I considered saying it again, but I knew it would come out wrong the second time.

We said nothing more after that and continued on our way, and I was well aware of the immediate danger, to me, not her. Nothing she herself had planned, said, or done. It was me, me and him, wandering through dark woods, one the hunted, the other the hunter.

Chapter 43

I gave Marla two aspirin, sat her on the couch, and placed an ottoman beneath her ankle. I went to the freezer, put ice in a plastic bag, pulled up a chair to sit on, and held the ice against her flesh and bone for several minutes, shifting it now and again over the injured area so the cold wouldn't burn her skin.

All that was fine and proper, but in the small warm silence of her apartment it was impossible to suppress the memory of what we'd done on that couch. It was like having a third person in the room offering us a platter of tempting images, sounds and sensations. Would you like to try another, Miss Tupo? Mr. Amado? It didn't take me long to start paying too close attention to the sound and rhythm of her breathing. I forced myself to get up.

"The ice is melting," I said. "I'll go get more."

The undisclosed issue about the boy was still on my mind and offered a path to a safer place. At the refrigerator I stopped and turned around.

"There was more you wanted to tell me," I said. "That speech. I think talking would help you get your mind off the pain."

"I never said I had a speech. You said that."

"Oh, I don't mean speech. Things, you know. There were things you wanted to tell me."

"I already did."

"You did, but—"

"But what?"

"I just thought… Ah, never mind, just this banged-up head of mine acting up."

I came back with fresh ice and sat down and applied it to her ankle.

"Is it feeling any better?"

"It's kind of numb."

"Numb is good, right?"

She looked at me, her mouth lined with irony.

"I'll take your word for it," she said.

"Fair enough."

Encouraged by her somewhat lightened tone I said, "Can I share something with you?"

"Do I have a choice?"

"You'll think it's silly, never mind."

"You have to tell me now because you've made me curious."

"It has to do with breathing. Still interested?"

"Breathing. I've heard of it. It's a good thing, right?"

"Ha, yes, but this isn't ordinary breathing. It has the power to take you somewhere else. All you have to do is inhale as you say a word, and exhale as you say another word."

I paused but got no reaction. Didn't she want to know what words?

"Okay, so first you breathe in *Jesus* and then you breathe out *Mercy, Jesus* on the inhale, *Mercy* on the exhale, and you do it over and over. Some people swear by it, say it brings them peace. So, what do you think? Are you willing to give it a shot?"

I was expecting her to laugh or change the subject, but she didn't say a word, and her numbness ramped up the gnawing dissatisfaction inside me regarding me and her and now this unsolicited arrangement and what it might portend, and I realized I was willingly complicit in whatever madness was primed to follow.

You see, I needed more, I wanted more, for her, for me, from the ever-changing here and now, though I had no clue what that more was nor what the moment entailed or promised, if anything. I knew for Marla *more* couldn't be me, and for me it couldn't be her, and I was determined to flesh that more out, summon it forth. I saw myself as a magician digging down into the magic hat that was Marla's psyche, climbing inside it and feeling around for some surprising wondrous thing to pull out.

And then, in a strange meek voice that set off a tiny alarm inside me, she said, "I'll try."

I closed my eyes and all I could think to do was demonstrate the *Jesus Prayer* as Callie had taught me. It didn't take me long to step outside myself and take a good hard look at the grotesque pantomime I was performing, and needless to say, I put an abrupt, ungracious end to it.

"I'm not good at this," I said trying to smile away the self-disgust.

Marla stared at me for a long while. The lines in her skin were receding, and her features were settling into a kind of smooth stoicism. I suspected she had arrived at an understanding about me and the peculiar circumstances that had brought us to this point. She seemed reflective and most likely disabused of any illusions she'd had about me. I considered that I might unwittingly be serving a useful purpose in her life after all.

I couldn't bring myself to say anything more. She didn't help matters with her silence. I concentrated on the ice. I stared at my hand holding the ice against her ankle. The ice became like a shield, or a hiding place, and we said nothing to each other.

I don't know how much time had passed when she pushed her hands down onto the couch to shift her hips and move her injured limb. I had kept the ice far too long on the same spot and it must have been hurting her. Cold drops were dripping off my hand onto the ottoman and floor. I got up and put the melting ice in the sink. I stared at the white tiled backsplash with the grimy seams that needed to be scoured clean.

I needed to be scoured clean. A thorough cleaning from top to bottom was what I needed. Who the hell was I to go around preaching Jesus? Stick to what you know, fool. I knew the swelling was down and that the aspirin had kicked in. There was no point hanging around any longer. Marla could get up and hop along on one leg if she had to. It wouldn't kill her. I did what I could for her and now I had to go.

When I turned around, I saw that Marla's eyes were shut. She was sitting erect, both feet flat on the floor, hands folded on her lap. She was taking deep, slow breaths. I drew closer and saw that her lips were moving in time with her breaths. I read the words on her lips and heard the whispers. I stood transfixed, mystified and a little unsettled as I observed her. I could hardly bring myself to breathe.

At one point she took a shuddering breath and opened her eyes. When she saw me standing before her she began to sob. I sat next to her on the couch. Should I comfort her? Was any of this real, or was it just another spectacle, a new game for us to play?

At times she appeared calm and ready to speak, and she'd look at me and try to smile, but after a few words she would begin to sob again. I took her hand but my touch made her tremble all the more and this caused me further confusion. At one point, in an almost desperate gesture, I put my arms around her as if to protect her from whatever sinister force was roiling within her to shatter her person into a thousand unrecoverable pieces. When she pressed her cheek to my chest and began to rock and wail like a keening widow, I envisioned how this day might end.

In an excited flush of terror, I saw myself tumbling down the long dark well again, condemned to lose all I loved and become for the rest of my days a madwoman's antidote to reality.

Get up, you fool, get up! Leave before it's too late!

But I couldn't get up. I closed my eyes and waited, and as the minutes passed, I began to breathe a new kind of air—rarified and pristine—and I felt as if I were anticipating some ineffable occurrence, something too large for my imagination to conceive. Another quarter-hour, maybe a half-hour passed. I was conscious of Marla's every tear and moan and breath, the small movements of her hands and limbs, the varying heated pressures where her body touched mine, and when she had drained herself to exhaustion, I helped her get up and she limped to the bathroom and splashed cold water on her face.

I handed her a towel and after she had dried her face, I asked her if she was okay but only because I needed her to say something I could comprehend. She smiled at me in the most unusual way, the way I imagined a woman brought back from the dead might smile.

My astonished look must have prompted her to temper her joy. With only the shadow of that remarkable smile left for me to contemplate, she touched my cheek and told me to go home.

"I'm fine now, Lucas. Really, I am, I'm fine."

When I was back on the street, I realized I'd forgotten to call for a taxi, but I had no interest in walking back to Marla's apartment, so I started walking down the street.

Chapter 44

The woman with the whining preschoolers, the shape-shifting pile of laundry, the washer-dryer thump and roll all seemed merged into one pale-lit groaning toiling entity. When she looked up I smiled to assure her I was no thug, but her harsh gaze suggested I go peddle my gallantry elsewhere. I located the laundromat pay phone and within minutes the taxi stopped out front and drove me through the dark Legacy City streets back to the park.

I was glad to see my car hadn't been towed or vandalized but that didn't keep me from experiencing a vague sense of having been cheated.

On my way home I stopped at a liquor store and bought a bottle of vodka. I sat at the kitchen table and started sipping straight from the bottle. All I wanted in the world was to have my family back, I said to the bottle, but the bottle laughed at me as its nimble fingers began unbuttoning Marla's blouse.

Then the bottle told me Niagara Falls was a fairy tale and the idea of restoring my family a pipe dream. I lifted the bottle and swallowed long and hard. I needed somebody to talk to. I thought of calling Virgil but Amy might pick up. I didn't want to talk to Amy though I liked her well enough. Virgil was always telling her he was having a drink with me even when he wasn't. I sometimes wondered if Amy hated me. No, I didn't want to talk to Amy so I didn't call Virgil.

I placed a kitchen chair at the foot of the bed facing the headboard and sat with the bottle dangling from my hand. In between sips I stared at the crucifix José had bequeathed us—the one that had hung over my parents' bed all those years in their Legacy City apartment.

"You must have made a chair like the one I'm sitting on," I said. "You must have measured and sawed and nailed and sanded just like me in eighth grade wood shop."

I closed my eyes and lowered my head and felt the shift of thorns claw at my skull and split open my scalp. I felt around the torn flesh with my fingertips and looked up again.

"How much did you charge? I mean, you didn't just give it away, did you?"

I took another sip and waited and studied the crown, the nose, the beard, worked my way down the bloody trail to the nailed-together feet.

"And when the rich man stiffed you, did you just let it go?"

I wanted to see the hidden eyes. I got up on my feet and moved closer and lifted the bottle and drank and stared a long time at the broken face.

"I need to know one thing, are you Mr. Galaxy, or am I?"

I stared until my eyes burned and then I paced up and down the apartment. I went to the kitchen table and picked up the small sheet Hadley had given me. The letters and numbers squirmed like maggots. Repulsed, I moved the sheet away from my face and then drew it close again real slow until the characters settled in. I walked over to the phone and noticed the *New Message* light flashing.

Marla, Marla, Marla...

She called after I left. Oh, I knew what she was going to say. She was going to explain what had happened, or what she thought or pretended had happened.

She was going to ask if I wouldn't mind returning to keep her company for a little while, maybe help her walk around her cozy apartment, maybe sit with her on the couch and discuss Law School and career aspirations, talk about the future and maybe say something about Hester Prynne and that scarlet letter.

I pressed the *Message* button and heard a faint sigh followed by silence.

"It's me."

I felt a stab of pain between my eyes as I frowned and leaned toward the Phone-Mate.

"Hadley told me she spoke with you in Greenwich... I really don't have much to say to you. Johnny's fine, okay? But you, Lucas, you must not call me and you must not come here. I don't want to see you. Please don't come because I will not see you nor talk to you. I need time and space. I don't know what's going to happen..."

Callie's voice faltered in the end, and I felt consoled by her moment of weakness, the way a drowning man might be consoled by the beauty of the sky as he breathes his last breath.

It took her a long time to hang up. I played the message over and over again at high volume, desperate to pry forth every unspoken word and thought. How many times did I hear her words and silence? I stopped finally and stared at the phone until the room began to spin.

When I had steadied myself enough, I picked up the telephone and began to dial Adeline and Stan's number. Halfway there my fingers locked and my head seemed to be everywhere but on my shoulders.

I hung up the phone, took one last punitive swig of vodka, stumbled across the living room and threw myself face down on the bed.

Chapter 45

There had to be some mistake. I passed the house and slowed down at the corner to check the sign: Stratford Street. Under the street lamp I took a closer look at Hadley's note, *137 Stratford Street*. So where was the grand old house? And where was Grace's Cadillac?

I circled the block to offer reality a chance to reset, and I checked off the tiny single-family cape houses one by one. Turning back onto Stratford there it was again, dingy and dispiriting, 137 Stratford Street. I drove down to the corner and made a wide looping left turn in the intersection and drove back and parked the rental against the curb opposite the house.

The brick and aluminum houses stood like battered sentinels on narrow lots separated by asphalt drives that had been spitting up gravel, dirt and weeds probably since World War I. Above the porch overhang of Adeline and Stan's purported residence a shallow gable with two compressed windows covered the house like a cap over dead eyes. In the middle of the tiny front yard a leafless tree extended one long limb toward the house like a beggar.

Was this all Stan had to show for the two businesses Adeline had boasted about?

It was about a twenty-minute walk down to the Falls from there, I estimated, and maybe a bit more to the Tower center where Stan's glassblowing shop was supposed to be located.

I leaned back the driver seat and scoped the property. The house seemed empty but for the thin lines of light at the corners of the window shades. After all the driving and the anticipation and the worry I couldn't bring myself to go knock on the door. I was drained.

A long while of should I's and shouldn't I's passed before a bulky Monte Carlo squeezed into the driveway. An old man emerged from the driver side and paused to press his hands against his lower back.

It was Stan all right. He stepped around the car and moved with a forward lean, his hand coaxing the metal handrail and brick steps closer.

I watched him disappear behind the incongruously elegant front door and then I stared for a while at the ugly little house. They weren't here. On my way to Stratford Street I had driven past a Hilton Hotel. I pulled away from the curb and headed back that way.

IT WAS STILL dark when I woke up from wandering through poorly lit hallways and entering rooms that resembled busy kitchens crowded with faceless workers. José had been in mid-monologue when I walked into the big room. People were zigzagging behind and before him, but he remained focused on the task at hand. He spread a white tablecloth over a small round table. There's a leak in the fuel tank, he was saying, and corrosion. The corrosion needs to be taken care of. He was emphatic about it. So many things need seeing to, he said. He left a cup of red wine in the center of the round table, told me to drink it, and walked away.

The morning was crisp and clear and long. The center opened at 9:00 AM, I was told by the front desk. That was when most of the shops opened, though not all, especially this time of year. Some shops—such as the glassblower's—could open at any time. Of course, in November there were fewer tourists and, most likely, the shop would open later than usual, if it opened at all.

I was hoping to avoid Stan because of the wedding and all that had happened, so I waited until 9:00 before getting in the rental and driving back to 137 Stratford Street. The driveway was empty and there was still no sign of Grace's car. I took a deep breath and walked to the front door and knocked. I couldn't hear any voices or detect any movement. I knocked again, harder.

The deadbolt slid open with a dull metallic thud. The door opened and it took Stan a moment to recognize me.

"Lucas," he said. "Come in, come in."

I think I was more surprised to see him than he was to see me. I stepped inside the small living room and listened for sounds. Stan's eyes were droopy and sad. It made me nervous.

"Stan, where are they?"

"Can I get you some coffee, Lucas?"

"No, I'm fine. Please tell me where they are."

"Callie and Johnny are fine. Walk with me to the kitchen. I was just about to pour myself a second cup."

A large leather-bound volume lay open on the kitchen table.

"Did you know that William Faulkner read *Don Quixote* once a year?" Stan said. "He found the book indispensable, and here I am at seventy-five reading it for the very first time."

"My father was reading it too, but he wasn't able to finish it."

"I have not had the chance to speak to you, Lucas. I am so sorry about your father's passing…"

I nodded. "Thank you."

After a respectful pause, Stan said, "I believe no true book is ever finished."

"I think you're right about that, Stan, but tell me, where are they? I don't see Grace's car."

"Adeline went to meet them for breakfast. I will take you to them soon, but please sit."

"I thought they were staying with you."

"Oh no, only for the first night. You do not imagine Grace would tolerate such modest accommodations for longer than necessary, do you?"

"Are they staying in a hotel?"

"Yes, the Hilton."

"The one near the Tower?"

"Yes, it is the only Hilton in town."

I felt the hairs on my arms rise. How close had I come to seeing them? How far apart were we as we slept in our separate rooms? Stan poured coffee into a Niagara Falls souvenir mug and set it on the table before me.

"In case you change your mind," he said. "That is your car out front?"

"It is."

"Good. In a short while then we'll drive down. But let them have their breakfast, if that is all right with you. They have been waiting for a fine day like today."

Stan set a bowl of sugar and a carton of milk in front of me.

"I have thought about you a great deal since I last saw you, Lucas."

"The wedding fiasco."

"A most unusual day."

"I drank too much."

"You were not the only one."

I studied the tumbling falls on the coffee mug.

"Callie has every right to be angry with me," I said.

Stan considered my words.

"In your absence she has forgotten how to smile," he said.

I frowned at the circle of coffee and looked up at him.

"My absence? I wasn't the one who left."

For several moments Stan nodded without speaking.

"I understand, my friend," he said. "I am glad you have come."

293

Something about Stan reminded me of Dr. Greene. Was it the long hard years, the big open books, the words that were always more than just words?

"So Johnny," I said, "he's been a good boy?"

"Oh, let me tell you, your son is a force of nature."

I had to smile imagining the chaos unleashed that first night by the one and only Johnny Amado.

"Stan, I have to ask you something. At the wedding, I believe you saw me as I was walking out onto the patio. Do you remember? I was walking with a tall woman with very short almost white hair. I was with such a woman, wasn't I?"

"Yes, you did not imagine it."

"I've made some bad decisions."

Stan closed the book and placed his gnarled blue-veined hand upon the engraved image of the mounted Knight of La Mancha, the mad and honorable righter of wrongs.

"I found you lying in the woods."

"So it was you. I thought so. Did you happen to see a man?"

"A corpulent man, yes. I have dealt with such men before. I have seen women like the one you mentioned also…"

"Where did you see him?"

"It was getting dark, and my concern for you led me outside. I looked out over the course at the trees. When I saw the man coming along the side of the building with a wild look in his eye, I felt something bad had happened to you."

"Did he say anything to you?"

"No, he didn't even look at me. He went inside. When I found you, I rushed back to the hall and spoke to the first waiter I encountered. He led me to the maître d'. I told him one of the guests had been assaulted out on the course, that you were lying unconscious among the trees. He asked me if I or anyone had witnessed this assault. I said no, I didn't think so, but I strongly suspected a man, whom I described to him in great detail.

"The maître d' nodded and made a phone call. Within minutes I was in a patrol car leading the officers to where you lay. An ambulance arrived. There were no flashing lights, no sirens. I overheard one of the police officers say you were drunk and had run into a tree and knocked yourself out.

"I told the officer I was sure you had been assaulted, and I described the corpulent man. He stared at me and began to sniff me like a dog. He patted me on the shoulder and said, 'You like dancing the polka, Grandpa? Would you like another drink?' They all thought it was very funny."

"It doesn't matter."

"Ed Rollo said to me, 'The man you think assaulted Lucas? His father is one of the richest men in the region.'"

"It doesn't matter. I won't ever see those people again."

Stan's face darkened.

"I should have pursued the matter," he said.

"No, Stan. There was nothing more you could do."

"His name is Caspar Barnum. You should at least know the name of the man who might have killed you. I would want to know."

"Caspar Barnum. Okay, Stan."

"I am sorry, Lucas, for everything."

I rose from the table.

"Can we go now?"

"Yes, of course, Lucas. Let us go."

Chapter 46

"That way to Main Street," Stan said as we stood in the Hilton parking lot. "It is not a long walk down from there, though a bit steep for an old man like me. Look, there is the Monte Carlo. And there by the fence, see, Grace's Cadillac."

I walked over to the Cadillac and peered inside. There was Johnny's car seat sitting all alone like a long-lost friend. My hands went up onto the top of the car and my eyes shut out the world.

I felt Stan's hand on my back. "Are you all right?"

I turned around and stared at him. Who was this man?

He patted me on the shoulder and said, "Allow me to go inside for just one moment. Wait here."

Stan walked into the hotel restaurant and returned a couple of minutes later wearing a broad smile.

"They left ten to fifteen minutes ago. Adeline is taking them for a stroll along the riverfront to the Horseshoe Falls."

I studied Stan to make sure it really was Stan. I scanned the parking lot, checked off the Monte Carlo, the Cadillac, the Dodge Colt rental. The cars were real, the parking lot, the Hilton, all real, and Niagara Falls somewhere behind those buildings and down below had to be real, right? I'd seen pictures. We walked toward Main Street.

"It is quite amazing, Lucas. The waters come all the way from the upper Great Lakes and pour 170 feet down into the river."

Would she recoil from me like Hadley?

"... a geographical marvel, really, 2,500 feet wide from Goat Island in the United States to the Canadian side. Yes, Goat Island."

Stan pointed—though there was no need—and I caught my first narrow glimpse of the bold and raucous poetry of the Falls. The walk down took much longer than I would have expected and we wasted no words as Stan dedicated himself to conserving energy.

The breeze flowing up from the Niagara River was cool and pleasant and our slow descent gave me time to reconcile myself to the idea that I had no healing words to offer Callie. I only had myself, with all my scars and deformities, and if that were not enough...

When we reached the bottom, we paused so that Stan could catch his breath.

"People come all year round," he said. "In fewer numbers this time of year... Some prefer it like this... Let's cross here."

"Is this why you settled here?" I said extending my hand toward the crashing waters.

Stan reached for a bench. He seemed to be in some distress and for an instant I was afraid he was going to collapse.

"Adeline loves me too much," he said as he sat down, "too much. I hardly understand it."

He put up his hand indicating I would have to wait a bit and took several deep breaths as he tried to regain control of his body.

"We had a big house... a beautiful house near Toronto..."

He raised his hand again and smiled, a little embarrassed. He pointed in the direction of the waters, as if to divert me from his difficulties.

"We came often as tourists. Three years ago, I said without thinking, 'Adeline, would it not be good to die in such a place?' She wept for me, my poor Adeline... And here we are."

I sat down next to Stan and we stared at the waters.

"Those are the American Falls," he said pointing, "and there, the Bridal Veil Falls. Very nice, very beautiful. But over there, those are the Horseshoe Falls, the most magnificent. Now you go, Lucas, I have already delayed you too much."

I left Stan and made my way along the river walk toward the Horseshoe Falls.

Will I have to master the art of walking on water?

The waters thundered and rose in sweeping mists. I gazed up and down the length of the river, my heart quickened by the raw power and beauty, and by the tantalizing proximity of new life.

I spotted a stroller and a woman. She was sitting on a bench staring at the waters. I slowed my pace. A man ran across the parkway, approached the woman and squatted before her. He held her hands and spoke to her with uncommon excitement, as if the vibrancy of the waters had permeated to his core. They got up and started walking toward me. The man pushed the stroller and continued to talk in an animated manner to the woman, glancing often at her, but the woman seemed far less interested in the man than in the waters.

As they approached, she turned her head suddenly and looked at me as if I were the source of some new sound only she could hear. I thought perhaps I reminded her of someone, or that she sensed in me a shared consuming need neither of us could fully articulate.

Her glance seemed to linger, though I'm sure it was only for a moment, and then she turned her attention back to the waters. As they passed by, I could hear the man speaking in a foreign tongue, and I wondered if she was listening to what he was saying. I turned to follow their progress, but they were soon swallowed by a restless sea of light and flesh and mist.

A horn blast like a terrible wail and the screech of skidding tires pierced my chest like a quick in-and-out knife thrust. In the middle of the parkway a stroller and young woman seemed to vibrate before a stalled car. I dashed out onto the street and began to run toward them. The world bounced as I sprinted toward the woman and her baby.

Breathless seconds later I stumbled and fell at her feet. She eyed me with alarm as she stepped back clutching her screaming baby to her breast. I glanced at the man as I got up from the ground, my hands on fire. A woman—the man's wife?—stood frightened by the passenger side door.

"Are you alright?" I said to the mother of the crying baby.

She nodded and the man said in a heavily accented voice, "Okay? You okay?"

She glared at him. "Sorry, sorry," he said and backed away bowing, praying hands seeking forgiveness. A dazzled looking boy and girl—twins maybe—were craning their necks out one of the rear passenger windows. The car backed up a few feet and curved painstakingly past the stroller and carried the shaken tourists away.

The woman thanked me. The crying stopped and she put the baby back in the stroller and they continued on their way.

"Lucas, are you alright?"

Adeline in blue. Halfway between her and the river walk I spotted Grace. She was staring at me with an inquisitive expression. Several feet behind, partly obscured by her mother's form, Callie occupied some hiding place. Her fingertips slid back and forth over Johnny's stroller handle.

"I'm fine, Adeline," I said as she hugged me.

She walked back toward the river walk, turned her head to check on me and smiled. She said something to Grace and they walked away together.

Callie crossed her arms over her chest as if overcome by a sudden chill. I looked down and saw that my shoelaces had come undone. My hands were scraped raw and my pants were torn at the right knee. I shook my head and slowly looked up and she found my eyes.

It was our first day again, like the day of fallen books and windblown sheets.

I slowed everything down, teased the life force pedal so the moment wouldn't die. I bent down to tie my shoe and when I got up I saw that she was still there. And the stroller with Johnny in it was still there.

Before taking a step, I looked to my right and then to my left. I wasn't going to be tossed, trampled or killed today. It would be such a waste after everything that had happened. When all was clear I started walking slowly toward her, breathing in and breathing out.

Callie didn't know what to do with her hands. Her mouth didn't know what to do. She kind of smiled. I think she tried to laugh but it came out wrong. She started to cry instead, so I ran to her.

Part 9

Grace

Chapter 47

Before I learned her name, before we had any way of knowing who we were to one another, her smile shattered the wall that separates souls and invited love to come along with all its unforeseen chaos and heartbreak. Then she forgave me and the memory of a later smile that burst into happy tears remains an unhealable wound in me, a stigmata of the heart.

Two weeks after we buried Callie and Johnny, Grace tried to kill herself. I found her dying in the condo where the four of us had been living for several months.

On their drive up to Canada to Adeline and Stan's house, Grace had barely spoken to Callie. At one point, at a rest stop, she had gazed at her daughter with dead eyes and told her she could think of no compelling reason to go on living.

"How can you say that?" Callie had countered. "What about Hadley? What about Johnny? What about me?" But Grace only drew further into herself and refused to speak the rest of the way.

After Niagara Falls Grace decided she would continue to live. She secured the condo and managed her Parkinson's and operated in the day-to-day world just enough to at least pretend life was worth living.

Then the accident struck like a cyclone and two of us were swept away and two of us were left behind.

I COULD HEAR Callie joking with Lauren on the telephone one evening and it reminded me of when they were part of the laughing girls' group back at Copernicus. Lauren's first child was to be named Calliope, but they would call her Callie, though Lauren admitted she had yet to run the idea past her husband, Franklin, the father of Johnny's presumptive bride-to-be, so she wasn't really sure that the name would hold up.

Callie had a big smile on her face when she told me all this and before you knew it she and Johnny were in Grace's Cadillac driving up north to the baby shower.

Some people take comfort in familiar sayings. An apple a day keeps the doctor away, and good comes to those who wait, and April showers bring May flowers. Predictability is reassuring when it holds form, but one normal April day it rained and then the rain stopped at night and whoever would have imagined it could drop to below freezing?

A witness saw it happen, the police officer said. The Cadillac was going at a normal speed down a curving merge ramp onto the interstate. The driver lost control of the car, the witness said. Something may have distracted the driver. It wouldn't take much at all, a small animal leaping onto the ramp, a wind-tossed wrapper. Everything can change in an instant, the officer might have said, but didn't.

And before the crocus bloomed Callie and Johnny were gone in a blast of steel and glass. Who would have thought such a thing could happen in April?

I was tracing a short in an attic when it happened. Among the rafters I lost my balance and cut my hand on a misaligned nail.

Hadley was coming down that weekend to visit Grace. She was bringing homemade chocolate chip cookies. She had a surprise to share with us, some very good news indeed. And Callie and I were going somewhere fun, the two of us alone. How long had it been? Hadley was happy for the first time since I'd known her, and she seemed to have developed a spirit of generosity of late and was going to spend Saturday night and watch Johnny and Grace too while we were away.

The pulldown ladder felt loose and rickety. I checked the fastenings to make sure the steps were sound. I observed the beaded metal pull string swaying and keeping time beneath the solitary attic bulb. I entered the low, cramped, suffocating dimly lit space, and my thighs knotted from the strain of prolonged crouching.

I lost my balance and cut my hand on a nail and couldn't remember when I'd last had a tetanus shot. I could smell burnt leaves in the attic, like the scent of death wafting in through the vents.

"Be careful," I had cautioned her before leaving for work. But it was only out of habit, a reflex triggered by repeated recollections of the Falls, the stroller in the middle of the river parkway, the woman holding her crying baby.

I had dreamed the morning away, my thoughts speeding toward quit time and me alone with my girl who forgave me and loved me before the moon, the stars, and all flowers.

I lost my balance and cut my hand, and the world came undone. "Pay attention, Lucas!" José always said. I should have paid closer attention, and maybe Callie sees the ice, makes the easy adjustment, eases into the merge in full control and proceeds without incident to Lauren's baby shower, then comes back to tell me how they all laughed like they used to at the dining hall and how happy Lauren was despite gaining all the weight. And then we'd all get to eat cookies.

But that kind of thinking…

Oh, that kind of thinking engenders monsters.

• • •

HADLEY had forever lost the opportunity to announce to her sister that she was with child. She and her mother stood between Coldwell and me to the left of the caskets. Glum Audrey, fidgety Ed, their daughter Lilly and Hadley's husband, Brock, hovered nearby. Adeline and Stan seemed to have aged ten years since I'd last seen them. They sat alone looking perplexed, as if they were watching the Horseshoe Falls rising from the guts of the earth and shooting upwards into the sky.

The guests moved counter-clockwise in slow, somber procession, as if impelled by some futile time and death-reversing impulse of the collective unconscious: Virgil and Amy, Cosmo Etienne, Rolonda and her husband, Dr. Marcus Belford, Jay Weller and Walter Dunst, Mr. and Mrs. Roseboom, Alfred the accountant and his wife, Jan the receptionist, and techies out of blue wearing ties and jackets. Marla Tupo was dressed in black and gray and wore flat shoes that made her look smaller than I could remember.

Some of the guests touched the mahogany caskets as they passed on their way to us. Some placed a white rose on the smooth shiny wood. Some knelt on the velvet kneeler to pray or to appear to pray.

Inés and Grant suggested I get away, maybe spend some time with them in Seattle. I looked at them as if they were out of their minds. Adriana, who left Enrique and the baby in Zurich, clung to me without saying a word for fear of breaking. When poor pregnant Lauren rushed toward me ahead of her husband, I thought again of babies and strollers and out of control cars and held her shaking swollen body until Franklin gently pulled her away.

It was all staged. None of it was real.

How could it be? I wondered as I watched Caspar and Artemis Barnum lower themselves onto the kneeler.

The wake was coming to an end and guests were streaming out into the night. The last few were going through the formalities, and in those final draining moments all I could do was stare at Caspar Barnum. I watched him embrace Coldwell and then spend a few moments whispering in his ear. Coldwell seemed puzzled and nodded absently and was barely aware of Artemis when she took his hand and patted it without saying a word to him.

Barnum spoke with chilling tenderness to Grace and Hadley, grasping both their hands at once and looking into the eyes of one and then the other reassuringly, as though having secured for them a safe way forward. He stopped before me and stretched out his hand. The fat knuckleless flesh floated before me like an obscenity.

"My condolences," he said and fixed his lips tight in mock sympathy.

Barnum's hand tired of the air and a smirk erupted on his face like a blazing sore. He moved on and spent a quiet moment with Ed and Audrey. I kept my eyes on Barnum and ignored Artemis, who stood before me issuing a cautionary remark.

Stan was staring at his feet. I was sure he had seen the Barnums. How could he not have? And yet, he appeared disinterested. I wanted to cry out, *Stan, don't you see them?* But Stan kept looking at his feet and Barnum walked out of the viewing room. Artemis followed him with a sudden burst of happy energy, her ass like a pompom shaking in the air.

The Barnums were still in the parking lot when I got outside. Bear was leaning against the Jaguar smoking a cigarette, and Artemis sat in the car with the windows rolled down because of the sudden and cruel warm front that had come and melted all the ice.

Without looking, Bear flicked his cigarette butt in my direction and got into the driver's seat. He waited for me to pull out of the parking lot, and then followed me for several green lights before turning left and disappearing.

Chapter 48

The television was on all the time. We preferred it that way. The snappy voices and sporadic commotions of a twisted world depicted on a monitor offered icy comfort. Still, it was always better stepping out than stepping in. That first step back into the condo was always the toughest, like stepping onto a sheet of ice. For the time being I was living on the edge of Grace's new world, Grace in her recliner like a raft stuck in the middle of a frozen sea beyond anyone's reach.

Hadley stayed with us for nearly two weeks after the burial. I wasn't sure why I stayed. Upon each return from the outside world, I was greeted by my pregnant sister-in-law, whose pitiful efforts to smile drove me crazy with suppressed anger and grief.

"How was your day?" she always asked, like a stand-in wife, regardless of how absurd we both knew the question to be. Did she expect me to open up to her as I had when she despised me? Oh, do you mean where have I been all day? Where did I go? What was I thinking about while I was out there?

Or do you mean why haven't I slit my wrists yet?

Hadley was harvesting time, picking days and filling life bushels to survive one more season of living.

The second week my returns to the condo became more predictable, and Hadley prepared dinner each night and the three of us sat together in the dining room with the living room television projecting a stream of empty voices and mindless rollicking exuberance that numbed our minds and hearts.

One day I told Hadley I'd found a room to rent and was going to move back to Legacy City. Hadley wondered if I wouldn't stay another week, that is, if I could manage it. She had to go home, but she and Brock would return in a week to move Grace to their place in Connecticut. Brock was having some alterations made in the house in preparation for Grace's coming.

I agreed to stay another week, but I knew the deal. Before long Brock would develop a mysterious condition that would require special attention, and Grace's move to Connecticut would be put on hold. Then what?

Despite my misgivings, I agreed to delay my move another week, though I had already committed myself to resuming work that following Monday. Yes, Hadley did realize Grace would remain in the condo by herself while I was working. Yes, of course, but in all likelihood, she assured me, Grace wouldn't even notice I was gone. All I had to do was look at her, Hadley said, and yes, Grace did in fact look to be borderline catatonic.

"Grace, I'll be back in a little while, okay?" I said.

Her right hand rose slightly from the recliner armrest as if in rebellion against the disorder, but her left hand quickly seized it as it began to shake and returned it to its place and lay upon it to keep it from rising again.

"I made you a sandwich. It's in the refrigerator in case you get hungry."

I left Grace on the recliner watching the Monday morning news with a glass of cranberry juice and chocolate chip cookies on a plate. I left feeling uneasy.

The week stretched before me like a death march. Hadley had left Sunday afternoon and I couldn't deny that already I missed her.

The idea of coming back to the condo after work and being alone with Grace was so distressing that I wondered if I would be able to keep my word and stay the extra week.

I could always stop at a bar after work. I could eat a cheeseburger, drink a couple of beers, and maybe when I returned Grace would be in bed. I could do that for a few days and maybe that would be enough to get me through the week.

But it wasn't going to be like that, was it? I had told Grace I'd be back in a little while. But what did that mean to her? An hour? A day? And what about dinner?

Hadley said Grace wouldn't even notice I was gone, but I knew that wasn't true. I saw Grace's bad hand move. I saw it try to will itself to health before my eyes. Before *my* eyes. Maybe Hadley really didn't understand what was happening to her mother. Maybe she couldn't or wouldn't understand. But I did.

When I returned the happy voice emanating from the TV might just as well have been reporting a walk-off home run by the Yankees.

"Norman Mailer has won the 1980 Pulitzer Prize for Fiction for his creative nonfiction book, *The Executioner's Song*. The work depicts the events related to the execution by firing squad of Gary Gilmore in the state of Utah in 1977. Gilmore was convicted of the senseless murders of a gas-station attendant and a motel clerk in 1975…"

Senseless murders, as opposed to sensible murders? Sanctioned executions and unsanctioned killings? Non-fiction categorized as fiction? Why? To make it less or more real?

It took me a few moments to consider the implications of Grace's absence. She wasn't in either of the bathrooms. She must have decided to take a nap. I knocked on her bedroom door but got no response. I tried opening the door, but it was locked. Grace never locked her bedroom door. I called her name and knocked harder. No response. I crouched and stared at the tiny hole in the middle of the doorknob, wasted a couple of seconds wondering what I could use to reach the turn-lock mechanism, slammed my shoulder hard against the door and popped it open.

Grace was lying on her bed unconscious, an empty bottle of valium on the night table and a near empty vodka bottle I'd recently purchased lying sideways in its own pool on the floor by the bed. I grabbed her by the shoulders and shook her. I shook her hard and shouted out her name.

I checked her breathing, slapped her face and shouted, *Grace! Grace! Grace!* But Grace was slipping away.

My mind in a muddle, I ran to the phone and dialed *911*, but the voice I heard angered me and I slammed the phone down and dashed back to the bed. I rammed my fingers down Grace's throat and she started to gag and vomit. I wrapped her in a blanket and carried her down to the hatchback and raced her to the Emergency Room.

Grace lived, and I told myself I had done the right thing.

Chapter 49

"Are you her son?" the doctor asked. I shook my head, he nodded his head, and then he explained a few things to me, which I failed to retain, remembering only that I should contact the family immediately and get some sleep.

It was late and the world was black when I got to the condo. The bedroom felt ice cold. My throat tightened as I looked at Callie's side of the room, her half of the bed, her pillow. I stooped down and opened the drawer of her night table and found her new address book.

I breathed in a faint trace of her favorite perfume as I flipped the pages that were filled with her neat handwriting, page after page of names and phone numbers and addresses. She had drawn tiny stars on every page, and I imagined how pleasing to her the moment of each star's rendering must have been. I marveled at the controlled loops and lines and dots and the little stars as if at a new kind of art. The star-covered pages scented of Callie trembled in my hands.

I walked to the living room to make the calls. I stopped and groaned and held my head when I saw the answering machine lit up like a fresh wound, the red number *1* throbbing, teasing hope and devastation.

What had I done? Had I missed my one and only opportunity? If only I'd let Grace die in her bed like she had wanted, if only I'd allowed her to fulfill her wish, if only I'd been here by the phone instead of at the hospital, I would have picked up the phone, I would have talked to her, we would have sorted it all out.

Oh, sweetie, don't you believe in miracles? They happen all the time, signs and wonders, things that confound the scientists, things the human mind is simply incapable of grasping. There was so much chaos and confusion, Lucas, people failing to understand one another, people being diverted by all the things that don't matter. You're right, darling, there was an accident, a terrible accident, and Johnny and I were taken to the hospital, but as a precautionary measure only. Do you hear me? A precautionary measure, so you mustn't worry, we're fine… It was another woman, Lucas, another baby, so very much like me and Johnny. A cruel and chilling heartbreaking tragedy, us, in fact, Johnny and I, if not for the grace of God. And I must tell you, Lucas, because I know you have so much trouble believing such things, but it was by the grace of God I saw the axe lying there on the frozen sea, and I heard it say, Chop! Chop! Chop! And I heard it go Chop! Chop! Chop!

I pressed the message button and turned my head away in disgust at the sound of Marla's dull lifeless voice. I began to howl and pound the walls with my fists.

In twenty minutes, I was outside her apartment banging on her door. She peeked through the door chain gap in confusion as though having been woken from a bad dream. She closed the door without uttering a word and then opened it wide to let me in.

Her eyes grew large as I grabbed her arm and flung the door shut. She was a strong, sturdy woman, but in my rage, I dragged her to the bedroom with little difficulty and threw her onto the bed. I pulled her nightgown up over her waist and pinned her down with my weight.

"Stop it!" she screamed. "What are you doing?"

I pressed my mouth against hers and she shook her head from side to side. In her seizure-like wildness her teeth raked my upper lip, and the sharp bruising pain thrust my fist up into the air like a hammer waiting to fall. When I saw myself in her terrorized eyes I froze and wondered what had become of Marisol and José Amado's son?

She lay panting and whimpering beneath me and I was consoled by the sight of her tears. I kissed her worried forehead, and when I saw my blood there, I shaped it into a cross, like a priest administering ashes of repentance. She recognized the crossing movement of my thumb on her forehead and it caused her to moan in soft surprise.

I stared at her, touched her eyes and felt her tears that became precious ointment to my fingertips. I ran my fingertips down my cheeks to my lips and tasted her strange sorrows. I got up off the bed and pulled down her nightgown to cover her and walked out of the bedroom.

"I'm so worried about you, Lucas. Stay here tonight. I'll sleep on the couch. It'll be okay, I promise."

I ignored her and opened the front door to leave. As I stepped into the hallway, I heard her call out to me, "Oh, Lucas, don't you know how much he loves you?"

What a strange and unexpected feeling it was to have my own words shot back at me like that. They pressed against my ears and lips, tasting of salt and iron. I licked the blood and felt it seep across my tongue. I thought of red roses and twinkling stars high above.

"I don't know anything about that," I said before closing the door.

Chapter 50

N o one wanted Grace, though to be fair, Hadley, Audrey and Ed did visit her at the hospital. On Saturday morning—a couple of days after I'd brought her back to the condo—I informed Grace that her daughter, sister, and brother-in-law would be coming by before noon to visit her. She showed no interest whatsoever and after breakfast got back into bed and was pretending to be asleep when they arrived.

Ed wasn't fooled one bit and sat on one side of Grace's bed complaining about President Carter the entire time, how he'd botched the hostage situation at the United States Embassy in Tehran, how he'd let the damn *Aye-rabs* piss all over the U.S. in front of the whole damn world, and it made me wonder if he really thought Persians were Arabs, or if he was just trying to coax Grace into correcting him, but she didn't and he kept hammering poor old Jimmy even after Grace opened her eyes and sat up.

All the while her husband was yammering away, Audrey sat on the other side of the bed, quiet as a hostage, staring at Grace's bad hand.

I think Ed became nervous and uncomfortable because once Grace got her eyes focused, she drilled him good, and he kept repeating himself and clearing his throat, and his words came bubbling up like a gooey regurgitation of half-baked premises.

Grace had those amazing eyes, of course, and probably a keener knowledge about Ed's inner workings than most of us other than maybe Audrey. Audrey glanced briefly at her sister's face when she emerged out of her fake sleep, but then went back to staring at the afflicted hand while Grace probed Ed with such raucous silence, I kept expecting him to flop his soft tanned hands over his ears.

At one point Ed got up and shook his head at me in what I interpreted to be a gesture of sympathy. With a flick of his head, he indicated that I should follow him to the living room. There he put his hand on my shoulder in a fatherly way.

"I cannot imagine what you must be going through," he said. He clenched his jaw and shook his head and seemed on the verge of tears. "Damn it, Lucas! It's so damn unfair, so horribly damn unfair! You're a brave young man, son, and a better man than I."

I guess it made Ed feel better about things seeing me as a kind of Gunga Din to his Rudyard Kipling, but maybe that was just me slipping back into the world of books. Ed embraced me far too long and then disappeared into one of the bathrooms and I could hear the faucet water running full blast. When I went back to the bedroom Audrey was holding her sister's bad hand and singing her a lullaby in a wispy voice and Grace was staring at Hadley.

Hadley was leaning against one of the walls watching her mother and aunt and crying softly. I touched her cheek and squeezed her shoulder. She cried all the time now, like my sister, Adriana, but this particular breakdown surprised me because she had always tried to be brave in front of her mother, though it was hard to tell if Grace cared one way or the other. Grace just stared at people and mostly you couldn't tell what she was thinking.

After she calmed down, Hadley informed me that Brock had been diagnosed with Crohn's disease. It wasn't a life-threatening condition, thank God, but he was in pretty bad shape. He was in a lot of pain and discomfort. And now, with Brock in such a bad way, and the baby coming soon, she just didn't know how they would be able to...

WE WERE like phantoms, Grace and me, becoming visible to one another only in brief dreaded glimpses. What struck me as odd was that Grace never probed me anymore the way she did everyone else.

I probably spent too much time pondering the irony of Grace's abandonment by her family and how I, the unwelcomed outsider, had in some sense become her sole lifeline to the world. During my most bitter moments I blamed Hadley and Audrey for not standing up to their husbands, but I never did find comfort in that.

Sometimes I'd think about Coldwell and wonder what he thought about this new state of affairs while lying spent alongside his younger, perkier wife.

I saw Callie and Johnny in every young mother and child and watched them with a longing heart until I sensed the discomfort, and then the river of loss would carry them away from me, and I would be left standing on the banks watching the river flow and flow.

And where was Grace in all of this? I often wondered what monsters had made her mind their dwelling place, and one day a compelling thought popped into my head: *Killing Grace would be a mercy.*

It was a revelation. When the thought first entered my conscious mind, I received it with guarded respect, as if it were a visitor coming over to welcome me to the neighborhood. I grew more comfortable with the idea and allowed it free entry whenever it might be in the mood for a visit. I could have—maybe should have—allowed Grace to die when her desire for death had overwhelmed all other options. But all was not lost, neither for Grace nor myself.

Hadley would appear at the condo every now and then to spend a couple of hours with Grace. It was a long drive from Connecticut and she was getting bigger by the minute, and Brock had okay days and bad ones. Hadley would take her mother's trembling hand and say, "The new baby is on the way, Mom, very soon. A baby girl, remember? A granddaughter!"

But it never ended well. Each time, pushed to her limit, Grace would finally look up and stare at her daughter, probe her, watch her daughter's hopeful expression wilt, watch her daughter turn away and waddle to the bathroom, hear her close the bathroom door and run the faucet full blast just like Ed did that one time.

It took me some getting used to not being on the receiving end of Grace's discontent. I'd discovered another Grace after Niagara Falls, and maybe she'd discovered another me. One moment in particular stood out in my mind. Grace had always had a painfully awkward way with Johnny, but I remembered how she smiled one day after we'd been living in the condo a few months. Even now the moment comes back to me with an intense clarity, Grace holding Johnny up by his wrists, helping our little boy drag one foot crookedly forward and then the other. I saw Grace's truest and loveliest smile in that timeless moment, and I understood how she might have once been.

And to think Johnny would have been walking on his own in a few weeks if not for the ice that came in April, if not for me losing my equilibrium. But who in his right mind would want to spend time dwelling on such things?

Every night I walked about the dimly lit condo past Grace's bedroom door, pausing to listen to her anxious whimpers and murmurings. One sleepless night I got up from bed and went to the bathroom and filled the tub with hot water. I filled it high, but not so high that the water would spill onto the floor after I got in. Then I went to the kitchen and got the carving knife set Callie had purchased for Johnny's first Thanksgiving.

That Thanksgiving morning, so soon after our reconciliation, and with my mind in the clouds, I tested the knife's edge with my thumb and sliced it down the middle. I could have used a few stiches. It wasn't intentional, I don't think. I wrapped the thumb tight and watched it float like some aloof and privileged observer beside the hard-working fingers of my left hand as I carved the turkey. When Callie asked me about it I told her it was nothing, just me being clumsy. It was an excellent knife to be sure, razor sharp— best carving knife ever—and I carved the legs and sliced the breasts with ease and put the dark meat on one tray and the white on another.

I took that same knife and again tested its edge against my thumb, but in a more prudent manner this time. I could tell it was just as sharp. I went to the bathroom, placed the knife on the edge of the tub and walked back to my bedroom.

I paused before the crucifix my father had left us. "Mercy," I said. "You're all about mercy, right?"

I took my pillow and sauntered over to Grace's bedroom, stopped at the door and listened for a few seconds to her tortured breathing. The obscured night light produced a candle-like effect, and the room seemed to shrink when I entered. I hovered over her like a giant, the pillow dangling far below from my hand.

Gradually her breathing steadied and a strange tranquility came over her. It was as if she knew I was there, and why, and was disinclined to dissuade me from doing what I had come to do. I breathed *Jesus-Mercy* as I grasped the pillow with both my hands. I adjusted my grip and repositioned and aimed the pillow and waited for peace to descend upon me. But I received no peace. I stood fixed and stiff, my feet nailed to the floor, my thoughts like roaming jackals.

Me and this woman and the pillow floating between us in the middle of the night with no one else alive in the universe, it seemed. How horrific, how hilariously absurd it all was, this cushion of death so soft and pliable hovering before me, between me and the woman, calibrating itself, aiming, slowly zooming in on the woman's sleeping face, like a cosmic camera designed to capture for some wandering alien race the moment of our own graceless capitulation and extinction.

I couldn't do it. I stopped to bury my face in the stale dry suffocating dough of the pillow and to muffle a cry for mercy and clarity.

Then I saw Grace's lips part just slightly enough to suggest she might have something to say on the matter after all—a recommendation, an opinion?—but all I could hear now was the growing howls and yelps of an approaching pack.

I scanned the dark walls and floor and ceiling of the bedroom and heard weird laughter and loud curses heaped upon the growing din. My bones began to rattle. Grace tilted her head toward me as if acknowledging the severity of the moment. I brought my head closer to hers to assure her that all would be well, but my mouth locked and the bilious words slid down my throat. The howls and curses escalated and the night erupted into a massive conflagration of rage, ignited, I knew, by my failure to comply.

The air was fast burning away, and the thickening horde bore down on me from all sides. I fell to my knees gasping, the air thinning with a distinct steady hiss beneath the roar, my hopes and faculties in dread flight, my mind in shooting pieces. If only I'd had the words, I might have rolled back extinction, warded off oblivion.

Fuérteme! Fuérteme! Fuérteme!

And Hell's fury fell on me like a thousand blazing knives. I collapsed and curled myself on the floor like a dying child.

Chapter 51

"But Virgil, even if it was a dream—and I'm not saying it was—what do you propose we do?"

"We go back."

"Go back where?"

"Where you need to be. Do you trust me?"

"I do, but—"

"Buts are tiresome, you know. Just follow me."

"All right, Virgil, I'll follow you. But what's that smell? Do you smell it? Burning leaves?"

"Oh, yeah."

"But they're not just leaves, are they Virgil? It's the smell of everything going up in flames."

"*Everything* is a big word, but yeah. Now pay attention, watch."

Boom! Boom! Boom!

"*That!*" Virgil shouted pointing to the Graddick mansion as it exploded into smithereens like a blown-up munitions factory, "and what *you* said."

The pool water was thick with algae and bacteria. No lost boy feet floating in the bobbing slime that I could see.

"The hedge," Virgil said tossing his head in that direction.

"Jeremy? Is Jeremy there?"

"What if I told you it was Jack or Jay? Would you protest, say that not okay?"

"Virgil, please, no word games today. We're talking about a lost boy."

"But didn't you say you trusted me?"

"I'm beginning to have concerns. I have questions."

"You *said* you trusted me."

"I do. I'm just having trouble grasping—"

"Here, grasp this."

Virgil pulled one of the hedge branches for me to hold. Together we pried open a passage through the hedge as flakes and dust fell from the sky like brown snow.

"Off you go," he said.

"Wait a second. What about you? Aren't you coming? This was *your* idea."

"For the love of… Do you trust me or not?"

"Virgil, you're my friend. You know I trust you, but—"

"Enough with the buts already! Listen to me, you *have to* cross the wasteland."

I looked at Virgil, who nodded reassuringly, and the hedge branches swung shut with a crazy loud *whoosh* after I went through them. As soon as I was on the other side I wondered if I had been tricked. That fellow didn't look anything like Virgil.

But the wasteland, though vast, seemed passive and only faintly ominous, and I was struck by a potent urge to dominate it. I started sprinting, determined to go for as long and hard as it took to get to the other side. A hundred strides in I staggered to a stop heaving and panting like poor old Stan reaching for a bench on the river walk.

"You don't have to run."

It was the same voice, only different. I turned to look. All I could see was the hedge behind me.

"You don't have to run anymore, you can walk."

So I walked for a long time and the stars flickered and faded and I lost all sense of direction. I was real low to the ground, my six microscopic feet tracing circles, my large-eyed tiny head chasing question mark-shaped clouds. Would I limp along a circular route on five legs or four? Would I rediscover the right way? Would I possess the wherewithal to know my final step? Would my antennae still flutter after all was said and done?

"Do you know what your name means?"

The voice was all around and everywhere at once. I thought I saw a talking tree. I did see a tree that may have talked to me and so I said to it, "Is it you?"

"What it signifies, you know, anthroponomastics-wise."

"Anthro what?"

"Your name, Lucas."

"My name?"

"Your name, your name, your name…"

I was the tree and the storm winds bent me till I tore free to whirl and dance and when I tilted too far, I fell in a spinning, rolling heap.

"How could you forget who you are?" she said

I reached for the stars with limbs and leaping roots and cried out in a new voice, "Callie, where did you go?"

ON HERALD STREET a lamp flicked on, then another, and yet another. I walked the cracked, uneven sidewalk and saw a small white speck growing and splitting into legs and arms and head, and sprouting pale luminous breasts.

"Where's Angel?" I said.

She turned without a word and jogged across the street—stiletto sandals in hand—and disappeared behind St. Corbinian's. I found her fake-bound to the wooden utility pole across the street from Babylon Elementary and Angel sleeping on the sidewalk a few feet from her with specks of old blood like tiny black stars across his wrinkled white shirt.

"Angel, wake up, we have to go," I said, and then I was lying on my back where Angel had been.

"He doesn't like it when it's the same," she said, "so he made a few edits, for whatever it's worth."

I jerked my head to look at her. She was licking blood from her upper lip. She drew her hands from behind the utility pole and pinched her cheeks.

"He says I'm too pale. He says I look like a ghost."

She pressed her fingers to her lips and spread blood over her cheeks like rouge.

"What do you think?" she said and resumed her false captive posture, shifting slightly to accommodate my view of the fire alarm box and tiny blurred panel window.

When I heard the low rumbling sound in the distance I tried getting up. My head wagged, and my arms and legs waved insect-like, but I was stuck to the sidewalk.

"He likes to change things up. He wasn't totally pleased last time as you might recall. I'm not saying it was all your fault. God knows I could have done more to help him achieve his goals."

I listened to the careening roar of an approaching train.

"But why would I? He tells me all I'm qualified for is porn, which is hilarious. I don't do porn. He says I should be grateful. But he's the one that should be grateful, being that I have to listen to all his bullshit. My artistry outshines his any day of the week, it's not even debatable. Don't tell him I said this, but he's a deluded wee-wee. He thinks he's Ingmar Bergman."

Artemis kept talking through the screeching roar of the train braking to a stop in the middle of Independence Street. I couldn't understand what she was saying. The train trembled and heaved like a great beast finally at rest after a long chase. I could see blurred faces behind the windows.

"See it?" she said.

"See what?"

"The knife with the shining cross-guard and the pretty pommel to boot."

"I don't understand."

The train began to pull away. I tried to yank myself free, tried to shout. A powerful spotlight burst with a loud pop, illuminating me. I turned my head toward Artemis seeking answers. She put her finger to her lips and turned an imaginary key to keep me from opening my mouth. Then with an exaggerated yawn she silently mouthed the words, *The Knife.*

The yawn did damage, caused the cut on her upper lip to reopen. She rolled her eyes. The wound broadened and blood seeped into her mouth. She slid her tongue over both lips, smacked them together as though she had just applied fresh lipstick, and smiled wholesomely. I could see sharp bloodlines outlining her pink teeth. The blood began to trickle in a thin line down her chin and down her ghostly throat.

The spotlight was eclipsed by an amorphous form, like a dense vapor wafting toward me. I ran my hands over the coarse surface of the sidewalk, heard a second loud pop and another spotlight flashed from a new angle rendering Bear's hulking figure. He was wearing a white suit with a black rose boutonnière on his left lapel, and his rifle was at the ready.

My hands continued scouring the sidewalk until they touched cold steel. My fingers felt along the thick textured handle and the flesh of my right hand settled securely against the cross-guard. I squeezed the handle and felt the sidewalk's hold on me loosen. I rose to my feet, the foot-long blade tucked behind me, unseen by my oppressor.

"You're *not* a team player," Bear said and stared at me with a look of grave concern. He seemed more in control than in our previous meeting, more sober and results-oriented.

"Do you even know who I am?" he said pointing the rifle at the sky and waving his right hand in the air, as though to indicate it all belonged to him.

"I had such high hopes for you, Ricardo. From the moment I saw you wrestling your kid out of that fine car of yours I said to Artemis, *he's* the one..."

He grimaced and shook his head.

"But frankly, you've been a colossal disappointment. And clearly, your inability to be a team player has rained down all kinds of shit on your parade, hasn't it? When she showed me the headline I cried out, *Mercy!* Imagine my consternation when I read those horrible words, *Mother and Child Go Poof on the Interstate!* I'm getting all emotional just talking about it. Can't imagine what it must be doing to *your* head. What kind of bullshit is that, right? Whoever thought April could be the cruelest month in *that* way?"

He stared at me, trying to read my thoughts. I could feel the knife pulling itself forward. It was a good knife, a loyal knife. I knew that now. It wanted what I wanted, but I held it back. Not yet, not yet.

"Still and all," Bear said, "there's something to be said for second chances."

He snapped his fingers and I heard yet another loud pop and a third spotlight flashed directly over Artemis, who gleamed like polished silver as she shaded her eyes with one hand and wiped blood from her chin with the other.

Bear swung the rifle in her direction and said to me, "Talk to me, Ricardo. What do you see? Be specific."

When he saw that I wouldn't look he frowned and said to Artemis, "How many times do I need to remind you, woman? Spread your legs! If we're going to accomplish anything worth a damn here today, you need to spread your legs so Ricardo can make a fair assessment."

"You mean like this, Bear?"

Bear ignored her and turned his attention back to me. He raised his hand to the side of his mouth and spoke to me in strictest confidence, "Crazy bitch thinks she's Liv Ullmann."

Then he looked straight up at the black sky. I watched his neck widen as he said, "You tell me, hon, feeling a bit drafty down there?"

"As drafty as an open window, Bear."

He grinned as he turned his attention back to me. "Did you know there are thirteen ways to look at a piece of ass?" he said.

He was so clever and pleased with himself that it made him chuckle in a good-natured way, but my lack of interest galled him and he became quiet and morose. Artemis snickered, and he seemed baited by her insolence and robbed of any prolonged enjoyment he might have been anticipating.

"She's ovulating," he said grudgingly, as though having been coerced into divulging this bit of information much too soon. "Says she's wants one of those pretty little men growing inside her to replace the one that died on you."

Bear waited for me to respond, but I was consumed by a vision of the long blade's smooth entry, and I could feel my restless blood tingling in my fingers and palm.

"What the hell's wrong with you, Ricardo?"

Artemis began to hoot and howl. Bear wiped sweat from his brow.

"This is bullshit!" he shouted as he cocked his rifle. "It's time we cut our losses. Drum roll, please."

I heard the drums and then I heard Artemis cry out, "But wait! There's been a mistake! He's not Ricardo Hatchback, he's Mr. Galaxy!"

Bear tossed a confused glance at Artemis, who kept a straight face. He turned back to me, ready to comment on what she'd said.

I gave him no time as I brandished the twelve-inch blade, which gleamed under the scrutiny of the spotlight. Bear was roused by the sight of the knife and roared his approval. "Who ever said you were a disappointment? I eat my words."

He seemed happy now and was laughing hard as he raised his rifle. He took aim at my chest and fired.

Click.

"Aw, come on," he grumbled.

Artemis giggled and clapped her hands excitedly.

Bear fired again.

Click.

"Son of a bitch!" he growled.

Click.

With a roar of spit and fury Bear charged me, the rifle lifted high over his head. When I saw that his attack was unfolding in slow motion I knew time had sided with me and that my moment of truth had arrived. I crouched low and lunged at his center, dodging the rifle butt and plunging the knife in his belly just as I had envisioned. I heard the tearing sound of his pants as the blade pierced the fine fabric. I heard the clink of metal on metal as the knife's cross-guard collided with Bear's jewel-laden belt buckle. I heard the deep clogging groan and the rifle's clatter as it fell to the concrete sidewalk.

I drew the blade out in a wild sweeping motion as Bear clawed and flailed as he attempted to crush me in his arms, but my right arm escaped his clutches and the blade swung back deep into his side. His hand grabbed at the new wound as I withdrew the knife, leaving me an opening. I shifted my body and plunged the blade again into his belly, burying it to the hilt with an upward twisting thrust that shot burning pain through my wrist and arm and into my neck and shoulder.

My hand was slick with blood as I waved the long blade at the night, the rest of me trapped in Bear's keeling embrace. He tried to lift me but stumbled forward and we fell together. The sidewalk shook as it slammed against my back and the great mass of stinking flesh knocked the wind out of me. I lay pinned beneath the monster in a semiconscious state, my face a hand's width from its bloody lifeless yawn.

When Babylon erupted in flames and the wail of distant sirens rent the night, I barely noticed. I thought of Icarus. What did he see as he sank into the ocean? Was the sky more beautiful when glimpsed at last breath? And the alarm? Who pulled the switch? I turned my head but Artemis was gone. The alarm box panel lay open.

The flames that were incinerating Bear licked at my flesh, but I didn't feel them. I thought of the departed train and all the ones I loved and my heart ached, but I felt no physical pain. All around, smoke was rising like incense. The stars were multiplying and swelling to near bursting. They glowed like bright laughing faces. I wanted to laugh but no sound came out of my mouth.

Above me and below and to my sides the flames were consuming all manner of matter and air. I felt my father's medal and crucifix like melting ice pooling in the center of my chest and I realized I was naked. Then, breathless, I watched the stars rain down torrents of shimmering light upon Legacy City, and all the flames were extinguished and a voice said—

"Lucas?"

Huh?

I got myself up off the floor and stared in bewilderment at Grace's face.

I leaned onto the bed and held her long thin body as she began to gurgle and groan as though she were drowning. I pried open her mouth to see if something had lodged in her throat, and she bit me. I yelled out in pain and it made her stop. I tried shaking the pain from my hand and she reached for me but couldn't bring herself to touch me. Her hands hovered near mine, vibrating like hummingbirds.

I got her up and led her to the bathroom.

"Wash your face," I said. "Would you like some coffee, some whole wheat toast with butter and jam?"

She nodded, embarrassed. I walked to the kitchen sink and ran cold water over my hand and began to prepare Grace's breakfast. I was setting the table when she appeared at the threshold of the kitchen wearing a light green robe over her pajamas. The robe was too short on her. It was Callie's.

"Lucas," she said again, her eyes closed.

How strange it was to hear her say my name. Her narrow shoulders seemed crushed beneath some invisible weight. Her hand trembled as it rose like the hand of a blind woman lost in a strange city.

"Lucas," she said opening her frightened eyes.

"I'm here, Grace, don't be afraid."

I took her long thin hands in mine and pressed them against my mouth. How unlike Callie's hands they were, and yet...

Chapter 52

Grace didn't belong to any church or denomination though she knew her parents had once been Episcopalian. Some things you didn't talk about, and Cam never showed any interest in joining a church anyway. I knew it was because of Callie that one day Grace asked me about her daughter's conversion, which back in Colts Brook had been viewed more as a passing fad than the life-changing event it turned out to be.

I thought a lot about Callie's conversion after she and Johnny were gone. I didnt mean to, I didn't plan it, I just did. I suppose I was hoping to find something, I don't know, comfort, consolation, answers? But there was never any way to filter out the pain from the hope, and in my telling that's how it came across to Grace. She was crying before I got to the end, and I wondered how many more incidents of grief multiplied we'd be able to endure.

The very next evening Grace was sitting in her recliner in the condo watching television. She called me over and asked me to turn the TV off. I sat down and she told me she wanted to go to Mass. I called the local parish to find out the times. She said she wanted me to go with her, so on a rainy Sunday morning we went together. It was my first time in church since José's funeral.

I called Hadley one day to see how she and the baby were doing. I also wanted to feel her out, hoping things had improved with Brock. She told me the baby had tested positive for cystic fibrosis and started to cry. I was surprised that I wasn't surprised. Who could possibly figure any of this out? All I could think to say was that researchers were getting closer to finding answers, that with early detection cystic fibrosis didn't have to be the horrible disease it used to be, that there was reason for hope.

"I know," Hadley whispered in a small heartbreaking voice, "I know."

I asked her if she was going to tell her mom, but she didn't respond.

I had to make a decision. Should I tell Grace about Baby Helena? I was a little afraid the news would set her back, but maybe if it came from her daughter... I decided to wait, see if Hadley would work up the courage to tell Grace.

One evening I stopped in the hallway to listen to Grace explaining the Rite of Christian Initiation of Adults to someone on the phone. Then she was silent for a long while. Finally, she said, "It's going to be all right, darling. I promise you, it's going to be all right."

I went to my room. I was writing at my desk when she knocked on my door.

"A few months ago, I tried to kill myself," Grace said. "If you hadn't intervened... You saved my life. I must tell you, though, for a long time I was far from grateful."

I stared at her.

"Did you know?" she said.

"Yes, I wanted to wait. I was hoping Hadley would tell you."

"Oh, Lucas, life doesn't get any easier, does it? God or no God."

"No, it doesn't."

"I'm glad you didn't let me die. I have work to do, right?"

I smiled a sad smile. "Yes, Grace, you do."

"They need me, Lucas. Hadley, Helena, Audrey, they all need me to be my best me."

MY SISTER INÉS'S husband, Grant, was a project manager at an up-and-coming company in Seattle called Microsoft. I'd finished up my Master's degree and Grant had said he could get me a job as a technical writer. The company had just signed a partnership with IBM and the sky was the limit.

That kind of sky meant nothing to me, but I needed a change of scenery, and I wanted to see my sister and nephews.

Virgil told me he would be leaving Galaxy Alarms sometime after the holidays. Amy's parents said they would be happy to help them with the down payment on a house on the condition they move down to Florida where his in-laws had retired to. That way Amy's mom could see her daughter and grandkids anytime she wanted.

"Is conditional love an oxymoron?" Virgil asked me.

I smiled and refrained from commenting.

"I'm hoping to run into Leo one day," he said.

"Florida is a big place."

"I think I'm destined to run into Leo."

"Hey, just no more crazy quests, okay?"

"Nah, man, you know me."

I did, and that's what worried me. I gave Virgil a big hug and left it at that.

Marla and I had lunch one day. I told her about Grace and Hadley and Baby Helena. Marla had become involved with a prayer group at her parish and had sort of patched things up with Rolonda Belford, though Rolonda didn't know what to make of the new Marla. It was going to take some time, Marla assured me, and I marveled at her radical serenity. Marla suggested I bring Grace to the next prayer group meeting, which I did, though I myself didn't stay.

When I'd first informed Grace of my plan to move to Seattle, I got the impression she thought I was looking to pawn her off, wash my hands of her. And maybe there was a grain of truth to that, but it was for both our sakes. How could I explain that being with her was like having the same old wound ripped wide open on a daily basis?

I knew Marla was going to be a good friend to her, an important friend, ironic as that might sound given all that had happened. Grace was only a few years older than Marla, and at this point Grace needed a friend like Marla more than she needed me.

I didn't give my two-week notice at Galaxy until I knew for sure Grace was ready. One day, after thinking much on it, Grace told me she understood. She said we were each other's grief mirror. She made me promise I would call her now and then. Her illness had stabilized. She was healthier in every way and strong enough now to help shoulder the sorrows of others.

SOMETHING I learned in those early years of love, separation and loss—something we all learn at some point, I suppose—is that in life you always have to expect the unexpected. My final act before getting on the road was to get a haircut. I didn't really need one, but my father and I had been going to Cardosa's Barbershop for so long that I felt almost obligated to do it.

Senhor Cardosa greeted me, as was his custom, in poor English, and I responded, as was my custom, in poor Portuguese. And then he said, "Mickey Mantle haircut?" waving his scissors at the 1961 picture of Mantle and Maris. I nearly fell out of my barber's chair. Had he ever said anything to me in twenty years other than *How is our champion today?*

"No, thank you, no Mickey Mantle haircut today. Just a little in the back and sides."

"Trim a little bit, then, yes?"

I told him I was taking a job in Seattle where my sister and her family lived. He smiled and nodded but didn't say anything. Then his smile faded. I could see it happening in the big wall mirror. I could see a shadow of melancholy descend over his features. The scissors and comb stopped moving, but his hands remained suspended in the air. He said in a low quiet voice intended for me alone to hear, "Before I come to America, I have wife and baby too. Before I come, she die, and baby die too. Like you, yes, like you. I know... I know..."

After he cleaned me up and shook the barber's cloth he walked to the wall and took down the picture of Mickey and Roger.

"Take," he said.

"Oh, no, I can't."

And how could I? How would the other kids, those other first generation American kids, ever know *Senhor* Cardosa was more than just another guy off the boat?

"Take," he said with a smile of encouragement. "I get more Yankees."

So I took Mickey and Roger with me to Seattle.

I FULLY expected my four-day cross-country drive to be peppered with the usual car failures. I didn't care. I envisioned with satisfaction the final agonizing throes of that hideous little car. It would be fitting to hear it cough its last toxic fume.

But wouldn't you know it, the little bastard drove for four days without a hitch. What was I supposed to make of that? And what are we to make of ourselves? We are sojourners in a strange world, laughers and weepers, survivors, pilgrims of hope or of despair, crafters of unfinished dreams, travelers making our own path toward the light or darkness.

I wanted to eat, drink and breathe America, its amber waves of grain, its purple mountains majesty and fruited plains, the whole big wide rippling continent nourished by the blood, tears, ashes and dreams of people of all stars and stripes and colors.

I wanted the long, quiet open roadways that peeled back memory and summoned dreams. I wanted new life fed on the blood of old wounds, wounds like water, bread and wine, wounds pulsing with the breath and song of all the beloved, wounds bleeding faith hope and love like roses.

I was wholly invested in the panoramic drama of the journey west, and then Minnesota reminded me how wacky life can be.

About a quarter of a mile after the *Welcome to Minnesota* sign I spotted a car pulled over on the shoulder, its left rear hoisted up on a tire jack. A man was tossing a flat tire into the trunk. He had a wolfish air about him that reminded me of Borders. I slowed down. I knew it couldn't be Borders because he was dead and had long ago taken down the tent he'd set up in my brain and packed up and gone away. But I slowed down anyway. The man was wiping his hands on a rag and staring at me the whole while as I drove past. I couldn't quite tell if he was mistaking me for someone else, or if he was just hostile by nature.

Somewhere between Minneapolis and St. Cloud I stopped for lunch at a combination roadside diner and gas station. The place was like one big skillet sizzling and smoking. A large man with his back to the counter was dipping wire baskets in deep vats of boiling oil. Truckers and men in hunting vests were paired off and talking in funny accents. I sat at the end of the counter on the only available stool. The torn vinyl of the seat was sharp against my right cheek.

I could feel someone staring at me from one of the three small tables set against the wall behind me. I tried to ignore whoever it was, but the unwelcomed scrutiny began to feel like a big hand sliding over the side of my head. I turned my head to see what the problem was.

It was a short guy with a wide waist and long thin strands of graying hair streaking helter-skelter over his pink balding pate. He was sitting facing me with his feet set wide apart. He had on black wingtip shoes and droopy pale blue socks and black dress slacks that rose high enough to display inches of shiny white shin. He wore a white dress shirt unbuttoned at the collar that spilled out over his left hip.

"The ribs," he said looking at me.

"Excuse me?"

"The greasy ribs with the fries, yum-yum."

He had shadows and bags under his otherwise neutral eyes. A big book lay open on the table with what appeared to be two rows of math formulas. It looked like an Algebra or Trigonometry textbook.

"The ribs, huh?"

"Oh, you won't regret it, believe me."

"I'm not a big ribs guy."

"What?" he said looking perturbed.

A man wearing a hunter's vest took a quick glance in my direction. He turned back to his partner and said something in a low voice. They both laughed.

"I prefer a good cheeseburger," I said.

Mr. Ribs grimaced and started flipping pages with a sense of urgency.

"The ribs are the best deal, hands down," he declared thumping the book shut. "Better than anything. Real greasy, real yum-yum. Always best to get your money's worth."

"Don't listen to him," one of the truckers chimed in. He was sitting at one of the other tables and was wearing a Minnesota Vikings cap.

All the one-on-one conversations came to a stop. All you could hear was the hard clear music of forks and knives and plates.

"Overpriced!" Mr. Ribs shouted. "Almost five dollars. Four-ninety-two to be exact."

The trucker wearing the Vikings cap cleared his throat. I turned to look at him. He was rolling his eyes and whirling his index finger over his right temple.

"Four-ninety-two," the cook said as he placed a plate before me. It was the tiniest cheeseburger I had ever seen in my life. It was the size of a chocolate chip cookie.

I started to laugh expecting everyone to join in on the joke, but everybody seemed to stop eating at the same time, and the diner became quiet as a cloister. I looked up at the cook and I saw Bear standing before me wearing a greasy apron. He was wiping his big beefy hands on his stomach.

"Four-ninety-two," he repeated in a neutral tone.

But it wasn't Bear. This man didn't look anything like Bear. This was all Borders's doing, I realized, his final farewell to the young man he'd had issue with.

Nobody's fault, Ah-ma-dole, ha-ha-ha.

I put a five on the counter and lifted the top of the bun. The small slice of cheese looked hard as plastic. I put the top of the bun back on the cheeseburger and got up to leave.

"Keep the change," I said to the cook.

"Didn't I tell you?" Mr. Ribs yelled as I was walking out the door. "Didn't I?"

"Harvey," warned one of the truckers.

"These people! They just don't listen!"

"Shut up, Harvey. Let it go."

About the Author

Given all that's happened, happens, and will continue to happen to us and the planet, I'm still more or less an optimist. Like many, I've enjoyed and endured my share of challenging and formative encounters and occupations. Among other things, I've been a landscaper, factory worker, darkroom manager, security systems technician, college writing instructor, tech writer and occasional alien. I'm a husband, father, grandfather, born and raised in the Ironbound, Newark, NJ several lifetimes ago, the son of Spanish immigrants who taught me how to be human.

Thank you for reading *Mr. Galaxy's Unfinished Dream*. If you enjoyed the novel, please take a couple of minutes to leave a review on Amazon. Your support would mean a lot to me. Knowing I've connected with a reader is always gratifying and humbling.

You can reach me through any of the following:
Author website: rgarciavazquez.com
Facebook: @rgvtimeleaper
Twitter: @rgarciavazquez2

22678365R00211